Of Light and Love

Of Light and Love

by E.V. Bancroft

2022

BUTTERWORTH BOOKS

Butterworth Books is a different breed of publishing house. It's a home for Indies, for independent authors who take great pride in their work and produce top quality books for readers who deserve the best. Professional editing, professional cover design, professional proof reading, professional book production—you get the idea. As Individual as the Indie authors we're proud to work with, we're Butterworths and we're *different*.

Authors currently publishing with us:

E.V. Bancroft
Valden Bush
Helena Harte
Lee Haven
Karen Klyne
AJ Mason
Ally McGuire
James Merrick
Robyn Nyx
Simon Smalley
Brey Willows

For more information visit www.butterworthbooks.co.uk

Of Light and Love
© 2022 by E.V. Bancroft. All rights reserved.

This trade paperback original is published by
Butterworth Books, Nottingham, England

Cataloging information
ISBN: 978-1-915009-25-8
CREDITS
Editor: Nicci Robinson
Cover Design: Nicci Robinson
Illustration: "Laura" by KC Lylark
Production Design: Global Wordsmiths

Acknowledgements

It isn't true that a book is a one-woman process, and I am so grateful to everyone who has given of their time and expertise to bring *Of Light And Love* to fruition.

Firstly, I'd like to thank Nicci Robinson from Global Wordsmiths/ Butterworth Books for providing the writing retreats, sharpening up the whole writing, putting me on the right (write?) track when I strayed, and leading me through the whole process through to publication.

Secondly, I'd like to thank my awesome beta readers, Annmarie Llewellyn, for going through in detail, and the Swallows critique group: Joey Bass, Valden Bush, Jane Fletcher, Lee Haven, and AJ Mason. I know the book is so much stronger because of all your input. Thanks also to Sue Llewellyn for marketing help and to Dave and Kev for being unstinting ambassadors for my work, even though it's not quite "their thing"!

I am grateful to KC Lylark for bringing Laura to life, and to Nicci Robinson for designing and producing the book cover; I love the chiaroscuro vibe!

I couldn't have done this without the support and understanding of Em and Mairi. By contrast, Jerry has continued to do everything to try and stop me from writing by demanding attention and strokes.

Finally, I'd like to thank you, the reader, for taking a chance on me and giving me such wonderful feedback. It's such an honour. Thanks.

Dedication

To everyone who is caught in the twist of grief.

And to Em, thank you for continuing to cope with me going through the vacillations of my writing process.

Prologue

THE AMBULANCE DOOR CLOSED with a clunk, emphasising the finality and shutting out Caro, leaving her alone, bereft. The paramedic started the engine and an Adele song clicked into life, as if this was just a normal day, which it was for him. The lyrics were something about it not being easy giving up your heart.

"Ms Fitzclare?"

"Huh?" Caro turned away from the vehicle and gazed into the deep brown eyes of the police officer who had already asked a hundred questions. She was questioned out.

The police radio blared with an all-units call. "Will you be all right on your own? Is there a friend or family member you can call to be with you?"

"I'll be fine," Caro said. What else could she do but lie? They clearly had somewhere else to be.

"Are you sure?"

Caro nodded. The woman opened her squad car door and settled herself into the seat. The crackle of the police radio was harsh and impersonal as the officer announced she was leaving, and the door shut, leaving Caro alone for the first time in many years. She stared as the red lights of the emergency vehicles blurred and disappeared, taking the love of her life with her. They didn't bother with the blue lights. There was no hurry; Yvonne was dead.

Caro slammed her fists against the doorjamb and howled. Pain spiked in her hands, but it was nothing to the agony in her heart. Anger melted into a torrent of tears. Unable to hold up against the crushing reality, her knees sagged. She slipped down the wall onto the cold, wet steps leading up to their house. She curled up on the step. It couldn't be true. It was just a hallucination. But the cement beneath her fingers was real, cold as mortuary marble. It was tangible. Yvonne was gone, and nothing would bring her back, no matter how Caro cried. Her sinuses stung and her throat

I

burned.

Eventually, she registered the rattling of the cat flap, followed by the soft padding of feline paws. The next second, there was a huff of breath and a wet nose probed at her neck. Caro turned to meet the wide green eyes of their cat, staring at her intently. Caro stroked her soft fur. "Oh, Artemisia, she's gone." The tears welled up again as Caro's tabby rubbed herself against Caro's legs. "I know. I still have you."

Then she mewed in that petulant way that said, "And you didn't feed me."

Caro half-smiled. "It's just cupboard love, then?" She didn't know how long she had lain there, but the cold had seeped into her bones, and she shivered uncontrollably. Maybe it was a nervous reaction. The shock that had numbed her blood was wearing off. With difficulty, she raised her head and brushed off tiny bits of grit that had made her face sore. Artemisia butted her forearms with her furry head and curled her body around Caro's arm in silent encouragement for her to rise.

Caro stood. Facing a future without Yvonne in it was unimaginable, unwanted, and frightening.

Chapter One

IN THE HAZE OF being half-awake, everything was peaceful. Until realisation came howling in, ripping off the roof of her grief, leaving her life in ruins like the aftermath of a hurricane. She dreaded falling asleep, and with her heart in tatters, she didn't want to wake to the devastation of her life. Again.

It had been over two years, but the raw pain lingered. Her friends had seeped away with well-meaning comments that she should move on. Grief had no expiration date. Caro wouldn't move on; she couldn't. Yvonne had been her everything. Beautiful, lauded, charming Yvonne. And now the chattering of Yvonne's media friends was gone, the atmosphere was as flat as the empty bottles of fizz. Only silence remained. When she stood by her kitchen window, staring at the empty bird feeders, the echoes of laughter from the dining room taunted her. She'd catch a glimpse of Yvonne's scarlet bath robe flash past on the landing, but when Caro focused, there was nothing there.

She dragged herself to her studio, fifty steps down the garden and placed to catch the northern light, but each step took her closer to her failure. What once had been her sanctuary was now her scene of torment. The daily drip of acid in her stomach, each day that passed just one more burn, confirmed her failure. Yvonne had been her muse, her life, her everything. Their life had been perfect...until it wasn't.

Caro ignored the incessant ring of her mobile phone. It would only be Rebecca checking up on her, which was really an enquiry about whether she had started painting again. And the answer was always no. That was the problem with having your best friend as your agent; their interests were divided, and Caro was never sure which Rebecca was speaking.

From behind the jars of dry paintbrushes, there was a purring sound, loud and insistent.

"Oh, Artemisia, don't knock them all over again. It took me ages to sort. Do you know how many different types of brushes I have?"

Artemisia stared, unblinking, and her grey and black tiger stripes came into view as she poked her head between two old sweet jars full of brushes. Caro snatched one away as it wobbled and placed it further down the paint-splattered bench. It had once seemed a sturdy part of her life, holding all the tools she needed for the job in hand, forgotten as the muse had taken her. Now, the bench mocked her, displaying what she couldn't use. When she painted, her whole life shrank into the pinpoint focus of the brush hitting the canvas, slow and soft, or hard and swift. The sum of all her emotions poured from her soul and into the sable brush.

That was all lost. Yvonne's death had ripped out not just her heart but her soul, her skill, and the very point of her being.

Artemisia nuzzled against her hand as if she could tell Caro needed the comfort. In all honesty, she wasn't sure how she would have survived if it hadn't been for her beloved cat, thrusting her face at Caro, demanding attention, snuggling up to her and rewarding her with a purr.

Caro stroked Artemisia, and she purred even louder. "You saved me, girl, even though I'm not sure why. I want to climb all the steps to my turret and slam the door." Her laptop sounded the arrival of an email, and she closed the lid. It was probably Rebecca again, or another demand for repairs or insurance. The house had been manageable when there were two of them, with Yvonne's steady salary and Caro's infrequent but large deposits. But now there was always something that needed paying for. "Somehow the bills still keep coming—a ping of email followed by a vacuum from the bank account each month."

Rebecca had said Caro ought to move to a smaller house with smaller bills, but Rebecca didn't understand. Caro couldn't leave. The house was a sanctuary and, if she was honest, her bedroom a shrine to her dead wife. Caro's portrait she painted of Yvonne took pride of place on the wall, so it was the first thing she saw when she woke. The rest of her treasured possessions and mementos, her half-finished lipstick, her earrings, and the paperback she'd been reading still in place on the dressing table, became a memorial. By keeping the objects that Yvonne had touched, Caro could keep a connection.

A rustling outside startled her. A flash of blue swooped to pick up a ball in the middle of Yvonne's borders—no, her borders. She banged on the studio window, but the boy in blue flipped her the bird before trampling the begonias and scrambling up the fencing. No wonder it needed replacing. "Bloody kids," she said. "Why can't they keep the ball in their own gardens?" They used to be so polite, waving shyly, but now they challenged each other to torment her. Yvonne would have sorted them out.

Caro pulled her sketchbook towards her. The pages no longer sat flat due to her constant turning as she stared, transfixed, at the last sketches of Yvonne. Naked with her back towards Caro in a three-quarter serpentine curve, Yvonne had curled her arms around her knees, after she'd drawn them up to her chest. In another, Yvonne was stretched out with her hands above her head as if stretching after a restful night's sleep. The final sketch was a mid-close-up of Yvonne with her eyes closed, leaning against the sofa after another hard day.

"I hate that one," Yvonne had said. "I look so old."

"You're stunning. Look at your cheekbones, the way the light falls and casts deep shadows."

"Look at the skin sagging around my neck like a scrawny chicken. It's no wonder the station has dumped me."

"What?"

Yvonne picked up her wineglass and swilled the contents around as though she were discussing nothing more important than the weather or what they were having for supper.

"Evidently, I am being replaced by a younger, less intelligent, prettier version. Meanwhile, my male co-host, whom I've saved umpteen times, gets the prime role."

Yvonne's flat tone had pulled at Caro's heart. She'd taken the sketchbook and wine from Yvonne's hands, straddled her, and placed her arms around Yvonne's neck. "That's shit. Paul Roper doesn't have the skills or emotional range you have. He can't do empathy to save his life. The only thing he can do is talk about sports."

"Exactly. I can't bear it, Caro. My life is gone."

"You still have me," Caro had said, but the blank look that settled in Yvonne's eyes suggested that Caro would never be enough. Caro had said nothing more in case that horrible truth was confirmed. "You've still got your voice acting work, and maybe you should go on the radio again. With your sultry voice, you'll have them all in raptures."

"You don't know what it's like. I feel like a desiccated husk. I hate getting old."

Their age gap had reared its head so many times. When they had first got together over a decade earlier, it hadn't mattered. Then, at thirty-nine, Caro hadn't felt young, but she was an artist, and it really didn't matter. Yvonne was fifty-four and for TV, that was ancient. But Yvonne had so much life to live. "You're not old. You're beautiful and talented. And people love you."

"No. They love my so-called fame. They want to be close to me so they can get themselves onto television some way or another."

When Yvonne had spoken like this, there had been no changing her mood and nothing Caro could have said or done would have connected or shifted Yvonne's downward spiral into deep shadow. Perhaps she should have known then that Yvonne wouldn't want to sit for her again. Everything was intertwined with Yvonne's loss of her job, her status, her sense of self.

With each stab of grief, guilt twisted around her heart like a double helix. She should have been there. Why hadn't she seen it coming? Had she been so selfish and self-absorbed that she hadn't noticed what was going on? The queasiness in her stomach had now become an acid burn. *I'm sorry*. Caro stared at the picture, scratched in quick curves and fuzzy at the edges, unlike her paintings, which were so precise. If she had known it would be the last time she drew Yvonne, she would have spent longer staring at those beautiful forms, the way the shadows fell across her body. She would have tried to capture Yvonne's essence: gregarious and full of life, not slumped on the floor.

No, she couldn't go there. Caro shook her head and closed the sketchbook. It was too intertwined with her guilt and despair, a daily reminder of what had happened. Artemisia wound herself around Caro's legs, a sure sign she was hungry. "Okay, come on, girl, let's get you some tasty tuna."

Artemisia pelted towards the cat flap as if she could conjure the food from thin air. The trouble was, she wasn't terribly bright; she hit the flap at full force before the lock clicked when it recognised her chip. Caro smiled and shook her head, then guilt smacked her across the face. How could she smile when Yvonne was gone?

She followed Artemisia into the kitchen and stopped when she saw the rapid stream of water seeping from the boiler. It smelt stale and was streaked with rust.

"Bollocks."

Caro dropped onto the stool. She had hoped the old boiler would last a few more years. How was she going to fund a replacement? This was just the next in a series of repairs and bills that needed paying from her non-existent income. Rebecca's other suggestion of renting out her spare room began to look unavoidable.

Chapter Two

LAURA REVERSE PARKED THE rented van first time in front of another van. *Ha!* She wasn't even sticking out into the road much, so she did a little victory jig in her seat. "Awesome. Cough up, mate." She held out her hand. Matt scowled at her but placed a pound coin in her palm. She scrutinised the Victorian terrace house on a busy street that would be their new home. The front garden was a typical student rent, unkempt with weeds poking out of the cracks in the concrete, and the recycling bins cascaded beer bottles.

"I think we've been spoiled by our previous flat," she said. "I can't believe we were there four months." She couldn't believe she'd only known Matt that long, either. They had just clicked, and he was like a little brother now, one who followed her everywhere.

She sighed. It had been fun doing the internship at the animation company, but she was looking forward to the next phase of her life. Laura picked up her gloves from the dashboard. "Let's get this party started." She glanced in her mirror at the stationary van behind and frowned. A woman retrieved a removal box and staggered to the front door of their new house. That was strange. "How many rooms has Rob let out?"

"Two."

Laura nodded to the other van. "Unless he's got a new girlfriend, we may be about to play musical chairs."

"What?" Matt's nostrils flared.

He jumped from the van and slammed the door behind him with such force that the whole vehicle rocked and Laura's belongings shifted and rattled in protest.

Laura turned to her homemade hand puppet, MiniMe, sitting between the two front seats. She picked her up and straightened her wool hair. Laura had hand crocheted her for her undergraduate degree but was hoping to use her in her master's.

"I'm not sharing with him," she said in MiniMe's voice. "He probably farts in his sleep." Laura threw down the gloves.

"You'd better take me with you if you want the courage to say what you need," MiniMe said.

"True." Laura slipped her hand inside the puppet. "Let's investigate."

She followed Matt into the house, but not before noticing the paint peeling on the open front door.

"Seems a bit of a mess. Not like your last flat," MiniMe said and canted her head at the door.

"Beggars can't be choosers. That was part of the internship deal so we could be close to work."

Removal boxes littered the kitchen, and there was washing up in the sink. Rob stared at Matt, whose face was bright red and blotchy, clearly trying to keep his temper and failing. Laura touched his arm. She didn't want him to explode again. It would take ages to talk him down from his anxiety. She stroked him with MiniMe's arm. Rob stared at the puppet, then at Laura, his mouth half-open. "Hey, Rob, have you let out the second room we asked for?" She smiled, not wanting to make him more irate. He looked ready to pounce.

Rob shrugged, but his face had a faint tinge of red that implied he was guilty. "I thought I was doing you a favour. Aren't you a couple? You always seem so close."

Why did people have to assume anything? Why not ask? Laura shot a quick glance at Matt to check he was okay. "Nah, Matt's not my kind of girl." Laura flashed Rob a saccharin smile.

Rob's mouth formed an O. "But you're too pretty to—I mean, wow, I would never have guessed. Hard luck, mate." He punched Matt on the shoulder.

They both glared at him.

"Stereotyping much?" Laura said, not believing she'd hear such stupid comments in this century.

Rob raised his hands. "Whoa, okay, sorry. Meant nothing by that. Jeez."

Meant nothing by the insult? Maybe Laura would be better off not living with this ignorant homophobic slob, anyway. It could be difficult living with friends of friends. As far as she knew, Rob and Matt shared little about themselves as they bonded over gaming. Perhaps it was a man thing.

"You gave away our rooms?" Matt faced up to Rob. He looked hurt and confused, as though someone had told him they didn't like Star Trek.

"Honest mistake, Matt. Only one room. I can't do anything about it now." Rob gestured beyond them. "Kaylee's already moved in."

"Nothing to do with her being pretty, is it?" MiniMe asked. Laura stared at the puppet as if she couldn't believe what she had just heard. MiniMe turned her head to glare back at her. "What? You do know this is you talking, don't you?" Laura laughed and grimaced at Rob as though she had no control.

He frowned at her. "You're fucking weird."

Like that was something she hadn't heard before. "Yep, that's me. How can we solve this? I can phone the accommodation office now and see if they have any alternative graduate places, but this close to the start of term, we'll be lucky. Otherwise, Matt, you'll have to sleep on the floor, and MiniMe will share my bed."

"I can't do that. We were supposed to share a house, not a room."

Matt turned blotchy again, and he tapped his thighs with his fingers. Laura touched his forearm to placate him. She pulled her phone from her jeans' pocket with MiniMe and wandered into what would become Matt's room. The dining room at the back of the house was converted into a bedroom, presumably to maximise the income. There was a double bed, desk, and small wardrobe crammed in and covering almost the whole of the floor space. No room to practise yoga here. A single, unhemmed curtain hung across the window, which overlooked a small yard, with just enough room for a bike rack. Matt followed her in and stood by the door, nibbling at his nails.

Laura squeezed his arm and waited until his eyes met hers before she smiled. "Don't worry, I'll phone the accommodation office." She pressed the button to make the call. "Oh, hi. Who am I talking to? Hey, Tracey, yes. My name is Laura Kingston López. I'm on the master's in animation. There's a misunderstanding about our accommodation, and my room is no longer free. Do you have anything else available?"

There was a clattering of keys down the line as Tracey entered something into her computer. Laura stared at the wallpaper that bubbled and creased by the edges, showing it had been hastily applied.

"The only thing I have is to the South of Bristol. If you're doing animation, you'll be based at the Bower Ashton Campus, so that'll be handy. The room has just become available and has a private bathroom, bedroom, and small lounge. It's on a direct bus route in and is five miles by bike on a Sustrans bike route."

Tracey's motherly voice reminded Laura of her own mum. A pang of homesickness filled her heart, and she pushed it down. She would phone her mum tonight as soon as she was sorted. No doubt she'd be driving her dad nuts, worrying about how her precious one was doing. "Wonderful, it sounds perfect," Laura said. Private bathroom, though? It was a rite of passage that students had to share, even graduates. "How many people share the bathroom and lounge?" She swallowed and hoped it wouldn't be over three. She didn't need horrendous morning queues for the bathroom, especially as she always left getting ready until the very last minute.

"No one. There would just be you."

A surge of happiness blossomed in her heart, and she gave Matt the thumbs up. "Wow, I've died and gone to heaven. How much is it?"

The price Tracey quoted was just in her budget. "I'll take it."

"There's only one thing before you commit. The owner is a bit eccentric and wants to keep her privacy at all times. And no men."

Laura drew out a breath. "Okay. She's not nuts, is she?"

"No, just a recluse."

There seemed to be a lot more that Tracey wasn't saying, but Laura had little choice. Matt needed to be secure, and he'd settle easiest amongst familiar faces. "I'd better get my full charm game on then."

"I'll let her know you're coming, dear. Her name is Caro Fitzclare. When do you need to move in?"

"Now. Today. I have a rented van to get back to the depot tonight. Can you call me back as soon as you hear from her, so I know whether I have a roof over my head this evening?" It always helped to be nice to people, as they usually responded in kind, and it was easy to be friendly with Tracey.

"I'll see what I can do."

"That's awesome. Thanks, Tracey. If ever you need a cartoon drawing, I'm your woman."

Tracey laughed. "Don't worry, I'll get back to you as soon as I hear."

Laura swiped to end the call and danced a happy jig. "I've scored my own private bathroom and lounge."

Matt looked devastated.

"Sorry, mate, she doesn't want any men in her house, so it has to be me."

He leaned against the door, looking rigid, with his hands by his sides.

"But I wanted to share with you."

"Yeah, I know, Matt. I did too. But Rob's friend has already unloaded. Hey, if she's straight, maybe you two could, you know." She wiggled her eyebrows. He snorted, but his shoulders relaxed. "You've known Rob for years. You'll be fine. It's me you need to worry about. Sounds like the landlady's eccentric. So, if I don't appear for lectures on Monday, just check I haven't been chopped up and cooked in the refectory pasties. Actually, if she's eccentric, maybe she'll be the first person to like MiniMe?"

"You're weird." He jumped back as she took a swat at him with the puppet.

"Let's get your gear in here, so I don't get charged an excess for returning the van late."

Rob came to the door. "There's a problem. The rent is based on four people sharing utilities, so Matt will have to pay more. You understand."

"No." Laura fixed Rob with a stare but smiled and poked Rob's chest with MiniMe. "The costs will be less if there are three of you, and you already fixed the rent with Matt. Given you let out my room, you can honour your word with the rent you agreed. Come on, Matt, let's clear out the van of your stuff before I complain to the accommodation office about dodgy landlords."

"But..." Rob said, then caught Laura's expression. He held out his hand to Matt. "All right. It's a deal." They shook hands, and Matt trailed Laura out to the van.

"Thanks, mate, I would have agreed to the increase."

"I know. But he's doing okay with the deal. If you grab your boxes, I'll take this." Laura picked up a cardboard model of the Starship USS Enterprise that had been carefully placed on the top of boxes abutting the front seats to protect it.

"Be careful with that."

"Yeah, I know." Laura hummed the original Star Trek theme tune and walked slowly into the house as if the model was a crown. She almost bumped into a woman coming out. This must be Kaylee and up close, she was pretty and dressed in docs, top hat, and a frilly dress. She squealed when she saw the model.

"Oh, wow, Star Trek. I love it. Is it yours?" Her eyes widened.

"No, it's his." Laura nodded to Matt, who was following her with a box of books and an anglepoise lamp balanced precariously on top. He stopped abruptly, and the lamp wobbled but maintained its position.

"Oh." Kaylee looked from the model to Matt, who was wearing an old Starfleet Command T-shirt, as if to confirm he was the Trekkie. "Did you make it?"

Matt's ears went red. He cleared his throat. "Yeah, when I was eleven."

Laura grinned, wondering how much she could tease him about the strange rise in his normal timbre but chided herself. It would do him good if he had something in common with a stranger who was about to be his flatmate.

"Who's your favourite, Kirk, or Picard?" he asked.

Kaylee's eyebrows shot up. "Janeway, of course."

Matt snorted. "She almost killed her crew, on more than one occasion—"

"But she always sticks by her principles."

"Can you two have this conversation later? We need to get you moved in, so I can get into my new digs." Laura didn't have time for one of Matt's lengthy Star Trek debates.

"Oh, hey, I'm sorry about that, I didn't know. I'm Kaylee, by the way." She kept her eyes on Matt.

They introduced themselves and carried Matt's stuff into his room. Laura looked for a place to leave the model without it being damaged. She stood on the bed to place it on top of the wardrobe and avoided staring too intently in the cobwebs. Spiders were fine as long as they didn't move. Matt followed Laura into the room and closed the door. She jumped off the bed. "You're in there, but you'll need to brush up on Janeway."

"I don't need to. I've seen every single Star Trek episode."

She punched his shoulder lightly. "That's a conversation you can have with Kaylee."

Two hours later, Laura stretched her back, pleased they'd squeezed in all his belongings, by using the floor as a bookcase for his lever arch files. He could sort them into alphabetical order later. "I'll have that coffee now, Matt. I need to phone Tracey."

She'd missed Tracey's call but had a text saying everything was fine and that Ms Fitzclare would be there to meet her at the house. After a quick slurp of coffee, she rinsed her mug in the grimy sink. "Right, Matt, shall we find out how odd this landlady is? Come and give me a hand unloading at my new place so I can drop the van off on time." Laura did some quick calculations. If she didn't have any late drop-off charges, she could afford a pizza for dinner and save the leftovers for tomorrow's breakfast. "If we get the van back this evening, I'll even buy you pizza." She picked up MiniMe and strode out of the front door, buzzing with delight. Her own bathroom and lounge. *Awesome.* Life was definitely looking up.

Chapter Three

TODAY WAS THE DAY. CARO sensed it would be different. She didn't know if it was the first heavy dews of autumn or the shift of the light from the glaring summer to the slanted sun absorbed through the thicker atmosphere. She paced the steps to her studio with a lighter tread. The garden smelled different too, more earthy, and the trees had scattered the first of their leaves as the chlorophyll bleached away, revealing spectacular tans and ochres. The dew soaked into her old sneakers, but she didn't care. Today she would start work again.

The air was musty in the studio, and she pushed open a window frame that had swelled with the extra moisture. It was too cold to leave the door open and even though she'd had the new boiler, she couldn't afford to run it until she made some money. A shiver of anxiety ran along her spine. She needed to paint soon or find another job. The thought of teaching art again made her cringe. She'd done it before she'd been famous and hated it. No, that wasn't strictly true. There was a satisfaction when someone who thought they couldn't recreate a likeness produced a ghost of truth. But mostly, the classes were stuffed with Sunday daubers who came with all their expensive kits and closed minds. They didn't really want to learn, just be congratulated on how brilliant they were.

She'd made canvases in the long fallow months of grieving. She had even done the quick wash in brown gesso to create a barrier between the oil and the canvas, so there was no excuse. She just needed to start. Her idea was to use the last sketch of Yvonne's face, lit from a single candle and throwing deep shadows in dramatic chiaroscuro. It would represent her life before, with Yvonne in the light and her life now, in the deepest black. It would be a homage to Yvonne in her last few months, with the vestiges of lines cracking her alabaster skin. People were much more interesting to paint when they were older, with their experiences traced upon their cheeks and temples. Their imperfections made them appealing, interesting, and unique.

E.V. Bancroft

Yvonne had never understood that. For her, it was always image and perfection in poise, presentation, and delivery. Nothing annoyed her more than overrunning the time segment. Yvonne would have hated what Caro was about to paint, as if Caro was emphasising Yvonne had overrun her own time.

Caro unscrewed the cap and inhaled the strong scent of turpentine, the drug of choice for an artist. Her fingers tingled with anticipation of that moment before creation. She imagined the finished picture, and her task was to recreate it as accurately as possible. She sketched a few curves to show the position of the planes of light. She loved the juxtaposition of the contrasting colours that reflected the drama in Yvonne, who thrived on attention and always captivated a room when she entered. Caro was the direct opposite, silent, observing, exploring her art. Their few arguments had been when she grumbled if they had to entertain again.

Caro shook her head. She would not be maudlin today; she was going to paint. She perched on her stool as she thinned the Vandyke brown on her palette. Normally she would mix her own tones, but she needed to get it down quickly, to confirm she could still do this and shore up her crumbling self-esteem.

Caro stood for the first strokes. Paint from the gut, her old tutors used to say, and she did, in wide broad movements, laying thin arcs of dark brown and obliterating the paler base layer. Her phone rang. *Damn.* She'd forgotten to put it on silent. It went through to voicemail. "Go away, Rebecca. I'm actually trying to do what you keep nagging me about. Now you've woken Artemisia. Go back to sleep. No, I can't stroke you, I've got paint on my hands."

The exhilaration of actually painting made her giddy and lightheaded. She attacked the canvas quickly with confidence, edging up to where Yvonne's face would be. In her peripheral awareness, there was a rustling, breaking twigs, and then a hammering on her studio door. She scowled and wiped her hands on a cloth, an old shirt that had once belonged to Yvonne. She swung open the door, catching sight of the neighbouring kids giggling and scrambling up the fence.

"Bugger off." She didn't care whether they were too young to know swear words. She looked down to see a pile of cat poo on the step, dried out and resting on laurel leaves. "You little bastards," she shouted and could hear the laughing on the other side of the fence.

Of Light and Love

Pain exploded in her brain. Caro felt like she was back at school being taunted for being different and artistic. She detested that feeling of exclusion and yet she hated being the centre of attention. She was so surprised when she got together with Yvonne, always in the glorious middle of whatever she was involved with. But as Yvonne had said, "How could I not fall in love with someone who paints me like a goddess?"

Caro cleared the muck up with some old newspaper, and the tell-tale sensation of tears prickled at the back of her eyes. *No.* She'd been doing so well but those little bastards had disturbed her concentration and her equilibrium. She would have a word with their parents and didn't care if they were some hotshot surgeons, they needed to keep their tribe in order. Caro washed her hands under the tap, startled at how cold it was, but she still couldn't put the boiler on. She wiped her hands and picked up her phone. Three messages and a voicemail.

"Hi, Ms Fitzclare, this is Tracey Coggins from the university's accommodation office. I hope your room is still available. We have a graduate student who needs lodgings urgently today. Her name is Laura Kingston López. She's a mature student on our Master's in Animation course, and she can do a bank transfer to your account today. I'm sending her over now, so I hope that's okay. If there are any problems, call me back as soon as possible."

That was a cheek sending someone over before she'd agreed. Her heart thumped. She didn't want a stranger in her sanctuary, leaving a mess in her kitchen and seeing all her things. Sweat trickled down the back of her neck. She clutched the bench and tried to force herself to breathe slowly. She could do this, she would just set down the rules and boundaries, and it would take the financial pressure off until she could paint again.

Caro appraised the painting so far. It was crude and poorly executed, with sloppy brush strokes. She was out of practice because she hadn't painted for two years. It would be like riding a bike; she would wobble a little before she found her balance. But the painting was flat, emotionless, and inexpressive. An icy grip of fear clamped around her heart. The skill shortfall wasn't the problem. She'd lost her muse and lost her way. Her confidence shrivelled when Yvonne died, and Caro couldn't express a passion she no longer lived within. Perhaps it would take her longer to spread her soul on the canvas. Caro couldn't let Rebecca sell anything she wasn't satisfied with, not that Rebecca would. Caro definitely needed the rent money. If she was frugal, it would be enough. She sent a quick text to Tracey, accepting it, and turned back to her painting.

Her hands trembled, where they'd been as solid as rock just a few minutes ago. She had been so confident, slapping on the paint, but now she was unsure and timid. She placed a tentative stroke. No, it was wrong. She scrubbed at it with her cloth and stared at the smears on the canvas. She dabbed again, but it was like an amateur violinist attempting Paganini's Caprice Number 24. The result was painful. She brushed out the marks and dipped the tip of her flat brush onto her palette. She added more paint, but it just congealed in a flat brown mess, so she snatched up a cloth and scrubbed and scrubbed at the canvas as if trying to eradicate the pain from her heart by obliterating the mockery of her daubs.

There was another hammering. *Those bloody kids.* She swung open the door. "Leave your shit somewhere else. You're ruining my—"

A younger woman stood before her, eyes bright and a huge smile on her face. When she met Caro's gaze, she froze.

"Ms Fitzclare? Sorry to disturb you. I've come about the room."

Caro shut her eyes. This was not a good start.

Chapter Four

LAURA STARED AT THE lean, wild-eyed woman, her dark hair hanging in a messy bun. She looked like a zombie from the movies Laura couldn't bear to see without getting nightmares afterwards. Her face was red with pent-up anger but drained as she realised Laura was clearly not who she was expecting.

"Oh, I thought you were the kids from next door. I'm Caro."

They shook hands. Caro's were rough with calluses, a clue that this woman worked with her hands. Laura peered past her into the cavernous studio, and the brown swirl on the canvas caught her eye. Caro must be an abstract artist. "And do they leave their shit around?"

"Cat poo on the doorstep. They think it's funny. It's disgusting."

"Maybe they're just bored," Laura said, attempting to placate Caro who looked to be on the verge of boiling up again, as though the memory turned up the gas on her rage. "I'm Laura. Is the room still free? I have my things in a van and a friend willing to help move me in."

Caro frowned. "Don't you want to see it first?"

What was it, a dungeon? The room she would have had in Bristol was worse. It could be awful, but she didn't have a choice. Anxiety prickled in her stomach. "Please."

Caro bustled past without saying another word and strode rather than walked back to the house. Since starting animation, Laura had begun to really notice how differently people walked to figure out how they could be depicted. She forced herself to look up in case Caro might think she was checking her butt. She did have a very nice butt, lean and muscular in her tight jeans. She hadn't intended to check out her new landlady, but she was far more appealing than Rob.

Laura followed Caro into the house that had obviously once been chic but now looked rather tired. The kitchen had marble counters and led into an open dining and living space, complete with old white leather sofas that had seen many days of wear, or maybe it was just the cat scratches and colour fading from the light streaming in through the patio doors. On the far wall was a massive TV and a library of DVDs and CDs, mainly classical and opera. Not Laura's taste, so she'd make sure to wear her headphones when she cooked, rather than blast up the volume. "What a lovely spacious room, ideal for entertaining." Laura could hardly contain her curiosity.

A shadow flicked across Caro's face, and her neutral mask dropped to reveal a glimpse of sorrow. "I don't really use this room anymore," Caro said. "Come through."

The speed with which she exited left Laura wondering if she had already seen too much of Caro's soul simply by casting her eye over the shelves and why Caro wanted to keep everything about her secret and separate. It looked like two cottages had been knocked into one large house. Laura followed Caro past some amazing sculptures made of scrap metal as they went down the corridor to the wing in what would've originally been another cottage.

Caro opened an old stripped-wood door through to a smaller lounge that could have been the sitting room of the original cottage. The room was cosy, with a cushioned window seat looking out to the garden and the studio. A battered but expensive-looking sofa bed, dark wood desk, and captain's chair filled the room. Bookshelves lined the walls, and Laura inhaled the wonderful scent of old leather and musty books. It was heaven, a place to lose herself in on a wet winter's night. She was tempted to trail her finger over the volumes lining the shelves, though that was probably not polite. You could tell a lot about a person by their book collection. There were a mixture of biographies of celebrities and art books, hundreds of them, including catalogues from various exhibitions going back several years, but they stopped two years ago. There was a story in that, one Laura would love to unravel and examine.

Caro stared at Laura with grey blue eyes that sparkled with intelligence. She must have spoken by the look she was giving Laura, clearly waiting for a reply.

"Sorry?" Laura asked.

"You can use the snug as your own sitting room. No sleepovers."

Laura gave a cheeky smile, trying to flush this woman out of her hiding place. "Not even my mum?" she said and turned on her full-wattage smile.

Caro's eyes widened. "That's all right if she's not noisy or messy."

Result. Laura tried to keep her cheesy grin to a polite smile. Her heart fluttered like confetti settling on a church path, anticipating her mum's delight. "She's sixty-two. I'm sure she won't be partying all night." Although she did do a mean karaoke, but Laura didn't bring that up.

Caro nodded. "Okay, if it's not longer than a few days."

"Perfect." Laura did a little happy dance in her head - her mum could stay, and she had just chipped away the first sliver of ice from this intriguing woman. "What a great room. Are you sure you don't want to use it? I'd be happy to share. Although if I spend too long here, I won't get my project done." Laura tried to contain her excitement, though she was itching to do a happy dance.

Caro raised her eyebrows. "It was never really my room, and I can't—" She bit her lip as though she had said too much and frowned as if she was cross with herself.

She turned around and paced up a set of steep, narrow stairs. a sharp contrast with the wide, elegant stairs in the other part of the house. Maybe Laura was being taken to the servants' quarters. That didn't matter if she could spend time in this wonderful room, so unlike the tiny space she would have had to share in Bristol.

The bedroom was simple, with wooden floors that looked like they were original and were varnished to a sheen. They squeaked as she moved across them. In the centre of the room was an iron-framed bed. *That would be good for attaching handcuffs*. Where did that come from?

"This is your room, and the bathroom is a family bathroom, but it's for your sole use. The bath is deep but don't fill it as it will take too much hot water."

"It's all right. I prefer showers." Laura twirled around and could hardly contain her delight. "You have a most beautiful home."

"If I have friends to stay, we'll all be in the other part of the house and won't disturb you. I eat early and want the place to be kept tidy after you finish. I don't want to come down to dirty dishes. And I don't want the smell of cooking to pervade the entire house, either."

Caro's reluctance to let out the room hung heavy in the air between them, but Laura had to make it work. "It's okay. I eat late, so I shouldn't bother you." She couldn't promise about cooking smells though. She loved to cook the Andalusian specialities that her dad had taught her, especially the ones which drew people to his restaurant. Perhaps she could burn candles to absorb the smells. Her mouth watered just thinking of preparing meals in Caro's huge kitchen.

"I don't want to be disturbed. At all. I need to get back to work," Caro said.

Her expression shifted from glaring to one of misery and then, just as quickly, the frown returned. What caused Caro to scowl? Why had she bothered to put her room up for rent when she could end up with a student, all bad rep, noise, and mess? But Laura would put up with a grumpy landlady when she could have her own glorious, individual space, with no one to "borrow" her food or bang on the door when she was showering, and her own library snug to curl up in. It was perfect. "Don't worry, I'll be at uni most of the time. I'm so excited about starting my master's program. I've been dreaming of this, and I've been saving for it for several years now." She thought Caro might enquire what she was doing, but she didn't seem to have any curiosity at all. "I'm doing a Master's in Animation." Laura needed to fill the void.

Caro shrugged. "Did the accommodation office tell you the cost per month?"

"Yes, Tracey told me, and that's fine. Would you like the deposit and the month in advance as she suggested? If I do that transfer now, could I move in today?" She said a little prayer for her dad, who had transferred the money to her account a couple of days ago. She was grateful she hadn't paid the deposit or first month's rent to Rob; she had an inkling that getting it back from him would have been difficult, if not impossible.

Caro nodded. "See you do. I'm going back to my studio. Be careful of my paintwork and use the back stairs."

"Sure." Laura went out to Matt, who was playing a game on his phone.

"I was just coming in to see if you'd been murdered," Matt said without raising his head.

"Yeah, right." Laura nodded toward his phone. "You were going to level up first, and I could have been lying there with blood pumping from my neck." She flung her arm across her forehead in a melodramatic style.

"Nah, I'd have heard the scream. I'm sure your ex-girlfriend told me you're a screamer."

Matt's snark showed he was settled with the arrangement. They both grinned.

"Ha-di-ha. You don't know her."

Of Light and Love

"You didn't deny it, though. So, what's she like?" He gestured to the house, making it clear he had moved on from her ex, Valentina. Laura shook her head, not wanting to think about Valentina or waste time on her lies, and betrayal, and the ever present hurt that lined her stomach like vinegar. "Frosty McFrost Face. I'm determined to get her to smile at me... Well, I would, but she's fled to her studio to avoid helping me move in."

"Yeah. Maybe I should have tried hiding in my room," Matt said. "Or maybe not."

"Let's do this, then we can grab a pizza." Laura spun like a ballerina as she made her way to the van doors. This was perfect, and it would be even better once she got McFrost Face to smile.

Chapter Five

CARO'S FINGERS TREMBLED AS she tapped out Rebecca's number.

She answered on the second ring. "Caro, darling, perfect timing. I was talking to Freddie about doing a retrospective of your work. It's the thing you need to get out of yourself. Some of the existing owners are happy to loan their pictures to the gallery for a few weeks. If you add just three little pictures based on the sketches you showed me, that would be perfect. I can see them now, dark and brooding with bright light on the face. It will give you a focus, and you can stay with us while the show is on. We'll go into town and have some fun like the old days. What do you think?"

Caro exhaled slowly, giving herself time to think so she wouldn't be sucked into Rebecca's latest project. "This isn't why I called you. There are people invading my house, and I'm petrified they're going to rifle in my bedroom. I'm hiding in my studio."

Rebecca took a sharp intake of breath. "Shall I call the police?" She dropped her upper middle-class braying and slipped into her natural Birmingham accent.

Caro gripped onto the bench and willed her heart to stop racing. "The student's got a man helping her, and he's all long legs and gangly hands."

Rebecca laughed. "Darling, you've had men there before. Yvonne had hundreds of men around."

"That was then, and this is now. I can't cope with someone invading my space, and now there are two of them trampling dirt all over Yvonne's carpets." Caro wasn't really concerned about dirt; Artemisia trailed muddy paw prints in the house regularly, as well as depositing the occasional furball. The whole idea that she had let someone into her sanctuary and that they might see her shrine to Yvonne gave her the shivers. She didn't want to change.

"I thought you said women only?" Rebecca asked gently.

"I did, and she is, well… I was quite horrible to her, and she made huge puppy dog eyes at me. I was such a bitch, and that isn't me. It isn't who I

27

E.V. Bancroft

am. Is it? Have I become a monster?" Caro willed herself to calm down and breathe more slowly.

"No, darling, you're not a monster, but you have become a hermit, and it's not good for you. You need to get out more, come to London. The kids would love to see you again," Rebecca said.

"They probably don't know who I am anymore." The reality hit Caro like the dropping of a guillotine. She had become so self-obsessed she hadn't even sent birthday cards or presents. Great godmother she was. She also didn't want to have the same conversation with Rebecca about getting antidepressants. Yes, she was depressed, and she didn't need anyone to tell her that. She'd seen it in Yvonne. She didn't want to take medication either. That's what had destroyed Yvonne. That and the alcohol. Caro shook her head as if she could eliminate the memory. She needed to step away from that well-grooved track. Again.

Exhaling heavily, as if she was trying to eject the uncomfortable thoughts, she brought herself back to the conversation. "The student's name is Laura. She lives in Spain although she sounds English."

"Is she cute?"

Caro blinked, recalling her wide, burnt umber eyes, glossy brown hair, soft curves, pleasing features, and gleaming olive skin. She could never understand why the tone was called olive. It was nothing like the colour olive; more a mix of raw sienna, phthalo blue, a touch of cadmium red, and the slightest hint of yellow-green. Caro would be fascinated to capture the richness of her skin tone and that wistful expression.

What was she thinking? "Don't be ridiculous, she must be ten years younger than me," Caro said.

"Hun, you waited far too long to reply. Do I need to point out Yvonne was fifteen years older than you?"

Caro's cheeks heated, and she was grateful it wasn't a video call. "That was different."

"How so? You need to look forward. It's been two years."

Something inside Caro snapped. Everyone thought she could talk her way out of grief, that sufficient time had passed. Grief didn't work like that. It danced to its own macabre rhythm, like a skeleton in a Día de los Muertos march. "Enough. I can't stand it. I can't do it." Caro ripped the ruined canvas off the easel and tossed it on the floor.

"Whoa, I'm not telling you to do anything. I just thought if your

28

lodger's nice or cute, why not enjoy her company?"

Caro had had enough of this conversation. She peered out of the studio windows and spied shadows in the snug, moving across the window as they carried through boxes. "I don't want her company. I've already told her she can only use the snug, not the lounge, and only cook in the kitchen when I'm not using it. She promised to eat late, and she'll be at the university most of the time."

"She sounds like the perfect lodger. You get the money you need and your own free time to concentrate on your work without worrying about boilers and oil bills," Rebecca said. "So, what's really wrong?"

She hoped that Rebecca would let it go, but they'd known each other too long and shared too many secrets. The fear spiralled in on itself tighter and tighter until she could hardly breathe. "I don't know. It's change. I feel as though I'm moving on, and Yvonne would hate it. It's like I'm forgetting her or betraying her memory. It's getting more difficult to recall her face with the same clarity. I have to look through the sketches to remind myself—"

"Nonsense. Yvonne would hate to see you moping around. She'd hate to see this shadow of your previous self. If the position was reversed, don't you think Yvonne would've moved on by now?"

Caro cleaned her brushes in thinners, annoyed she'd left them too long and the paint had caked on, clogging the bristles. "That's not the same, and Yvonne was so different from me. She loved people, loved being around them and being the centre of attention. I hate it. I don't want other people. And those bloody kids are getting more courageous with their taunting. I can't even concentrate because I'm just waiting for them to bang on the door again."

"Talk to the parents," Rebecca said, adopting the commanding voice she used with her own children.

Caro didn't want the confrontation. She just wanted to be left alone, to howl at the storm. "The parents are some liberal doctors from the hospital who think their kids can do as they want. They don't believe in discipline or getting children to respect other people's property and privacy." Caro tossed the ruined brushes in the bin. What a waste of time and money.

"You could tell them you can't work if you're being disturbed. How would they like it if they were in the middle of surgery and someone burst in? You can say your agent is requesting, no demanding, that you work."

Rebecca was right, but that didn't mean Caro was going to challenge her neighbours. The truth was pulling her into a maelstrom, she was too exhausted to escape from. Caro cleared her throat. "I can't work anymore. Every day, I come into the studio, but nothing comes. I've sorted everything, prepped all the canvases, but I've lost my muse and confidence, and I'm too numb to express any emotions. I don't have it anymore." Everything else was an excuse, maybe a valid reason, but the crux was she couldn't paint anymore. It wasn't physical. It was that her whole essence was tied up in being an artist. It was how she had related to herself for so long that it had become ingrained. Facing an empty canvas was like staring at the abyss, knowing she was about to fall but unable to do anything about it. Unbidden, tears came rushing up, and she blinked to dam them.

"It'll come back to you. You've got so much skill and talent. You're a household name. Most artists would kill for that. How many people can claim that a poster of one of their paintings outsold Van Gogh's sunflowers? Doing the retrospective would inspire you. Or you could experiment with something new."

Rebecca's relentlessness was part of why she was so successful as an agent, but Caro needed someone to understand, not judge or cajole. "That's the trouble with you. I never know who's talking, my best friend or agent. I can't do it."

"Hey, hey, don't worry. Look, I'm busy this weekend, but I'll come down the following Friday, and we'll go away for a few days to the coast, body boarding at Croyde or Woolacombe. We'll have fun splashing in the waves. You can laugh at me when I struggle into my wetsuit. I've been eating too many canapes recently, or maybe it's the champagne. I'd love to escape from London for a few days."

"Okay." There was no point arguing. Rebecca would arrive and whisk her off whether or not she agreed. Caro peered at her house. Figures moved in the kitchen area. "What do I do? She's in the kitchen, but I want a drink."

"It's your kitchen, darling. Just go in, smile, and get yourself a cup of tea. You don't have to stand and chat, although it would be nice if you made her welcome. Perhaps you could apologise for being horrible to her earlier."

"I'm not a complete imbecile," Caro said.

"No, darling, but don't forget to smile. You can be quite intimidating when you scowl."

Caro raised her eyebrows out of the frown Rebecca had guessed was there. "Remind me why you're my friend."

"Hun, you love me. I look after you, and I keep you on the bent and narrow. Now go in there, grab your drink, and smile."

Rebecca ended the call with a kissing noise. Did she think Caro was some ogre? If she ordered another kettle, she could make herself tea in her studio, without having to interact. "Smile on, tits out," Yvonne always said before any big event or going on air. Caro stiffened her back. She could do this, though she wouldn't be baring her breasts to anyone anytime soon.

Chapter Six

LAURA SAID GOODBYE TO Matt, Rob, and Kaylee after they'd shared pizza, with her leftovers wrapped in aluminium foil. She couldn't stop the pang of envy at the camaraderie in the bright, noisy house. Matt seemed settled, and he and Kaylee had been arguing the finer points of a particular Star Trek episode as she left.

Now it was her job to explore new worlds and boldly go for twenty minutes through the deserted streets to her bus stop. She splashed through the puddles, her Doc Martens distorting them as they reflected the lights spilling from the flats and boarded shops. There were the usual crude drawings and tags on the shutters but also two pictures of women that were really great street art. Great art, full stop. Since Banksy, people were prepared to see graffiti as art, even if he mocked the art afficionados when he could.

Laura pulled her jacket around her shoulders, aching from all the lifting today, and she hopped from foot to foot to generate some warmth. She definitely needed to sort out her bike. Finally, the bus drew up with a hiss and a clatter, and she jumped on board, scanning her ticket. "Hi. It's getting cold out there," she said and smiled, hoping to coax a response from the driver.

He stared, obviously not used to people actually talking to him. Eventually, he nodded as if satisfied she didn't pose a threat or cause a nuisance.

Laura scanned the interior. There were no other passengers. "I'll see if I can find a seat then."

He didn't even break a twitch of a smile. Laura swung from pole to pole and let the momentum carry her onto a seat as the bus lurched forward. Had she pissed him off? The bus had recharging stations, so she plugged in her phone. She'd be able to call her mum when she got back and made a mental note to ask what the Wi-Fi code was. Surely Crusty Caro had broadband? She hadn't thought to ask earlier, and she'd be stuffed if she didn't. She'd have to WhatsApp call her mum from the campus. Laura leaned her head against the window, ignoring the condensation that dampened her hair, and tried to make out anything in the dark, but all she could see was her own lonely reflection and the lights of the bus.

"Can you let me know when we get to the bus stop by the church, please?" she called out. The driver didn't reply, and her heartbeat thudded. Nothing was familiar from earlier. Had she taken the wrong bus? She was about to shout out again when she spotted the pub two stops before hers. She perched at the edge of the seat, ready to exit.

The vehicle drew to a stop. The driver glanced behind but said nothing. Laura bounced up the length of the bus and jumped down to the pavement. "Thank you. Good night." The doors shut behind her. She'd had her fill of grumpy people and confrontation today. Never mind. A strong coffee and a chat with her mum would restore her equilibrium. She'd probably be fidgeting to know how Laura had got on today.

The lane was pitch black, and she was glad she had charged her phone as she scurried up the road, convincing herself she was hurrying because of the cold. She didn't consider the country being dark at night. In Granada, the Alhambra was always lit up in the evenings. A sliver of homesickness washed over her. She missed her parents.

Laura tiptoed into the kitchen to switch the kettle on and put her pizza in the fridge. The kitchen was quiet, the only light coming from the microwave. Had Caro gone to bed? Laura glanced at her watch to see it was only ten. Okay, so she'd have to get used to being quiet in the evenings. As she waited for the kettle to boil, Laura took her jotter pad out of her backpack and tore off half a piece of paper to scribble a note. *Please help yourself, Laura x.* She placed it on top of the wrapped pizza. Maybe the kiss was over the top, but she had to start somewhere in Mission Thaw.

She padded down the corridor, taking care not to stomp, and dragged herself up the back stairs, feeling wearier with every footstep. Relieved they'd made the bed before she left, she dropped onto the mattress and revelled in its thickness. She stretched out and snuggled under the duvet. It would be eleven in Spain, so her dad would still be front of house at the restaurant, but her mum would be free. "Hi."

"Sweetheart, how are you? Are you all settled? I've been thinking about you all day. How's Matt? Is it okay at Rob's? It's lovely to hear your voice. I know I shouldn't worry, but I do."

"Oh, Mum." There was something about hearing her voice, so bubbly and full of joy, that meant home and safety and being loved. Or maybe she was exhausted, emotionally as well as physically, after the trial of a day. Laura teared up, and she choked down a sob.

"What's the matter?"

"I'm not at Rob's house because he'd already let out my room, assuming Matt and I were a couple, so I had to find somewhere else. It's stupid, but it fed into my whole rejection stuff."

"That bloody woman has a lot to answer for. I'll never forgive her for hurting my baby girl."

Laura snorted a snotty laugh. "I'll be thirty in a few weeks' time." She didn't think her mother would call her baby girl if she knew what she and Valentina had done in bed. But the breakup still hurt. Her confidence was crushed, and she shouldn't need to speak through a puppet to put her point across.

"I know, I know, but you'll always be my baby girl. Now, tell me what's wrong. Where are you staying tonight? Did they find you a hotel? If you need more money, just tell us and we'll transfer it."

"You've both already sent me enough, thanks. It's just..." Tears spilled over her eyelashes.

"Honey, tell me about it. Please don't cry, you'll set me off and you're so far away. I just want to give you a big mum hug."

"I need a mum hug," Laura said before explaining what had happened. "The place may be beautiful, but Caro doesn't want me here, and she doesn't want to interact at all. What is it about me that people don't even like me, let alone love me?" She was whining but couldn't seem to help herself.

"That's not true. Everybody loves you. You're lovely, kind, and intelligent. Who wouldn't love you? And I'm not counting Valentina. She was just a selfish bitch."

It wasn't like her mum to swear or say a bad word about people, and Laura could feel the swell of her mother's anger, even though it had happened months ago. "I know people like me, they just don't love me in that way. I thought I'd found my soulmate, but she had other ideas." Laura thought about her plans to propose to Valentina, where they would hold their wedding venue, and how they would spend their lives together.

"Sweetheart, that only means she wasn't the right one for you. Don't give up on love. Look at yourself, you're not even thirty."

Laura chuckled. "Only for another month or so. Then I'll definitely be on the shelf. Who meets the love of their life this late?" Laura only said it to hear her mum's nostalgic story about meeting her dad.

"I was thirty when I met your dad. When we shared tapas over the bar. I knew he was the one for me, and we've been happily married ever since."

"I know, but you two are ridiculous. They could use your story as a Hallmark movie for the holiday romance that lasted."

Her mum laughed because she couldn't deny it. When Laura was a child, she'd thought everyone had a loving family like her. They were busy but always made time for her and for each other. It wasn't until much later she realised how lucky she was. She loved her mum like a sister, friend, and mother all at once. The conversation and the caffeine had revived her.

"Come on, show me round your room," her mum said.

"Okay, hang on." Laura reversed the camera and did a quick tour of the room and bathroom to the sound effects of lots of oohs and ahs. After she went down the stairs and took her phone into the snug, her mum let out a squeal of delight.

"That's lovely. You're so lucky to be there. What a beautiful place. And you say it's only five miles from the campus?"

"Yeah. There's a bus at the end of the lane that goes directly to the entrance, but I could also get my bike out."

"It seems perfect. And you'll see Matt and your friends when you go into your course. Who cares if your landlord is grumpy? If she keeps out of your way, which is what she wants, then it seems like you're onto a winner."

"Thanks. I knew you'd make me feel better. Did I tell you I love you?"

"I love you too, but I miss you. I hope you'll be able to get back for Christmas. It won't be the same celebrating without you."

Laura stared up at the tower of moving boxes. The thought of unpacking them made her groan. She sat up. "I know, Mum, I'll do what I can. I just don't want to meet up with Valentina and Gonzalo or my old work colleagues. It's humiliating."

"*They* should be humiliated. They had the affair, not you."

"I know, but the rest of society seems to delight that a queer girl went back to the light, to the straight and narrow."

"Bullshit."

Two swear words in one conversation? "I'll let you know, Mum. In the meantime, my newest project is to get Grumpy Caro to smile at me. I'm calling it Mission Thaw."

"That's my girl. Don't worry, she's only your landlady."

Laura grabbed a tissue and blew her nose. "I know, but I don't understand why she doesn't like me."

"It's nothing to do with you. She may have had no choice about taking a tenant. Maybe she's short of cash or overextended herself in her big house. All fur coat and no knickers."

Laura laughed at her mother's strange sayings. They were always quirky and had an innocence about them. "I think she must be an artist. I glimpsed a painting on an easel in her studio. Perhaps I could get her to talk about her art. That's something we have in common. She said you could come over though and stay here, so I guess she can't be all bad."

Her mum squealed with delight. "I'd love to see you and visit where you live."

"I could show you around the campus, too. It's wonderful. It's set in parkland. And we could see the suspension bridge, and the museums, and the art galleries. I was going to drag Matt to London, but he's not interested, so we could go instead."

"I'd love that. I've missed them all."

They said goodbye, and Laura wandered back upstairs to her vast bedroom. She looked around the strange room that would be her home for the next few months and snuggled under the fresh smelling duvet, warmed by the conversation with her mum and grateful for her love. Maybe Caro just needed someone to show her affection. She would definitely try to get Caro to smile, starting tomorrow.

Chapter Seven

THE FOLLOWING EVENING, CARO walked into the kitchen and stopped abruptly. Laura was singing and dancing as she listened to music on headphones and stirred whatever she was making on the hob. Her energy was warm, a flash of magenta and buttercup yellow. Caro sidled around the kitchen island to the kettle, but it was empty. She needed a chamomile tea to help her sleep. Who was she kidding? She would never fall asleep and mouldy weeds wouldn't help.

The rich scent of Laura's food assaulted her nose, the individual flavours of garlic, onions, and olives, and she salivated. It smelled delicious. Laura was gyrating, completely engrossed in what she was doing. There was something so appealing in Laura's vivacity and joy in such a simple task as preparing food for herself. Caro hated making meals and as often as not, didn't bother to cook. Yvonne had always loved to entertain, and cooking was how she wound down.

Caro used to bake but hadn't for many years. She'd loved how different ingredients changed the texture and the colour of the food. It was like painting with tastes, and she loved to add unexpected spices into cakes and biscuits. That was then, and this was now. Caro had left the kitchen door open and, attracted by the glorious smells, Artemisia came sauntering in, affecting nonchalance. But she didn't rub against Caro's legs like she normally did, demanding food and attention. Instead, she went straight to Laura at the hob and nuzzled her head against her jeans. What a traitor.

Laura bent and stroked the cat and rubbed behind her ears. "How lovely. Hello, beautiful. Aren't you handsome? I wonder what your name is, you elegant cat."

"Artemisia."

Laura turned quickly, her eyes comically wide. She tapped at her headphones. "Oh, hi, Caro, I didn't hear you. I hope it's all right me cooking now. I thought you'd finished for the evening?" She looked up with her pleading puppy eyes.

E.V. Bancroft

Caro rolled her shoulders. She should apologise, as Rebecca had suggested. "I was just coming for a chamomile tea before I go to bed." She was being such a coward. Why didn't she just say it and be done with it, and they could start anew? Yvonne would have already made her welcome and probably offered her a glass of wine or something stronger.

"Sorry for disturbing you when I arrived," Laura said and smiled. "You didn't want my peace-a offering then?" She nodded at the leftover pizza placed on a plate.

What a terrible pun. Caro would not encourage that, and she needed to set boundaries. This arrangement had to be strictly business and professional. But the smells were heavenly and were making her stomach rumble. "I don't eat pizza." That wasn't strictly true, she just hadn't eaten pizza for over two years.

"Okay, I hope you don't mind then, but I gave a little to your cat."

"She doesn't like strangers." As if to prove Caro wrong, Artemisia mewed up at Laura and nuzzled her cheeks against her legs, claiming her as the newest servant. "Traitor," Caro said, not able to control a slight smile.

Laura lit up. "Do you need some water?" Laura snatched up the kettle and filled it, placing it carefully on the heating element before switching it on. "You have a beautiful cat. I didn't catch what you said her name was?"

"Artemisia."

Laura smiled. "As in Artemisia Gentileschi?"

Caro had to close her mouth. She didn't expect a younger person to be interested in painting. They were normally into installations and multimedia, not skill and graft. "You know Gentileschi? She's my hero."

Laura grinned and stirred her supper. It smelt so good Caro licked her lips. It had nothing to do with the fascinating woman in front of her, just the delicious scent.

"She was a fantastic painter, and it's amazing she could do that in Renaissance Italy. I think my favourite is of the two women, Judith and her maidservant. Their look of surprise as though they'd been disturbed," Laura said and licked the spoon in a tantalising way.

"Well, they have just killed Holofernes." How refreshing to talk about art. "Which version are you thinking of? She did a few variations."

"The one in Florence."

There was no hesitation, and Laura genuinely seemed interested. "I prefer the one in Detroit," Caro said, trying to test the boundaries of her knowledge.

"That's similar to the one in Cannes, yeah. My mum took me there."

"Really?" Caro grasped the edge of the kitchen counter.

"My mum used to be a painter. She went down to Spain on a painting holiday and met my dad there. She gave it up to help him look after his bar and restaurant but any opportunity she got, she'd take me off to see the galleries in Europe. It was wonderful. But why do you prefer the Detroit version?" A thin line of concentration appeared between Laura's brows on her flawless face. No, not flawless, there was a slight scar on her forehead, but that made her more intriguing.

"I love the really strong contrast between dark and light in that version," Caro said, tamping down her curiosity.

"Oh, the chiaroscuro. Yeah, I love that. There's something so compelling about darkness and light. There's something so fundamental about it, like watching a distant thunderstorm with a house in bright sunlight in the foreground."

Caro couldn't believe Laura was talking about her passion. A thrill ran up her spine. No, she needed to keep this businesslike. She clamped her mouth shut and nodded to the kettle.

Laura gestured to the pan, as if she misunderstood her meaning. "Would you like some Spanish meatballs? I've made too much for me to eat."

"No, thanks, I was going to bed."

"Sure. Let me pour your tea out." Laura drew down a mug from the overhead cabinet. Yvonne's mug.

"No, not that one. Mine is the Zeltser Gallery mug."

Rebecca had given it to her. It had been one of her husband's early mistakes. Most of Freddie's clients expected champagne when they came to the gallery, so they offloaded the mugs onto all and sundry. They had given Caro two, although Yvonne had broken one when she had come off the phone to her producers in a rage.

Laura handed over the mug with the tea bag in it. She stared deep into Caro's eyes, and Caro was reminded how stunning and intriguing this woman was. If she could capture the light and shade on her face—but it wasn't polite to ask. Besides, she had to finish her final pictures of Yvonne for Rebecca. If she could paint anymore. The very thought of picking up her brush caused her heart rate to rise. Laura stared at her, as if waiting for her to speak. "Thanks. Sorry if I didn't make you very welcome yesterday. I'm finding this quite difficult."

Laura positively glowed. "I understand. I'm sorry if we disturbed your work."

What work? Caro stared at her, unsure what to say, feeling exposed. She couldn't admit to that, so she cupped the tea in her hands. "Thanks for the tea. Can you make sure the kitchen is clean when you finish? Good night."

"Of course. And Caro, thank you."

"What? Why?"

"For opening up your home to me. I bought you a little thank-you gift." Laura handed over a purple orchid from the countertop.

The flower was beautiful and must have been quite expensive for a student. Caro put down the tea to receive it. The poor unsuspecting plant didn't know what it had coming. "Thank you, but you shouldn't have. I'll only kill it. I kill all houseplants. I don't mean to, but I do."

Laura grinned. "Well, let's see if we can keep it alive together then."

Caro nodded and turned away. She wouldn't say it had been a pleasure, but Laura seemed nice, and she smiled as much as a celebrity on the red carpet. They wouldn't be doing anything *together*, but the fact that Laura was so pleasant should make their living situation bearable. Caro had no doubt she'd still kill the orchid. She just hoped she wouldn't kill the friendly atmosphere Laura was clearly trying so hard to cultivate.

Chapter Eight

LAURA STRETCHED HER FINGERS out and rolled her shoulders. Eight straight hours of lectures was a killer. But they had to do that in order to squash the programme into twelve months. Ravi Kumar, the balding, rotund lecturer, seemed to droop. Poor guy was probably exhausted.

"Before we finish, just a reminder that I'll need to have your project ideas submitted by the end of next week."

Everyone groaned. Laura glanced at Matt, whose eyes had glazed over at having to concentrate so long. "Can we do a joint project?" she asked.

Kumar fixed her with a stern gaze. Okay, so she'd just shaken a snake's tail. *Note to self: don't ask difficult questions at ten o'clock at night.*

"No, Laura, you cannot do a joint project. This isn't a high school piece. This is graduate level work we expect."

Laura swallowed hard but smiled wider. "I understand that, Ravi, but with a joint project I'd expect to do a ten-minute piece, not five." She was conscious of Matt sitting beside her, jiggling his legs under the desk. He was fully alert now. She placed a hand on his thigh to still his trembling limbs.

Ravi sighed as if he was dealing with a first grader. "No, Laura, I know what you're trying to do. Each piece must be unique, and your critique is to assess what you've achieved in *all* aspects of the project."

Laura nodded. She'd planned to pitch their project to studios. She squeezed Matt's arm and leaned into him. "Don't worry, we can still help each other out." The fear in his eyes betrayed how well he thought his project would fare.

"Before you go," Ravi said, "I want you all to learn how to draw even if you plan to do your project on the computer." He swung around to glare at Laura and Matt. "Every animator should be able to sketch, and I expect to see your sketchpads as part of your portfolio."

Sketchpads? Laura hadn't used a pencil since her undergraduate days. She cleared her throat. "Can we draw using Procreate or a similar program?"

Ravi seemed to evaluate her. "Fine. Use a computer if you must. I expect you to draw anything and everything. Not just characters in motion, but water, trees, life drawing. The key is to observe everything and translate that observation onto paper or tablet." He checked his watch. "Now, if there's nothing else, that's all for this evening. See you on Thursday for your next session. Goodnight."

Laura stretched again. She would definitely need to do some yoga this evening. She turned to Matt, who was staring ahead, not even putting his notebooks into his rucksack. He looked so pale, and the freckles across his nose and cheeks formed an angry constellation.

"I don't know what to do," he muttered.

"We can talk about it at the pub. My bus isn't for another forty minutes." One thing she hadn't considered when moving to the country was that the buses after ten at night were scarce. Soon, nights would draw in and it was getting colder, so she really needed to get her bike sorted.

"Kaylee's going to cook tonight for Rob and me," Matt said, still gripping his backpack.

Laura felt the sting of rejection, and her already defeated self-esteem withered a little more. She wouldn't let that happen. This was just the long-term impact of Valentina's betrayal. It wasn't the same just because it started with them having a few innocent drinks together after work, then going away together on a conference. How ironic that she'd stayed to work and gain promotion so that she and Valentina could settle down. Matt wasn't Valentina, and he certainly wasn't her lover, but the exclusion still stung. "I thought we could talk about the projects and how we approach them, because we can still help each other. With your technical skills and my creativity, we make an awesome team."

They'd worked well when they were both interns at Aardvark, the large animation studios where they'd met. Matt was a whizz with the computer modelling. She hadn't broached it with him yet, but she hoped she could persuade him to work on her pitch to the Granada studios she used to work in and to come over if they took up the idea.

Matt beamed. "Yeah, I'd love that."

"I'll pop into Aldi and pick up some garlic bread. I'll just have to get going before midnight to catch the last bus."

Matt relaxed his shoulders. "That'll work."

They strode down under the underpass to Matt's house. "What project do you want to do?" Laura asked.

Matt fidgeted with the hem of his sleeve as though he was hiding his hands. "I'm not creative at all. I can't think."

Laura tried to think of something he could relate to. "What about a space opera, the first five minutes anyway, a bit like Star Trek?"

"But we're not allowed to do fan fiction."

"No, it won't be. You just think about key characters and develop it from there. Every story is one of only seven plots, so they say."

Matt's cheeks coloured, and he stiffened. "Star Trek is different."

"Okay, keep your hair on. How about you tell me your favourite Star Trek episode, and we can develop something from that?" By the time they arrived at Matt's house, Laura had talked through a rough idea for Matt, and they'd agreed to work on it ready for a presentation the following week.

"Great, you're here. I'm just putting on the pasta now. Hey, Laura, do you want some supper?" Kaylee asked from the kitchen.

"Thanks. I come bearing garlic bread."

Kaylee dumped a jar of Bolognese mix into a pan at the same time as the pasta. Laura cringed. It would be overcooked, but she was a guest, and beggars couldn't be choosers. She took the opportunity to chat to Kaylee as she popped the garlic bread in the oven.

A few minutes later, they tucked into the garlic bread as they squashed together around the tiny table. Four was really tight, and Laura sat side-on so she didn't knock against Matt.

"So, Laura," Rob said. "How's your bitch of a landlady?"

Laura bristled. If Rob hadn't been so greedy, she wouldn't be with Caro.

"She's a nightmare," Matt said.

Laura put down her fork. "Hey, she apologised for being shitty the other night. Maybe she's just got stuff going on." She realised she was quoting her mum.

"No need to be a bitch, though," Rob said as he shoved another spoonful of pasta in his mouth. He turned to Kaylee. "This is awesome, thanks."

Kaylee smiled. "Just thrown together."

Laura nudged Matt.

"Um, yeah. Thanks."

Laura watched between the two men, clearly wanting to make an impression on the pretty girl in their mix. She expected them to snarl at each other any minute. "Hey, Kaylee, do you have all the Star Trek episodes? We thought Matt could base his project on the programme."

Kaylee brightened. "Only Janeway."

Laura nodded, delighted to see Kaylee was eager to help. "Matt is going to take Picard, his favourite, and change him a bit, give him a new identity—"

"He could call him Dick Hard," Rob said, then coloured up as all three stared at him. "Joke." Rob shrugged.

Laura ignored Rob's inappropriate behaviour. "Yeah, well, as I was saying, we can develop the project from that basic idea."

"That sounds cool." Kaylee smiled at Matt with a distinct sparkle in her eyes.

"Matt thought maybe there could be a challenge between his Picard character and a Janeway-type character on how they should fight the aliens. But they succeed when they work together." They hadn't discussed any of this on their walk home, and Matt gawped. *Play along with me, Matt, I'm trying to get her hooked for you.*

Kaylee huffed. "Janeway would win."

"No, it needs to be cooperative at the end." Laura grinned. "Are you going to Comic Con in London?"

Kaylee shook her head. "I can't afford it."

"Matt and I have tickets. I can't go now, so you're welcome to have my ticket."

Matt opened his mouth to protest, but Laura kicked him with the side of her foot. Then he twigged. "Yeah, George Takei is going."

"Wow, that's awesome." Kaylee bounced in her seat. "Are you sure you don't mind giving up your ticket, Laura?"

She minded very much, but it was a minor sacrifice to edge Kaylee towards Matt rather than the idiot, Rob. "It's better than it going to waste. I haven't booked our coach tickets yet, but you should be able to get a cheap deal."

Kaylee jumped up and squeezed around the table to hug Laura. "Thank you, thank you, thank you."

Rob glared at Laura, smelling a rat, but she smiled sweetly at him. "Hey, Rob, have you played the latest Call of Duty?"

Of Light and Love

Rob seemed torn between being annoyed with Laura and wanting to talk about his favourite topic. He had been amazed when Laura said she worked for the famous Granada gaming company, Domingo Studios. It'd had three huge hits, one of which Laura had worked on extensively with Gonzalo. She ignored the vision of Gonzalo and Valentina in bed together; she had a new life and a new project. Laura checked the time. "I'd better go, I've a bus to catch. See you. Thanks for supper, Kaylee." Delighted to escape having to make small talk with Rob, she got up and grabbed her rucksack.

Kaylee beamed at her. "Anytime."

Laura closed the door behind her to stride out into the dark, pleased with the evening's work. She'd tipped things in Matt's favour; it was up to him now to develop it. Laura had a bus to catch and a second project to consider: Mission Thaw.

Chapter Nine

THE HOUSE WASN'T THE same. There were sounds of activity, a clunk of a pan on the stove and a dropped fork. Caro hoped Laura would wipe down the floor with kitchen towel. Yvonne was always so particular about her kitchen, though the whole house was her pride and joy. She loved to cook and chat to Caro, who had lounged on the sofa reading an art magazine or talked to the guests when they were entertaining. Where had all those people gone? Onto the next celebrity they could suck dry, no doubt.

Caro was hiding in her bedroom because Laura was fixing herself some food. Even at the end of the house, the cooking smells seeped through her senses. Maybe she'd got used to being on her own, being able to talk to Yvonne with no one listening. It wasn't normal to talk to a dead wife, but it comforted her. She was petrified Laura would go into her room and see her shrine to Yvonne. To the right of the bed was a dressing table with various photos and mementos from their twelve years together, ticket stubs for the opera and the ballet, the gold necklace Caro bought for Yvonne on the Ponte Vecchio in Florence, and a treasure trove of trinkets and reminders that kept Yvonne central in her life.

Caro picked up the photo of their wedding, where they were both laughing. Yvonne stared, beautiful and arresting, into the camera as though she was peering into the soul of the viewer. Caro gazed at Yvonne, her expression one of deep adoration. They had been so happy, but now she struggled to picture Yvonne's face without having to resort to photographs, to recall her sultry tones without playing some of her videos on YouTube.

She traced her thumb over Yvonne's face. "I'm sorry. I hope you don't think I'm forgetting you. The house isn't the same anymore. There's a strange energy about the place. It's not Laura's fault. It's just she's so young, and exuberant, and smiley, it doesn't feel like ours anymore. I'm sure you won't mind, but I really didn't have a choice. I can't afford to keep it with no income coming in, so it seemed to be the best of an awful situation. I didn't want to let it go. The house was always so precious to us, our little oasis of sanity in the madness of the world."

There was the clattering of plates from the kitchen, and Laura sang as she cleared up. Caro could imagine her gyrating with that blissful, and so compelling, expression. She diverted her attention back to Yvonne's picture. "And Laura has been tidying the kitchen as you would like it, and she knows not to use your mug now. But she never uses a tea pot. She always makes tea in a mug. I'm not sure you'd approve, but I think you'd like her. She's intelligent and has more than a passing interest in the arts, and she's funny when she's not trying too hard. It sounds as though I'm trying to convince you. But I don't feel I can relax in the lounge anymore, because she demands a conversation when all I want to do is sip my gin and tonic and listen to my new soundtrack, Donizetti's Una Furtiva Lagrima."

Caro put down the photo and stared at her painting of Yvonne. She was stretched out, legs akimbo, almost entirely in darkness with a single low light source from the left highlighting the planes of her flesh. At the apex of her thighs, nestled in the dark curls, the glisten of sex reflected light. Her expression was of unadulterated pleasure, satiated after orgasm. This was Yvonne at her most vulnerable, painted from a sketch Caro had made just after they had made love. That passion flowed through every brush stroke.

It was one of her best paintings, but she would never share it with the world. Yvonne had always been delighted Caro hadn't painted all her wrinkles, but Caro liked it because it encapsulated Yvonne. A part of her hidden in the shadows, enjoying the simple pleasures of cooking and gardening but she was never completely unguarded. Caro had been treated to glimpses of that wonderful soul but never the whole person, despite being together for twelve years. She was almost as old now as Yvonne had been when they met, when Yvonne was in her prime, appearing on TV daily. And each weekend, they held parties for her media friends that resulted in much drinking and snorting. But they all drifted away when Yvonne's vibrancy faded, like the old masters that bleached and dulled.

Caro's phone rang. It was tempting not to answer, but Rebecca would keep calling until Caro picked up. She strode to the bed and snatched up the phone. "Hello."

"Caro, darling, I hope you haven't forgotten we're all going bodyboarding this weekend. We've hired the usual apartment overlooking the beach at Morte Point. You don't have to board. You can sit on the terrace and read or paint."

Caro rolled her eyes. "That was all of half a minute before you mentioned the p word. That has to be a record, even for you."

"I know, darling. I just think some time away from that mausoleum of a house of yours might set you free."

Caro slipped off her slippers and sunk onto the mattress on her side of the bed. "I love my house just as it is, thanks. Well, I did, but it's not the same since Laura moved in."

"Oh, dear, wild student parties and dishes in the sink or rancid food clogging up the—"

"No, nothing like that." Caro leaned against the headboard. "She even asked when recycling was due so she could put the bins out on the lane. She's very considerate. It's just it's not the same, and she smiles too much and tries so hard to be obliging. It's infuriating."

"Caro, you are funny. Stop being such a grump. I bet you haven't apologised to her."

Caro crossed her legs. "I did."

"What did she say?"

"She apologised too and thanked me for opening up my home."

"She sounds like the perfect tenant. So, what's really the problem?"

She'd always been completely honest with Rebecca. That was probably why they got on so well, despite living in very different worlds now. "I don't want to change."

"Life moves on and however much you cling to the past, it's gone, locked out. Change is inevitable for all of us," Rebecca said quietly. "So, do you still have your wetsuit? We'll pick you up around Friday lunchtime. I'll bring salad, but if it's decent weather, we can sit outside on your deck overlooking the valley, before driving on to Morte Point. It will be wonderful to breathe something other than this smoggy London air. Freddie will have to go back on Monday, but Zoe and Jack will be with me the whole week."

Ah, now Caro understood. Rebecca needed a companion to help look after her teens, whose posh boarding school seemed to have constant holidays. "Are they on half term already? It's only the middle of October."

"I know. It's ridiculous, isn't it? They only went back after summer a few weeks ago, and they've got two weeks off already. They're driving me nuts. I can't believe how much mess they make—and the noise!"

Rebecca was hardly selling it as a relaxing break, but Caro reluctantly agreed. Would it be safe to leave Laura on her own in the house? Calm settled on her stomach. She trusted Laura, and Artemisia would enjoy the attention. The cat would probably be spoiled completely while she was away. Caro felt safe with Laura.

On Saturday morning, Caro slipped on her wetsuit, surprised by how much weight she must have lost because it was no longer snug. She seriously wondered about her sanity as she stood in the swirling waves, her fingers completely numb, her shoulders tensed, and her neck twisted to view the rush of coming waves. Salt spiked up her nostrils, and the sand gritted beneath her feet.

"Now, Aunty Caro!" Jack launched himself off and paddled as fast as he could.

Caro followed suit, thrusting herself on the board and splashing hard with her arms, only for the wave to roll out below her and leave her stranded like a piece of flotsam while Jack and Freddie hurtled towards the shore. Frustrated, she stood again with the water waist-high, waiting for the next large wave. They seemed to be a metaphor for her life, which was passing her by. And yet, as her toes curled in the sand being sucked from under her feet and the waves buffeted her body, she was prodded to be present, to breathe in the freedom of playing in the sea, and to share the joy with her found family. Caro inhaled the harsh salty air.

Zoe came up to her, whooping with joy and beaming from the euphoria of her previous ride. She splashed Caro playfully. "Aren't you getting cold?"

Caro splashed her back and they laughed, invigorated in the connection and the being here, sharing a moment, a memory. "I'm waiting for the right wave."

Zoe pointed out to sea. "Look, Aunty, there's a big one coming, let's go."

They launched together and magically, the wave caught underneath her board and pulled Caro towards the shore, sucking her along in an exhilarating wave of delight. Zoe rode beside her and they tumbled off the wave with a crash and hiss as the sea spat them out.

"Awesome." Zoe high-fived Caro. "Come again?" Zoe asked, breathless.

Her glee was infectious, and it was so tempting to go again, but Caro shivered when the wind flapped her wetsuit and ruffled her hair. She was too old for this; she no longer had the padding or youthful exuberance to keep her warm. "No, I'll go and help your mum with the food."

"The wine you mean," Zoe said as she dragged her board back towards the waves.

Although she was probably right, Caro didn't want to encourage her goddaughter. "Enjoy."

Zoe waved and waded back to join her brother and dad. Caro watched them for a few moments, standing against the surge. She heaved herself against a powerful rip that tried to pull her back towards the sea, then turned and trudged across the strand, granules of sand rubbing between her toes. Her hair was stiff with salt and her cheeks burned with windblast, but she still smiled. She felt alive for the first time in years, but as the thought occurred to her, the habitual dread sucked at her delight like the receding tide.

Caro hadn't thought about Yvonne for the last couple of hours, and now, despite being surrounded by kind people, she felt so alone. Rebecca's family was lovely, but there were a stack of family in-jokes she wasn't party to, and she didn't understand the memes her godchildren quoted. Rebecca and Freddie seemed to be in on it all because they joined in. Or maybe they had just been dipped in Gen Z culture so often they had taken on the hue.

Her mood darkened for the rest of the day. The teens went to the sunroom in the evening to play board games, and Freddie and Rebecca were grateful just to relax. Caro couldn't work out why she was still out of sorts though. She felt she was intruding on their precious family time, even though she knew Rebecca was glad for the dilution of the full teen onslaught. Caro could go back with Freddie, but that would be rude and would also leave Rebecca in the lurch. Rebecca wasn't very good being a full-time mother, probably because their lives revolved around a vibrant social scene in London, schmoozing the art world. She had never gone back to her promising career as a sculptor, despite that being the rationale for boarding the teens.

Freddie was a superb cook, and he even left freshly prepared meals for them after he returned to London, which Caro was very grateful for as Rebecca was no cook and Caro didn't want to have to cater for the opposing veganism of Zoe and the omnivorous tastes of Jack. Freddie didn't seem to mind though and faced it like some medieval challenge. Rebecca often kissed him and placed her hands on his hips as though she was about to ravish him.

Caro couldn't cope being on the outside, witnessing the happy family, so when they discussed going for a long bike ride the following day, Caro opted out. She needed time alone. When the family had gone, she took out her sketchpad. But as she picked up her charcoal, an overwhelming sense of dread overtook her, like the waves that had tossed her about the previous day. The pressure of the audience expecting her to produce something was too intense. She would simply have to tell Rebecca she couldn't do this anymore.

Nausea crept up her chest and into her throat. What would she do instead? Being an artist had been her identity all her adult life. Art *was* her life. Without it, what was she? A has-been? Maybe her birth family of overachieving bankers and lawyers were right, and she should get a proper job. The thought of teaching the bored or the know-it-alls made her sweat.

At supper, she was even more withdrawn. The teens excused themselves as soon as they could, and Caro put off saying anything until after they had cleared away and loaded the dishwasher.

"Are you all right?" Rebecca asked as she filled their glasses with more cabernet sauvignon.

Caro didn't reply and carried their glasses into the lounge area. Freddie put down his book and saluted her. They shared a smile, but they wouldn't be smiling in a minute. Her heart beat a fast rhythm in her chest. When they were all settled on the comfy armchairs, Caro took a large swig of wine for courage. "I've got something to say."

Freddie and Rebecca turned towards her and stared intently.

Caro swallowed. "And you won't like it."

Rebecca tapped her fingernails against the glass.

Had she guessed already? "I can't paint anymore." This was like confessing her sins, and she was looking to them for absolution. How easy to say a few Hail Marys and be done with it.

"What do you mean?" Freddie asked.

His thick eyebrows drew together, and he managed to look both irritated and concerned.

"I no longer have the skills or the inspiration. Going into my studio every day is like locking myself in purgatory. The more I try, the

54

worse it becomes. I know you want me to do three more paintings for the retrospective you want to run, Rebecca, but I just can't. I end up with coloured sludge all over the canvas. I've lost all my passion, and everything is lifeless and dead. Like Yvonne. I know you don't believe me, but she was my muse and my joy, and each painting was a love letter to her, about her. And it was great when people shared that, but I can't put myself through that anymore. I'll have to get a proper job. Won't my parents be pleased? They'll be delighted to say I told you so."

Rebecca slammed her wineglass on the coffee table, and a red wave flowed up and ebbed without teetering over the top. Her eyes were wide and wild.

"Nonsense. That's confidence and practice. It's the inspiration you need, and I understand that. Maybe you just need a different environment. You're doing so well here. Yesterday, you seemed more engaged than I've seen you in years. Even the kids noticed, and they're self-absorbed teenagers."

Freddie reached forward to enclose Caro's hand in his own. "Caro, sweetheart, what will you do? If you lived in London, I could set you up in the gallery, because you know as much about art as anyone. In fact, if you wanted to work a few days a week, come and stay with us and work in the gallery on those days."

Caro ignored the glower that Rebecca gave him and felt grateful that Freddie heard her plea. This was hard enough, and she didn't want to anger or upset her best friends and chosen family. Rebecca snatched up her wine and took a large slug while Caro smiled at him. "Thanks, Freddie, that's kind of you, but I haven't thought about what I want to do instead. I don't want to teach, but I don't want to have to sell my home either. It's where I feel closest to Yvonne, where I can commune with her."

He nodded and sipped his wine. "Okay, but the offer's there, anyway."

Caro felt a genuine rush of affection for his generous, compassionate heart. It's what had drawn in Rebecca. She'd even converted to Judaism for him. Not that they seemed to go to the synagogue that much.

Rebecca tapped on her wineglass. "I understand you feel under pressure, and I'm sorry if that has come from me."

If? Caro wanted to challenge, but she just nodded.

"Perhaps in the retrospective, we could just focus on those last few sketches you have. I know you won't want to sell them. There are also a couple of artists who've adopted your style. I could feature them too, and we could pose it as part of your legacy. What do you think?"

Caro rolled her wineglass around in her fingers, creating an eddy that reflected the churning in her stomach. "I wouldn't have to paint anything?"

"No, nothing at all, unless you want to, of course. You'd only need to attend the opening. Would that work? There'd be no pressure, and everyone would be happy."

Caro exhaled, and the tension in her shoulders dissipated. "What do you get out of it?"

Rebecca flushed, as though Caro had discovered how she'd achieved her magic trick. She replaced the wineglass on the table.

"I've taken on the two artists who emulate your style, and it would be good for them. And I know two current owners of your works are quite keen to cash in on the capital gain, so they'd be happy to offer them for sale via Freddie's gallery. Freddie would get commission on that, and you don't have to paint. If you wanted to sell a few sketches, perhaps you could make something out of it too. In fact, you've got half a wardrobe of sketchbooks. We could definitely sell some of those, and maybe do a run of prints from them. Think about it, darling."

Caro raised her glass to them both. She appreciated their ideas. Selling off some old sketches would bring in some cash until she decided what she wanted to—or could—do. "Okay, I'll do it."

Rebecca came around and kissed her on the cheek. "Wonderful. It's the perfect solution."

Caro sighed, hoping she wouldn't regret it. She might not need to rent out her home anymore, which should be a cause of celebration, but a pang of fear gripped her heart. The house would be empty without Laura. She would miss her. There was no need for Caro to change their arrangement. It suited them both. She loved that Laura filled the place with light and laughter, and she looked forward to their conversations in the kitchen. But Laura would leave when she graduated. Caro sipped her wine and sat back. Everything was temporary, changeable, shifting between contrasting states. Where there was laughter, there would be silence. There was no light without shadow, no joy without loss.

Chapter Ten

A FEW DAYS AFTER Caro returned from Woolacombe, Laura cycled her bike after her first foray on the British roads, although fortunately, almost all of her journey was on the cycleways. Part of her was still smarting that Matt said he and Kaylee would spend the afternoon together, but she couldn't complain since she'd pushed them together. Everyone was getting on with their lives, and she was no further with Mission Thaw. She suppressed the lingering loneliness with every push on the pedals. "This too will pass," she said like a mantra in time to the circle of the wheel.

As she cycled the last few yards up the drive, she couldn't believe how sweaty and sore she was. She'd definitely make use of the cream that Ben, one of the guys on the course, had given her. She must pick up a new jar to give back to him. She rounded the corner of the house and had to slam on her brakes. Heaps of leaves and a rake were strewn across the driveway. Laura put her feet down and slipped off the saddle. She saw a puff of condensation emanating from the bushes. Caro turned round to face Laura, a look of irritation on her face that slipped into recognition.

"Oh, it's you."

Standing in her gardening clothes and bright orange crocs with muddied, thick gloves and strands of her hair falling out of a bun, Caro really shouldn't look sexy, but she did. She was so lean and graceful that it really didn't matter what she wore. Laura chastised herself. She was trying to be friendly, not letch after her landlady. "Yeah, I picked up the bike from my friend's house this morning, and this was the first time I've ridden it. Would I be able to keep it under cover at all? If not, can I just chain it round the back?"

Caro wiped her face with the back of her glove and smeared some mud across her cheek. Laura stifled a smirk. Should she say anything? She pointed to the spot on her own cheek, but Caro scowled at her.

"The back of the garage has a lean-to wood store. You can lock it in there but not near my studio."

She got it. Caro's studio was off-limits, along with her bedroom, which, of course, it should be. "The wood store's perfect, thanks." It would be covered and hidden from thieving eyes. She wheeled the bike around the back of the garage and stared. A lace of webs stretched across the wood store door, but she could just about cope with spiders. She steeled herself and opened it, flailing her hands in front of her. Thick, sticky silk gloved her arms, and she shuddered and shook her hands to free herself. She couldn't actually see any spiders, which was a relief. Judging by the veil of cobwebs draped over the stacks, the wood hadn't been disturbed for years. That was odd about the house and Caro, as though they were trapped in a time loop, waiting to be brought back to a state of animation. There was evidence of life and order once, but now all was silent, even morgue-like.

Laura leaned her bike against the wall. She took off her bright, wearable chain and out of habit, locked the bike. It was probably secure in the country, but she didn't want to take the risk.

Laura released her backpack from the pannier rack and slipped it over her shoulder. She ignored a scurrying movement in the corner. *Creepy.* As she stepped back out into the garden, a ball sailed over the fence from the adjoining property. There was a banging on the other side of the fence, and a girl peeped over it. Her eyes went wide when she caught sight of Laura.

"Hi, what's your name?" Laura asked as she walked towards the ball that had flattened some plants. She didn't imagine Caro would appreciate that.

"Amelia. Can I have my ball back?" She looked about nine.

"Hi, Amelia, I'm Laura. Do you like football?"

The girl nodded. "Riley and I play all the time, but we keep losing them in here, and she scares us." Laura could imagine that Caro could terrify though she didn't need to imagine; her first encounter had been pretty terrifying. But she hadn't seen fury in Caro again during the past month of lodging here.

"How come you don't control the ball?" Laura asked. Another smaller head popped over the fence. It was a boy about two years younger than Amelia. "Are you Riley?"

He nodded and looked shy.

"Don't you practise how to control the ball so you can make it go where you want it to?"

"We don't know how," Amelia said.

Laura grinned. She toed the ball up with her right foot, did a few foot stalls to keep the ball in the air, caught the ball in the crook of her neck, flipped it over and did an around the world before she lofted it over their heads and into their garden. All that messing around with her dad and cousins over the years had paid off, and the look of amazement on their faces was worth it. She did a little bow.

"Wow, can you show us how you do that?" Amelia asked.

"Okay, but you'd need to get permission from your parents first. I'd have to come around to you."

"Yes, yes. Wait there," Amelia said and dropped from view. "Come on, Riley."

Laura wandered over to Caro, who was giving her a curious look.

"Nice bit of juggling, and if you can get the little buggers to stop their ball from coming into my garden, I'd be eternally grateful."

Laura grinned. "I can't promise anything, but I'll see what I can do. Of course, it might make them spend even longer playing ball. Where should these leaves go?"

Caro's eyes widened. She obviously hadn't expected Laura to offer to help.

"The compost heap at the top of the garden behind my studio. But—"

"Don't look in the studio. I know." Laura dropped her bag and scooped up an armful of crackling brown, orange, and yellow leaves to take them up the garden. Despite the curiosity, she kept her eyes strictly focused on the brick-enclosed compost heap that seemed to contain years of garden leavings. Another example of maintenance and structure. What had happened? Caro had said "we" a few times, presumably a husband or partner, but what had happened to them? Had they left Caro like Valentina had left her because she'd had an affair, or had Caro's partner died? They weren't at that stage where she could ask. The woman would just clam up completely. But they were making progress; this was the first time Caro had let her help. Step one in Mission Thaw accomplished.

She wandered back to pick up the next armful of leaves and was conscious of Caro watching her, but her expression was difficult to read. Laura smiled and after a second's hesitation, Caro returned it, but it didn't reach her eyes.

As Laura returned with the third load of leaves, Amelia popped her head above the fence again.

"Mum says you can come over and play with us."

"Great. I'll just finish putting these leaves in the compost for Caro, then I'll be over."

"Be quick. Please," Amelia said.

"Maybe you could help me?" Laura asked.

Amelia frowned as if Laura had asked her to pick up cat poop with her bare hands. "No, it's okay. We'll wait. Mum says you can come through the side gate. She'll unlock it."

"Great. Why don't you try to keep the ball up for fifty times without it touching the ground until I get there?"

Amelia looked as if Laura was mad. "Fifty?"

Fifteen minutes later, Laura knocked and went through to next door. The garden was a war zone, bikes were littered across the lawn, along with a trampoline, a slide, and a sand pit disgorging toys. Against Caro's fence, a football net had been erected. No wonder their ball kept going into her garden.

A harassed-looking woman in her late thirties greeted Laura at the gate. "I'm Gemma, Amelia and Riley's mother. I hear you have some cool footballing skills. Honestly, if you can keep them occupied for half an hour, I'd be grateful. I'm on nights, so when I'm awake, I need to get all the chores done before I go off again."

"No problem, Gemma, happy to help. I'm Laura. I've just moved in as a lodger with Caro next door. I'm a master's student at UWE."

"She let you in her house? We've been here eighteen months and have never been invited inside. We tried to be friendly when we first arrived, but she's never made us welcome, and she terrorises the kids."

Laura didn't want to gossip. "Would it be all right if I reposition the goal? I think part of the problem is that the balls go into Caro's garden, and it disturbs her when she's trying to work."

Gemma looked at the net as if she had just noticed its position. "Oh. I didn't think of that. Do you need a hand?"

"That would be awesome. Let's put it against the back fence."

Gemma helped her lift the unwieldy structure to its new home.

"Thanks. Do you mind if I leave you to it? I'll just be in the kitchen." Gemma indicated the kitchen window.

"Come on, come on," Amelia said, dragging Laura by the arm towards the footballs. "Show us that keepy-uppy thing. I managed thirty-two, and Riley says he did forty-one but he's a liar, liar, pants on fire."

Laura laughed. "Maybe he can show us?"

They spent about half an hour playing, and Laura demonstrated how to trap the ball in parts of the body. "You can't use it in a game, but it's great to know how the ball reacts to different parts of the foot."

They ended with some defence tactics and shots at goal. Laura handed back the ball to Riley after he'd successfully toed a ball past her and into the net and done a victory dance around the lawn.

"Who taught you?" Amelia asked.

"My dad. He's passionate about football and has always supported Real Madrid since he was a kid."

"Who's your favourite player? Mine's Ronaldo," Riley said, coming to a stop in front of them.

"Yeah, he's skilful, and he used to play for Real. Benzema's my favourite, because he uses his brain, and he does tons of assists as well as scoring goals. Lots of them."

Laura shivered. The sweat from cycling had cooled, her legs chafed, and her butt was sore. "I need to go now. Next time I'll show you the Ronaldo chop."

Riley nodded. "Wow."

"Thank you," Amelia said.

Laura basked in the warmth of the approval and waved to Gemma as she let herself out of the side gate. It hadn't been hard to get the kids on side. If only getting Caro warmed up was as easy.

Chapter Eleven

THE FOLLOWING DAY, CARO rifled through her old sketchbooks, some of which went back to her days at the Slade Art college and her postgraduate degree at the Royal College of Art. As she stared at sketches she had done of her fellow students, including quite a few of Rebecca at the flat they'd shared in London, she couldn't believe she had once just picked up a pencil or charcoal and delineated something so quickly. For some sketches, she remembered what she was thinking or listening to as she'd done them. There were also the ones with one lecturer who had said they couldn't use over twenty strokes to conjure the entire picture, then only ten, then five. It forced them to really observe what they were looking at and to be economical with their marks. It stood her in good stead. Maybe she should try practicing again. But the problem wasn't physical. It was emotional, and she hadn't been able to unpick the knot that was all tied up with her grief over Yvonne. She couldn't go there.

She laughed at some later sketches of Artemisia as a kitten. Caro was sure she had an entire book of sketches somewhere from then. Those would probably go down well, and Rebecca could probably get them printed into cards, and notebooks, and whatever else she thought would sell. Rebecca had a real knack for making money and had always put Caro in front of the right people. She owed her career to Rebecca. Guilt at letting her down trickled down her spine. She would find that other book for Rebecca but for now, she would send these as a sweetener. Rebecca could scan them and say whether they would be appropriate.

Grateful she could actually *do* something, Caro got up from her chair and replaced the sketchbooks on the shelves above the bench. She walked out of her studio and almost stumbled into Laura, who had her iPad in her hand and was staring at Artemisia, stretched out on the path sunning herself in the milky autumn light.

"What are you doing?" Caro asked, sharper than she intended.

"Oh, hi, Caro. We've been told we have to sketch anything and everything for my course."

"On an iPad?" Caro could hardly keep the disdain from her tone. What did they teach at university these days?

Laura grinned. "Sure. I'm using Procreate."

Caro snorted. "You can't sketch on anything but paper with a pencil or charcoal. You need to feel the emotions in your sketching. How can you feel emotions on a screen?"

Laura just smiled up at her, apparently not fazed. "If it's good enough for David Hockney, it's good enough for me. Anyway, I've done nothing on paper since I was at art school. I can't afford the materials and have nowhere to store any artwork."

Caro shook her head. "Great art reflects life and all its emotions. It's the artist expressing what they are, what they stand for, or what they object to. How can you do that on an iPad?" Caro asked, aware of the chasm between their experiences. She felt so old.

"I've never claimed mine is great art. I worked in a factory-like environment for a games company that's now branching out into animation. I want to be there at the forefront."

Caro shuddered. "I can't think of anything more soul-destroying. Why would you want to do that?"

Laura cocked her head to one side. "Because animation is about telling stories, and I want to tell my story."

Caro nodded. Yes, that made sense. Laura was intriguing, and Caro was being pulled into her atmosphere like gravity. "In that case, why animation? It must be one of the least efficient ways of telling a story, at what, twenty-four frames per second? That's a lot of work for very little reward."

Laura smiled. "That's why my friend Matt and I are making computer models which we programme to tell the story. Once you've set it all up, it's much more like making a movie, and what could be more fun that shooting your own movie without having to use actors?" She grinned again.

What was with all the smiling? How irritating, as though she was trying to ingratiate herself with Caro. But she clearly had an opinion based on a thought-out process and wasn't just jumping on some bandwagon. "How does it work?" She ignored the smirk teasing at Laura's lips. Very cute lips, if truth be told. What was she doing? How did her lusting after her much younger tenant hold Yvonne's memory dear? Rebecca's words that

Yvonne would have moved on already echoed in her head. She inhaled deeply and observed as Laura showed her the programme. Caro was taking in the choice of brush and opacity but was drawn to the curve of Laura's neck as she curled over her tablet, how the autumn light danced highlights on her skin tone. Laura's lovely smooth skin and the downy hairs on her arms fascinated Caro. She would need a very fine brush to capture the likeness.

Laura looked up at her and caught her gazing. She probably thought she was checking her out.

Caro's cheeks flushed. "What?"

Laura raised her eyebrow and had the vestiges of an amused expression. "I asked if you wanted to try it."

"No, thanks. The layers could be interesting to work with, but it's too mechanical and not organic enough for me. Besides, it looks as though it is too easy to mix with the palettes that are there rather than really observing the actual colours. Look at the way the light is catching the underside of the leaves, giving them a soft glow." Caro pointed at the last few leaves clinging to the branches, haloed by the oblique autumn light from behind.

"Oh, that's easy. Change the opacity of the leaves and place a sunburst behind."

Laura's enthusiasm was catching, and Caro could easily have asked more, but she needed to keep a distance and stop being drawn into the warmth of her sun. "Maybe some other time. I need to get on. Don't dismiss organic sketching until you've tried it."

"I could also say that about using digital." Laura grinned again. "Have a good day."

"Thanks." Caro gripped her sketchbooks, turned, and fled. What was going on? She went upstairs to what had been Yvonne's study, where she had the scanner and printer. Everything needed a good dusting. Yvonne would have hated it being unloved. She'd spent so much time here when she wasn't at the TV studios. She was always organising some event or entertainment or another, and this had been her battle headquarters.

The machine came to life with a groan and clunk, and Caro scanned the first of the cat sketches. She was particularly pleased with this one, as she had used just three strokes. A very long one for Artemisia's outline, including her ears and mouth, and two for the whiskers. She loved the simplicity of it, but maybe it wasn't suitable for a professional exhibition.

Rebecca had such a good nose for what would sell.

Caro flipped through some of the early sketches of Yvonne. She had always painted what she wanted and somehow, Rebecca knew who her work would appeal to, like those who reacted against the nineties Brit art world of Damien Hirst and Tracey Emin. Caro's followers wanted a work to be a highly skilled depiction of what it was supposed to look like, teeming with emotion and passion. That the subject was a beautiful woman didn't harm. At first, it had seemed strange, as though Caro was sharing Yvonne and her body with the world, and she didn't want to think of dirty old men lusting over her and pretending it was in the name of art. But she couldn't really complain since Yvonne loved to have her body admired, and she trusted Caro to do it in a way that was tasteful. Caro had always basked in that trust and taken great pains to drape and light Yvonne so everything was suggestion, and it was so much more tantalising for being hidden in shadows.

After she had scanned three pictures, she sat at the old desktop computer and pinged off an email to Rebecca. "Will this suffice? I have another whole sketchbook of Artemisia somewhere, if you want some more."

Five minutes later she received an email.

Gimme, gimme, gimme. Yes, more of those and perhaps some of the early sketches you made in college but none of me, thank you. I have no wish to be objectified. It would be useful to show your development in sketches, and the cat ones are perfect for greetings cards. We can put them all in the corridor between the two main halls. I thought your pictures could be in one gallery, the new artists' work in the other. I'd love for you to meet them. When can I have the originals? And send what you have. Or better still, when can I collect them?

Rebecca's enthusiasm was like being trampled by a herd of elephants. Once she had something set in her mind, she was off and running. Caro picked up her phone and called to make the exchange faster and easier. "I'll have to find it first. It's somewhere in the house, but I'm not sure where. It might be in one of the spare bedrooms. Let me see if I can find them first before you go into ultra-planning mode."

"Perfect," Rebecca said. "Don't be too long about it. This is going to be a fantastic show. Freddie's looking forward to it too. Maybe you should stay with us for the duration, and we could meet up with some of our old college friends?"

Caro didn't want that written into the contract. "No, that's too much, but perhaps I could stay for one or two nights?"

"Wonderful."

Caro had the distinct impression that's what Rebecca had been planning for all along, and she'd just been played. She felt invigorated to be taking action, like stirring dried-up paint and helping it to flow onto the canvas. She was beginning to move, but she couldn't suppress the jitters that something bad would happen, that the other shoe would soon drop.

Chapter Twelve

HALF ASLEEP, LAURA STUMBLED into the kitchen to fix her coffee solo, the thick, bitter coffee she loved, with beans she had brought with her from Spain. She was debating whether she could afford to go over during the Christmas holidays when she noticed a sketchpad and pencils by the kettle. On a pink Post-it note in large, loopy handwriting was the instruction, "Play." She snatched it up and clutched the book to her chest. It was not so much the sketchbook itself, although that was lovely, but that Caro was finally thawing.

Laura had no lectures, so she'd planned to sketch out the characters for her animation project. One of her characters was a cat, so Artemisia would be perfect to practise on, if she was around. She peeped out of the window to see the cat sitting on the stone patio at the back of the house licking her paws. Perfect. If she took out some treats, maybe she could entice Artemisia to stay while she captured her in pencil.

She opened up the sketchpad. The serrated edges of the ring binder had trapped slivers of paper underneath the rings, indicating that a couple of pages had been removed. Caro talked of working and made her way to the studio daily, but Laura had never heard or seen any evidence of work being done, apart from the glimpse of canvas on the day she'd arrived.

Laura picked up the pencil and as she waited for the kettle to boil, placed a few light marks on the paper trying to capture Artemisia, who wouldn't stop moving. She imprinted a few wiggly lines, then jumped as Caro whispered in her ear, "Observe."

Laura could feel Caro's warm breath, stirring a buzz of excitement deep in her belly. No, she should *not* be responding that way to her landlady. It was inappropriate. Mission Thaw was supposed to be about Caro melting, not the other way around.

"Think of the basic structures. Follow the line of her spine, and imagine rough ovals for her head, shoulders, and her hips. It might be easier to hold your pencil differently. May I?"

Laura nodded, not wishing to break the moment as Caro's hand gently grasped hers. Caro's fingers were cool and soft against Laura's warm skin, and she shifted Laura's grip slightly. Laura hoped her heated skin wouldn't give her away. "Thanks, that makes a difference."

The sweet scent of expensive perfume tickled Laura's nose. Strange. She wouldn't have thought Caro would be one for sweet scents, more musk or spice, but it suited her, and Laura tried not to be obvious as she inhaled the intoxicating aroma again.

They both laughed as Artemisia tried to scratch her ear and missed. Caro's laugh was warm and rich, like liquid chocolate. "She's a beautiful tabby." Like her owner, she was a contrast of dark and light.

"She is," Caro said. She withdrew, as if she suddenly realised how close she was, leaving a cool space behind Laura. "I only came down for tea. Are you having breakfast?"

Laura nodded at her coffee. "No, I'm good to go. The kitchen's free now. I was going to spend the day drawing my characters." She tapped on the sketchbook. "Thanks for this."

Caro nodded, but she seemed to freeze up by the second, as if she regretted her lapse. "I'm going to London today. I'm catching the 10:13 a.m. train and will be home around nine this evening."

"Vale. Are you going to any museums?"

The scowl she received was a very clear signal to mind her own business.

"Isn't vale Spanish for okay?" Caro asked. "But your English is excellent, are you bilingual?"

Laura smiled. "Yep, my mum's English and my dad's Spanish, so I flip between the two. Do you need me to do anything around the house when you're gone?"

Caro exhaled as if she was about to say no. "Could you put my washing into the airing cupboard and feed Artemisia."

"Vale. Where's the airing cupboard?"

Caro frowned slightly. "Up the main stairs, and it's the third door on the right."

Laura nodded and picked up her coffee and sketchbook and pencils. "Great. Enjoy London."

Caro raised her eyebrow, as if that was an impossibility. Laura would love the chance to bunk off to London and explore the museums and the art galleries. They were so different; Caro was moody, depressed almost, but she was thawing, and Laura notched up her laugh as a real step forward, even if she had retreated immediately. Knowing Caro needed to get on, Laura stepped away to the back stairs and her own room, her heart skipping.

A couple of hours later, Laura stretched her back. Happy with her main characters, she decided she would continue sketching Artemisia, who was basking in the late morning sun in the main lounge. If she was careful not to disturb anything, Laura was sure Caro wouldn't mind—she *was* doing more of what Caro had encouraged.

She needed to sort out the laundry first, so she hung up her cycling gear and T-shirts in the utility room. Then she picked up the neatly folded pile of Caro's clothes. She was tempted to run her hands over the material but resisted the impulse and wandered up the main stairs to the unexplored part of the house, glancing over her shoulder as if someone was watching.

Upstairs smelled different and slightly musty. It needed a good airing. Closed shutters at the end of the corridor gave a gloomy air. She couldn't be bothered to search for the light. Did Caro say third on the left or right? If they were locked, Laura would know she was in the wrong place. She padded along the thick carpet, which absorbed most of the sound. At the third door, she paused and opened the door with its brass handle. She pushed at the stripped oak door and entered a room, not a cupboard.

She blinked. The curtains were drawn, but the dim light revealed a massive room with a large modern bed taking up the central area. To the right was a door ajar, revealing a marble bathroom with travertine tiles and brass taps. In contrast with the mustiness, it smelled luxurious. To the side of the bed was a dressing table full of knickknacks, lipsticks, and mementos. But what held Laura's gaze was a large painting, created in sharp contrast of light and shadow. A woman leaned back amongst tousled sheets, her arms raised above her head in an alluring pose. The perspective was interesting as it was at the same level as the woman, as if someone had painted it from the bed, accentuating the mound of Venus covered in dark curls and... *Oh*. That was incredibly erotic, and Laura lifted her gaze up the body to the face, partially in shadow but with the soft gaze of post-coital haze. That face. She'd seen it before but couldn't remember where.

Laura knew she shouldn't, but the painting was breathtaking, mesmerising, and incredibly arousing. She took a photo with her phone so she could do some research later, she told herself. As she slipped it back into her back pocket, she realised she had creased the washing. She backed out in respect, then wandered to the correct door, completely distracted by what she'd seen.

Why was that face so familiar? She was sure she'd seen it before. Maybe someone on TV? But it was more likely a painting. Her mum would know, but she couldn't betray Caro's trust. Laura shook her head. She wouldn't be like Valentina. Some of her own secret research would satisfy her curiosity. Then she would delete the photograph. She smoothed the clothes and placed them on the shelves, and her mind worked overtime trying to put a name to the face. She closed the airing cupboard door and made her way down the stairs. Artemisia joined her and curled around her legs as if deliberately trying to trip her up as she stepped down. She lifted her foot to climb over her, and Artemisia hurtled downstairs as if she'd been scalded.

"I didn't touch you!" Laura followed her into the kitchen. "Would you like feeding, Arty Farty?" She stroked the cat and walked to where the kibble was kept in the kitchen cabinet. She poured it out without paying much attention. The chiaroscuro style of painting was familiar. It reminded her of the conversation she and Caro had had about the contrast of light and dark. She took out her phone and enlarged the bottom right corner. *Bingo.* The signature looked like it was Carolyn Trent-Parker, written in large loops. Wow, Caro had an original CTP. She was probably the most well-known and expensive modern British artist. Her mum had taken her to a gallery in London in the late noughties, and there were some paintings by Carolyn Trent-Parker. They had both raved about the trompe de l'oeil precision of the painting, as though you could actually touch the skin and it would be warm. Connections fizzed in her brain. It couldn't be, could it?

Laura ran back to her room. She opened a new tab on her laptop and googled the artist. The picture she'd seen was similar in style, but it wasn't in any of the catalogues she could see. Her heart raced when she opened an article with a photograph of Carolyn Trent-Parker and her wife. There was a younger Caro with a stunningly beautiful woman whose face graced most of her paintings, including the one in Caro's bedroom. Laura clutched her chest as if she needed help to push air into her lungs. Caro really was Carolyn Trent-Parker. Why hadn't she made the connection before, that was so obvious now? According to Wikipedia, she hadn't painted since the death of her wife two years ago. So much made sense now. *Oh, my God, I've been getting sketching tips from one of the best artists of her generation.* Her mum would be ecstatic, but she couldn't tell her. Laura was using a sketchbook that belonged to a truly wonderful artist. She did a jig around the bedroom then threw herself on the bed to stare at the picture on her phone.

"Have you seen this, MiniMe?" Laura showed the picture to the puppet.

"Sexy lady," MiniMe said.

"She is, but it's the artist who interests me. From this picture it seems she's into women." A ripple of possibility ran through Laura, which she quickly dammed. But an interrupted ripple comes back stronger. Could there be something there? Caro was undoubtedly sexy, although she seemed completely unaware of that. But beneath the surface was a caring, passionate soul that was even more attractive. It didn't harm she was a fabulous artist either. Okay, she was smitten with Caro. This had to stop. She was her landlady, her immensely talented landlady.

The painting was wonderful, erotic, and beautiful. But she couldn't say anything because that would show that not only had she broken Caro's trust by going into her room, but she'd invaded her privacy by taking a photo. She would delete it, just not yet.

The world needed more stunning paintings like this one. Laura had a new mission. She would bring up CTP in conversation, but more importantly, had to get Caro painting again.

Chapter Thirteen

THE FOLLOWING MORNING WHEN Caro made tea, she saw Laura had left the sketchpad with a note saying, "Play too?" Caro chuckled and flipped through the sketches, then paused and trailed her finger on the page. Laura was good. She had captured the essence of Artemisia in simple clean lines. There was no hatching or broken lines, just clear strokes. It wasn't an insult to say it was like a cartoon, simple and powerful in its simplicity. Laura *was* an artist. Just because cartoons and animation were popular media didn't mean they couldn't be artistic.

She was also a force to be reckoned with. She'd won around the kids next door, and her constant smile and positive attitude were enchanting. She was adorable. Caro wasn't always thinking about Yvonne like she had. Now she'd begun to view Yvonne from the perspective of distance. Caro looked forward to their breakfast conversations over Laura's strong, black coffee, and she enjoyed hearing Laura singing and moving around the kitchen in the evenings, even though her music wasn't opera. They were complete opposites, and she was so young, in her twenties still. How strange that they had formed a friendship.

She sipped her tea, and an idea filtered through and solidified. She dug in her robe pocket for her phone, snapped the sketches, and pinged them over to Rebecca. Yvonne liked Caro to be available at all hours, and she hadn't been able to kill the habit of taking her phone with her everywhere, even if she ignored it half the time. "Rebecca, I have an idea. I can't find the extra sketchbook of the cat pictures, but I've just sent you some recent sketches. What do you think?"

There was a pause. "Very cute, but this isn't your usual style. There's no definition or detail. Don't take this personally, but they look like cartoon drawings."

"More like Picasso's rendition of Don Quixote. It has sparsity of line yet depicts the essence of the subject."

"Have you been reading Freddie's verbiage? Save it for the brochure."

Rebecca inhaled. "Are you exploring a different style, darling? I'm really glad you're sketching again. It's a start, but it isn't what people are expecting."

"Are you saying you don't like them?" Caro asked.

"Of course I do, but I'm trying to put together a cohesive exhibition. These are pretty, and they would make some interesting coasters and tea towels, but they don't compare to your detailed sketches. Perhaps we could include them in a future exhibition where you're exploring different areas."

"How much do you think the original sketches would fetch?" Caro took another sip of her tea and waited for Rebecca's reply.

"Well, your normal sketches fetch up to five thousand, depending on whether they relate to one of your famous paintings. I don't know, you've put me on the spot here. Freddie would be the one to ask. Perhaps a thousand."

"If they were sketched by an unknown?"

"Ha! I knew it. They didn't have your signature style all over them. I'm not stupid, you know." Rebecca's exhalation was audible.

Caro grinned, enjoying her friend's discomfort a little too much. "I never said you were. How much would they be worth otherwise?"

"They may sell for up to a hundred each, or a small royalty for any prints or novelties."

"Is that something you could do?"

"Whose work is it? Given it looks like Artemisia, is it your tenant?"

"Got it in one."

"Why would you help her? Don't take this personally, but you're normally so self-absorbed, you don't see much beyond your nose."

Ouch. That was harsh, but probably close to the truth, and certainly in the last couple of years. She hadn't been there for Rebecca when she struggled as the children turned into stroppy teens. Shame prickled the periphery of her consciousness. "Sorry. I probably have been self-centred recently."

"I'm not having a dig. We've known each other too long. It's a surprise, that's all. Isn't it the requirement of any artist to have a selfish streak, otherwise they wouldn't prioritise their work? They'd be looking after their family and supporting their spouses. It's why so few women in history have ever made it in the creative industries. Society always expects us to put our needs behind everybody else's. "

There was wistfulness in Rebecca's tone, as if she was referring to herself. Caro had a few of Rebecca's best pieces in her hallway. "Like you?"

Rebecca took a sharp breath. "Why are you helping your tenant? Is there something you need to tell me?"

"What? No. She's just friendly. I like her, and she's done a lot to make things easy around here. But she's says she's skint and could do with a bit of extra cash. If the sketches were worth something, it might give her a small income that could help. I feel sorry for her when she arrives home drenched because she's cycled rather than taken a taxi or bus home."

"When have you ever showed compassion and empathy?"

"You make it sound as though I'm some grumpy old sod."

There was just a slight hesitation before Rebecca spoke, implying she agreed with the description. Caro supposed she deserved that.

"The best way to help your 'just friends' tenant is to find more of your old sketches, as you promised, I might add, and sell one or two off in the exhibition. If you felt so inclined, you could donate her some cash."

Caro could imagine Rebecca doing air quotes around just friends. Her gut tightened. "I can't tell her who I am."

"Whyever not?" Rebecca asked.

"Because I'm not that person anymore, and she mentioned her in passing the other day, so I pretended ignorance."

"Of course you did. But you are that person, that amazing, talented artist."

"Not anymore. I'm lost without my muse." She struggled to speak beyond the lump in her throat, but she needed to acknowledge it and own who she was now. A has-been. Ironically, she had more sympathy now with how Yvonne felt when she was dropped from her TV show.

"You'll recover your mojo...or maybe you'll finally realise you don't need that external stimulation to produce wonderful paintings."

"But how can I paint when I feel nothing? My paintings are all about brooding emotion, intensity, and passion. My libido is non-existent, and I'm numb most of the time." Caro heard a sound behind her. "Oh, I need to go. Do what you can with those sketches. Bye, Rebecca." She ended the call. *Damn, how much had Laura overheard?* It was bad enough to spill her insecurities to her best friend without involving her lodger. She switched the kettle on to give herself time to compose herself. And was it really true that her libido was non-existent? She'd certainly stirred when Laura entered the room. "Mug of sludge?" Caro asked.

"Ha! It's better than your dishwater any day."

Caro held her breath and took down the cat mug Laura had claimed as hers. Would she refer to her conversation with Rebecca?

"Did you see my note?" Laura asked.

"I did. And I love your sketches. They're so neat and quirky. You should definitely keep the sketchpad. It would be a waste otherwise." She decided not to say anything about Rebecca, so she didn't raise Laura's hopes.

Laura cleared her throat. "You should sketch and show me how it's done."

Caro raised her eyebrow. "Why would I show you how it's done?"

"Because, because..." Laura swallowed audibly, as though she was trying to build up her courage, "you're Carolyn Trent-Parker, the foremost artist of your generation."

Caro threw up her hand to stop her. Laura knew or had guessed. Caro couldn't cope with Laura asking about who she used to be. That artist had died with Yvonne. Now she was just Caro Fitzclare, a woman struggling to keep herself afloat and decide what she wanted to do for the rest of her life. "Enough. I am only interested in your programme and how you get tone."

"I can show you this afternoon, if you're free?" Laura said, trying to hide her obvious delight.

Later that afternoon, Artemisia was nowhere to be seen, probably fed up with the attention and wanting to reassert her rightful place as queen of the house. Caro and Laura strolled outside into the dank autumn air, and the faint aroma of decay released as they trod on the fallen foliage. The light breeze held the hint of ice as it skated over their cheeks.

"Shall we paint the leaves?" Caro pointed at the vegetation scattered on the ground in a multicoloured carpet. Caro retrieved an old, faded deck chair from the shed, and Laura perched on a stool Caro took from her studio. She sat close so they could both see the iPad.

Laura handed the iPad to Caro and gave her a short tutorial. Caro really shouldn't feel stirring below her belly when Laura pressed closer to her body when she changed a setting, or when her warm breath sent goosebumps trailing down her arms.

After half an hour, when Caro had produced a technically accurate rendition that lacked soul, she snorted in disgust. "How can you get passion into a computer 'painting?' It's like paint by numbers. Sorry to be rude, but you can't draw or paint anything meaningful without passion."

Their eyes met, and Laura tilted her head to the side. "Is that why you don't paint anymore?"

Anger gouged a gorge in Caro's chest. Laura must have heard her conversation with Rebecca. "That's none of your business." Her eyes blurred and, despite staring upwards and blinking, tears trailed down her cheeks. And not just a few tears, this was full sobbing, ugly crying. Laura crouched by her side and, to crown her humiliation, Caro clung onto her and cried onto her shoulder.

After her sobs became hiccoughing gasping, Caro said, "I can't paint anymore. I'm not CTP, so I don't want to talk about it. When Yvonne died, I lost my wife *and* my muse."

Laura whispered comforting words, but Caro had to explain so she could retreat inside and wallow in her shame. Two years of holding back the grief. She had cried when she lost Yvonne, but this was the first time she had cried for the loss of her talent, her skill, and her status as an artist, for the loss of her essence. "I made some sketches before Yvonne's death but every time I try to paint, it's like I'm trapped in my guilt that I didn't see, that I didn't know how upset Yvonne was at losing her looks and being too old to be the early evening news anchor anymore."

"That's not your fault." Laura squeezed Caro tighter.

"But I didn't know how she felt about it. I was supposedly the master of capturing emotion in paint, but I didn't see her pain, I didn't hear her pleas."

"Surely Yvonne wasn't that old? Did it matter?"

"She was fifty-four and still stunning, despite the signs of aging, but the TV station dumped her for a younger woman. The irony is that Yvonne was the more skilled and professional anchor than her male co-host, who was two years older. Yvonne couldn't cope with not being beautiful enough and being ignored. She didn't see what I saw: a beautiful, mature woman whose face showed the creases of a life lived well, who was interesting, intelligent, cultured, and the very centre of my existence on every level."

The core of the problem was that Caro had put Yvonne onto a pedestal and didn't see her for who she really was. She would never make the same mistake again. Ever.

Chapter Fourteen

THE FOLLOWING EVENING, LAURA was cooking a few Spanish staples to make her feel less homesick, berenjenas con miel and tortilla Española. She'd soaked the aubergine in milk for nearly two hours in the fridge and was waiting for the omelette to firm up. So far, she'd been good at not prying, apart from her mistaken entry into Caro's bedroom. A flash of shame that she had yet to delete the photo made her cringe. As did the fact that she'd caused Caro's meltdown yesterday. She'd seemed humiliated afterwards and had fled. But Laura was touched that Caro had let down her walls and been vulnerable. It showed a trust, a trust that Laura couldn't ever envisage for herself. That just led to heartache. But if it meant that Caro was going to open to her, she was grateful to make a friend. It helped her feel less homesick.

She wandered around the kitchen dining area as she waited for her food to cook. A thin layer of dust had settled on the mantelpiece above the wood-burning stove. Maybe she should offer to help clean this area too. A massive TV dominated the chimney breast and on the mantelpiece ledge, the only item that didn't seem to be shrouded in the light dust was a photograph of Caro and her wife that had been placed there since yesterday. There was joy in Caro's eyes as they laughed. Laura would love to see that same joy in her art hero's eyes now, rather than the shut-off distance or the inconsolable sorrow of yesterday. She gazed at Caro's dark hair and blue eyes and realised how beautiful Caro was. Guilt joined shame at her intrusiveness, like she was trampling on flowers growing in a temple. From what Caro said yesterday, she felt responsible for Yvonne's death because she hadn't recognised her wife's anguish. What happened to her?

Laura heard the click of Caro's bedroom door being closed and the squeak of floorboards as she walked down the stairs, so she rushed back to the stove just as the tortilla was about to catch fire. It served her right for prying where she shouldn't be. She placed the tortilla on a breadboard, then started cooking the aubergine. The smell was one of herbs, and cooking oil, and home. If she closed her eyes, she could almost imagine she was with her dad, correcting her and encouraging her to taste and experiment.

"Good evening. I thought I'd grab a tea," Caro said. "That smells nice."

"Would you like some? I'm just about to make a salad."

Caro paused, her mouth open as if she was about to reject the invitation, then she smiled slightly. "Thanks. That would be nice."

A thrill ran through Laura. Trying to tempt Caro to open up or share food was like leaving breadcrumbs for a tiny songbird. She would sidle up and then the slightest noise or interruption would send her fluttering for the hills. As Laura chopped up the salad, Caro fiddled with the knives and forks, straightening them out on the dining table neatly.

"I'm sorry about yesterday. I feel mortified." Caro addressed the tablecloth and didn't look at Laura.

"Why? I feel honoured you trusted me enough to be vulnerable."

Caro snorted, then retrieved the condiments from the cupboard. She turned and waited until Laura met her eyes. "How did you figure out who I was?"

Shame laced a collar of heat around Laura's neck. "I'm sorry, I accidentally went into the wrong room when I was putting away your laundry and saw your painting. I'm not great with left and rights. It is a stunning painting though—"

Anger flashed in Caro's eyes, and she panted, as though she were trying to control her temper. "That's incredibly intimate and personal. That painting has never been made public. There are only three people who've ever seen that painting: me, Yvonne, and now you."

Laura placed the knife down and gave Caro her full attention. "I was thrilled to have seen it, and I won't tell anyone about your secret masterpiece." So why exactly had she kept the photo? She was so glad she hadn't shared it with her mum. She still needed to delete it though.

"I don't know how you got from the painting to CTP. It could have been by someone else or purchased from a gallery."

Laura decided to tread carefully. "You were so insistent about not going into your studio, you have a cat called Artemisia, and you're deeply interested in art. Besides, I googled CTP and saw photos of you and your wife."

Seeing the anger simmer in Caro's shining eyes, Laura recoiled a little and shrivelled. "Sorry. You asked."

Caro slammed her hand down on the table, dislodging the cutlery she had arranged so precisely. "What are you, some sort of fangirl that you check me out and google me? I can't stand that. I need to feel safe in my home without unrealistic expectations and hopes of who I was. I told you yesterday, I can't paint anymore, and I don't want any pressure on me either. I'm not who I was. I am an angry and bitter failure. If you cannot accept me as I am now, then we cannot live in the same house."

Laura's hand flew to her chest, then she raised her hands to placate Caro. She couldn't bear to be ejected. Her fear of rejection squealed like a banshee, warning her it was happening again. She loved it here, and if she wanted to stay, she had to be careful about what she said in the next few moments. "I don't judge you or have any expectations of you. I'm hoping we can do some more iPad sketching again, even if it's not real art." She grinned and dished out the aubergine onto a serving plate, hoping that Caro wouldn't retreat into her room again. Caro's expression was closed and wary.

Laura sat down and offered the serving spoons to Caro to help herself to salad. Caro took a small quantity of leaves onto her plate, the smallest piece of tortilla, and a tiny portion of aubergines. It was hardly enough to feed a sparrow, and Laura hoped that was not the excuse for Caro to flutter away to her nest. "Doing the sketching is helping with my project. In animation, everything has to be made from nothing. My friend Matt has devised a generic two-legged and four-legged model which can be dressed in different skins, depending on the character."

Caro took a forkful of food and nodded. "People walk differently depending on their size and shape and their emotional state, so how do you deal with that?"

Laura's shoulders relaxed. "Exactly. We've been working together on doing a series of walk and run cycles which can be adapted on whether you have a short woman or a tall man, an angry dog, or a slinking cat. I'm hoping to use it for my master's degree and the project I want to pitch to the studios back in Granada."

Caro swallowed and looked up. "What's it about?"

"It's based on my puppet, who's part of a family. Her thing is that she says things that no one else will, and she challenges the status quo, about corruption, climate change, and bullying. She has a cat who talks to her."

Caro frowned. "What's with the puppet thing?"

"She says things I won't say."

"Why not? Do you need people to love you all the time?"

Laura blushed and faltered, surprised at Caro's directness. "I... Well, yes, I do want people to love me."

"Why should their opinion matter? Especially people you don't know."

Laura had the uncomfortable feeling that she was referring to the two of them. Caro didn't need or want Laura's opinion on her as a person or an artist. She wasn't happy about the challenge, but maybe that's what she needed. "It can also be entertaining and humorous."

Caro raised her eyebrow, something Laura had noted was her tell that she was sceptical about something.

"If you don't believe me, come to my birthday party. Everybody has to do a turn, sing, or recite poetry, and amaze us with their brilliance. I was going to do it in the pub in Bristol, near where my friends live. Would you come along?"

Caro shook her head. "I don't think so. I'm probably old enough to be the mother of most of your friends and sitting in a noisy pub is not my idea of fun."

"What if I held it here? If you would agree, of course." She thought Matt and the others would come along just to be curious and hopefully because they wanted to support her. But of course Caro would need to approve, and she doubted she would.

Caro opened her mouth, then closed it. "I don't normally have men in my house as they're noisy, smelly, and take up too much room. I like Freddie and his son, though, and Yvonne was friends with everyone." She sighed and shut her eyes. "No more than ten people and stay in the snug."

"Wow, really? That's awesome." Laura resisted doing a happy dance.

Caro shrugged. "When is it?"

"My birthday is twentieth of November. I'm a Scorpio. I always think we get a bad rep, but actually we're very loyal and sensual." *What the actual fuck?* Where did that come from? Was she just going to blurt random stuff now?

Caro's eyebrows shot up, and Laura blushed. But Caro didn't know she loved women. She hadn't mentioned anything. That thought stirred an excitement she had tried to squash down. Caro was so out of her league, not to mention eleven years older. "Sorry, I wasn't, I didn't—"

"Twentieth of November could work. But I don't want anyone to know who I am, not that they'd care, and no one's allowed in my room or studio. Including you." She fixed Laura with a scowl.

Laura raised her hands. Her head was spinning between the threat of being thrown out and the invitation to bring her friends here. But they'd made progress. She couldn't wait to tell her mum. Or would that be against Caro's wishes? She would definitely delete the photo, though—after she'd stared at it some more. The emotional intensity was raw and compelling, strong and layered like an onion. Laura was developing a crush on Caro; she was so talented and intriguing and when she smiled, she was as sexy as hell.

Stop it. Why was she going down this path? There was no way she would follow her lustful thoughts again as that just resulted in hurt, and it would bring nothing but trouble. She should put the brakes on right now. It was that easy. Wasn't it?

Chapter Fifteen

CARO HID IN HER room the next morning. She couldn't believe she'd invited a group of strangers into her home. She could rationalise the madness to herself because Rebecca said she should mix more, although a bigger part of her wanted to do it to please Laura. There was something enticing about her eternal sunshine, but Caro didn't entirely trust it, especially since Laura needed to rely on her puppet to say things she couldn't say. How ridiculous to feel like this. The solid steel door to her heart that clanged shut when Yvonne died was unlocked, and Laura had cracked it open, just a tiny sliver, to allow in hope and possibility.

"I blame you," Caro said when Rebecca picked up her call. She slumped down on the bed, which squeaked in protest. Artemisia jumped up and butted Caro's hand until she started stroking her fur.

"Darling, how about 'Hello, how are you?' I'm assuming if you're annoyed that your lodger has done something she shouldn't? Has she kidnapped Artemisia? You know that cat is her own mistress?"

Caro laughed. "No, more me taking a leave of my senses."

"Care to tell what you've done?"

"I'm about to let ten strangers into my house, and it's all your fault because you said I should mix more." Caro tried to keep the panic out of her voice. Artemisia mewed at her rough stroking. "Sorry," she whispered and tickled her chin. Artemisia stretched and shifted to the other side of the bed.

Rebecca chuckled. "That wasn't quite what I had in mind, but how did your young tenant persuade you to let down your defences? Did she melt your heart with her sugar and smiles?"

Caro's cheeks burned. "I don't know. I have this really weird compulsion to please her, and I hate it when she gives me her puppy dog eyes."

Rebecca was closer to the truth than Caro wanted to admit. She played with the tassels on a cushion on the bed. She'd never really liked them; they were over-fussy, but Yvonne had loved the whole boudoir vibe. Caro glanced up at her painting. It was so clear they had just made love, and Caro remembered with startling clarity the drive to capture the moment.

"Are you sure you're not falling for her?" Rebecca asked.

The question jolted Caro back to the present, and it took a second to catch up with Rebecca's crazy notion. "Don't be ridiculous. She's my tenant, and she's only just turning thirty, and she'll be going back to Spain when she's finished her master's and—"

"Those all sound like excuses to me. Do I need to point out that there was a fifteen-year age-gap with Yvonne?"

Caro pulled at the tassels, hard. "That was different. I was mature for my age, and Yvonne was eternally youthful. I doted on her."

"I know, darling, but I'm just saying, don't write it off with this new tenant."

A flash of anger rose in Caro's throat. She couldn't stand Rebecca's patronising attitude. "She has a name."

"Yes, I know. Do you and Laura have a little tête-à-tête over the teapot, or is she mooning over sharing a house with CTP?"

Caro wasn't about to admit that she timed her tea breaks to when Laura would be in the kitchen. It was just to check up, of course, and to make up for their inauspicious start. Delicious aromas wafted into the room, as if on cue, and Artemisia jumped off the bed to seek out illicit treats. "Artemisia's just gone downstairs so Laura must be cooking. That cat is such a traitor. Whenever there's food Artemisia disappears and inevitably, she gets a titbit or two from Laura." Caro was the same as her cat. Laura was a superb cook and conjured up really tasty dishes with very simple ingredients. She needed to treat Laura to an expensive meal as a thank-you for the meals she'd shared.

"What are you going to do about the feelings you have for the lovely Laura?" Rebecca said, bringing Caro back to their conversation.

Caro stopped twiddling the strands of thread. "I don't have feelings for her."

"You talk about her a lot, and you've said how attractive she is. Why not have a fling? Where's the harm?"

Caro sat up straight. She should nip this in the bud before Rebecca bulldozed her into something she didn't want. It was one thing for her to daydream about Laura, quite another for Rebecca to manoeuvre her into something. She counted down on her fingers. "One, I talk to her because she lives in the house. Two, she's attractive, but that doesn't mean I want to go to bed with her." Even as she denied it, a shiver of delight ran up Caro's spine at the possibility. "Three, I don't do flings. Four, what if it all goes wrong and we're stuck living in the same house?"

"All I'm saying, darling, is why not be open to whatever happens? Now, for the reason I thought you were calling me. I hope you're going to say you've got more sketches for me. Unless you've got a full painting, of course."

Caro could almost hear Rebecca's grin, and she pushed down a surge of guilt. "I've had a look, and I can't find the sketchbooks. They're not in my studio or the closet in my room."

"What about all the boxed files in Yvonne's study?"

"I had a quick look." She had only given them a cursory glance because they contained Yvonne's things, not hers, and she couldn't bear to rifle through them even now. She vaguely remembered Rebecca had helped her sort out some old sketch books, and they'd stacked them at the back of the closet in the study.

"Maybe have another look around? I need all the exhibits finalised by the end of this week if we're going to stage the exhibition in Freddie's gallery. I must get back to work for the clients who are actively working and earning money. Talk to you soon, and don't worry about the invasion. Just send them into the snug."

And Rebecca was gone, leaving her usual storm debris that Caro would have to pick over. Was she right about Caro having feelings for Laura, even though she differed completely from Yvonne? She had been the drama of a thunderstorm about to break, bristling with pent-up energy before sparking and crashing in a deluge. By contrast, Laura was a slow, sunny day and cerulean sky. What did that make her? Caro snorted. She was foggy grey and green like an English November. She needed to be less gloomy and look for those sketchbooks. No time like the present.

A shiver shimmied down her spine as she stepped into Yvonne's study. But for the thick layer of dust, it could have been Yvonne had just popped out for a minute. If she had a little more money, she might consider hiring a cleaner. She would never want one to go into her bedroom though. Laura was wonderful at cleaning her own areas, and she also cleaned the kitchen diner and the main living room too. What was she doing thinking about Laura? She was always in the periphery of her thoughts, skirting around unbidden, but *not* unwelcome.

There were sketchbooks at the bottom of the closet. Caro sat cross-legged and pulled the first one out. Most were organised by year but a few were organised by theme, including one whole sketchbook of Artemisia when she had been a kitten, charting her development from all fluff and mini tiger to a mature cat. Rebecca could definitely use something from that one. Now she had to search for some early sketches for the works that Rebecca said were going to be included in the exhibition. Her back ached from leaning forward, reminding her she had done very little exercise for quite a long time. Her core muscles were soft and underused. Maybe she should join Laura when she did yoga in the main lounge. She'd said there was more room to stretch out than in the snug, so Caro had relented and had needed to avert her eyes when Laura moved into downward dog.

Caro pulled more sketchbooks out and flipped through them, reliving her memories. She reached towards the back and knocked against another volume. One must have been caught, but as she extracted it, she saw it wasn't a sketchbook but a notebook with Yvonne's writing on the front. Caro felt the rush of nausea and her hands trembled. She calmed her thumping heart before she opened it up. *A journal.* She lifted the pages to her nose, but there was no trace of Yvonne. Caro swallowed hard. How magical and sad to see Yvonne's confident handwriting, to read things she had never read or known before. It was like accessing her soul. A sliver of guilt slipped down her spine. She traced the lettering with her index finger, trying to imagine Yvonne writing the dates of the journal on the cover. Was she going to do this? It seemed like prying, and didn't they say you should be careful seeking out what you weren't meant to see?

Caro breathed in sharply and flipped open the cover. Most of the comments were about her work colleagues but as time went on, the entries became shorter and darker. With a deepening sense of dread, Caro turned to the back pages. The last entry was three days before she died. Caro brought her hand to her mouth, trying to keep down the scream.

The writing blurred through her tears, and she couldn't really read much beyond a few sentences.

There is nothing work-wise to inspire me, just a few jobs reading audiobooks. Nobody seems to want a serious, respected journalist, just some blond bimbo half my age. I've got a constant headache, and I know I'm drinking too much, and that's no good for my complexion either. At this rate, I'll end up with a drunkard's bulbous nose and vein-lined cheeks. C doesn't understand. She can't see what I see. She's too infatuated. It's cloying and claustrophobic. If I don't get out, I'll scream.

Shaking from head to foot, Caro leaned against the closet frame. It couldn't be. She couldn't stop her teeth chattering, and the last few sentences in the journal turned around in her head, wearing a groove in her memory. The heaviness in her stomach turned to acid as questions tumbled out in quick succession. Yvonne must have been feeling desperate, misunderstood, and trapped to write those words. Why hadn't she said anything? If Caro had known maybe she could have done something about it, helped, or got professional help.

With rising nausea, Caro recalled one of their arguments.

"I'm not one of your perfect paintings, I can't live up to your expectations," Yvonne had shouted after Caro had suggested she didn't drink any more wine.

"No painting is perfect. If it were, no one would ever paint again. There is always a discrepancy between what you envision and the painting on the canvas." Caro had desperately tried to right the boat of their relationship, as it seemed close to capsizing.

"It's a bit like relationships then," Yvonne yelled, then in a calmer tone she had said, "I am blemished with an angry, depressed side."

Caro had wrapped her arms around Yvonne, and she eventually relaxed into the embrace. "I know you have your dark patches, but those are insignificant to the radiance of your light."

Caro had forgotten about that argument, or maybe she had blanked it out. She'd been entranced by Yvonne's light and her vivacious, entertaining self. Now she saw that Yvonne had tried to tell her, but Caro hadn't seen, hadn't wanted to see. Blood roared in her ears, draining Caro of knowledge, of certainty, and her carefully constructed narrative.

Caro retched. The perfect life she imagined they'd had was nothing more than a mirage now that she understood Yvonne did not feel the same. And what was wrong with being infatuated? She loved Yvonne. But it seemed she didn't know Yvonne at all. She slammed her fist against the wooden architrave. Damn Yvonne, why hadn't she told her explicitly? Now it was all too late. Time had stopped, her life had dropped and shattered into a thousand pieces, and she couldn't put it back together again even if she tried.

Was her whole life and relationship with Yvonne a lie? She had thought it perfect, not cloying and claustrophobic. She dropped her head into her trembling hands. Was anything about their life real? She felt she was discovering a treasured masterpiece was by Barker of Bath, a copy of love. No, it was more like an Escher painting that seemed like a rising staircase but from another angle, was actually a staircase coming down. Perspectives changed and skewed by that small phrase, "*If I don't get out, I'll scream.*" The conclusion of the coroner's statement turned in her brain. Accidental death. But the mocking echoes whispered that it was no accident. It had been a deliberate act of desperation because there was no escape. Now she had proof their relationship had been a lie. No, not a lie. She knew Yvonne loved her, but their love wasn't enough. It was never enough. Even if it had been an accident, that Yvonne felt she had to numb herself with alcohol and medication was distressing. Caro shook her head. Surely better to have no relationship than be trapped in a miserable one? Caro thought Yvonne had always loved her adoration and devotion.

Her life and certainty suffered a seismic shift. Her world twisted, the perspective all wrong. Couldn't they have discussed it after twelve years together? Caro stared at the blurred words. Clearly not.

She didn't realise she was screaming until Laura came hurtling through the door, her expression wild with concern.

Chapter Sixteen

LAURA RUSHED TO CARO and knelt beside her as Caro clutched a book to her chest and rocked forwards and backwards like a crying child trying to sooth herself. Laura wrapped her arms around her and gently ran her fingers over Caro's back, saying soothing words into her ear until she slowly calmed down into soft sobs. "Do you want to talk about it?" Laura asked.

Caro trembled from head to foot, but met Laura's gaze, her raw emotions carved on her face. "I can't."

Caro, normally pale, had turned ghostly grey as though her blood no longer flowed through her veins. She trembled in Laura's arms like a bird fluttering to escape, and for many minutes said nothing and just leaned against Laura. She was almost a dead weight, as though her life force had gone, her core collapsing like a building in an earthquake. They sat still for so long that Laura lost all feelings in her legs, and when Caro finally moved and Laura could shift her feet, her limbs tingled as the blood returned with pins and needles. Eventually, Caro's breathing slowed to normal, and she looked up, shame and torment warring on her face.

"Sorry, I'm stopping you from doing what you were supposed to be doing today."

"No worries. How about we go downstairs, and I'll make you a cup of your disgusting slop water you call tea?" Laura asked, feeling completely inadequate in the face of anguish she could do nothing to soothe or contain.

Caro nodded and let Laura pull her up. She was so curious to know what had Caro so distressed and figured it had something to do with the book she held tightly to her chest, but she wouldn't push her. She couldn't bear to see Caro like this. Strong, aloof Caro so completely undone and not in a good way.

Laura didn't let go of Caro's hand and pulled her gently down the stairs. As they walked down the corridor, she was aware how soft Caro's cold hands were except for the callouses where she must have held her paintbrush. When they got to the table, Laura reluctantly released her. Caro slipped into a seat, and as Laura switched on the kettle and pulled down the mugs, her mind was racing. Whilst she loved to see Caro opening up, she hated to witness the pain and anguish that made her so vulnerable.

What could Laura do? Her mum always said she walked to ground herself. Laura had to do some more sketching today to build the environment for her animation, and she needed distant views from a hill from different angles that she could adapt. Caro stared at her cooling tea. Laura couldn't leave her where she was, so sunken and upset. "I need to do some sketching from a hillside for my project. I've seen some paths leading up the hills through some woods, but I'm not sure how to get out onto the hillside itself. Would you be able to show me?"

Caro raised her head and met Laura's gaze, as though she'd only just realised Laura was still there. Laura hoped Caro didn't think she was being insensitive, but Caro was struggling, and if she wouldn't open up, surely she needed a distraction. Laura always found that helped. After Valentina left, she devoted her time and energy to learning some of her dad's special Spanish recipes. She put on three kilos in weight in two months, so it wasn't the healthiest solution, but it helped to give her a focus.

"I'd really like you to come. I'm taking my new watercolour pencils so you could tell me what I'm doing wrong." She grinned. Her mum had sent them as an early birthday present, and she was eager to try them. How better than to get an unofficial masterclass from the great artist, CTP? She had yet to tell her mum, who would be thrilled to learn about her landlady's identity. Looking at Caro, she could no longer equate this woman with the CTP fantasy. Caro was a wounded woman, with all the niggles and nuances of a regular human being.

"Watercolour pencils? You're living dangerously. We'll have you painting before you know it." Caro gave a watery smile.

Laura's heart thumped. She wanted to put her arms around Caro again. "Absolutely. You can tell me what I'm doing wrong there too."

Caro nodded as if accepting the fact but not committing to any action. Perhaps she realised it was one of those half-jokes that had a serious intent below them. Caro seemed stunned and still recovering from the shock that had her so distressed, but she was trying to shake it off.

"All right. We can walk through the woods and along the hilltop. That should give you different angles and perspectives so you can translate it into three dimensions."

"Perfect," Laura said. "I'll get my walking shoes and coat. Would you like to use my iPad?"

"You can bring it, but I might just walk."

Laura almost skipped back to her room to pick up her wet-weather jacket and her rucksack with her kit. She almost forgot the iPad but shoved it in her bag at the last moment. When she got back downstairs, Caro had a cape on and was carrying an old leather rucksack decorated with splatters of paint and a shooting stick with a small stool attached. Was she going to paint? Laura's heart skipped but was unsure whether to say anything. Shyness overcame her. Here she was, a nobody, going out to paint with the great CTP. She blinked at the frown on Caro's face. No, she was painting with her landlady and, she hoped she could say friend. "Ready to go?"

"Don't you have a stool or even a sit mat?" Caro asked.

"I've brought a plastic bag." Laura shrugged. She didn't care. She would happily put up with a wet butt to go out painting with Caro.

Caro raised one eyebrow. "Wait here." She wandered to the cupboard by the front door and, after rummaging around, pulled out a green sit mat. "Eureka," she said, transformed from the woman who had been so shocked a few minutes ago.

"Thanks." Laura accepted it respectfully.

"Let's go out of the back gate, assuming it's not too overgrown," Caro said.

Fortunately, the nettles were dying back, and Caro led them through a gate that opened out onto a stony path, winding up the hill across a rough grass field. The path entered the wood, and Laura absorbed the multicoloured brilliance of nature and scuffed her feet through the leaf litter. The air sagged with unshed rain like melancholy at the passing of another year. As they walked, the musky, sweet smell of decaying leaves stung her nostrils, reminded Laura that she hadn't smelled anything like this for a long time. She thought of their visits to her grandmother here when she was a child. They didn't see the sharp contrast between the seasons in Granada. It became less unbearably hot in the autumn, but she'd never experienced the damp, colourful autumn as she had in England.

They were both breathing hard as they came out of the wood onto a wide meadow and continued climbing. They stopped near the top and turned to admire the Severn estuary and the distant hills of Wales. "This is beautiful," Laura said, trying to catch her breath.

"I thought you could start here, then we'll move along the ridge."

"Aren't you going to sketch?"

"No. I'll just sit here while you christen your new watercolour pencils."

Caro put down her backpack, flipped open the worn leather padded seat, and pushed the spike into the soft ground. Laura sat in front of her by a couple of paces and laid down the portable seat pad, which was more comfortable than a plastic bag. She patted the mat before she lowered herself. "Thanks for this." She glanced up at Caro, but her eyes were closed, and she'd raised her face up to the sky.

"You're welcome."

Laura mapped the landscape out in her mind's eye and thought about how she could adapt it. She needed this for the scene when Charlie, her main character, was being chased by the big dog and its master, and he treads in a cowpat. It wasn't high art, but the story was relatable.

Laura was pleased at how the drawings for Charlie had turned out, capturing the essence of MiniMe in simplified form. Next, she would programme the walk and run cycle. She tilted her head and appraised her sketch. The colours weren't right. She'd drawn the outlines and attempted to hatch in with different colours before applying the water by sponge to activate the watercolour. She took a photo on her iPad to remind her of the actual colours.

She inhaled deeply. How wonderful to be in the countryside alongside such an appealing, complex woman as Caro. Laura turned to watch her soaking up the weak afternoon sunshine with her eyes shut. Laura noticed the silver trail of tears on her cheeks and reached out as if to touch her but held back. "Caro, is there anything I can do?"

Caro's eyes flicked open, but she didn't look at Laura. "No."

"Is it about what had you so upset earlier?" Way to go, bringing up the awkward moment.

Caro nodded and stared out at the Welsh hills.

"If you want to talk about it, I'm a good listener," Laura said. What an idiot. She needed to learn when to keep her mouth shut. This wasn't the time to be flippant.

Caro cleared her throat. "If you mix a little red in the background, it should help the green of the meadow zing."

Laura appraised her picture and when Caro said it, it made perfect sense, so she added a touch of red to the trees and the contrast gave the scene a more three-dimensional feel to it. "Thanks. That's so much better." She would stick to safer topics in the future. Caro would tell her if she wanted to. She breathed in the smooth balm of the fresh air.

"Sorry about earlier," Caro said after a long period of silence. "I discovered something which has turned my whole world upside down, and I'm having problems processing it."

Laura nodded and snuck a quick glance at Caro, but she was staring out into the distance.

"I found a journal of Yvonne's and an entry a few days before she died. She wasn't as happy as I thought."

"That must have been hard to read." Laura didn't know exactly what Caro was trying to say, but her heart bled like the watercolours she was applying to her picture, mixing and merging in a wet mess. "How did she die, if it's okay to ask?"

Caro stayed quiet. Shit, she'd pushed too hard.

"She died of an overdose. A mix of paracetamol, antidepressants, and alcohol," Caro whispered. "The coroner said it was accidental, but I've always had my doubts. And this seems to prove it. I didn't know how unhappy she was. I never knew. I was too selfish and self-absorbed to see what was under my nose. The irony is, I prided myself on my powers of observation."

Laura quieted her breath and stilled her hands.

"She was my soulmate, my muse, but she was unhappy, felt trapped with me. I...." Caro shook her head as if trying to pull herself together. She stood and pulled the shooting stick out of the ground. "We ought to move on, otherwise the light will have shifted too much."

"I can light the scene within the computer programme," Laura said.

Caro stared at her, mid-way between closing her shooting stick. "Of course, you're only doing this as a means to an end, not for its own sake."

Laura's blush crept up her neck to her cheeks. Not only had she been insensitive about a very painful matter, now she was insulting Caro's passion. "That's not true. I would love to paint properly, but I don't have the skill. I'd like to learn."

"Maybe we need to get you painting in future then."

Laura tried to still the thudding in her heart at the thought of a future doing this again, and she followed Caro, who strode towards the kissing gate at the edge of the field. They followed a narrow path that led around the edge of a disused quarry. As they passed the fenced-off rim, a bird of prey rose and flew off. Laura thought she could include it in her project, especially as Matt was working on flying creatures. She had said birds, but he said it could apply equally to bats or butterflies, with a different flight cycle, of course.

Caro stopped at the far end of the rim, ducked behind a straggly bush into a patch of grass with a clear view, and stretched out her shooting stick. "Does this work for you? If we go further on, the bushes and trees will obstruct our view."

Laura turned and gaped. "It's perfect. All the same features from a different perspective. Thanks for bringing me up here. I would never have found this spot, but it really helps to overlay to give the 3D."

"You're welcome. It was one of our favourite walks."

Laura's smile fell. This must be so hard for her, but she was putting on a brave face. "All the more reason to thank you then."

Caro shrugged and, to Laura's delight, pulled out her sketchpad and charcoal pencil and chalk. Was she actually going to sketch? Not wishing to startle her, Laura sat to Caro's side, so she couldn't see what Caro was doing.

Within minutes, Laura was engrossed in trying to recapture the same features as before. They were higher up, so she observed more flat planes. It must have been half an hour later when Laura glanced to the side. Caro was staring at her, pencil in her hand. "What? Have I got paint on my nose?" Laura asked.

"No. I was captivated by the look of concentration on your face and how the shadows fall."

"Oh, wow. Have you sketched me?" Laura's heart fluttered, and nothing would have been able to stop her wide smile. "Can I see it?"

"No. You're too bright and full-on sunshine to be drawn in black and white."

Laura glowed from the inside. Caro was not only sketching, but she'd also drawn Laura and paid her a wonderful compliment. How she would have loved to have a copy of that so she could show her mum. She basked in Caro's approval. Laura's crush was getting more entrenched by the day.

Later, as she was going through the events of the day in her head, laughter bubbled to the surface, and Laura skipped into her bathroom to clean her teeth. She hadn't experienced such joy since she first met Valentina. But this was deeper and not just physical but a pull to the whole of Caro. It couldn't go anywhere, obviously. Somehow, she had to reconcile the paradox of wanting to get closer to Caro but needing to pull back before she got hurt. Her heart didn't want to stop, whatever her mind was telling her.

Chapter Seventeen

CARO POTTERED IN THE studio all morning, building up to this moment. She had mixed the tones deliberately brighter with cadmium red and yellow ochre. She studied the picture she had sketched of Laura when they had sat up on the hill a week ago. Since then, their paths had hardly crossed as Laura had been staying late at university. Caro had missed her. She looked at the simple lines on the page and remembered the curve of Laura's neck, the fuzz of downy hair on her skin that caught the light, and her gentler, softer lines. She was nothing like as sharp or as classically beautiful as Yvonne had been. Laura was more voluptuous, and her dark, expressive eyes twinkled with merriment. She was like a younger, softer Penelope Cruz, with an air that she had a secret thought she wasn't revealing. That's what Caro had to reproduce in her painting. She observed the sketch again and envisaged the finished picture. She measured some basic proportions and scaled them onto the canvas she'd prepared with a desaturated green. Laura would need to be built in layers, much as she had layers herself. Laura could dazzle with how she presented, but Caro realised there was depth to her and the more she saw, the more she wanted to uncover.

Caro splayed a few strokes of paint on the canvas. She wondered how she could depict Laura's essence with her soft intensity and relaxed spine as Laura had been so engrossed in the landscape. The bright surface beauty was easy, the ephemeral, intriguing subtlety was trickier. In minutes, Caro had the first darker planes—not black, Laura could never be black—but a rich, ultramarine blue lightened with titanium white.

Once absorbed and painting from her feelings, using her whole body for the largest strokes, she worked quickly. This was not the detailed hyper-realistic nature of her previous works. This was loose, playful, and bold. After many hours, she didn't know how long, her legs ached with standing. Dark shrouded the windows, throwing the light in the studio into sharp relief, drawing her eye to the radiance of the portrait. Caro dropped her hands to release the tension in her back. She stepped back, stretched her hands up high and studied the painting. Laura was half in profile, half forward in the difficult three-quarter pose, staring out to something off canvas to the left, a slight flick to her lips and eyebrows. Caro realised the emotion she had evoked wasn't admiration or lust, but love. She staggered back and reached for her stool. That couldn't be.

Caro hadn't thought about Yvonne all day and expected the howling pain of loss to come rushing in as she realised, but there wasn't the usual tsunami of grief, just a wistful acceptance. *Oh.* Since she'd read Yvonne's journal, Caro had been quietly re-evaluating their relationship and her life. What had been a slight crack in her understanding now became a huge fissure. With every minute, Caro drifted away from who she thought she was, and Yvonne receded into the background of her past. Each time Yvonne faded a little more, guilt twisted a knot in Caro's stomach, as though she was betraying her. It was ridiculous but knowing it didn't change what she felt.

Now there was Caro's painting of Laura, exposing her emotions for everyone to see. What feelings *did* she have for Laura? Caro enjoyed her company but was it more than that? She looked forward to their conversations over coffee and in the evenings, and she admired Laura's understated beauty. Laura's joy was infectious, but was it more than affection for a friend? No, surely she was imagining it. Maybe it was just the relief she felt at actually putting brush to canvas. A thrill went through her; she was painting. Caro hadn't noticed the time. She picked up her phone and turned down the opera blaring out.

There was a missed call from Rebecca and many texts from Laura. "Tea?" sent at 11:12 a.m., "Would you like a sandwich for lunch?" at 1:07 p.m. "Hope you're okay. Just shout if you want anything brought out. L xo." And finally, about half an hour ago at five, "Hope it's going well. Just a reminder it's my party tonight so you don't get freaked when you come into the house. They're instructed to come in and not stray. I'd love it if you joined us."

Caro sighed, regretting giving Laura an invitation to her friends. They'd talked about it a few nights ago, and Caro was still uncomfortable about it. She'd never been a social animal and would disappear as soon as she could if Yvonne's friends were here. No wonder they had all stopped coming around after she died.

She should have remembered the party was today. Laura had scrubbed and cleaned until the place gleamed yesterday. It was a long time since the house had more than a cursory dust and hoover, and Caro was gratified to see it shining brilliantly like it had done in Yvonne's day. Wait, today was Laura's thirtieth birthday. Caro blushed; she was so self-absorbed she hadn't got Laura anything. Caro could pay for the party food, but that wasn't special. She stared at the painting. Could she? Would Laura see that love was blended in the brush strokes, or would she take it at face value? No, she was bright and emotional, she would sense it. Did that matter? Laura was straight, and Caro wouldn't act on anything, or had Laura meant more when she'd asked about her mum coming to stay? Caro didn't believe in flings, and her soulmate had been Yvonne, and she was gone.

Guilt overtook her. She should have bought a card. Giving the painting would be much more than a card. Rebecca would go berserk. If her fans still followed her, they would probably pay thousands of pounds for this, or maybe they wouldn't, given this was a distinct style. But she didn't care; it felt right. Was it too revealing? One person would tell her at a glance. She snapped a quick photo and sent it to Rebecca with the caption, "Any good? C xx"

It took all of three seconds before Caro's phone rang. Rebecca screamed down the phone when Caro accepted the call.

"Caro, darling. I love it. Interesting new style, and how wonderful you're painting again. We can't include it in the retrospective. Everything is finalised, and the catalogue has gone for printing. Thanks for the last sketches, they made all the difference. Now." She paused, presumably as she enlarged the picture to look at it more closely. "Do you want to tell me something?

Shit. "What?" Caro tried to affect nonchalance, but her best friend knew her and her paintings intimately.

"Despite the style difference, the feeling I'm getting is the same tentative, budding emotions I got from the pictures you produced when you and Yvonne first got together."

Caro rubbed the bridge of her nose. "Bullshit. It's just exuberance at painting again."

Rebecca snorted. "Fool yourself, if you must, but you don't fool me. I'll ask Freddie what he thinks when he gets home. I bet he says the same as me. Are you falling for your little tenant? I told you there were feelings there."

"No, I'm not. I wouldn't do anything. She's too young, she's straight, and she's not Yvonne."

"Sweetie, you need to be open to love again. This picture is like the first flower blooming after rain, delicate and precious. Don't deny it. And if it means you paint again, I'm all for it. We can consider another exhibition in a few months if you do a few more. Do you want to ask Freddie what his customers think? He probably has a few buyers who could take it immediately."

"It's not for sale."

"Are you going to hang it in your bedroom instead of the one of Yvonne?"

Caro gaped. How could Rebecca even suggest that? And how did she even know about that painting? Rage exploded within her, and she swallowed the urge to snap and snarl. "When did you see that painting? And the answer's no. How could you think that? Yvonne was my soulmate."

"Whoa. I stayed with you after Yvonne died, don't you remember? No, I guess you don't. I didn't pry. I know how private you are. Although I'd love to get my hands on that picture. Why don't you want to sell this?"

Caro tensed her shoulders. "I'm going to give it to Laura—"

"You can't." Rebecca cleared her throat. "I mean, would she realise how generous a gift it was? If she tried to sell it on eBay, it would completely devalue your brand, and we've worked so hard to build it up. No, hun, surely you see that won't do. It will impact the value of any future paintings."

Rebecca had a point, but Caro didn't want to countenance that. "How about I stipulate she never sells it, or if she wishes to, she has to sell it via you or Freddie?"

"All right. Talk to you soon. Love you. Ciao." Rebecca ended the call without waiting for Caro to reply.

How ridiculous that she needed permission to gift her own paintings? She could see it was crude compared to her old style. Maybe Laura wouldn't want it. She could always keep it for herself. Caro's stomach grumbled. She'd had nothing but juice and a granola bar all day, and exhaustion had sucked the energy out of her. Maybe she should go in and risk running into Laura's friends. She stared at the painting, hoping the emotion had morphed.

Of Light and Love

It hadn't.

Her phone buzzed. This time, Laura called. Caro looked towards the kitchen, which was lit up with what seemed hundreds of candles. Laura's flickering silhouette appeared at the window, and she waved. Caro waved back before she realised what she was doing, and she couldn't help but smile.

"Hey, how are you doing? I've still got your lunch sandwich in the fridge. Would you like a cup of tea? I can slip out now before my friends come, if that's still okay?"

"That would be lovely. Could you bring it out? I'd like to show you something. And of course, you can still have your friends over." She could almost feel the smile on Laura's face, even over the distance.

"Give me two ticks." Laura waved as she finished the call.

Sudden panic hit Caro. Should she do this? She would lay herself open and be vulnerable. Would it be too big a gift, as Rebecca suggested? She didn't need to give it to her, she could say she was just asking her opinion. What a coward.

A few minutes later, Laura carried over a tray holding two cups and two pastries. That was presumptuous but very welcome. She opened the door to let Laura enter, and cold air rushed in along with Laura and her traitorous cat.

Laura looked delighted to see her but stumbled and almost dropped her tray as she caught sight of the easel. The tray slipped onto the bench, and tea slopped over the sides. Laura covered her mouth, and it took a few moments before she could speak.

"Oh, Caro," she said, her pitch much higher than normal. "That's stunning. And you're painting. I...I don't know what to say. I thought you didn't want me to see your sketches because you weren't happy with them—"

"I wasn't. Do you like it?"

"It's gorgeous. Well, apart from it being me, of course! You've made me so noble, so soft, so, dare I say it, sexy. And although the style is different and colours so much brighter, it's still obviously done by you." Laura slumped onto the stool, her gaze transfixed on the picture.

Caro shuffled with a nervousness she wasn't used to feeling. "If you like it, I thought I might give it to you for your birthday."

Laura turned quickly. "No, you can't possibly. That's way too much.

It's beautiful, but I can't take that. If you sold it, you could afford to repair the roof. You could probably have a whole new roof."

She was so adamant Caro had to bite her bottom lip to hide her disappointment. Didn't she like it or want it? She admonished herself to stop being so ridiculous. It made more sense to do as both Laura and Rebecca suggested.

Laura seemed to glow. "I can't tell you how flattered and honoured I am. My mum would love it too. Could I take a photo of you by it to send to her? That would make my birthday. If you really want to give me something, I'd love the sketch when we were up on the hill."

"I don't like my photo taken." Caro caught the pleading in Laura's expression. "Okay." She tried not to feel deflated. It was probably the adrenalin from painting having worn off. Exhaustion settled in her bones, but she stood as Laura instructed.

Laura showed her the photos. She was so close Caro could smell her fruity shampoo. As she stared at the photo, Caro realised this was the first one she'd been in since before Yvonne died. She couldn't believe how she had aged. She looked so much thinner, gaunt almost, and had shadows under her eyes. Caro turned away, neatly cut the sketch out of the sketchbook and signed it with a signature she hadn't used in years. It felt rusty and unfamiliar, like returning to her childhood home after many years away. She could do more of this.

"Would you sit for me again?" Caro asked, a little unsure of herself.

Laura smiled. "Of course. I'd love to. I can't tell you how much it means you're painting again. It's a truly wonderful birthday present, the best I've ever had." She accepted Caro's sketch. "I will treasure this always. Thank you." She stretched on her tiptoes and kissed Caro's cheek. "Now I'd better get back to party prep and check those candles. I don't think my landlady would like it if I burned the place down!"

She turned but not before Caro caught the deep blush in her cheeks. When she'd left, with Artemisia in her wake like one of the pied piper's followers, Caro touched her cheek. Her lips had been so soft, much like Laura herself. But now Caro felt too awkward to join Laura's party. Maybe she would just hide in her studio all evening. The day had been exhausting and exhilarating in equal measure.

From the house, she heard a squeal of delight and excited voices. Laura was probably telling her friends about the picture now. The rapture on

Laura's face was worth all the anxious deliberation. She was delighted with the sketch and the photo, and Caro still had the portrait. A painting for the first time in years. She smiled as she cleaned her brushes and hummed "The Barber of Seville." She glowed from within, fuelled by elation. Today had definitely been a good day.

Chapter Eighteen

AN HOUR LATER, CARO watched the figures criss-crossing the lit kitchen window. Part of her wanted to be included; everyone was laughing and seemed so animated. It was reminiscent of Yvonne's parties, except there were no flashy cars in the drive and Laura's friends probably wouldn't drink expensive champagne. Her stomach grumbled. She was unsure if Laura had fed Artemisia, who would hate having her routine upset. Maybe she should rescue the poor cat before she let her displeasure be known by shredding something she shouldn't…like her sketchbooks.

Inhaling to give herself courage, she left the studio, locked the door, and carried the tray to the kitchen. She entered the back door and almost tripped over someone's bag. Laura glared at a gangly young man and rushed over to her.

"Hey, let me help you with that. I've told them they shouldn't be leaving their stuff everywhere. Are you going to join us? We're just about to have something to eat and start the performances. Let me introduce you to everyone."

Caro smiled at the curious faces staring at her and was relieved when they turned to the buffet spread out on the kitchen island. There was a mix of sweet and savoury, a palette of different colours, and some wonderful smells emanated from it all.

"I asked everybody to bring specialities to nibble from their home country," Laura said. "We've got some Japanese sushi, Indian samosas and snacks, crisps and Twiglets from the UK, Canadian maple leaf cookies, Italian pizza and, of course, Spanish meatballs and tortilla."

Laura handed Caro a plate and a piece of kitchen towel instead of a napkin. Yvonne would have shuddered at the thought of offering anything but the best serviettes to guests, but the students tucked in with gusto. She should have contributed to the feast if she was going to eat it. But she could still raid Yvonne's wine stash. "I'll get some wine. Any preferences for red, white, or fizz?"

There was a bit of an uncomfortable shifting and staring at feet, and Caro was unsure what she had said wrong. Didn't the young drink wine nowadays?

Laura flushed, which gave her skin a glow. "Sorry, I said they could only bring a couple of cans of beer each. I didn't want anyone getting drunk and trashing the place." She looked really uncomfortable.

"Thanks for being so considerate, but if anyone would like a glass of wine, you're welcome to join me. I'm planning to open a bottle each of red and white, and I don't really want to drink it on my own." Caro smiled and received eager nods in return. She didn't know where all the wine glasses were. Rebecca had helped to sort out her kitchen after Yvonne died and two years on, she still couldn't find anything. She opened various cabinets aimlessly and came across a mixture of wine glasses and tumblers.

"Does anyone mind if they're not in proper wine glasses?"

Nobody objected, so Caro stepped down the stone basement stairs. Apart from the cobwebs draped across the wine racks, everything was as it had been. Caro leaned against the doorjamb for a second and closed her eyes. She inhaled to ground herself. "Sorry, Yvonne. I'm sure you won't mind. They seem like a nice group."

She turned at footsteps echoing down the steps. Laura was caught mid-flight in the light spilling from upstairs. "Are you okay, Caro? I wondered if you needed help?"

Caro stiffened her shoulders and handed over a bottle of red. "I'm fine. Take that up and let it breathe for a few minutes."

Laura grimaced, and the effect of the light on her face turned it quite spooky. "I hope that's not a really expensive bottle, because they won't care."

"*I'll* care. Now, a nice pinot grigio, I think." Caro followed Laura upstairs and put out the bottles on the counter. She dusted them with a piece of kitchen towel to remove any traces of cobwebs, as if she was removing any sign of Yvonne.

Laura rummaged around the drawers to find a bottle opener. "I have the key to our troubles."

Caro twisted in the corkscrew and whispered, "How does this evening work?"

"Part of the deal of coming here is everybody has to do a turn while we eat." Laura grinned. "Don't panic. You get a free pass—unless you want to perform?"

"Oh, God, no." Caro took a stool by the counter, leaving the assortment of chairs to Laura's friends, who had arranged them in cinema style looking towards the blank TV.

She should have taken down the photos but was relieved to see Laura had done it. How considerate of her; she really took Caro's privacy seriously. She marvelled again at Laura, such a wonderful young woman for whom these people had turned up willing to humiliate themselves in the name of entertainment.

Most of the students sang or played guitar. Laura's friend, Matt, and his girlfriend, Kaylee, did a scene from Star Trek. Caro watched from the sides, curious at the display. She had no desire to be involved but was fascinated by this younger crowd doing an old-fashioned kind of entertainment. The last performer was Laura. She had that bloody puppet on her hand. What did that say about her self-esteem?

"Thank you for coming to my birthday bash and entering the spirit of the evening," Laura said, fixing everyone with a look and a smile.

Even Caro was warmed by the welcome and this was her own home.

"I'd like to thank my wonderful landlady, Caro, who's given us access to her home and also provided some very nice wine."

They all turned and clapped. Heat rushed up Caro's neck and cheeks. She hated being the centre of attention and made a dismissing motion with her hand, trying to signal to Laura to hurry up.

MiniMe turned her head to stare at Laura. "I think she's saying you're a bit slow. Get on with it." People laughed.

"Okay, okay." Laura was laughing too, as if the puppet "speaking" was nothing to do with her.

"So, you may think you know Laura." MiniMe said. "How many of you know that Laura swings the other way?" MiniMe scanned the crowd. "Has she told you she likes nothing better than to have her hand stuck up my woo hoo? If that doesn't give you a clue, I don't know what does."

Her friends laughed. Caro's heart pounded. Laura was gay? If she was a lesbian or bisexual, had she actually been flirting with her all along when she'd thought Laura was fangirling on her? She sifted through the interactions and conversations since Laura had been here with a different perspective. Was Laura interested in her?

Caro's body tingled all over. Her heart raced and possibilities expanded, but she quashed the feelings. She remembered Yvonne and knew she couldn't act on anything. For a few exhilarating minutes though, she felt alive with the thrill and anticipation. Was this the reason Laura wanted the party here? Their eyes locked and although Laura was addressing the entire room, Caro felt she was talking to her. There was definitely a message there. After about ten minutes, joking about university and people Caro didn't know, MiniMe turned her head to Laura.

"Laura, we know you can be sly and smart, but is it true you are fluent in two languages?" MiniMe asked.

"Yes," Laura said, frowning slightly.

MiniMe stared at Laura and then turned to the crowd, holding her hand to her mouth as if she was telling them a secret. "So, it's true, she's admitted it. She's a cunning linguist."

Laura's friends fell about laughing. They clapped as Laura and MiniMe took a bow.

How was Caro supposed to address something raised by a puppet? It gave Laura ultimate deniability if Caro mentioned it. Laura had an intoxicating exuberance that seemed to light the darkest corners of Caro's heart, and she yearned for more. But she was so much younger and, in some ways, quite innocent, and that was endearing rather than immature; she hadn't yet been tainted by all that life could throw up. She was a joy to be around.

But Caro felt so old. She couldn't cope with someone eleven years her junior. Yet, as Rebecca had pointed out, she and Yvonne had a large age gap between them. That didn't seem to matter so much though, maybe because Caro was besotted with Yvonne, and Yvonne had loved the adulation. Well, Caro thought she had, until she had been proven wrong.

Laura was different. Maybe they could admit that they had more than friendship. Caro felt that way, and her body certainly agreed.

Chapter Nineteen

LAURA WENT TO BED humming, convinced she wouldn't sleep with the adrenaline buzzing in her veins. It was too late to phone her mum, but she couldn't wait to tell her about Caro's picture. She sent a text asking her mum to call when she woke up. She was lightheaded with the thrill about Caro's portrait of her and wanted to discuss its merits with her mum. The picture wasn't like Caro's usual work, and she was flattered and delighted, but the style change disappointed a tiny part of her. Caro was such a hyper-realist painter like the Renaissance masters or even Gerome. It wasn't as big a transition as Picasso's work from realistic altar boy to the abstract paintings of prostitutes, but it left Laura feeling uncomfortable, as if she was responsible for the shift somehow. This portrait was speedy with just a few strokes to represent her, almost like a caricature, but it captured Laura's essence and was unmistakably her. There was something else that was so appealing, and that was passion.

Exhilaration whizzed up Laura's spine, and she hardly dared guess what it might mean. Did Caro think of Laura as more than a friend? Laura had given enough hints this evening. She was cowardly to come out via a puppet, but it was the only way after Valentina's betrayal stole her confidence and self-esteem, as well as her happiness. Laura knew she ought to have a proper conversation, but it would take courage to make herself vulnerable, to trust again.

"Trust is earned one truth at a time and lost in a heartbeat with one careless act or thoughtless action." She could almost hear her mum saying it. In Valentina's case, it had been one selfish action. The old vision of finding her post-sex with Gonzalo looped in Laura's brain. The only good thing that came from the whole thing was the business finding the money for Laura to study abroad. It had come from Gonzalo's budget as COO. It was the least he could do. She shook her head to clear the memory. She didn't want to relive that nightmare that still haunted her sleep. Not that sleep came, she was too buoyed up to settle, but she didn't care, even though she would suffer the next day.

Annoyingly, Laura couldn't get hold of her mum in the morning, so she headed off to uni for a day of lectures and working on her project. She wheeled her bike out of the wood store, trailing one hand in front of her face in case a cobweb had appeared overnight. She was used to this procedure now, and she clenched her teeth and shut her mouth, as if that would stop the nasty eight-legged creatures.

Despite her eyes being gritty through lack of sleep, she felt alive and buzzing. She still couldn't believe Caro had given her such a wonderful birthday present. Surely it meant something for her to give her such a valuable gift, that Caro must like her.

The bike wobbled when she first set off but with each push down on the pedals, she became more confident and stable. The ride was a bit like her could-be-more-than-friendship with Caro, wobbly to start, but she was sure that interest had sparked in Caro's eyes when she came out last night via MiniMe. It had taken time to establish their rhythm, but now they were speeding along. The tyres thrummed on the cycle track, and the occasional bird twittered its disapproval at being disturbed. Laura laughed and pushed harder, the cold giving her cheeks a glow. It was exhilarating, the speed, the sense of danger, the freedom. She could not keep her smile tethered if she wanted. She was drifting upwards like the balloon taking off in Ashton Court, light and bright in the still morning air. What a fantastic ride to uni, what a fabulous sensation, to feel cared for, and maybe, just maybe, her crush on Caro was reciprocated a little bit.

At the end of her final lecture of the day, Laura turned to Matt and grinned. "Hey, are you ready to skin the rig? I've mapped out Charlie."

"I'm seeing Kaylee," Matt said, not looking at her.

Laura shouldn't be disappointed he never had time to spend with her anymore, and she tried not to take it personally. They had planned to do their projects together, but she'd had to do all the modelling herself, because he hadn't been there to share his expertise on the computers. Laura had learned so much more from her mistakes and had researched extra instruction from YouTube. She'd set up all the keys to tweak each part of the body of the model and was pleased with her results, proud even. In some ways she was glad she'd ended up working alone, as she had a real sense of achievement. And it was lovely to see Matt so smitten with Kaylee. "Okay, I'll have a go. Do you reckon it will work if I just replace the skin of the standard model with Charlie's and tweak the scale?"

Matt looked anywhere except at her, but he nodded his head vigorously. Was he feeling guilty that he had abandoned her on the project?

"Sure. Have you programmed the walk and run cycle yet?"

"That's my next job. I'm pleased with the field scene." She smiled, remembering the scene was based on her walk, where Caro had sneakily sketched her. A shiver of excitement went through her. That sketch was stunning, and she'd sent a photo of it to her mum. In response, her mum had sent her a string of heart emojis.

"What are you grinning at?" Matt asked.

Busted. Laura affected an innocent look. "Nothing."

"Is it a good time to ask if you're in a good mood?"

Laura cocked her head to one side. "I'm always in a good mood. What's eating you?"

"Would you rent my room? I've moved in with Kaylee, and we could save loads if you shared with us. Rob agreed. It would be awesome."

"Thanks, Matt, but I like where I am." *I also have an insatiable crush on my landlady, who painted my picture and gives me goosebumps when I look at her. I look forward to seeing her every day, and I'd miss that. And Artemisia, and the wonderful snug, and Amelia and Riley, who are finally showing footballing skills.*

Matt looked shocked. "It would be easier to work on our projects together."

Laura inhaled and steeled herself to tell the truth, without the need of a crocheted puppet. "I don't want to play third wheel with you and Kaylee, and I'll fight with Rob over the TV and his snarky comments. Also, I'm intrigued by Caro and want to get to know her better. We've been sketching together, and I like her."

He frowned. "I thought she was Frosty McFrost Face?"

Laura cringed. She really hadn't spent much time with Matt if he was that out of date. "Caro apologised for that, profusely. You know that, you saw how she was at my party. She's really interesting, and she's tutoring me, and she's got a great cat, and there are friendly kids next door. Not to mention I have my own bathroom and lounge." Not that she'd spent much time in her side of the house. When she was at home and wasn't working, she hung around the kitchen chatting to Caro.

"Okay. See you later." Matt left, and the doors swung behind him.

Laura made her way to her favourite place in the computer lab and threw her bag down on the seat next to her to create a barrier from anyone else coming near, so she could concentrate on programming the walk cycle.

Five hours later, she had a rough walk cycle for Charlie. It wasn't right, and she couldn't see what was wrong, whether there was a problem with the programming or her understanding of the walk cycle. She rubbed her face in her hands. Her stomach grumbled. Time to go home and sort out food. She copied over the work onto her laptop. It was much slower and didn't have two monitors, which was ideal to view two profiles simultaneously, and that made it trickier to work on. She let out a huff of frustration. The travel time would give her a much-needed break.

Before she headed down to the bike shed in the pitch-black, she sent a text to Caro. *Spanish meatballs?* They hadn't had the opportunity to speak since the party last night, and a frisson of excitement skittered through her at the thought of seeing Caro again. Laura rubbed her eyes just thinking about how late it was before she'd finished clearing up last night, but it had been so worth it to have such great memories, and she would never forget the look on Caro's face when she realised that MiniMe had revealed Laura's sexuality. After the initial shock, Caro seemed curious, and that was a good thing, right? A text pinged, and her heart skipped.

Yum. Yes please, but I must pay for the food. C.

I have some left over. They just need reheating. See you soon L x.

Was it too much to put a kiss at the end? She was just being friendly. Who was she kidding? Yes, she was crushing on Caro, but it was harmless. CTP, the famous artist who hadn't painted for years, had painted Laura, *and* she'd given her the preliminary sketches. Who wouldn't be buzzing at that?

After dinner, Laura asked Caro if she could watch her animation videos on the TV in the lounge. "It's not right, and it would help to see on a big screen."

"Sure," Caro said. "What's the problem?"

Laura shrugged. "I'm really struggling with this. I thought I'd followed what they'd said on YouTube, but if it's right on the side profile, it's wrong on the front view." Her stomach muscles quivered as she teed up the character, Charlie. Revealing her vulnerability was not one of her strong points, and she so wanted to impress Caro. Would Caro think she was crap at her chosen field of study? It really mattered what she thought, she wanted Caro to think well of her. She pressed play.

"Can you do one frame at a time?" Caro stared at the screen.

When she concentrated, Caro had a habit of nibbling her lower lip, which was very sexy and *very* distracting.

Caro leaned forward, still gazing at the screen. "Okay. That's one problem. There's no anticipation. You need to show that with a tiny weight shift before she starts and then, after the head bob, there needs to be a bit of overshoot and settling."

"What do you mean?"

"Watch me." Caro stood up. "Do you see before I start, I breathe in as if I am tensing my muscles, then as I go through the motion, my head rises as I straighten my leg and bobs down again, but it takes a millisecond for my hair to catch up and it swings slightly before it settles. You need to shift the hips up and down more."

Caro walked in front of Laura from left to right, then away and back towards her. Caro swung her hips in an exaggerated fashion, and Laura licked her lips. Her belly buzzed low down and her core throbbed. She crossed her legs as if that would stop the feelings.

"Do you see?" Caro asked.

"Sorry. I—" Her face burned. It must have been obvious that Laura had been checking Caro out, but she didn't react. Hadn't she noticed Laura was burning up?

Caro stepped over to the coffee table where Laura had set up her computer. "Show me on the programme."

She sat next to Laura on the sofa and leaned over so close that her warm breath caused goosebumps to trail a path down her neck. Caro's sweet scent made Laura giddy. All she wanted to do was pull Caro in for a kiss. *Focus.*

"See here. On this frame, you need to show a bit of tension," Caro said.

Laura tweaked the handles that controlled each of the limbs in 3D. Within twenty minutes, they had smoothed out the walk and it looked more natural. "Thanks, that's so much better. Now it just needs some personality and maybe a bit of a bounce."

"Can you put personality into animation? Just kidding. I love animations, especially Pixar. I loved watching them with Rebecca's children. Of course, they're too cool for animations now, so I don't have an excuse anymore."

Sweat beaded on Laura's forehead. Caro never mentioned a lover. "Who's Rebecca?"

"My friend and agent. I'm godmother to her children."

Laura smiled. "Phew, I thought you might have a lover you were going to bring back and chuck me out of the house for."

Caro stared at her, her mouth in a grim line. "I had one soulmate. I don't sleep around."

When would she learn not to be flippant around Caro? "I did too, and I don't have one-night stands or short flings either," Laura said.

The air seemed to crackle between them, as if one was expecting the other to speak, to do something, or acknowledge the significance of what they'd just said. Or maybe Laura was indulging in wishful thinking again.

"Awesome. You never need an excuse to watch animation. My favourite is *The Incredibles*. I have a thing about Edna. 'No capes, darling.'"

Caro laughed with such a silky and sultry sound; Laura would love to hear that again.

"When you say you have a thing, do you mean you fancy short dark characters with swinging hair?"

Was Caro flirting with her? Did she have any idea she was turning Laura into a liquid puddle of longing? "Yes. It seems I do, but not necessarily short." Her mouth seemed to speak even without MiniMe attached to her arm. In fact, she fancied longer hair falling out of a messy bun that kept flopping over Caro's eyes, but she couldn't say that.

Caro raised an eyebrow and nodded towards the computer. "Run it at full speed, and let's see how it plays out on a second viewing."

Had she gone too far? Laura obliged, and now it definitely looked more natural. "Thanks, Caro, that's awesome." *And so are you.* She had to be careful. Her crush could get the better of her and blossom into something more solid. She was kidding herself—she was already infatuated.

Chapter Twenty

THE FOLLOWING DAY CARO didn't recognise the lounge. Laura had made quite the nest for herself in the lounge, with Caro's agreement. The TV was on with the computer maquette mid-cycle, a mug was on the coffee table, thankfully with a coaster or Yvonne would have gone nuts to think her table was ruined. Laura must have been in here for hours. Caro had come back for her second tea, and Laura still hadn't moved.

As Caro entered with her empty mug, Laura stood up from the sofa and clenched her arms above her head, wriggling her spine so her buttocks wobbled. They were round and plump, ready for the picking, and voluptuous like Botticelli's Birth of Venus. Oh, she shouldn't be looking. *What are you doing to me?* Caro couldn't remember the last time she'd had even the tiniest churn of arousal deep in her core. Now Laura had caught her watching.

"Have bottom the size of Brazil," Laura said.

Caro frowned at Laura's strangely posh accent and wanted to roll away from this conversation.

Laura laughed. "Don't you recognise the quote?"

"What?" Caro felt the blush of discomfort. Was Laura mocking her? "I have no idea what you're talking about," Caro said. Didn't Laura understand she rarely watched films or YouTube?

"What? You haven't seen one of the greatest movies of all time? Definitely from your era. The quintessential classic romcom?" Laura seemed genuinely shocked.

Cheeky Madam, she made it seem as though she was a grandma. Didn't she understand she had no interest in such things? "No."

Laura stood up from her place on the sofa. "Caro, we're going to have to educate you. Life is more than opera and art galleries, you know."

Caro's cheeks burned and despite herself, she was throbbing in places she hadn't felt in a very long time.

"You've never seen the movie, *Bridget Jones' Diary*?" Laura asked.

Caro shook her head. What did that have to do with bottoms?

"Don't you know it's a requirement that every Brit should be able to quote from all Richard Curtis films."

Laura turned back to the TV with that delicious, plump round bottom and bent down to pick up the remote control from the floor. Now Caro was hot all over and licked her lips.

"Do you have Netflix?" Laura asked.

"Not anymore. I cancelled it after Yvonne died." She found it easier to talk about Yvonne without wanting to curl into a ball every time she mentioned her name.

"I'll set the TV up with my subscription," Laura said.

"How can you afford a subscription to Netflix? Sorry, that was rude."

"No, it's fine," Laura said. "I need to watch old movies for my course. We'll definitely have to have movie night, especially as we're coming up to Christmas. Let me see, all the Bridget Jones ones, *Notting Hill, Four Weddings and a Funeral*."

Laura seemed ecstatic, like she did when she reeled off her favourite foods, and to her, presumably, films were as nourishing as food.

"I've heard of that one." Caro smiled.

"That's a start."

"Isn't that the one where they quoted from the poem *Stop All the Clocks* by W H Auden?" Caro was grasping at the only information she had of these supposed classics. How could something in the nineties or noughties be considered a classic? Laura slapped her forehead in apparent despair. "Yvonne used to watch all those things with her work colleagues." Caro felt like she was confessing a major crime, not her choice of popular culture.

"Were you never interested?" Laura asked and took her dirty mug to the dishwasher.

Caro followed Laura into the kitchen. "Not really. They used to go out after work."

"What was the last movie you watched?"

Caro blinked and cast her mind back. "*Brave* with Rebecca. We said the film was for the kids, but we enjoyed it."

"Great movie. Spunky young woman protagonist. I love that one."

Laura's eyes gleamed in delight with an intensity that was appealing and unsettling all at once.

"Okay, I think from now until Christmas break when I go to Spain, we should have a movie night every Friday, when we can catch up on your education."

Caro couldn't think of anything but Laura's Botticelli buttocks. She would love to capture Laura in all her luscious glory, so different from Yvonne's TV skinny body. Laura was all curves and voluptuousness. "Could I sketch you?" Perhaps that was a bit of a non sequitur; Laura seemed to start and whipped her head around. Sometimes she reminded Caro of a cartoon character, all wide eyes. Her actions were so evocative, it was hard not to smile.

Laura's expression changed to pure delight. "Vale, of course, yes. When, now?"

Caro raised her hand. "If you're willing, I thought it might be good to draw as you work at your computer, cook, or even when you're playing football with the kids next door."

Laura grinned and wiped her hands on a tea towel. Caro wished she'd use the hand towel, but it really didn't matter, she reminded herself. Yvonne wasn't here to complain.

"Ah, action shots, except at the computer. Make sure you get my best side, though," Laura said.

"They're all best sides." That came out of her mouth without thinking. She moved to the kettle to distract herself. "Would you like your sludge?"

"Yeah, my usual, thanks."

Caro switched on the kettle and attempted to calm her thundering heart and unpick why she had just been so forward. She never just launched herself at people, certainly not beautiful younger women. Laura was unsettling. Caro's stable routine had been rocked, and she was having to re-evaluate who she was in the world. The catalyst had been Yvonne's journal. Her words haunted her, but was that an excuse to flirt with Laura? She needed to control herself.

She was aware of Laura's warmth behind her. "You'd been so long I wanted to check you were okay?"

Laura was so intuitive and empathetic, it was a little disturbing. Caro smiled at Laura's worried expression. "One sludge coming up. Would you get the milk for me?" There was something about Laura that lifted her spirits, made her want to see the delight in her eyes.

Laura danced as she got the milk from the fridge, then twirled around and bowed as she placed the plastic container on the counter. Caro's heart lifted and her chest expanded. Laura's joy and exuberance were intoxicating. "Could I sketch you cooking?"

"You know I don't stay still?"

"I've noticed, and I'd like to experiment with capturing the movement, if you don't mind? I think it's seeing all your walk cycles. Maybe doing a series of overlapping images a bit like Duchamp's 'Nude Descending a Staircase.'"

Laura nodded. Caro loved that she didn't have to explain art to her. She was knowledgeable about the old masters but still absorbed all modern aspects of life and culture too, eternally curious and interested. It's probably why everyone seemed drawn to her; when Laura listened, it felt as though you were the most important person in the world.

"Of course. But can I keep my clothes on? I've never taken to the naked chef thing. Too many opportunities for disaster with spilt oil on my special bits. I'm going to have a break from the run cycle this afternoon. I've nearly finished my storyboard and I want to get that done today, then I plan to make some polvorones. They're a holiday speciality. You're not allergic to almonds, are you?"

Caro was still too busy imagining all those special bits to think about biscuits. "No. But you're always making me things. You really must let me pay for your ingredients. I'm not sure how I'll cope when you go to Spain for Christmas."

"You gave me that wonderful sketch. Cooking for you is nothing compared to that." Laura bit her lip and looked a little unsure. "Why don't you come to Spain with me?"

Caro almost choked on her tea. Laura was just inviting her willy-nilly to her family in Spain. That wouldn't do. It would upset her routine and order. "I can't. I always spend Hanukkah and Christmas with Rebecca and her family. Her children pretend they're too grown up, but we enjoy playing board games together. Good job it's not Monopoly anymore. It was boring when they were young, so I used to cheat." Caro sighed when she saw Laura's disappointed expression. "But I would like to paint in Spain sometime. The light can be amazing up in the hills."

"I'm glad you're not on your own at Christmas. I talked to Mum about it last night, and she said she'd love to have you over. The Spanish go to the restaurant before Christmas and the expats love to go over Christmas itself, so you never know quite who will turn up, or how drunk they'll get. Brits abroad don't have the best reputation."

Caro was intrigued and touched that Laura worried enough about her to ask her mum, but socialising with strangers? She shuddered. She could think of nothing worse than a room full of people she didn't know. It was like dropping back into Yvonne's parties, drunken, loud, and noisy. She'd locked her door after one party when she'd seen a couple trying all the doors upstairs. Caro shooed them downstairs and told them to go back to their spouses. There was nothing she hated more than infidelity. It would have shredded her if Yvonne had ever done anything like that. In her darker moments, Caro wondered what Yvonne saw in Caro. She was not glamorous or involved in media. Maybe because of that Yvonne knew Caro had depth, was real and she became her anchor to all that was tangible.

"Would you look at my storyboard? I'm trying to prepare everything, because I've arranged to make a pitch to Domingo Studios in Granada over the Christmas holiday," Laura said.

Caro frowned. "I thought you said they only did video games?"

"Yeah, but they're branching out into animation, which is why they agreed to me doing the master's. I signed a contract to say I'd work for them for three years afterwards, which I'm happy to do, but I want to develop my own story, so I've got an appointment the day after I get back to pitch my idea. Ideally, I want one fully rendered scene to show them the aesthetic. I thought I'd do the chase through the field scene that ends with the dog owner stepping in the cow pat."

"It's a little coarse, isn't it?" Caro hoped that didn't sound as judgemental as it came out.

"Kids love it," Laura said. "I showed Amelia and Riley an earlier version, and they thought it was hilarious."

Caro thought about how Rebecca's children would react. Jack would think it was funny. Zoe would probably think she was too mature. That reminded her, she needed to order their Christmas gifts. What did you buy for teenagers who wanted for nothing? She was tempted to buy them chickens from Oxfam that would provide a family in Tanzania with eggs. Or maybe a toilet. She could almost imagine their disgust if that's what she donated on their behalf. She looked up to see Laura chewing her bottom lip. "You're right. Kids love that kind of thing. And I'd love to see your storyboard. I'm not sure what I could offer as input, but I'm delighted that you've asked me."

The anxious look dropped away, and Laura's face lit up with a smile that could power a village. "Thanks."

Laura extracted multiple pages from her backpack. They were covered in squares of drawings, like a comic, with three lines under each picture titled shot, action, text. It intrigued Caro that each shot was detailed and could have been live action. Yvonne had been offered movie scripts, but she'd always been drawn to the journalistic side.

Caro followed the storyline, studying each picture, and could see how the physical humour would work. There was also a beautifully interwoven life message. "I can picture that. That should wow anyone. If your studios in Spain don't like it, I'm sure I could talk to some of Yvonne's old colleagues and get you a pitch to the channel bosses." Heat rose from her neck to her hairline. That comment had come from nowhere.

"Oh, wow. That's so kind, Caro. I know Domingo Studios has a hold over me, but I'd prefer to work on my own stuff rather than another game or someone else's story."

"How did you cope with devising games? You don't strike me as being a violent, shoot-'em-up kind of person," Caro said.

Laura shook her head. "I'm not. My game was a world-building game."

That wasn't what Caro expected, but she should have known better. Laura was such a good soul, and lightness emanated from her. She was dreading Laura going back to Spain to live, but that was just selfishness on Caro's part since she couldn't commit. She couldn't ask Laura to change her life for Caro. That wasn't fair. "Would you need some sort of establishing shot?"

Laura cocked her head to one side. "Like the equivalent of a drone shot, you mean? Yeah, that could work. I haven't worked out how to programme the cameras yet, but I'm hoping Matt will show me."

"You don't talk about Matt much. I thought you were going to work together on your projects?" Caro asked.

Laura's smile dropped. "He's really involved with his new girlfriend. And it's great to see him so happy, but I miss him. He's like a little brother to me, and we got on so well when we worked as interns, really clicked, you know? I definitely miss his expertise. But I'm also learning a lot by doing it wrong."

The urge to reach out and comfort Laura was almost overwhelming, but she quelled the unwise desire.

"Would you come with me to the opening of my retrospective art show in London next week?" Caro asked. "I've never been on my own before, and I'm dreading it."

Laura bounced up and down on the sofa. "Yes, yes, yes. I'd love to. Could we go to some of the galleries in London and make a day of it?"

Laura's excitement was contagious. Visiting London would be very different with her. Yvonne had always wanted to go to the most expensive boutiques and meet up with her media friends for lunch at exclusive restaurants. Laura would probably be happy with a bacon butty whilst sat overlooking the Thames. Caro needed to break the mould and do something different. Also, Laura's interest in art was genuine and wide-ranging, Caro would be fascinated to observe Laura's take on some of her favourite paintings.

She met Laura's smile. "Why not?"

Laura took her storyboard back. "Awesome, and thanks for the input. I've been struggling on my own."

"I'm sorry you miss Matt," Caro said.

The look of sadness in Laura's eyes was fleeting, but it obviously marked a sharp wound. Caro knew so little about her past. She had been self-centred and absorbed again, never once asking her about any part of her life, other than her mum. "Are you all right?" Caro asked.

Laura jumped up. "Of course. I'll just tidy up in here before I start the polvorones."

"I'll help." Where had that come from? Caro never volunteered around the house, but she so wanted to see Laura's normal smile return.

It took about half an hour for Laura to regain her equilibrium. When she buzzed around the kitchen dancing to whatever was in her headphones her mood really settled again. Caro picked up chalk and charcoal on rough paper and stared as Laura moved. She fixed her with squiggles and curves that represented her spine, hands, and hips. Her flow was evocative and erotic, like a middle eastern dance routine devised to titillate and provoke. Caro's libido came rushing in like a hot tide. With every moment, Laura came closer and Caro lost a little more of Yvonne. Could she let go? Could she move forward if she relinquished her tight grip on the past? Or, given Laura would leave in a few months, was the hope of anything new extinguished before it started?

Chapter Twenty-One

"WOW, THIS IS AMAZING," Laura said, staring at the picture in the National Gallery.

Caro bubbled with laughter at her enthusiasm. Joy shone from every pore and in the gleam in Laura's eyes. How refreshing to be around someone who expressed their delight and fun and didn't care about behaving in a serious way around fine art. That they were both drawn to the Gentileschi Self Portrait as Saint Catherine of Alexandria was not surprising.

"Her use of light is ace," Laura said, leaning forward over the ropes to take a closer look.

Artemisia gazed out of the painting with a wistfulness that was so hard to recreate. "It's the expression that gets me," Caro said. Light seeped in from the glass ceiling in the long gallery, bathing the room, picking up the warmth of the terracotta walls, and offsetting the gilt of the frames. Caro had been here many times but never with such an enthralled companion before.

She needed the distraction. It was a great idea of Laura's to make a day of it before the opening of Caro's retrospective this evening, but maybe they should have done the tourist parts after the exhibition, because Caro's attention kept drifting to the impending opening, the crush of people, the expectations and small talk, and her speech. Would they like the exhibition? They should do, given that it comprised her old works, or was it out of vogue now?

Laura placed her warm hand into the crook of Caro's arm. "Are you okay?" Laura asked.

Caro inhaled sharply and pulled Laura closer. A heavy lump settled itself in her stomach. "How do explain I can't paint anymore? I don't want to talk to anyone. And Rebecca's still pissed off with me because I'm not staying with her and doing the rounds of our old college friends. I can't stand their pity and the discomfort of not knowing what to say."

Laura squeezed her arm, and the warmth of her touch settled the buzzing in Caro's stomach.

"What's the minimum you have to do that will keep you clear of Rebecca?"

"The only thing I have to do is give a small speech, I suppose. Freddie and Rebecca can do all the sales talks. And Rebecca will probably want to push her new artists."

"Do you want to practice your speech now?"

Caro shrugged loose of Laura's grip. "Not really, but we ought to go. Do you mind if we walk? I need to clear my head."

That Laura understood Caro and sensed her anxiety was a revelation. Yvonne could never comprehend how Caro hated being the centre of attention and just jollied her along with "Smile on, tits out" as a pep talk. But Laura seemed to be watching Caro's creeping dread with close attention, ready to protect. "Thanks for understanding, Laura."

They locked gazes, and Caro was drawn into Laura's deep brown eyes, keeping eye contact for a few seconds longer than expected between friends. Because they were really friends now. She looked forward to early morning tea and chats about art and politics and Laura's project. She could even cope with the teasing about her lack of knowledge of current culture.

They walked via Piccadilly Circus and Regent Street, with Caro pointing out the sights, although most of the shops seemed to have changed hands from when she was here twenty years ago. Not that they'd frequented Mayfair very much. That area had only become more familiar after Rebecca married Freddie.

"Rebecca's husband, Freddie, owns the gallery. He's posher than the queen, but he's a really kind man," Caro said as they avoided a group of tourists.

Laura looked a little anxious now, as if it was catching. "I'll chat to him all evening, then."

Caro shook her head. "No, you'll be lucky if you get to speak to him at all. He tends to act as a walking sales brochure, entertaining potential buyers and pointing out facets of the art even I wasn't aware of when I painted them."

Laura grinned. "Bullshits, you mean?"

"No. And don't say that to him. Be nice. Be you, not that bloody puppet."

Laura flung her arm over her eyes in mock dramatic fashion. "Caro, how could you? I'm wounded. Anyway, who says I'm not a potential buyer?"

Caro laughed. "Says the woman who cycles to college in all weathers to save herself fifteen pounds a week—"

"— and who's getting buns of steel because of it."

Laura flexed her buttocks, causing Caro to swallow hard. She really shouldn't be staring. "I'd like to paint you on your bike."

"Sure. Oh wow, there's Hamleys. Have we got time for a quick whizz around? Um, judging by your face, that's a no. Can we come up to London again? This has been fun."

"We could have a quick look if you like," Caro said, but Laura was already dragging her along.

"No, come on. I shouldn't have said anything. Do you want anything to eat before we get there?"

Caro tried to squash down the sickness. "I couldn't."

"Shall we grab a sandwich for afterwards then?"

"Why not." Caro glanced at her watch. Only fifty-three minutes to go until the doors opened. If they didn't get there soon, Rebecca would send out a search party. "Freddie has lent us his driver for afterwards, so we don't have to catch the train back."

"And he's going to drive us all the way back to Bristol?"

Laura seemed almost as amazed about being provided with a driver as she was by the Artemisia paintings.

"He's not going to drop us on the motorway, if that's what you mean," Caro said.

Laura's eyes widened. "Will he need to stay over for the night? It'll be late when we get home."

Laura was such a kind soul, always concerned for the welfare of others. Caro rarely heard anyone else worry about such things. Yvonne never did when the channel sent her home with a driver, thinking nothing of keeping the driver waiting for a couple of hours while she and her friends made a detour to a club. "If you like, we can ask him, but he'll probably want to drive back to London." So much for no men at home, but somehow Laura had softened her up, and her friends had behaved really well at the birthday party.

Caro's heart seemed to match the quickened pace as they approached the Zeltser gallery. Each step closer magnified the terror. Caro pulled at the bottom of her suit jacket. The satin was cool to the touch, and she smoothed down the creases before opening the door to the gallery.

"Here's the star of the show. Caro, lovely to see you. Rebecca can stop pacing now." Freddie gave her a kiss on both cheeks and hugged her. "How are you doing, sweetie?" he whispered.

Caro managed a faint smile. "Honestly? Shit scared."

"No need, darling. They're going to love you, and I promise you can escape as soon as you've done your speech. Terry will be waiting outside the back entrance and will take you all the way to that sweet little cottage of yours. If you need a little courage, please feel free to imbibe, just not too much that you slur your speech, of course. And who is this wonderful woman?"

Laura looked up from scribbling her name and email address on the list of guests and placed the pen down on the table.

"You don't need to do that, Laura. Freddie can always contact you through me. Freddie, this is Laura, my tenant, who has been instrumental in getting me here today. Laura, this is Freddie Zeltser, who owns the gallery and has squeezed in this exhibition to put pressure on me to paint," Caro said.

"Tut-tut, Caro, don't tell porkies." Freddie bowed over Laura's hand as if he was an old-fashioned courtier.

Laura was only partially successfully in hiding her smirk, and her eyes glistened with mirth. She seemed to avoid looking at Caro.

Freddie brushed his lips against Laura's hand. "Delighted to meet you. I hear you've also encouraged our CTP to start painting again. Thank you, not just for the sake of British art, but also because it means my wife isn't griping at me about it every day. You are a marriage-saver too."

Laura laughed. "My pleasure. It's lovely to meet you too. I've heard a lot about you."

A waft of cool air swirled around them as the door opened and shut behind them.

"It's all lies, I assure you. Now if you'll excuse me, I think we have our first guests arriving. Enjoy yourselves as much as you can, Caro." Freddie bowed again and turned to greet his guests in a loud welcome.

A waiter dressed in black and white approached them with a trayful of champagne.

"You can leave that with us, thanks," Laura said and grinned, but the waiter merely blinked and gave a polite smile. "Ooh, tough crowd." Laura took two champagnes for them both.

Caro's hand shook as she accepted the glass and sipped at the drink. The bubbles went up her nose, causing her to cough. How embarrassing to choke at her own exhibition, though there was hardly anyone here.

"Shall we go to the bathroom?" Laura asked.

Caro nodded, taking Laura away from the main gallery to the back stairs. Once she had swigged some water, she hung her head over the sink. "I can't do this. It's all too much."

Laura grasped both of Caro's hands, held them in her own, and waited until Caro met her eye. "Caro, you're an amazing woman. You've come so far. The people coming here tonight are all on your side and want the best for you. All you need to do is stand up and thank them for coming. I should have bought MiniMe along; she'd give you courage."

Caro smiled, then turned to face her reflection in the mirror, checking her hair didn't look too out of place.

"No, thanks. I'll stick with the champagne courage. Shall we go?"

Laura squeezed her hands. "You'll be awesome. I'd love you to show me all the Artemisia sketches."

Caro doubted she'd be awesome, but she'd get through it, thanks to Laura's support. Even a few months ago, she couldn't have imagined ever facing a group of people, would not have thought she could paint again, or feel genuine delight, yet she had enjoyed today, sharing her world with Laura, who'd been so enthusiastic. Around Laura, the light was changing from dark shadow to mid tones. Now she could see an aura of the sun.

As they stepped back into the gallery to face the crowd, Caro smiled. She could get used to having Laura by her side.

Chapter Twenty-Two

OUTSIDE, THE FROST FORMED a dense carpet on the lawn. Laura inhaled the thick aroma of the coffee needed to tingle her senses awake and sipped. By the flicker of the fairy lights she had insisted they put up, she observed how Caro ate her breakfast so daintily, nibbling at her toast without dropping crumbs everywhere. "I don't know how you can eat breakfast."

Caro raised her eyebrow but continued to eat. "I don't know how you can't. Breakfast like a king and all that. Have you got plans for the weekend?"

Laura looked up from her online search. "I need a beach scene for the finale of my project. I've been looking up the buses to Clevedon and Weston-super-Mare. But I don't think either is like a typical Spanish beach."

Caro wiped her hands on a piece of kitchen towel. "No. One's rocky and one's mud. Why do you need a Spanish beach?"

"Like I said, I'm hoping to sell my project to the Domingo Studios in Granada."

"Why not try for a UK studio? I was serious when I said that I could contact some of Yvonne's old colleagues to see if they'd be interested in sponsoring the project. I think it could do well, and there are several well-known animation studios in and around Bristol."

Laura warmed herself in Caro's enthusiasm for her to stay in the UK. Did that mean that Caro liked her? Laura was still surprised she'd found the courage to kiss Caro's cheek. She really liked her, but she had no idea what would happen after her course finished. She'd expected to go back home to see her parents. But Caro thinking about her *not* going back to Spain was heartening. Maybe she thought there could be a *them*. Or was Caro just being polite, accommodating, and British? "That'd be great, thanks. I may need to pitch several times before I get a bite. But I can't afford to repay the tuition fees that would get me out of my contract."

Caro blinked, as if debating something. "What if you could repay your fees? Would you stay?" She nibbled her lower lip.

"Is there something I'm not getting?" Laura held her breath while she waited for a response, her heart thumping like the frenzied bass beat in a club.

Caro folded the kitchen towel and flipped it over. "If you stayed in the UK, I could draw you more often."

Trying not to let her disappointment show, Laura nodded and tried not to sag. Caro was just after a model. That made sense. She'd recently rediscovered her painting, but Laura wanted to be more than Caro's muse, and it wasn't practical. But she was touched Caro would even think about paying her fees. She'd obviously done well financially with the exhibition. Post-Brexit, Laura would need a work visa to stay in the UK, but maybe she could commute regularly. If it didn't work out with Domingo, it could be her Plan B. Even if Caro didn't want her for anything more than modelling. The serpent of disappointment coiled around her throat, making it difficult to speak. "Thanks. I'd love you to explore whether I can pitch to a studio here."

Caro broke into that rare and delicious smile that warmed Laura's heart. Like the oil paintings she created, Caro had layers upon layers of complication and a heady mix of dark and light. Laura loved the contrast, especially when she came out into the dazzling sunlight.

Caro had folded the kitchen towel into a piece of Japanese origami. "If you want a deserted sandy beach, I could take you to Sand Bay. The water is still the sludge of the Bristol Channel, but there's sand, and we could sit on the dunes and sketch, if you like."

Laura's heart hammered in her chest. The air between them was charged, as though Caro was offering more than a lift to the beach. "I don't want to ruin your day."

"I planned to paint today, so this is the perfect opportunity to go somewhere different, and if you don't mind, I could sketch you while you draw?"

This wasn't the first time Caro asked her permission, but there seemed to be more significance in her intent. Was she reading too much into it? Laura leaned back on the kitchen stool and posed. "Draw me like one of your French girls." She batted her eyelids, then sat up again as Caro clearly hadn't got the reference. "*Titanic*?"

"Pardon?"

Sometimes they seemed so much further apart than eleven years. They were on opposite sides of a cultural divide. "Did you never see the film *Titanic* with Kate Winslet and Leo DiCaprio?"

Caro shook her head. "Yvonne saw it with her friends. I can't think of anything more tedious than sitting for hours watching a film about a ship sinking and seeing everyone die in the end. She said she enjoyed it, though."

"Not exactly a romantic, are you?" Laura spoke without thinking and regretted it when Caro winced.

"No," said Caro. She collected up her breakfast plates with a clatter to stack them in the dishwasher.

"Sorry, I'd love for you to paint me or sketch me anytime," Laura whispered, hoping she hadn't offended Caro.

Caro shrugged and closed the dishwasher with a snap.

"Would you like me to make a picnic?" Laura smiled and was rewarded with a softening expression on Caro's face.

"Sold. I'll get my easel and kit. I might paint if it's not too windy. Bring a scarf."

Laura didn't even know Caro had a car and was surprised when she reversed a bright blue Mercedes sports car out of the garage and retracted the roof. She'd always wondered why British people bothered with open tops when the weather was so cold and miserable most of the time.

Caro fiddled around and pointed to the heated seats. "You'll need those."

Laura stroked the leather interior, inhaling its luxurious smell. "This isn't what I expected."

"What did you expect, a Toyota Corolla or something else very practical?"

Laura blushed. "Well, yeah. It's very sexy, and of course, you're sexy, but you're not flashy." That had just slipped out. Her cheeks felt so hot, she probably didn't need the car heater.

"Thanks. I think. But you're right, it's Yvonne's old car. I guess I like to have a connection to her still by driving her most treasured possession."

Caro's words crushed Laura a little inside. "Do you believe you only have one soulmate, and that was Yvonne?" Laura asked.

"Yes. I did. Now I'm not so sure there is only one. I've been reassessing. I thought she was mine but according to her journal, I wasn't hers. If I wasn't hers, then she can't have been mine. Or maybe someone can be a soulmate at one time of life but as we change, what we need changes? Some grow together, others apart." Caro slowed down and looked both ways for traffic. "I didn't think I could live without her, yet here I am, a shadow of my former self."

Unsure what to say, Laura stared out the side window as Caro pulled out onto the main road. She closed her eyes and leaned against the seat, which warmed her bum and back. The wind whipped at her hair, and she was glad for a scarf.

Caro looked across at Laura. "But recently that's changed. Life feels good for the first time in years." She accelerated as they left a village, pushing them back in their seats. "That's largely thanks to you. You've opened a door I thought was closed forever."

Laura's heart pounded. "Thanks." She wasn't brave enough to say that the feeling was mutual. She needed to say what was on her mind, but first she needed to pick through her emotions.

Her stomach lurched in an uncomfortable queasy way. The more she was pulled in towards Caro, the more she liked about her. Beneath the gruff exterior was a passionate, talented woman with a good soul. But the closer she got, the spectre of Valentina's betrayal and abandonment grew and stifled her. As the possibility of a relationship with Caro became more real, the greater her fear loomed over her waking thoughts. What would happen when she left for Spain? Would Caro come too? Could she come too? It was all too difficult and complicated. She didn't want to be hurt again. Valentina's affair had taken too much out of her. Being betrayed felt worse than a bereavement when you knew the person loved you. That wasn't right for everybody though. Laura had seen how devastated Caro had been when she thought she was responsible for Yvonne's death. Wherever it came from, grief wasn't a competition.

"Are you okay?" Caro asked.

"Always." Laura smiled, but her heart didn't reflect it.

Caro fixed her eyes on the road ahead. "You've never spoken about your relationships. Have you ever been in love?"

Laura sighed. It had to come out sometime. She hated being so vulnerable and admitting her failure and stupidity. "Yes. I was with a woman called Valentina for three years, and we lived together for two. I thought she was my soulmate. We had a lot of fun together, working and playing hard. I was going to propose, and I'd already worked out which venue I wanted. My dad was going to cater, and my mum would help choose my dress." Laura stared out at the green hedges.

"What happened?" Caro asked.

Laura squirmed. How could she have been so stupid and not known what was coming? Valentina was always ambitious. "She started getting close to one of the bosses, Gonzalo. At first, I thought she was angling for promotion, then he made her his assistant, and they started shagging. According to the office gossip Valentina had chased him and pushed him into the affair." Laura took a second to compose herself. The raw and hurt hadn't really faded. It had healed, but the scar remained, indelible and distorting her skin, her heart for life. "I found them in bed when I came home from work early. I was devastated and humiliated. I had to work with them and see them flirting and fawning over each other. I needed to escape, and that's why I requested coming across to do the animation master's, and the studio agreed to pay, and I filled up the time with an internship till it started." Laura stared up at the glowering grey skies and attempted to blink back the tears.

Caro squeezed her hand. "That's shit. I'm so sorry, Laura."

Her hands were warm and her touch surprisingly gentle.

"I know. I'll never get over it or trust again," Laura said.

Caro's face fell. "What, you'll never love again?"

Laura's heart raced. Was Caro remembering Yvonne, or was she also feeling the same stirrings as Laura? "I don't think so. But they say never say never, which is what Sean Connery said when they asked him to do another Bond film. He shouldn't haven't bothered." Laura shouldn't really deflect, but she didn't want to continue this conversation and expose more of her pain.

Caro squeezed her hand, sending tingles through Laura. Her crush needed to be kept in check. This couldn't go anywhere, whatever her heart was saying. But she couldn't deny her feelings were growing stronger, and she loved being close to her and in her company, even when Caro was grumpy.

"I've no idea what you're talking about," Caro said and put her hand back on the steering wheel.

"I know."

They were silent for the rest of the journey as Laura sifted through her feelings. Caro parked on a virtually empty road by grass-fringed sand dunes and closed the car roof. They took out their backpacks, climbed the concrete steps that acted as a flood barrier and made their way through the sand dunes. Laura inhaled the salt air and was battered by the sting of sand on her cheeks. "It's windy. I'll sketch using my iPad. I want to work out how to capture sand granules."

"Yes, I think I'll sketch rather than paint," Caro said.

They took the shooting stick and canvas stool and climbed into the sand dunes, which hid them from view of the road, but they could still see the beach. In the distance, a couple were walking their dogs, and they pulled at their coats to protect themselves from the wind. The beach was a wide expanse and a long way to the churning estuary but tempting though it was to rush towards the water, signs depicting a person drowning in sand were placed at regular intervals. She shuddered involuntarily. She couldn't think of anything worse than drowning in sand.

Laura set up her iPad. She stared down at the sand and tried to figure out how to replicate the granules that could be affected by the wind. After a few false tries, she inserted a flexible layer in the programme that would simulate pouring sand.

Caro huffed in exasperation, and Laura looked up. Caro was battling to hold down the pages of her sketchpad with bulldog clips on each side. A few strands of her hair had fallen from behind her ear and were stuck against her forehead. Her cheeks were pink with the wind, and her lips were parted. She looked stunning, and Laura wanted nothing more than to lift the strand of hair, tuck it back, and press her lips against Caro's.

She moved closer. "Another disadvantage of paper sketchpads," Laura whispered.

Caro stood up, affording Laura slight protection from the wind. "You won't say that when your iPad gets sand in it," Caro said.

"True." Laura nudged closer. A tingle of excitement ran up her arms, and Caro stared at Laura's lips. Laura licked them involuntarily and saw Caro's heartbeat pick up. So she wasn't the only one affected by this. Laura shivered.

Caro opened her arms. "Come," she whispered. "Keep warm."

Laura stepped in until their bodies touched, and she snuggled against Caro. Their breasts met and even between layers of clothes, Laura's nipples hardened and her arousal surged. So much for keeping the crush under control. But this was too much. Caro leaned down, meeting Laura reaching up, and their lips almost met. Caro's beautiful lips looked so soft, Laura wanted to kiss them.

"May I?" Caro asked in little more than a rough whisper.

"Please."

Caro tasted of salt and gentle breezes. A hair found its way between them. Caro pulled it back behind her ears without breaking contact and kissed her, leaving Laura breathless. Laura moaned and licked Caro's lips again. Caro's lips parted, and she deepened the kiss, sending shivers to Laura's core. Laura sighed, and when Caro murmured, Laura's arousal stirred even more. They stopped to take air, and Caro's lips were swollen, pink, and beautiful.

"I want to make love with you right now," Laura said before her brain engaged.

Caro's pupils darkened. "Appealing though that is, sand will get into more than your iPad, and we can't have that. Perhaps we should just go home and have our picnic?"

"Um," said Laura. "Although I'm not hungry for food."

"Me neither." Caro kissed her again. "It seems I can't get enough of you. You've dissolved all my defences."

"Good, let's go."

Caro gathered her belongings and grabbed Laura's hand, who had to snatch up her canvas stool as she was pulled away. This felt so right. Laura shivered again, not with the cold, but with the thrill of anticipation. They headed back to the car and icy drops of rain splattered on her skin and cooled her ardour, dousing the spark of arousal and washing away her certainty.

"Just in time." Laura shivered again. She couldn't believe how cold it felt in the damp atmosphere, and it seemed to reflect her sudden change of mood. The further they left the beach behind, the more her doubt and panic grew. Her heart and body pulled her one way and her fear the other. She wanted to have sex with Caro, or was it to make love? No, it couldn't be that. She wanted to make lust with Caro, but was that enough? She'd never been one for flings, but Valentina had spoiled relationships for Laura.

She stared out the side window of the car. Caro looked to be concentrating on driving through the sleet that strummed on the roof. What they didn't tell you about sports cars was that all the spray from vehicles in front caused a tidal wave on the windscreen, making it hard to see the road ahead. Laura couldn't face Caro. She had to tell her how she was feeling, but how could she say this scared her and the fear of being hurt was pulling her down. MiniMe could explain and would probably make a joke about it, about her failings, but Caro didn't like talking through a puppet and she was right. Laura should grow up and communicate like an adult. But that required the vulnerability of trust. Trust that she would expose how she really felt and not be abandoned again, trust that they could work something out when she returned to Spain and Caro wouldn't give up as being too complex.

"Are you okay?" Caro asked and placed her hand on Laura's thigh.

Her smile was genuine and caring. Laura nodded, not trusting herself to speak in case her doubt and fear came tumbling out. She wasn't brave like Caro, who had moved so far from the deep shadow of grief. She was emerging into the pale light of hope, which was reflected in her paintings. That she was painting at all showed Caro's bravery to trust and be vulnerable again.

Caro ran her thumb up Laura's inner thigh, and Laura tried to control her body from reacting. Fear of being hurt and desire intermingled. She trembled all over. This was too fast. It couldn't last. Better to stop it now before anything started. She consciously slowed her breathing to a normal pace. Just as well she was going home tomorrow, so she could reset. The distance would ground her, so she could find the firm, safe sand between the dunes and the suffocating sinking sands out beyond the tide. She needed to find that middle ground, to be solid and secure and unravel the vulnerability cautiously like a safety rope. Caro deserved more than the fear Laura was throwing at her. "When I quoted from *Titanic*, the main character is throwing away her stuffy conventions and asking the painter to draw her nude," she said.

"Oh." Caro glanced at her. "Is that what you'd like?"

Laura nodded, arousal buzzing deep and low in her belly. That situation felt more controlled. It would give her distance, but she could enjoy watching Caro at work. She loved to watch that slight frown between her eyebrows as Caro observed and estimated proportions, and angles, and planes, and how light would fall and be reflected in the tones from deep shadow through the mid-tones to the saturation of bright light. Laura could dazzle her with joking and sunshine, so Caro wouldn't see the hurt behind the brightness. And she knew she needed to let Caro in, let her see all of her, and to trust that Caro would not betray her, desert her, or abandon her. Being painted meant what they had was real and tangible. "Maybe when we get home?" Laura asked.

Caro glanced across at her. "That would be wonderful." There was an unmistakable gleam of desire in her look, no doubt reflected in Laura's own expression.

Yes, painting was safe and perfect. Feeling she had been saved from drowning in her fears, Laura breathed in deeply. She could do this.

Chapter Twenty-Three

CARO DROVE THE CAR into the garage and switched off the engine. "Do you want to brew yourself a coffee and warm up? I'll just dry off the car," Caro said and smiled, but Laura didn't reciprocate. She just nodded and headed into the kitchen. Caro took a few minutes to polish with a chamois leather, giving herself time to understand what had happened, to recover from the emotional whiplash from Laura's apparent change of mind. Where had the happy-go-lucky sunshine gone? In the car, Laura had withdrawn into her shell as if she was regretting their kisses. But she'd kissed Caro with a fierce passion that was electric and so arousing that Caro had found it difficult to concentrate on the way home. What was going on?

The leather squeaked as she polished the now-dry bodywork. Painting would be a great diversion. Caro would go straight to paints without sketching beforehand to get an immediacy and fluidity. It may not be any good, but it would channel her sexual frustration onto the canvas. And if Laura didn't want to sit in the nude or sit at all, Caro would lock herself in her studio anyway.

Caro hung up the chamois leather and went to the studio to switch on the heaters. The cold seemed to affect Laura. Perhaps she would be more comfortable in the lounge. They couldn't go into her room. It was still full of Yvonne's things, and it would feel like betraying her, something she would never do. But she found it hard to remember Yvonne's face. Now, she had become exactly as the painting, but it no longer seemed right to her, so obviously on display in her bedroom. She would have to move them over Christmas, something to occupy her before Laura returned. She needed to let Yvonne go.

Caro had been brought to life again in Laura's presence. She was like a drug she didn't want to give up. But if Laura needed more time, she would respect that, despite the disappointment. Caro assumed it would be her holding back, but strangely, it was Laura.

She went into the kitchen through the back door. "If you're having second thoughts, it's fine. You don't have to sit for me."

Laura shook her head. "No, I'd like to. Maybe we could have our picnic first?"

Caro exhaled as the spark in Laura's eyes returned.

"Happy to sacrifice myself, by eating your delicious food," Caro said, trying to add a lightness to the conversation.

"Good. I'd hate for tortilla to go to waste. I've also left some meatballs and tortilla in the fridge for you while I'm gone, because I know you won't feed yourself," Laura said.

"Thanks, that's kind. Although starving won't be an issue. I'm going to Rebecca and Freddie's, and Rebecca always completely over-caters, deliberately I think, so she can pack me up a Red Cross parcel when I come home."

Laura placed aluminium foil packages on the counter, while Caro took clean plates out of the dishwasher.

"How long will you stay with them?"

"Two, maybe three days. No more. There's only so much teenage angst and family drama I can cope with without wanting to escape to my studio. And Artemisia gets antsy."

"You wouldn't like it in Spain then. There always seem to be loads of cousins and hangers-on wanting Dad's wonderful cooking. Although Mum always cooks a traditional British Christmas meal on Christmas day with all the trimmings. She has yet to persuade any of my Spanish cousins that brussel sprouts are not torture, but it doesn't stop her trying. Dad calls them boiled farts."

"I'm with your dad," Caro said and placed the food on her plate. She inhaled the earthy scent of potatoes. Laura had said that traditional tortilla didn't have onions, that was Tortilla de Patata con Cebolla, but Caro didn't care. She loved all Laura's cooking, and the smells were enough to make her swoon. No onions were good if they were to kiss again, but that wasn't a given. "Tell me about your Christmas in Spain," Caro said, wanting to commit it to memory so she could imagine Laura when she was away.

"Sure, I'll switch the lights on, so it feels more festive."

The tension in Laura's shoulders dropped as they chatted over their indoor picnic. The Spanish Christmas sounded chaotic, but Laura clearly loved it, hence her insistence about decorating the kitchen and lounge. How different from her social events with Yvonne, the ballet, the Messiah at Bath Abbey, and the dinner parties.

It was a long time ago, a lifetime ago, and Caro had moved on though she didn't know how far. If the opportunity arose, would she really sleep with Laura? Certainly, her body was interested, although there was more than physical attraction. "Do you want to talk about what's going on?" Caro asked, stretching out to stroke Laura's free hand.

Laura shook her head and swilled her coffee around her mug. "I can't, not yet. It's my shit to deal with. But I'd love you to paint me."

Caro's libido danced in anticipation of capturing Laura's likeness. If nothing else, Caro needed to paint out the stirring of kundalini awakening and tap into her creative force.

After Caro had cleared up the plates and reloaded the dishwasher, she turned to Laura, who sipped her coffee and watched Caro as if deciding what to do. Artemisia jumped up into Laura's lap. She had no doubts when her back was turned, Laura would let her prowl on the counter. "I'm going to the studio. If you wish to come, please wear something comfortable, and there's no pressure to do anything."

"Do we have to have opera?" Laura asked.

"Bring whatever soundtrack you like, although I'm not keen on thrash metal."

"Thanks. I'll finish my coffee and come over."

Caro's heart quickened as she picked her way over the wet grass and pushed the damp and swollen studio door open. A blast of heat stifled her. Caro needed some air or she wouldn't be able to breathe, let alone paint. She opened one of the side windows a crack and arranged the tableau. She draped the chaise longue in red velvet, but that wasn't right for Laura. It was too old-fashioned. Laura was smooth honey and needed a sumptuous cloth.

She pulled out some slightly creased cerulean satin from a drawer. She smiled faintly, realising it looked like satin sheets rumpled after vigorous love making. She trailed her index finger across the slippery material that purred luxury, and sensuality, and an invitation to make love. A frisson of pleasure shimmered through her.

Normally she arranged the light source so there was one powerful light, like from a candle or the glow of a machine so she would get the hard light and strong contrasts that had typified her style all her career. But that didn't suit Laura's sunshine and softness. Caro finally settled on the top left configuration typical of many paintings using diffuser screens.

Caro was about to extract oil paints, but they weren't calling to her. Oil was too slow and wet for too long. Laura deserved to be shown in the quick drying vibrancy of acrylics. She got on her hands and knees to open the lower drawers and retrieve her professional grade paints. They were neatly arranged and labelled, but she didn't remember doing it. It must've been an exercise when she was still in the thrall of grief.

She set up the canvas on the easel and rolled her shoulders like a fighter preparing herself for a bout. Excitement, adrenaline, and the overhanging arousal from earlier thrummed through her body. She was ready, but a glance at her phone showed nearly half an hour had passed, so maybe Laura wasn't coming after all. She battled not to feel the crush of disappointment.

Caro inhaled and steeled herself. She wouldn't waste the momentum and decided to paint the background first. It had always been her preference and then, when the background was dry, she would layer fresh paint on top. Acrylics were more forgiving than oils. If she started now with the satin and the chaise longue, she could transpose a sketch she had already completed of Laura and insert that into the painting if she didn't come in the next few minutes.

Caro rummaged around under the painting bench and found her latest sketchbook. She slowly turned the pages, and with each one, she ran her finger along the paper as if to trace out her love. Laura was all curves and voluptuous sex appeal, but she didn't seem to be aware of it at all. She looked so natural in all the sketches, laughing as she played with the kids, dancing as she cooked, and still, focused concentration when she sketched or read. Flawless, but for an old scar on her forehead. Joy radiated through her actions and expressions that were beautiful and fleeting. If only Caro could touch that joy, capture that exuberance.

She applied the basic background and planned which of the sketches she would bring to life. There was shuffling and a knock on the studio door. Surely not the kids next door, they hadn't been tormenting her for weeks thanks to Laura.

Laura was here. The tingle of excitement buzzed in Caro's chest, and adrenaline vibrated throughout her body as Caro opened the door. Laura wore a coat over jeans and sweatshirt, like any other day. She was biting her lip and looked younger than her age. She was so adorable, with that soft down on her skin.

"You came, thank you," Caro said.

"I've never done this before. I had to have a long talk to MiniMe before I built up the courage."

That bloody puppet. "I told you, there's no pressure, and I only want you to do what feels comfortable. If you're not, it will show in the painting. You'll be rigid, and it won't feel right. Stay clothed because you shouldn't need to build up courage to do this. That way, it's no different from when I've sketched you before."

It felt different though, more charged, heavy with potential and pent-up desire. She needed to set Laura at ease. Caro smiled and Laura reflected it shyly, averting her eyes. Laura's shoulders relaxed. Maybe the satin wasn't appropriate, and she could repaint just the undraped chaise longue. "That's better, much more you. Let's just do a series of quick paints with you sitting, or reading, or standing, whatever feels comfortable. Oh, I see you have your little shadow."

Artemisia entered, looking very haughty as though she was offering the world treasure by gifting them her presence.

"It's nice and warm in here." Laura rubbed her hands together. "Thanks."

For the first time, she met Caro's eye. There was a trace of fear, but her pupils were also large with desire. The warm heat of arousal burned low in Caro's abdomen and spread throughout her body. "Let me take your coat," Caro said.

Laura shrugged off her outer layer and handed it to Caro, who carefully hung it up. It seemed representative of setting aside the first layer of fear and distrust.

"I'm glad you've pulled the blinds down. I'm not sure I really want Amelia and Riley peeping in. They're not ready for this. The world's not ready for this. I'm certainly not."

"I want you to be comfortable," Caro said and locked the door. "At the moment, you're anxious, and I'm not sure if it's about the painting or something else."

"I can't do it in the nude. When I think of all your famous paintings of Yvonne, she was tall, lean, and classically beautiful. I'm not."

Ah, so she was self-conscious. "You are stunning, all luscious contours and irrepressible joy. You are the birth of Venus, beautiful and erotic, and you radiate light and exuberance. I would love to paint you nude if you're comfortable, but if you're not, we'll paint you how you are. Did you bring your music and a book?"

Laura held up her phone and iPad. "I've got a book on Kindle and playlist all sorted. I think you'll like it as well." She grinned.

Caro was sure there'd be plenty she would definitely not like. But if it made Laura relax, it was worth it. "Sure. Do you want to sit on the chaise longue? You can move the drape." Caro wouldn't care if she tossed the drape at this stage, if she would just relax.

"But you've arranged it. No, that's fine and what a beautiful colour. It matches the blue in your eyes."

Her smile was positively coquettish as she sat carefully not to upset the arrangement. Was she flirting? Caro had never been good at reading those signs and was hopelessly out of practice. Before she replied, Artemisia jumped on to Laura's lap, kneaded her knees and rubbed against her hand. Laura laughed with such playfulness, Caro wished she could capture that, there and then. "There's no mistaking who her favourite is," Caro said, which made Laura laugh again.

"That's because she gets lots of fuss and kisses, don't you, my little Arty Farty?" Laura kissed the cat's head and rubbed her ears. Artemisia purred loud and consistently.

"You *cannot* call my cat Arty Farty."

"Why not? You love it, don't you?" Laura scratched under Artemisia's chin, who shuffled to give Laura better access. "Are you ready for the music?" Laura pressed play.

To Caro's surprise, classical guitar music emerged from the iPad. It was complex, clear, and enchanting, evocative of flamenco dancers.

"One of my cousins, Pedro, plays Spanish guitar. This is his compilation," Laura said.

"That's fabulous." It genuinely impressed Caro. "Just keep on playing with Artemisia, and I'll start." If she could just recreate Laura's smile. Without conscious thought, she dipped her paintbrush into the mid-tones and started with the basic planes of Laura's body using rapid, confident movements. Like finding home after years of travels, she eased herself in. Laura was a delight to study, and Caro absorbed her, like a sponge soaking up her essence. With a quick check for proportions, Caro swilled out her paintbrush and carefully wiped it before mixing a darker tone on the canvas. Instead of her usual harsh lines of contrast, the changes were subtle, soft, and fuzzy.

It seemed like only minutes later before the magic that she could never explain emerged. It happened only when she was in flow, and the portrait built itself in tones and layers. Amazingly, Artemisia even stayed relatively still, her face angled to allow Laura's petting. Laura's hair had fallen forward, giving just glimpses of her face and with a few deft strokes, Caro had portrayed her. It was undeniably Laura, the way she held her head and the posture of her body. She started another quick study, short and sketchy as the first. Finally, Caro stepped back and stretched. "How are you doing?"

"Great. It's not a hardship to play with her." Laura smiled, joy dancing in her eyes. "Are you done?"

Caro studied the work that she had channelled. the portraits were good and wouldn't take much to complete them. "For now. We could both do with a break."

"Can I see?" Laura seemed nervous again.

"Sure." Caro dropped her paintbrush in the water, stepped back, and let Laura take her place.

Laura covered her mouth. "Oh, Caro, they're stunning, and I love how you've got Arty preening at my touch."

"I'm glad you like them." It felt strange when her work was praised. Sometimes, a picture came through her as though another hand guided hers.

"I love them." Laura wrapped her arms around Caro. "You're so talented."

"You're both wonderful subjects to paint."

Caro returned the hug and melted when Laura grazed a kiss across Caro's lips. The push-pull was hard to cope with. But the kiss must mean Laura had resolved her internal struggle, didn't it? Caro had a choice: clamber on board and ride the wave to take her who knows where, or struggle to fight the turmoil. Excitement made her choice, and she surrendered to the surge of emotion. She had no option. She hoped she wouldn't drown.

Chapter Twenty-Four

LATER THAT EVENING, LAURA finalised her travel arrangements with her mum. She also hoped to get some solidity on the thoughts thrashing around her brain. "Caro kissed me," Laura said. "It was mortifying."

"Mortifying?" Her mum sounded puzzled.

Laura tickled Artemisia behind her ears, giving herself time to sort out her thoughts. "I loved it; it was wonderful. But I couldn't show her how I feel about her, and I closed it down. I think I've hurt her."

"Why can't you show her?"

"Because it can't go anywhere. She'll never leave the UK, and I can't stay here." Laura twirled her fingers around Artemisia's fur.

"What about a long-distance relationship?"

"I know. I thought about that. If I get the project with Domingo, I could maybe work from the UK, and go to Spain to see you and have meetings." It all sounded so rational when she said it out loud.

"I don't understand what the problem is."

"I'm scared." Laura had been avoiding acknowledging the truth for the past few days. Weeks really.

"What are you scared of?"

"I don't want my heart broken again. Caro really isn't the lovey-dovey kind, so I don't know what she thinks about me, and she's still hooked into her dead wife. But she kisses so passionately, like her paintings, so strong and stormy." Laura was grateful she could tell her mum anything. "I'm petrified that passion will burn itself out, and now she's found her art again, where does that leave me?"

"With a wonderful person waiting for you in the UK, or she can come over to Spain. I can't wait to meet her."

Panic washed over Laura at the thought of her mum and Caro meeting. "Mum, you cannot fangirl on her; she hates that. She almost threw me out of the house for doing it."

Her mum sighed noisily, as if the notion had never entered her head. "I won't. The only thing I really care about is how she feels about you, how she treats you, and that she makes you happy."

"We're not at that stage. I can't commit to her. I like her a lot, but what if it all goes wrong?"

"If it all goes wrong, you come home and we eat pistachio and mango gelato and watch all the Marvel films together. Again. And you'll throw yourself into work. Have you got your presentation sorted?"

Laura smiled. Her mum had been wonderful after Valentina. She'd even suffered the whole of the Marvel catalogue, though she'd been puzzled about the characters and the plots. She had cried when Tony Stark died. Laura was more upset about Natasha sacrificing herself, but that was because she had a crush on Scarlett Johansson. "Thanks, yeah. Caro's going to make suggestions too." That wouldn't be nerve-wracking at all. Laura brushed some cat fur from her jeans.

"Good idea. Didn't her wife work in the business?"

Her mum must have been doing research since Laura had told her who she was living with. "Yeah, and she's asked if I want her to check with Yvonne's old contacts about getting to pitch my project."

"That would be wonderful."

Laura's heart seemed to shrink in her chest. Didn't her mum want her in Spain? "Except I wouldn't be at home with you and Dad."

"Oh, honey, you need to move away from home—"

"I did, and look where that got me." A sudden flash of rage surged up. "I can't do it. I won't do it."

"You need to have an honest conversation with Caro, and I don't mean via MiniMe either. Just tell her you're feeling confused and you really like her, but that you're terrified too. Then maybe you can discuss how you go from there. I need to go, love. Your dad's calling me."

It seemed obvious and logical when her mum said it, but Laura wasn't sure she had the courage to love or trust again. She couldn't imagine Caro having an affair, but she hadn't thought Valentina would either. She continued her packing and debated whether she should talk to Caro. What should she say? She hated blowing hot and cold, but she didn't want Caro to know just how much she liked her. That really wouldn't work, whatever her mum said. She'd also promised she would pose nude. Maybe they could do it tomorrow before she left. It would be weird to be remembered that way, as if she was fixed in time.

Of Light and Love

Laura tossed the last of the presents she'd bought into the case, planning to wrap them at home. She needed to see Caro now.

When she went downstairs, the kitchen diner was in darkness and there was no reflected light coming from Caro's bedroom. Peering out in the darkness, the blinds of the studio were still drawn but lines of light rimmed the edges. Without really thinking, Laura made her way down the frosty path to the studio, trying to avoid the wet grass seeping into her canvas shoes. She knocked, but there was no reply. She knocked again and heard shuffling and a yawn.

"Come in." Caro rubbed her eyes after she opened the door.

"Hey, sorry, were you napping?"

Caro stretched, showing off her slim body. "God, you make me sound like an old woman. I might have dozed off. I felt tired painting you earlier. I haven't stood that long for a while."

"They're beautiful pictures. Thank you for being patient with me while I sort my head out. If you have time in the morning, I could sit for you before my flight. I'm happy to do it in the nude, but maybe you could even out some lumps and bumps."

"Your body's beautiful," Caro said without a moment's hesitation. "So is your soul and your personality."

The burning of a blush travelled up Laura's face. "Thanks."

Caro eyed her with the intense gaze as though she were studying her like a specimen. "I could paint you now if you like."

"Aren't you tired?"

"Funny, I've got a second wind."

Caro smiled, and Laura's resolve melted. Her body hummed in all the right places at the anticipation of taking her clothes off and being seen and studied by Caro.

"I promise the painting won't be public unless you're happy with it. In fact, I'd like to keep it just for me," Caro said.

A tremor went through Laura. How could she say no to that? "How do we do this?"

"If you want to change into this robe, I'll get my paints set up. Acrylics again, I think." Caro turned to her bench.

Laura shrugged off her hoodie, and the cooling air blew goosebumps onto her skin. Her pulse quickened, and her lips were dry. Stripping her inhibitions with her clothes, with all her vulnerabilities and insecurities laid bare even if she didn't believe in forever, she could gift this moment to Caro, and her feelings would be recorded in a permanent reminder of now.

Chapter Twenty-Five

CARO FIXED THE PREPARED canvas onto the easel and scanned the studio, carefully avoiding where Laura was undressing. The studio was transformed now. Working in acrylics, there was no longer the heavy, heady smell of turpentine, and she had a Christmas candle burning so warm clove and cinnamon filled the air. Laura's Spanish guitar music played on a loop in the background, creating a romantic ambience.

Laura had insisted that she trail fairy lights around the edges of the windows. Caro had tried to complain that it would affect the light, but Laura just grinned and told her to switch them off when she was actually painting. Caro had also noticed, but not commented on, the Santa gnome complete with ceramic sleigh that had appeared in the flower borders. Yvonne would've hated it, dismissed it as juvenile and tacky, but it made Caro smile. It was so Laura. *Laura, Laura.* She was turning Caro's world on its head and rattling the rusted parts of her. A warmth deep in her belly grew, awakening all her senses, and her nerve endings tingled with expectation and joy.

Caro couldn't remember feeling like this with Yvonne. Winding back her memories, she realised she'd never felt like this. There was always adulation but never equality. With Laura, there was joy, laughter, and pure delight. Caro wasn't just renewed with her, she was reborn. She had the chance to become a better version of herself. She inhaled sharply and steadied herself against the bench. All that meant she loved her, didn't it? The realisation pulsed through her, strong and sure, like a heartbeat.

She shook her head. No, Laura was going back to Spain. It couldn't work. There was only this month, this day, now, to savour Laura and capture on canvas her desire and dismay at the ephemeral nature of it all. Life was lived moment by moment, slipping frame by frame for each day, and the animation reel would roll on until "That's all, folks." From now on, Caro would relish every day.

"I'm ready."

Laura's voice was husky and on a lower register than normal. Caro turned to face her and wished she could freeze this vision of Laura exuding anticipation, arousal, and a tinge of anxiety. Wrapped up in the robe, Laura reached her hand towards Caro as though she felt it too, and the air was thick with tension. Laura's robe parted, revealing a hint of cleavage, and the dark curls at the apex of her thighs glistened with desire.

Caro swallowed and squashed the craving that shimmered throughout her. "Stay like that. It's perfect," she said. "You're beautiful."

"With my clothes on? Are you saying don't remove my robe?" Laura's eyes betrayed her hurt.

"You're stunning with or without your clothes, but this is more provocative." How typical of Laura to be insecure when she had nothing to feel insecure about. She was such a lovely woman from her soul outwards. Caro had to clamp her lips together so she didn't spill the words she wanted to say that kept reverberating around her brain. She couldn't say them, because it would raise expectations, and this couldn't go anywhere. "Trust me, you're gorgeous."

Laura smiled, as if what Caro said had finally sifted through her defences. *How weird.* Caro's defences were nothing to the protective armour around Laura's heart. She had obviously been badly hurt, and now she played the clown so people wouldn't look too deeply. But Caro wanted to delve below the surface and reveal those glorious layers.

"I'm not sure I can hold this pose for long," Laura said.

That was fair enough. Holding a limb up for any length of time was torture. "Okay, I'm going to lie on the floor. I'd like you to come towards me as though you'd like to devour me. Imagine, if you must." Caro removed the canvas and placed it on a tabletop easel that she'd carefully angled on the floor. She dropped a cushion beside it and slipped onto it. Laura was now higher than her and fixed, as if coming towards her with intent, but the desire in her pupils wasn't fake. Every pore tingled, and the temptation to reach out and touch her was tantalising. She rearranged the fall of the robe and the back of her hand brushed against Laura's skin. "Are you too hot?"

Laura blushed from her chest upwards. "No, I just... I haven't been touched in a long time, and you're turning me on." She burned an even deeper shade of magenta.

"Good, that's the idea." Caro felt the pulse of arousal curling up from her core as Laura licked her lips and moved one pace forward so she was virtually on top of Caro. Yes, this would definitely do. She quickly mixed the mid-tone of Laura's golden skin and marked a few proportions on the canvas. Fantastic.

"What did you say?"

She must have said it aloud then. "You're just perfect in every way. Delectable."

"How quickly can you finish?"

"I've only just started."

"Hurry and finish then, although you should be naked too." Laura grinned that cheeky way of hers that got her what she wanted.

She was dangerous, and Caro couldn't say no. "Would you feel more comfortable if I *was* naked?"

Laura's eyes widened so large, it was almost comical.

"Or were you just joking?" Caro asked.

"I...I was, but I'd like that."

Caro shrugged. "Okay. I guess it's warm enough in here."

She smiled and pulled her sweatshirt and T-shirt over her head, fascinated by Laura's reaction as her eyes drifted down from Caro's face. Naturally lean, Caro was neither ashamed nor proud of her body. It was just the package that contained her essence, but the soft murmur of delight from Laura when she undid her bra and let it fall was almost enough to undo her and entice her to pull Laura into her arms. No, better to wait, to be deliberate, and let Laura set the pace and take control.

Who knew painting could be a form of delicious foreplay? She unzipped her jeans and quickly dispatched them and her knickers to a moan from Laura, who was unashamedly absorbing Caro's nudity. It wasn't just Caro's heart that was pulsing when she whispered, "Better?"

"Torture."

"Good. For me too. Do you still want the robe?"

Laura stretched up so she could shrug the robe off her shoulders. "Is it still provocative enough?"

She reverted to her previous position but what had been a smouldering ember in her eyes was now a flame of lust. Caro coughed. "Yes, you could say that." She picked up her brush again. It had dried already, so she swilled it around the water, the lights and candle reflecting as the paint swirled in the liquid. Caro was conscious of Laura watching her every movement and she caught her eye. Slowly, she drew out the brush, swept the bristles against the side of the jar, and gently wiped it in an old cloth.

"You even make cleaning your brushes seem erotic."

It sounded as though Laura was grumbling, but Caro didn't care. "Good. Keep that look, yes, with your lips parted as they are. What are you doing to me?"

"Hurry and finish. I don't know how long I can wait before I act. Do you know how sexy it is to see you naked and concentrating? I wish I had a photo of you just now."

Caro flooded at the thought of that. She thought she might have an orgasm just thinking about and watching Laura. "Maybe when you're away I'll paint a nude self-portrait."

Laura moaned. "Oh, please, I'd love that."

Then the magic happened, as it always did when Caro got lost in her painting. She became one with applying the paint and the intensity of concentration, and she dropped into the flow, where time stopped still, until she noticed Laura was trembling. Her arms probably needed a rest. "Do you want to stop now? I've got enough that I can finish later, and I think you've been super patient."

Caro dropped her brushes in water; they could wait. She rinsed the paint off her hands and her body where some had splattered. As she stood by the sink, she felt Laura's warmth behind her, before she enfolded Caro in her arms, and her breasts squashed against Caro's back. The nipples hardened to nubs, and Laura rubbed her sodden hair against Caro's butt. Caro arched back into the touch.

"God, you're so wet. Spread your legs," Laura whispered.

Caro hadn't expected Laura to take charge. The confidence of youth was so arousing, Caro thought she might scream in frustration. "Please. Just hurry."

"Patience, patience. You've kept me hanging for the last hour, I think you need some of your own medicine." Laura trailed her fingers around Caro's nipples and tweaked her hard. Caro spasmed and thought she might come on the spot. Then she felt warm, soft lips on her nape, and she liquified with desire. When Laura blew cool air over the same place, Caro shivered all the way to her toes.

"Hmm, you like that, don't you? And how about this?"

Laura circled her soft fingertips down from her belly and stroked all over except where Caro wanted it, where she needed it. She was ready to explode. "I need you inside me, now, before I come. That would be embarrassing."

She felt rather than heard the chuckle as it vibrated through their bodies.

"Are you sure you don't want me to do this?" Laura skated her fingers against Caro's engorged clit.

Caro moaned and arched into the touch. "Yes, yes, everywhere." Caro had never been so quivering and desperate. Laura licked her neck and Caro grunted, which turned into a pleasured moan as Laura slipped her finger between Caro's throbbing folds and pushed, setting up a steady rhythm. Caro wouldn't last. It was too long since she'd had someone inside her, and Laura was clearly skilled. She slipped in another finger to join the first and thrust in a slick cadence, faster and more frantic with every pulse, matching Caro's thundering heartbeat. Just when she thought she would teeter forever on the edge, Laura flicked Caro's clit with her thumb, and it was all too much. The last of Caro's defensive walls cracked and shattered into thousands of crystal shards, and she was falling through a flood of kaleidoscopic bliss. Her legs gave way. Laura held her up from behind and pressed her against the sink.

"You okay?" Laura whispered.

Caro could only nod, unable to organise words into a coherent sentence. She twisted and gave an embarrassed grin when she eventually gained her senses and realised what a muddle she was in. "Oh, dear, that was quick."

"We're not one and done," Laura said.

She stroked her clit, sending shivers of delight through Caro.

"I think we need to christen the chaise longue."

Caro leaned against the sink for strength. "Agreed, but I want to swap."

"No complaints from me."

Laura pulled herself away from Caro with a final tweak of a nipple that sent a tremor through her, fuelling her desire again. There were no complaints from Caro, either. Far from it. She pulled Laura towards her, and they kissed hard and desperately. Her craving for Laura coiled up her spine like a kundalini snake stirring her chakras.

"I've wanted you so long," Laura whispered.

Caro couldn't focus on Laura's face. It was the ultimate close-up, where breath, and sweat, and hot skin sizzled against hot skin. "You have? Me too." Caro pushed Laura back onto the chaise longue, rumpling the material even more, but she didn't care. She buried her face in Laura's ample, Rubenesque breasts and inhaled her scent, slightly earthy and spicy, like the burning candle. She licked a salty path down Laura's glistening skin, so soft and smooth. Laura whimpered when Caro tweaked her nipples and simultaneously flicked her swollen clit with her tongue. Laura bucked her hips trying to capture Caro's tongue, but she traced a trail up Laura's inner thigh, stopping short of where Laura wanted.

"You're so wet," Caro said. She raised her head, unable to resist the temptation to tease and to drink in the sight of Laura's dips and mounds. Caro savoured Laura's taste, tangy and sweet, and inhaled the heady spiciness of her scent. To taste a woman after so long was an intoxicating and sensory delight. Laura echoed her moan.

"Don't stop." Laura pulled Caro's head to her clit. "Fuck me. Please."

And Caro did, with tongues and fingers as deft as the guitar player still coming through the sound system. She licked and sucked with a rising rhythm as fast and passionate as any flamenco guitarist, until Laura shuddered, and cried out, and tightened around Caro's fingers.

Laura giggled. "Come up here, I want to kiss you. That was fantastic. I don't know what to say. Wow. Who knew there was such a seductress in the studio? Caro, thank you. That was amazing."

"It's all you," Caro said and rested her arms either side of Laura's head. She leaned down and kissed her, gently this time. She wiped a stray hair from Laura's flushed cheek and stared into her unfocussed eyes, holding back the words she wanted to say.

Laura giggled again. "I don't think I'll ever be able to listen to my cousin's playing in the same way." She stroked Caro's cheek.

Caro bit her lip and wondered if her face was much more wrinkled than Laura's previous lover, if Laura found her wanting.

"Come and lie with me."

Caro might have guessed Laura was a cuddler, and she was happy to snuggle up and wrap her arms around Laura's body. They lay there for a while until the candle had guttered and failed and the same loop of the guitar playing became irritating.

"Come to bed with me?" Caro asked. She remembered her room was a shrine to Yvonne. Not the best idea. "To your bed?"

Laura stared at Caro for a second as understanding settled. The glow on her face faded. "Okay," she whispered, after what seemed to be an eternity.

Caro rose and picked up her painting and set it up on the full easel, seeing where she needed to finish off. Laura came and stood beside her to stare at it.

"Oh, my god, I look so horny," she said.

Caro wrapped her arms around Laura and drew her into a sideways hug. "Ha. I was thinking it should be called *Desire*, or maybe *Anticipation*."

"Lust would be more appropriate." Laura shook her head and bit her lip and curved her arms over her very ample breasts, protecting herself.

She stiffened and withdrew from Caro's embrace to snatch up her robe, leaving an emptiness where there should have been warmth. Fear slithered over Caro, and she pulled Laura to face her. "What's wrong?"

"It's just it seems like a companion piece to the one you have of Yvonne in your room. Except this one is clearly just before sex, rather than after."

The air was crushed out of Caro's lungs. How could she convince her? "Laura, I can't undo the life I had before with Yvonne, and I wouldn't want to. That piece is called *Sated*, and now, knowing how Yvonne felt, I wonder if that's how she felt about me, sated as in weary and jaded—"

"But I can't compete with her, in looks, or style, or status—"

"You don't want to be like her, you're not her, you can't compare yourself at all." Caro stroked Laura's cheek. "Yvonne was alabaster, cold and unattainable. I don't love you because you remind me of Yvonne, but because you are *you*, soft, warm, and so present emotionally." Caro realised she had let the L word slip but didn't want to take it back. She couldn't untell a truth.

Laura just stared at Caro, her mouth and eyes wide. The silence between them seemed interminable, and Caro wished the ground would swallow up. "Sorry, I shouldn't have said anything." She felt like she was trying to scrabble in the air beyond the cliff like one of Laura's cartoon characters, but she wouldn't fall as long as she didn't look down. She looked down.

"Thank you for saying that," Laura whispered.

"It's all right. You don't have to say anything back." Caro's cheeks burned, and she turned to pick up her clothes. She was stupid to be vulnerable. What fantasy had Caro been pursuing to make love with a woman eleven years her junior, a woman who had been very clear she was not available emotionally? Caro dug deeper into her contempt with herself and unearthed the sickly feeling she had betrayed Yvonne. The clogging, cloying emotion swamped her, like drowning in treacle.

Caro hurriedly pulled on her clothes. "I guess you'll need to finish packing. What time's your flight tomorrow?" She snatched up the paintbrushes to clean thoroughly, wishing Laura would leave so she could get over the mortification of having revealed her love and not having it reciprocated.

"I... Thank you. Yes. Ten forty-five," Laura said as she turned.

The robe dropped to the floor with a thud that reverberated in Caro's chest. She sucked in a breath. Laura was scrambling into her clothes as though she couldn't escape fast enough. Caro wanted to hold on but knew she had to let her go. "Do you need a lift?"

"I'll get an Uber."

Laura handed back the robe, and their eyes met for an instant. Her expression was one of misery.

"Sorry," Laura whispered, then fled.

Well, that went well. Caro cleaned and tidied for another hour, giving Laura time to clear up and get out of the kitchen. When she was finished, she checked how dry the painting was. She flipped it over and stowed it amongst the rejected stack against the wall. She didn't want to be taunted by her foolishness. Maybe she would paint over it later and cover her humiliation. But for now, she needed to crawl into bed and hide.

Chapter Twenty-Six

LAURA COULD HARDLY CONTAIN her excitement when she saw her mum waiting at the entrance hall at Málaga airport. She sagged into her mum's embrace. Her mum smelled the same as always, of the Adolfo Domínguez rose water perfume. It wasn't Laura's taste, but it represented home. She inhaled deeply and blinked back happy tears as they held each other close, diverting the flow of passengers like a rock in a fast stream. She knew her dad wouldn't have time to come too, but that gave Laura and her mum the chance to talk for the ninety-minute drive back to Granada.

As they walked out of the terminal building, the warmth awakened every cell in her body. The temperature was a pleasant seventeen degrees rather than hovering around freezing, as it had been when she left Bristol. The quality of light was different too; in Bristol, fog dripped. But here, there was bright, oblique sunshine. She was home. She could breathe. "Thanks for picking me up, Mum. I can't tell you how lovely it is to see you."

They let a car pass, and her mum gave her another squeeze. "I can't believe you're actually back home. I want to keep you here. I've missed you so much, our chats as we prepare meals and even cleaning the restaurant in the morning."

"That's because Paulo really doesn't want to clean and only does a half-hearted job." Laura grinned. Paulo had been taken on when his parents died, to help around the restaurant and was now part of the family. Laura loved that people flocked to her parents for their love and acceptance. Everyone wanted to be near them. They always had enough love to go around. They would never be wealthy because they preferred to help people, whether that was giving a homeless person a free meal or giving old furniture to a young family to set up. They never had a minute to themselves, so this short haven of time with her mum on the drive back was perfect. Except for her mum's driving.

"Shall I drive?" Laura didn't expect her offer would be accepted, but she had to try, if only to salve her nerves at the anticipation of the drive

163

ahead.

"Nonsense. You've had a long flight, and it's confusing driving on the wrong side of the road. Besides, you're not used to my car."

"Mum, it was a short flight, and I don't have a car in England—"

"But you cycle. I don't want you veering us into the path of oncoming traffic."

"I cycle mainly on cycle paths. Part of the trip to the campus is lovely, going through parkland. The autumn has been glorious, all golds and russet." Laura grinned, thinking Caro would insist on her describing the exact colours and tell her how she should mix them. Then her panicked exit flooded into her memory, and she burned with shame and embarrassment.

"You'll be out of practice then if you haven't driven since..." Her mum trailed off, clearly not wanting to refer to when Laura had last driven. "It's only been ten months, Mum." Her life had changed so much. It had turned upside down, and she'd been shaken around until she didn't know which way was up. But she'd resurface and bob along the surface, even if she was hurting underneath.

Laura slung her bag in the back with all the other detritus of old coats, half-opened packets of serviettes with the name of the restaurant printed on them, and umpteen bills and letters her mum kept in the car. Laura moved a large box of provisions from the passenger seat and jammed it into the back so she could sit in the front.

"Ooh, sorry, I didn't want to miss you, so I shoved the box there. I had to collect some things for your dad before I picked you up. All set?" Without waiting for a reply, her mum pulled out into the path of a car, which blared its horn. "Asshole. Didn't he see my indicator?"

Laura didn't point out that he had the right of way. Her mum alternately stamped on the accelerator and brake and swerved her way around a guy on a moped. Laura waited until they were on the main road. "I'm in trouble, Mum." Laura almost hit the windscreen as her mum slammed on the brakes and pulled over.

"What do you mean?"

"I think I'm falling for Caro."

"Oh, I thought it was something serious. Don't do that, Lolly, you'll be the death of me."

Laura cringed at her childhood nickname but let it pass. "It *is* serious."

"Okay, but why is that a problem? Someone who makes a sketch of you with that sort of emotional intensity feels something for you. Who could help adoring my beautiful Lolly Lumpkin?"

The pet name seemed ridiculous. "Please don't call me that in public. Especially not if ever you meet her," Laura said.

Her mum twisted in her seat to face Laura. "You used to love it—"

"When I was seven." Laura sighed. "I thought this was just a crush, but I think I have genuine feelings for her. I even thought about delaying coming home so I could spend more time with her." Perhaps that hadn't been the most sensible thing to say. Hurt flashed across her mum's eyes, but she quickly masked it. "But I couldn't do that to you. I love you too much."

Her mum tried to disguise the delight in her eyes, but Laura caught it and it made her smile.

"And last night, she told me she loved me, and I panicked. I couldn't say it back."

"If you didn't say it, then you don't love her." Her mother was very practical about such things.

"But I do." That much was clear, like wiping a dirty lens and seeing for the first time. This was so much more than a crush, more than just sex. Caro had melted her defences. She wouldn't have laid herself bare for anyone. Caro had met her vulnerability and raised it with passion and hot sex.

"So why didn't you tell her?"

"I was too scared, and then she looked so hurt. She'd been open, and I may as well have slapped her in the face. But it doesn't matter that I love her. It wouldn't last. I'll be coming home in the summer, and I didn't want to fall for her. Maybe I don't really love her, and I've just been carried away with all her attention. I've been away from home, and it's hard. What if that's all this is about? Or what if she's just a distraction from Valentina? And it's not like either of us are interested in something short and sweet."

Her mum pulled the car back onto the road, and they drove in silence while cars swished by them on the motorway.

"I read online her wife died of an overdose. The coroner said the overdose was accidental, but the media speculated otherwise."

Laura sighed. "Yeah." She told her mum about Caro finding Yvonne's journal and how devastated she was to read its contents. "A tiny part of me thought, if their life wasn't so perfect, maybe she'd have room in her heart for me, but I felt really bad for thinking that."

Her mum pulled into the fast lane without indicating. "You want to be loved. You deserve to be loved. Maybe Caro is the one who can do that properly."

"She'll never leave her home and studio. Her life is there, but I need to come back to Granada. If my pitch goes well tomorrow, I'll have my own project to work on after I've finished my master's." Laura glanced at her mum, whose look of empathy and love made her want to fling herself into her arms, but then they'd be sure to crash. She fiddled with her seat belt. "But the biggest issue is me. I'm not good enough to be loved by anyone, and I don't trust myself to let someone in again, not fully. I'd just be waiting to be betrayed or rejected again." Maybe that was why she hadn't said she also loved Caro. Getting the rejection in first meant that Caro wouldn't get the chance to hurt her.

"Bloody Valentina. If I ever see her again, I'll ring her neck."

Laura blew out a long breath. "If she got the promotion she was pushing for, she'll be at the pitch tomorrow. I hate that. I'm pissed off with her, but part of me wants to see her. I don't know if I'll be able to work with her, though, with *them*." Laura's rambling bubbled out unrestricted. "This is the best shot for getting my project financed. No one else will give me the time of day. Actually, that's not true. Caro is trying to get me an opportunity to pitch with a UK studio. I'd hate Valentina having anything to do with my project being accepted or rejected, and I don't want to see them together smooching in the canteen. That's all making me feel sick too." Laura held her head in her hands, but the erratic swaying of the car forced her to look up before she vomited. She had no idea how'd she feel if she saw Valentina again. Would the hurt come rushing back, or would her attraction override that? It would be nerve-racking enough. She wanted to speak to Caro, to be grounded, to explain what she felt. She slipped her phone out and sent a quick text.

Hey, hope you're okay. Sorry about panicking yesterday. Can we talk later? Mum's just driving us home. Miss you. Laura XO.

Her finger hovered over the phone. She reread it twice, then hit send. She needed more courage to speak her truth, to own her feelings. And eventually she would talk to Caro, if it wasn't too late.

Chapter Twenty-Seven

ARTEMISIA MEWED AND SCRATCHED at Caro's door for the first time in months. She was probably missing Laura as much as Caro. She slipped out of bed and let Artemisia in. Immediately, she sprung up onto the bed and stretched out where Caro had planned to sit. "Artemisia, move over. Let me in."

The cat stared at Caro, then licked her paw and wiped her ear, ignoring her. Trying not to disturb the spoiled moggy, Caro contorted herself so she could get onto the bed. How could a small creature take up so much space? There was no duvet to spare, but with Laura gone, she was apparently worthy of the cat's favour again. She stroked Artemisia's head.

"Do you miss her too, even if she calls you Arty Farty?" Artemisia purred and sounded like a sawmill. "You little traitor, you like her too." She ruffled Artemisia's fur and was rewarded with a nuzzle as the cat kneaded Caro and stretched to take even more space on the bed. "How are we going to survive? She's only been gone two hours. I need to get a grip. She doesn't love me." Artemisia purred louder. "Yes, she loves you." If only Caro could wriggle into Laura's heart the way Artemisia had done so easily. "How will we fill the day today? I suppose I could order the rest of the Christmas presents, or I could do the self-portrait." She looked down at her pyjamas that were now two sizes too big. She'd shrunk over the last few years in confidence as well. She had started to feel good about herself, about painting again, but that was seeping away. "But not in the nude."

Laura's rejection stung, however much she tried to persuade herself it didn't matter and that she'd expected it. Laura was just being overfriendly with her landlady. But friends didn't ripple with desire like Laura had done, nor did they make love with as much passion as they had shared. Friends didn't make love at all. So, she freaked out when Caro mentioned the L word. They were clearly not in the same place she thought they had been.

Caro padded downstairs to the empty kitchen and made herself a cup of tea. "Sorry, Yvonne, did you think I'd forgotten you?" she whispered to the empty room. "Was I just a foolish old woman chasing after Laura? She's the first person that's got beneath my skin since you've been gone, and she lights up my days. I actually thought we might have a future. What would you have said? She's very young, just turned thirty. Would you be jealous?" She tried to imagine Yvonne standing across from her with a slight frown on her face, but it was getting harder and harder to envisage her at all.

Caro stroked Laura's small mug. It still smelled of coffee. She smiled at the word fridge magnets rearranged to spell, "The aliens eat cheese." Each new sentence Laura came up with was ridiculous. She needed to distract herself. A self-portrait then. In acrylics again, as the fast brush strokes suited her new style.

The studio was tinged with the lingering odour of sex. It seemed crazy that was only yesterday. She'd been exhilarated when she came at Laura's hands, like she was riding a huge wave. Why had she said anything at all about love? Laura's soulmate had betrayed her recently, so it was little wonder she wasn't open to anything. Caro had ruined everything.

Time to paint.

She placed a prepared canvas on the easel and dusted off the mirror before she perched it in place on the tabletop. Her eyes were sunken, advertising her lack of sleep. Her face was as gaunt as when Yvonne had just died. So many grey hairs streaked the dark. No wonder Laura didn't fancy her. But she'd definitely been turned on. That was desire in her eyes that Caro had pictured in paint. Desire couldn't be faked.

She picked up her chalk and sketched out the basic proportions of her thin body and pinched face. She loved this moment, when marks were made on paper and a structure began to emerge. With the skeleton on the page, she added in the planes of her face, checking the crucial distances between her mouth and nose. Each time, she had to reset to the same position.

Around mid-afternoon, she assessed her progress and was relatively happy with it. Studying the painting, she realised she looked forlorn. That was about right. Her phone buzzed with a text. *Laura?* Caro wiped her hands on a cloth and picked it up.

Hey, hope you're okay. Sorry about panicking yesterday. Can we talk later? Mum's just driving us home. Miss you. Laura XO.

Did that mean she *did* have feelings for Caro? Or was she simply sorry for hurting her? A shoot of hope pushed up amongst the weeds of doubt. Of course they could talk later. It had to be good news, didn't it? Otherwise, Laura would simply avoid her until she returned after Christmas. Now Caro just wanted the day to be done, but Laura probably had lots to occupy her when she arrived, seeing her parents and any other friends and relatives who were around. All the more reason to lose herself in her painting for a few hours.

Caro finished the portrait and as she reviewed it, the overwhelming emotions that engulfed her were sadness and possibly yearning, though that could have been her interpreting her current feelings? She took a picture and sent it to Rebecca, who would give her an honest opinion even if she didn't want to hear it. She then set to carefully cleaning her brushes, something she found relaxing and meditative.

She picked up her ringing phone moments later.

"Caro, what's happened? I love the picture, but it makes me want to weep. I haven't seen you like that since Yvonne first died. Are you all right?"

Caro replaced her brushes in the jar and twisted the jar so the label displayed forward, whilst deciding how to reply. Shame and humiliation choked her throat so she forced the words out as fast as she could. "I've been stupid. Laura and I had sex, and I told her I loved her, but she panicked and ran away as fast as she could. She's in Spain now until January."

Rebecca took a sharp intake of breath. "Oh, hun, that's not stupid. That's brave. It's so hard to put yourself out there," she said gently. "I'm sorry you didn't get the response you wanted. I wish I could hug you right now. Why don't you stay longer with us and get out of the house?"

Caro looked up at the ceiling to stop the tears from flowing. "It's too late to put Artemisia in the cattery, and she hates it anyway. I'll just come to you as arranged from Christmas Eve to Boxing Day. But thank you. And aren't you supposed to be pleased I'm painting again?"

"Not when you seem so bereft, no." There were muffled voices in the background. "Sorry, hun, I've got to take Zoe to her school concert."

Caro sniffed and straightened up. "Don't worry, I'll be fine. I hope the concert goes well. Is she still playing the flute?"

"No, she's more interested in a boy who's playing the violin and wants to sit in the front row so she can watch him."

Caro smiled. "You're encouraging her to be a stalker."

"I think it's called puppy love, and it's harmless—I hope. Take care, and let's speak tomorrow. Love you."

The line went dead, hitting Caro with a vast wall of loneliness. Everyone else was involved in family life. She ought to visit her own family but didn't want to face a barrage of questions about when she was going to get a "proper job" or to listen to her siblings boasting about their lives.

While she waited for Laura's call, she rang Yvonne's old friend and colleague, Jeff Summers, who headed up the Nutty Squirrel Studios, to secure a pitching opportunity for Laura. It went through to voicemail, so she left a message. She went back into the house to listen to carols and read a book. The old grandfather clock mocked the slow passage of time, and she read and reread the same paragraph without taking it in. She went into the kitchen. Reminders of Laura were everywhere: her mug in the cupboard, her tin of bitter coffee. Caro undid the clasp and inhaled the scent of roasted beans, feeling foolish as she did. She was glad no one could see her. Upstairs, Artemisia mewed by Laura's door.

"She's not there," Caro said and opened the fridge door, debating what to make. On the top shelf was a clip-top box with a yellow Post-it note. "Caro, emergency food, as you probably won't cook. More in the freezer, Laura xo." She melted at the thoughtfulness. Caro guessed it would be Laura's wonderful Spanish meatballs. Her breath caught to think Laura had gone to the trouble. Was that a nonverbal expression of love or just Laura's kindness? Caro traced the letters of the note, and they blurred as she read them again. This was ridiculous. She needed to get a grip.

Caro placed the box in the microwave and watched it turn, like her emotions going around, going nowhere. She took a fork from the drawer and didn't bother with a plate. As she ate her delicious food with its wonderful herbs and aromatic smell of garlic, she could almost see Laura cooking and dancing to her music as she chopped and stirred.

Laura sprinkled fairy dust wherever she went, and now there were reminders of sparkling confetti hanging around the place. But what did it signify? Caro still hadn't come to a satisfactory answer when she stacked the dishwasher.

Her phone buzzed.

RU free? Laura x

Of Light and Love

Her heart skipped a thrilled dance and she replied then waited for the FaceTime call, trying to calm her excitement, not wanting to be hurt and disappointed again. Caro smiled for the first time since Laura had run out of her studio. How wonderful to see her face again. "Hi, thanks for the meatballs."

"Hey, you're welcome. It's good to see you. I miss you, but it's lovely to be back in Spain. Let me show you around." Without waiting for a reply, she switched around the camera to show the white walls, and dark furniture, and marble tiles shining with the reflected light. "This is my room, and the landing. Oh, here's Mum. This is Caro."

The screen was filled by an older, rounder version of Laura, with creases around her eyes from years of laughter. Caro warmed to her immediately. So different from her own snobbish mother, Laura's mum seemed warm and welcoming, like a hug in human form.

"Hello, Caro, it's lovely to meet you."

Caro smiled. "Likewise. I bet it's great to have Laura back again."

"I can't tell you. It's been so long, and we've missed her so much. Thank you for looking after her so well."

"Laura's done the looking after. She's a wonderful cook. I've just eaten some of the albondigas she left for me. They were delicious." *And I've missed her so much my heart feels ripped out of my chest, even though it's only a day and I'm being ridiculous.*

"Quite right too. I know she loves spending time with you, sketching and being your model. What? It's true."

"Stop it, Mum," Laura muttered off-screen.

Laura's mum disappeared and the phone bobbed down a dark passageway as Laura made a hasty retreat. "So that's Mum. I'm sorry if she overstepped the mark."

Caro laughed, although Laura seemed embarrassed by the exchange. "Not at all. She seems lovely." Hearing Laura's voice thrilled her and seeing her wander through her old house tugged at her heart. She missed her so much.

"I'll take you downstairs to the kitchens and the restaurant."

Laura introduced Caro to various cousins, and friends, and finally, Laura's dad, who was busy cooking but stopped to have a word. It was probably the last thing he needed when he was working.

"Thank you for looking after our girl." He shot a smile at Laura so

171

laced with adoration, it warmed Caro's heart. Behind him there was a clatter of pans. He sighed but didn't berate the culprit. "I'll have to go. Nice talking to you."

"I'll take you outside," Laura said.

The buzz of activity subsided as Laura strode to the patio and the covered pool. Caro half-wished she'd gone with her. Rebecca wouldn't have minded, and it would have been better to be amongst a host of people, as long as Laura was there, rather than spending most of Christmas on her own.

Laura uncovered a pool chair and sat down. "I wish you were here," Laura said and picked at the hard plastic chair. "Although I know it's pretty chaotic, and you'd probably hate that."

"Your parents seem wonderful. They clearly adore you."

Laura smiled. "I adore them too. I'm so lucky to be surrounded by love."

Caro inhaled sharply. That word. So easy with the family but so difficult when it was personal to her.

Laura must have thought the same. "I'm sorry about yesterday. I panicked. I love being with you, and I want you in my life. What I don't know is if I can trust again, to fully commit, yet. But I really miss you. I feel so conflicted."

"When you say yet, what do you mean?" Caro grasped onto hope like she was drowning in the pool, and Laura held her lifeline.

Laura made an exasperated sound. "Sorry, I need to get my head together, not mess you around. If I get over myself, I can envisage being in love with you, but you shouldn't wait, because I may never be ready. I'm sorry. I don't want to hurt you."

Laura gave a sympathetic smile that seemed laced with apology and yearning.

Caro deflated, but she needed to be honest, however it might come across. "I miss you. The house is empty without you, and Artemisia's pacing up and down looking for you. She went walkabout after I fed her because I'm of no further use to her."

"I miss her too. I wish you were here, then I could show you around properly, and hug you, and make everything okay. And we could practise my presentation again." Laura grinned.

"We can do that now," Caro said, not wanting the call to end. She wanted to stretch it out because she had no idea when they might next speak.

Laura sat up straight. "Really?"

"Sure, why not? I'm not going anywhere."

They spent the next forty minutes going through the detail and all the while, Caro curled up inside, knowing she was lost on Laura, this bright, funny woman who was so passionate about her work. Caro was in deep, and the waters were closing over her head. But she could do nothing but tread water and hope that Laura caught up.

Chapter Twenty-Eight

LAURA SAT WITH HER dad after the restaurant closed, both drinking a Solera Gran Reserva. Although Gatsby Gin was her drink of choice, the smooth brandy slipped down well.

"Nothing but the best for my girl," he said and topped up her glass. "If you taste the best Spain offers, perhaps you won't run back to England to escape that Valentina woman who broke your heart." He hugged her again. "You're getting so thin."

Laura snorted. "Tata, you can't possibly say that, but thank you for caring." She kissed him, and his sweaty stubble reminded her of safety, security, and love. "Will you listen to my presentation in Spanish? They normally hold their business meetings in English for their international workforce, but I want to be prepared."

"Of course." He raised his glass. "My talented daughter can hold meetings in two languages." He sipped from the glass and smacked his lips. "When you get this project, have you thought about where you might live?"

Laura's heart picked up pace. Didn't they want her here? "*If* I get this project, I wondered about doing some of it remotely and maybe spending time in England and some time in Spain."

Her dad almost choked on his brandy. "No, Lolly, what I meant was your mum and I thought we could convert the old storage barns into a small house for you, so you can be independent. It's a bit further to commute than the apartment you had with that woman, but you won't have to live above the restaurant, and it would be nice to have you close by." He smiled when she jumped up to kiss him on the cheek.

Laura put her arms around his neck. "Thanks, Tata, but that's where you planned to build your house for your retirement."

He shrugged. "De nada. Andreas will probably take over the restaurant when I retire, so we might just do a house swap."

Laura took her seat again. "Then I'll be living in the paddock with my cousin's brood, who would consider me their inbuilt babysitter. Are you thinking of retiring?"

He stared at her over his glass, his brown eyes twinkling. "Not yet. But what's this about living in England? It's your famous artist, isn't it?"

"Caro, yes. Did you ever think of moving to England with Mum?"

He smiled that indulgent smile he adopted when talking about her mum. It was sweet after thirty-two years of marriage.

"If she wanted to, I would have started all over again in the rainy country. She always wanted to come here. She said the light was great for painting."

Laura took a sip of her brandy and rolled it around her tongue. It warmed her on the way down, giving her courage. "Except she gave it up."

His smile dropped. "I know. I tried to persuade her to continue, but we were just expanding then and couldn't afford extra help, so she helped in the restaurant. It's my only regret. But you wouldn't have that issue. In fact, we could clear out the second store for a studio for her. It's the one your mum used occasionally."

"That would be amazing, Tata." She hugged him again, buzzing with the possibilities that Caro could come here. Maybe it could work, just as it had for her parents.

"I'd better call it a night. I have an early start. Thanks for everything." She kissed her dad again and pondered the options as she wandered up to bed.

The following morning, Laura's mum dropped her off at Domingo Studios. Laura was delighted to see Jenufa, her favourite receptionist, was working and when Laura approached, she left her desk to greet her with an enthusiastic kiss on each cheek.

"How are the children, and is your dad okay?" Laura asked.

"It's like having three children in the house with him. He never clears up and says the most inappropriate things, but I wouldn't be without him. Can you sign here?"

Jenufa smiled and tapped the visitors' book. As she returned to her seat behind the tall, polished dark-wood desk, her smile dropped. "Both Valentina and Gonzalo will be there."

The dread must have shown on Laura's face because Jenufa gave her a sympathetic smile before she spoke into the intercom. "Señora Kingston López is here."

Of Light and Love

She looked back up to Laura. "If it makes it easier, things are not all sweetness between them. Don't worry. Tú puedes!"

Laura fiddled with her computer bag so Jenufa did not see her shock and hurt. She raised her head and smiled. "Thanks for the vote of confidence, Jenufa." She wished her confidence matched her bright tone.

The door opened, and Valentina clacked across the floor in nail-sharp stilettos and a tight smile as false as the padded bra she favoured. Her eyes glittered with what seemed to be arrogance but also a touch of fear. Laura could be brave. Her mum believed in her, so did Caro and Matt, and Ravi had given her some suggestions for her presentation. The animation school would love to say their MA student had a commercial project lined up on graduation. She would be fine.

Valentina avoided eye contact as she offered her hand to Laura's in a limp handshake, barely long enough to be polite. Laura wanted to forget where those fingers had once been.

"Come with me, please," Valentina said and turned around.

Don't look at her ass...or her hips swaying. The corridor was both familiar and remote, as though Laura had been here yesterday and also in a previous lifetime. A few of the pictures had changed for the newest popular game releases. Laura grinned when she saw that the poster of the game she had devised had pride of place at the end of the corridor, alongside the awards it had won.

Valentina opened the door of the conference room and stepped aside for Laura to enter. "You remember how to set up," Valentina said. "Coffee?"

Setting up the equipment was supposed to be Valentina's job, but she seemed as awkward as Laura felt, and wanted to keep the interaction to a minimum. "Yes. Solo, thanks."

"I remember."

Laura set up her computer and linked it to the projector, something she had done umpteen times, but now, she was on the other side. On the outside. She took a calming breath and straightened the suit she was wearing because she wanted to appear professional, and jeans and T-shirt didn't cut it. She believed in her project. It would entertain kids, and she'd woven life lessons into it that would appeal to their carers. She had this.

The studio team filed in as she triple-checked her notes, not that she needed them. She knew the pitch by heart, in English and Spanish. Laura raised herself to her full height and made eye contact with everyone in the room individually. Domingo Rodriguez, the head of the studios, nodded at her. So they'd brought out the big guns for little her. If her heart had been thudding before, it was a pneumatic drill now. Next to him was Gonzalo. *Shit.* Although she expected the chief operating officer would be there, her knees trembled. She leaned on the table and clenched her jaw tight, so she said nothing. Was he looking smug because he had stolen her soulmate and ruined her life? No, Valentina had chased him. And her life wasn't ruined. Not anymore.

Laura felt like running but took a deep calming breath. She was here, this was a great opportunity, and she wanted to make the most of it for her future. Valentina sat down at the edge of the table, placing her long legs elegantly left over right, and her top leg swung slightly, as if trying to hypnotise Laura. She used to find that intensely erotic but not now.

She shifted her gaze away and smiled. There were two other people Laura didn't know. She had to ignore all her feelings that swirled around her chest and bubbled up as if they would throttle her. She exhaled slowly. "You've got this," Caro had said when they spoke last night. *Focus.* "Buenos dias."

"In English, please, Laura, for our American friends," Domingo said, gesturing at the two individuals Laura hadn't recognised.

"Of course," Laura said and smiled at the newcomers. She explained her concept and detailed the storyboard for the pilot project and themes for five others, and how it fitted into the current marketplace. She played the showreel of her finished scene and was delighted when Domingo laughed. He'd always been like a big kid and personally liked to play all the games before they were released. "Think of it like *The Simpsons* in Spain."

"But there's a female protagonist," said one of the guys she didn't know.

Tempting though it was to snark, Laura nodded and forced a quick breath to centre herself. "Correct, and in the second series, Charlie's little brother gets more of a role, and you see how she leads him astray. The outlines are in the handouts."

Thirty minutes whizzed by. Laura shook hands with them all, and they said they'd be in touch. Domingo Rodriguez smiled at her and held her gaze. That was a favourable sign.

She strode towards the exit, aware of being shadowed by the click-clack on the marble floor. Valentina. Laura lengthened her stride.

Valentina gripped Laura's arm. "Can I have a word?"

Laura turned back and frowned. No, she didn't want to have a word. Being in the meeting had made her realise she could ignore her and Gonzalo. She'd given neither a thought whilst she delivered her pitch.

"I'm sorry I hurt you. I made a mistake. Gonzalo has gone back to his wife and kids. Do you think we could try again?"

Laura couldn't speak and tried to process the words Valentina had spewed. She didn't know what to say. Once she'd wanted to be with her, but it was too late, and was so wrong. She clenched her hands into tight fists. "You realised you've made a mistake, or you're terrified of being alone?"

Valentina averted her gaze.

"I might not be coming back to Spain." She cursed herself for saying that. It was none of Valentina's business, but she had wanted to show she had other options. Although Laura couldn't really imagine herself staying in the UK, except if Caro... But no, she'd blown that by running out. She was right not to trust again. Valentina proved it by this supposed change of heart that was more to do with Valentina being rejected than Laura being special. Rage rolled off her in waves.

Valentina held up her hands as if trying to quell Laura's anger. "They're going to offer you a contract for your project. Domingo loved the proposal you sent through before the meeting. He wants it for the flagship show of our new animation department. You'd be foolish not to take it."

"I didn't need to do the pitch?" Laura couldn't believe what she was hearing.

Valentina squeezed her arm. "No, except that was a job interview. They're looking for someone to lead the whole animation department. You."

Laura shook her head. "That's ridiculous."

"I know, that's what I said. I mean, you'd want to run the project, not establish an entire department. You're more creative than administrative."

Laura glared at her and shook her hand away. "You have no idea who I am or what I can do. I've changed. I never thought you'd be so self-serving to sleep with someone to get ahead. And now they're offering me a big job, you come hurrying back. You betrayed my trust, and you expect me to trust you again?" She shook her head and huffed. "Did you even miss me? Have you been desperate for me to come back?" She waved her hand at their surroundings. "And who the hell has this kind of conversation in a corridor after a business meeting? If you're trying to make me feel warm and special, you've failed." Laura blinked as the truth washed over her. "I never really loved you. I thought I did, but now I know what love really looks like, and what I had for you was a pale imitation." She stepped to the side and strode past her. "I need to go. Mum's waiting." She pushed open the door to reception, dangling her visitor badge to Jenufa as she passed.

She opened the door of her mum's car. "Hey, Mum."

She looked at Laura, anticipation written in her expression. "Well?"

"Not what I expected at all." Laura slammed the door and took a few moments to calm down and for her heartbeat to return to normal.

Her mum squeezed her hand. "I'm sorry, darling. Didn't they like it?"

"They did. Can we get out of here?"

"Vale, but do you want to tell me what's going on?"

Laura explained about the presentation and what had just happened with Valentina.

Her mum harrumphed with disgust and drove a bit too close to the kerb for Laura's comfort. "What a sly, power-hungry woman she is. I hope you said no."

"Of course I did. I'm not stupid. I wouldn't trust her with my bus ticket."

"Good," her mum said. "Let's celebrate. I think we should look around the Christmas markets."

"Perfect." What would be nicer than to have her project validated and have complete clarity over her ex? The flicker of doubt she'd had when she first saw Valentina again was snuffed out. Today had confirmed she was over her and felt nothing but contempt and sadness. Now she'd seen so clearly what she felt for Caro was real. The contrast was as sharp as dark and light. She was in love with Caro, but had she blown it? "I'll just text Caro and let her know how I got on."

Her mum chatted on happily, and Laura wondered how she could persuade Caro to come to Spain. Laura should feel elated, yet there was an ache in her heart about how she had left. Would Caro want anything to do with her anymore? If Caro forgave her, Laura would explore potential painting studios up in the hills, particularly if Caro didn't want to be in the backyard of the restaurant. It could be perfect. Laura shook her head. She had to live in the present, not in the fantasy. And she had to talk to Caro, to apologise. But would Caro accept it? She wouldn't blame Caro if she wanted nothing more to do with her, if she said she couldn't trust her. Laura wouldn't trust her own behaviour, so why would Caro? Regret, hope, excitement, and yearning warred within her, churning in her stomach. She had to be brave, set aside her fear. She had to woman up and tell Caro she loved her. She would tell her on Christmas Day. That's what they did in all the romcom movies.

Chapter Twenty-Nine

Christmas Day, Granada, Spain

LAURA'S DAD PUSHED HIS chair back and announced to all in his best English accent, "I'm fed up."

Her mum leaned over and kissed him on the cheek. "The saying is I'm full up, and you know it."

Her dad grinned and kissed her. "I know, my love, but it always makes you smile."

Laura couldn't remember how many times she had seen the same scene played out, with her parents being overtly affectionate, not caring about their audience. She loved it and was grateful for a happy, loving home, but there was always a tinge of poignancy.

Her parents were a wonderful love match, despite the opposition of both their families initially. The families accepted them both when it became clear that this was more than a holiday romance. Laura wished she could have the same love herself, but it wouldn't happen. She rose and cleared the dishes. The couple from Birmingham, Wendy and Dave, who'd missed the flight back home, also stacked a few plates.

"That was lovely. Thank you for inviting us to share your Christmas dinner," Wendy said.

Laura's mum turned to Wendy. "You're very welcome, Wendy, dear. Don't clear up. It won't take long for Laura and me to get the dishwashers working. I'm surprised they haven't gone on strike, it being Christmas and all."

Wendy looked horrified. "Don't you pay them overtime for working at Christmas?"

Laura's dad's deep laugh seemed to caramelise around his words. "We have industrial dishwashers in the restaurant. They're used to heavy loads, and machines don't need time off at Christmas." He slammed down his fist on the table as he laughed.

It really wasn't that funny, but his laugh was infectious, and everyone started bubbling up.

Laura carried the crockery to the kitchen and wondered how Caro was doing and how soon she could phone her. She'd said they ate late at Rebecca's, after opening the presents to stop the teenagers being grumpy at having to wait. Laura glanced at her watch again, but only five minutes had passed since the last time she'd looked. Why couldn't she just be present with her family? She hadn't felt this separate before, not even when she was with Valentina.

She stacked the plates and set the machine going. This must've been the smallest Christmas dinner her mum had cooked for a long time. After COVID, her mum hadn't seen her two sisters in nearly two years, one of whom usually came over with their tribe. When Laura asked her about whether she missed them all, her mum just smiled and said, "I won't leave your dad to cope for more than a few days at a time. He gets stressed and no one knows how things work the way I do."

Her mum didn't want to be away from her dad for long was what she meant. Laura couldn't live in the UK, because her family was too important to her. But didn't being in a relationship mean you put them first? She wanted to be with Caro *and* be close to her parents. Was she just being selfish? She couldn't bear it if she never saw Caro again. She missed her so much, it hurt.

Someone knocked on the restaurant door. Laura wiped her hands on a towel and made her way to the front, but her father beat her to it. She couldn't see who was behind the door.

"What are you doing here?" he asked in Spanish.

Her dad was never rude. Who was it?

"I'm not sure she wants to speak to you," he said, still not revealing who was behind the door. He turned to Laura. "Valentina says she needs to speak to you. Shall I send her away?"

Laura loved her dad's protective streak. He would've fought dragons for her. And that's what Valentina was, all hard scales, sharp claws, and breathing fire. "No, it's okay, Dad. I'll meet her by the pool."

"Did you hear that?" he asked and closed the door. "Goodbye."

Laura's heart thundered in her chest, and Christmas pudding churned in her stomach. When she got to the pool side, Valentina had made herself at home on an uncovered garden chair, like she hadn't left, and this was an ordinary afternoon. She rose when Laura approached and kissed her cheeks. Laura stood rigid in her clutches. "What do you want? Haven't you done enough damage? Wasn't I clear the other day?"

Valentina dropped her arms. "No, I'm sorry I made such a mistake. I knew you'd be here today, and I just needed to see you and talk to you. I've missed you, and I was so stupid. Come home with me, and we can make plans for when you finish your degree."

Did the woman never take no for an answer? No wonder Gonzalo hadn't been able to keep his trousers zipped. Just when Laura thought she'd untangled the knot, Valentina would pull harder. Laura thrust her hands in her jeans pockets so Valentina wouldn't see them shaking. "Why would I come back to you, Valentina? How can I trust anything you say? I've found love now, real love, and what we had didn't compare. You've had a wasted journey."

A flicker of annoyance crossed Valentina's face before she smoothed it out. "It wasn't easy coming here. I knew your dad wouldn't be pleased to see me, but I needed to see you. Please come home."

If she'd said that nine months ago, maybe even six, Laura would've said yes in an instant, but she'd moved on. Valentina was a career-climbing manipulator, interested in herself alone. This was obviously about the role Laura had been offered. "No, it's too late. I don't love you anymore, if I ever did. You infatuated and dazzled me, then you betrayed me. I can't forgive that. We can be civil to each other at work when I return, and that's it. Goodbye, Valentina."

Laura held out her hand to shake, as if to close a deal, but Valentina pushed it away. "You'll regret that."

Laura snorted. "Threatening me is a bit of a turnaround from your declaration of love. Goodbye." Laura turned and went through the fly screen door into the sanctuary of her family to pick up her phone and call Caro. It went straight to voicemail, so Laura took a walk to give herself time to think.

Wandering in the hills cleared her head. When she stared at the mountains, stark and white, it felt like home. But there was an unsettling gap in her heart that she couldn't ignore. She climbed higher, and when she had a strong enough signal, she phoned Caro.

"Hey, happy Christmas, I miss you. Sorry again for running out on you. I wish you were here," Laura said brightly, though she didn't quite feel it.

E.V. Bancroft

"I wish I was there, too. I love Rebecca and her family, and they always welcome me, but this year I felt more of an outsider than before."

It was wonderful to hear Caro's voice. Laura took in a deep, fulfilling breath. She was inhaling Caro's love, that gave her life and oxygen. Maybe next year, Caro would live here, for some of the time. She paused and looked at the lights scattered around the hillside. From a neighbouring house, she could hear families chatting, and arguing, and having a good time. The smell of garlic and herbs wafted across the valley. She scrambled up to a viewpoint overlooking the surrounding mountains. *Caro.* She loved her, really loved her. Her relationship with Valentina couldn't have been a clearer contrast. Caro chatted about Christmas and painting and asked Laura about her day. She was enthusiastic and inspired, and it thrilled Laura to the core.

Reluctantly, she headed back to her house in case her mum worried where she was, though she wanted to stay there, talking to Caro, as long as the signal held. What was wrong with her that she had to steel herself to go back into the family? She adored them, but there was a part of her that was missing. That part was Caro. In the last few months, she had got used to Caro's quirky ways, and she'd missed their chat in the morning over the kettle. And their lovemaking. Laura would never forget how beautiful Caro was when she finally let go and her troubled, sad expression was replaced by passionate delight.

"I'd better go, Laura. Rebecca wants me to lose at charades. I'm always hopeless. I never know the films and TV shows they're referring to, especially the kids."

"Just go with it, literally. I can see we'll have to continue our education when I get back. I'll call you later after you've wowed them all." And before she really registered it, the call went dead. She needed a drink, or maybe two, so when she spoke to Caro later, she could tell her how she really felt.

After many hours and even more glasses of alcohol, Laura staggered to her feet. "I'm going to bed. Night-night."

"Take some water, love."

She kissed both her parents and wove her way upstairs, concentrating hard to ensure she didn't slip. She still had a scar on her forehead from where she'd fallen as a child. The marble flooring was very unforgiving.

It was time. Caro deserved to hear what was in Laura's heart. No chickening out this time, and no relying on MiniMe.

Chapter Thirty

Christmas Day, Berkshire

REBECCA'S LARGE LOUNGE WAS a mountain of paper, books, and games and the usual detritus of opened presents and discarded wrapping paper. The teenagers clutched their new prize possessions but were being held back by their requirement to be polite and stay in the room.

"Off you go," Rebecca said and shooed them away with her hand. "We'll sort everything out later."

They didn't need a second telling, and Zoe and Jack rushed off to the snug with their new video games.

"Kids, honestly! They're not happy unless they're umbilically joined to their tablets or PlayStations."

"But we had an interesting conversation at lunch," Caro said. "I love that they care about the environment and challenge what the government is doing versus what they're saying. It shows that they're thinking about things that matter, so I don't blame them if they want to chill out with their bloodthirsty games. Or maybe they're not so bloodthirsty."

Laura's words replayed in Caro's mind. "I made my living designing games and none of them were evil or shooter games." Laura was creative, different from Caro, and she may never win the plaudits that Caro had received, but were they any less deserved? Why was fine art more acceptable than animated games?

Caro sighed. Even amongst her adopted family, she yearned for Laura's company and chatty commentary. She would be great with the kids. Caro was infected with a listlessness she couldn't overcome. It was crazy to miss her this much, especially as they had spoken last night. Yet she kept glancing at her phone, hoping for a text. It had to stop.

"More?" Rebecca tilted the bottle she was holding, yet another that she had raided from Freddie's wonderful wine cellar. "Come on, you're not driving anywhere. Besides, if we spread it over several hours, you won't feel hungover either."

"That's fine for you to say with your metabolism, but it seems to affect me far more than it used to. I suppose wine is stronger than the weak beer we had at college."

"It is. Who would've known we would've ended up here?" Rebecca gestured at the spacious room in the old mansion.

Caro wondered what legacy Rebecca would have left if she'd continued her sculpting. Not that she complained, and it helped that she had married well. Freddie was a kind man and would do anything for his family. That included her, and her heart warmed.

Freddie re-entered the lounge with a large sack for recycling as Rebecca poured Caro another drink.

"Here, let me help," Caro said. She was a little unsteady, but it didn't take long to clear the mountain of mess and stack the presents in neat individual piles. Caro was delighted with her tickets to the Royal Opera House. Of course, the unstated condition was that Rebecca would use the second ticket. It would be a nice excuse to come up to London and visit the galleries and museums, and they'd have a long lunch in one of the latest popular restaurants.

Freddie settled himself on the sofa next to his wife and interwove his fingers with hers. Rebecca took a sip of her wine, as if she was fortifying herself. An icy hand of dread clutched Caro's heart. What were they about to say?

"Has Rebecca told you about our idea for another exhibition of your works? The retrospective provoked more interest, and the world is ready for your new style. I think we should link up with the Tate. I've chatted to my contacts there, although there's a much longer lead time than if we mount it in my gallery. It would be nearly two years rather than a few months."

The spike of excitement at being shown in the Tate was quickly chased away by reality. They were being crafty by dangling the possibility of the Tate in front her, so she would agree to the principle of another exhibition. "You can't do that, Freddie. If it bombs because no-one likes it, I'd hate for you two to be out of pocket."

Freddie sipped his drink. "Well, my wife agrees with you, but I have a hunch about this. It will not only give you more exposure, but it'll also bring in a whole raft of new fans."

Of Light and Love

"I love your work, darling, but I think the style is too different. Your old fans may not accept it. It's unlikely these new paintings will fetch the same prices. I think we're better to keep it in house," Rebecca said.

She came over to Caro, poured her another half glass, and perched herself onto the arm of Caro's chair. Symbolically, it was as if she was taking sides.

"People accepted a change of style in Picasso," Freddie said.

He knew how much they both hated Picasso's reputation as a philanderer. He looked faintly ridiculous with his red Christmas hat slipping off his greying hair, at odds with his deep frown. He didn't like to be challenged in his domain.

Caro raised her glass to him. "Freddie, I'm not Picasso. I'm one exhibition away from having to teach or take commissions."

"Maybe you should take commissions."

Of course Rebecca would jump on that. It would make her additional income so she could take a cut. Caro frowned. "No. The temptation to paint the facade of the great and the good in the light but show their true animal nature in the shadows is too high. The prime minister would be a chameleon and the home secretary a wolf, but that wouldn't go down well with the intelligentsia, the only ones who can afford to commission my works. Talk about biting the hand that feeds me."

Rebecca quirked her eyebrow, clearly amused. "Maybe you should do it anyway, just for fun."

Caro and Freddie both said no. But the idea percolated for the rest of the day. She could do satirical paintings of the great and the good if she challenged everyone in equal measure. Caro could imagine in some perverse way that they would like to have their portraits painted as it would show they'd made it and would be conversation pieces. One of Oscar Wilde's best quotes came to mind: "There is only one thing worse than being talked about, and that's not being talked about."

If Caro could persuade Laura to stay in the UK, they could travel up to London together and explore the galleries and museums when she wasn't painting celebrities. She was disappointed she hadn't heard from the Nutty Squirrel Studios yet, but they were probably closed for Christmas. She was sure Laura's project would be perfect for their portfolio, and they already had great access to TV stations and other distribution channels with their popular Nutty Squirrel animation.

It could work, if Laura could "get over herself," as she'd said. Laura had called briefly after her Christmas lunch, but Caro hoped for another chat before she went to bed. She didn't want to call Laura because she'd be busy with her family and guests. It just highlighted again how lonely Caro felt as she slipped into her pyjamas.

Her phone rang, and she smiled when she saw the number. *Think of the devil.* "Hi, Laura, Happy Christmas, again. How are you doing?"

"Caro, Caro, my wonderful Caro. How is my treasure?" Laura said then burped.

Caro shook her head and chuckled. "Are you drunk?"

"Hmm, maybe a teensy bit. We've had quite a lot to drink, but I wanted to call my favourite person and wish her a very Happy Christmas, again. I miss you."

Favourite person? That was probably just the drink talking. But Laura was funny when she was tipsy.

"I might have had a tiny bit too much, but I've been trying to get up the courage to tell you I love you. And I'm in love with you. And I want to be with you."

The dam around Laura's heart burst, and all the emotions cascaded around Caro, seeping into all the crevices of her soul. She laughed but a thrill shimmied down her spine. They were the words she had been longing to hear. But it was probably just the drink talking. "That's wonderful to hear, but you need to tell me when you're sober, otherwise I can't trust it."

Laura took a sharp intake of breath. "You don't trust it? You don't trust me?"

"Of course I do, but I trust you sober talking more." Caro kept her tone gentle and light.

Laura exhaled noisily. "Oh. I can't do that yet... That might have to wait until tomorrow. Night-night, I love you."

"Good night. I love you too." Caro signed off with a smile but wasn't sure how much of the conversation Laura would remember. She did a giddy little jig around the guest room, fighting to keep the cheesy grin off her face. Her heart lifted, and even the fairy lights on the house opposite seemed brighter. What a wonderful Christmas present; Laura loved her.

Chapter Thirty-One

EARLY THE FOLLOWING MORNING, Caro paced the suburban streets around Freddie's mansion. Curls of mist swirled around her feet as nebulous as her confusion. Would it be too early to call Laura now? Probably she still had a hangover if she had drunk that much. Did Laura really love her? Or was it just the drink talking? Caro needed to know but couldn't ask. If Laura didn't mean it or didn't remember, Caro would look foolish, pleading, or desperate. She couldn't do that. Laura would have to say she loved Caro in her own time...when she was sober. Oh, how Caro wanted it to be true. Like the sun lightening the clouds and trying to pierce through the mist, Caro needed clarity and warmth.

She rubbed the tops of her arms and quickened her pace. All the houses were sleeping with their shutters down and gates closed, hiding their silent SUVs. Up ahead, a fox jumped up a wall before being swallowed into the shadows. Caro shushed her boots through the fallen leaves in a steady rhythm. Does she love me, does she love me? She didn't dare believe. She glanced at her watch again. Only five minutes had passed.

A pale beam of weak winter light broke the clouds. She took it as a sign to call Laura. The ring tone seemed distant, an echo of its normal self. After the third ring, Laura answered.

"Dígame. Oh, Caro, it's you. Hey, what're you doing up so early?" Laura groaned at the end of the phone, and there was a rustling of sheets.

Caro's throat constricted, and she cleared it to speak. "How are you feeling? How's the head?"

"Don't. Hang on. Let me grab some water."

There was a pause and the sound of sloshing liquid. Good, Laura had taken water to bed with her.

"Sorry, Caro. I had rather a lot to drink last night."

"I know, you called me," Caro said, her throat tight and scratchy.

There was a slight pause. "Did I?"

Caro sagged and leaned against a wall. She didn't remember so how could she mean what she'd said? There was no way Caro was going to bring it up now. Her excitement and anticipation dissipated into the mist. Perhaps it didn't mean Laura didn't love her, but that she hadn't expressed it yet. Not properly anyway. Who was she kidding? Believing something just because she wished it? That way lay fantasy and delusion.

"You've gone really quiet. Did I say or do something I shouldn't? If so, I'm sorry."

"No, nothing like that."

"Did MiniMe tell rude jokes?"

It was unbelievable that a grown woman had taken a puppet with her for a holiday. What would she do on a date? Would it be sitting at the table like a threesome? Caro shivered. Deflection was preferable to indulging in her disappointment. "No."

"Caro. you sound upset. What did I say? I'm sorry if I hurt you."

"No. It's nothing. What are you up to today?"

"The restaurant is closed, so we're going to visit my cousins in the hills for a couple of days. It's unseasonably warm up there, so we'll be able to sit out. The phone signal is pretty rubbish though so it's better to FaceTime."

"Sure." Now there seemed to be nothing to say. The declaration of love was sealed up in a box along with all the other things Caro had planned to tell Laura. The silence spun for a few awkward seconds. So unlike their normal conversations.

"What are you doing?" Laura asked.

"Freddie and Rebecca are entertaining neighbours today so I will hide in their guest room as long as I can or play board games with the kids. I'm going back home tomorrow. I can't wait to see Artemisia."

They slipped into a chat, comfortable and familiar and ultimately meaningless, but the daily lubrication of connection wasn't the same as having Laura here with her. Could she persuade Laura to stay in the UK? Was it fair to do so? If not, could they embark on a long-distance relationship? There were so many questions and no answers, but she wanted this, and she wanted Laura. Laura was the light. With every joke and laugh, Laura took a searchlight, shone it in Caro's dark places, and showed that she was safe. She didn't remember the last time she anticipated being with someone so much. There was nothing she would love more than to wake up to Laura's smile every morning.

Is that what Laura wanted though? Should she ask? "I'm hoping we will always be friends."

"Of course, I love the time we spend together. I'm sure we'll continue with that."

Laura's response was quick and certain, that was something. Caro cleared her throat. "I was wondering—"

"Caro, sorry I'm going to have to go. My mum's calling me. What were you wondering?"

She couldn't be that vulnerable. She had already put herself out there and had got nowhere. "It doesn't matter."

"Vale. Ask me next time we speak. Have a great day, bye."

The line went dead. She didn't even wait for Caro to say goodbye. Caro pulled her scarf tighter to keep out the swirling mist and headed back towards Freddie and Rebecca's. She was being a fool, wishing it was so, wanting it to be so. If Laura really felt anything for her, she would tell her in her own good time. She had already said that she couldn't commit because she had been hurt by her previous partner. Caro was merely entertaining a fantasy, like the Disney movie they would doubtless watch this afternoon. It was time to act her age and not that of a lovesick teenager. If she pulled back now, maybe she wouldn't get her heart broken, and she could focus herself on her painting, on her legacy.

Who was she kidding? If Laura didn't want to see her anymore, her heart would be ripped out. Her heart that was still scarred from losing Yvonne. She couldn't lose Laura too.

Chapter Thirty-Two

LAURA LEANED BACK AGAINST the cushions and shifted her gaze onto the scene of the cerulean sky and the ochre soil. She could almost hear Caro's voice, telling her to be precise with the colours, to be aware of the shifting of tints on each plane. She chose a titanium white for a harsher feel to reflect the intense winter light.

Caro would have been able to mix that to perfection. Laura was using the oil paints her mum had given her for Christmas. It should be relaxing, but every decision, every mix of tone or swirl of paint reminded her of Caro. Thoughts of Caro filled her head and heart, constantly wondering where she was and what she was doing. Painting was so intrinsically linked with Caro, it threw her absence into sharp relief. Laura stared out at the distant mountains where the snows smothered the tall peaks and considered how she could recreate them in oils. Caro would tell her to squint to let the definition blur so the blocks and colour would imprint onto her mind, and like the artistic duckling she was, Laura narrowed her eyes and absorbed the pixilating shapes.

Laura squeezed some paints on a palette and stirred them with a knife. Satisfied she had replicated the blue-white of the mountains, she took up her brush and loaded it with paint.

Her phone rang, and she saw it was Domingo. Laura threw down her brush, not caring if the bristles buckled, and snatched the phone up. "Dígame, hola."

"Hello, Laura. I hope you had a good Christmas."

Why was he speaking so formally and in English? Was he about to deliver bad news? Laura held her breath, which made it difficult to reply in a calm and professional manner. "I did, thanks. And you?"

"Yes, thanks. But it's good to get back to work."

He had a reputation for being a workaholic, so she wasn't surprised he had called her today just before New Year's Eve. She wiped her hands on a rag, glad he hadn't video called as she almost certainly had paint on her clothes and her face where she'd brushed her hair off her cheeks.

"I wanted to phone and congratulate you on the great pitch. Domingo Studios would like to fund your project."

Laura blew out her cheeks and fought to control her smile. Be cool, be professional. "That's fantastic, thanks, Domingo. I can't tell you how much that means to me. That's so exciting. I'd love to get started when I've finished my master's. When would you like me to start?" So not cool at all. She couldn't help herself. She couldn't wait to tell Caro and her mum the awesome news.

"I'm glad you are so excited about it, and yes, we'd like you to start on it as soon as you can, but ideally before the end of your course so we can pitch it to various TV channels in the summer for a Christmas release next year. There is something else."

Laura dropped her shoulders, and her smile slipped. "Oh?"

"If this goes well, we would like you to spearhead the whole of the new animation department. I won't be able to finalise the details yet, those will need to wait until my assistant is back early in January, but in principle, are you interested?"

"Oh, wow." So, Valentina was right then, they did have designs for her future. She was grateful for the heads up because it had given her time to think of the pros and cons of the role. If she could delegate most of the admin, it would mean she could focus on the department's direction. The only downside, apart from having to see more of Gonzalo and Valentina, would be if Caro didn't want to come out to Spain. But surely she would see how amazing it could be to paint in Spain. Laura sat up straighter, as if she was already assuming the role. "That sounds great. I'd need a good admin assistant. That's not my strong suit."

"Agreed. You can have Valentina. It's too difficult with her and Gonzalo hardly speaking. I've told them they need to put their differences aside—"

"Not Valentina. Would Jenufa be available?"

Domingo grunted. "Leave it with me. I'll get back to you in January. Congratulations again."

"Thanks so much, Domingo," Laura said as he signed off. She double-checked the line was clear and let out a huge whoop that had her mum rushing outside. Laura jumped up and down and danced around the terrace. "They want my project, they want my project!"

Her mum hugged her, and they did an awkward jig, embracing each other.

"Congratulations, my clever girl. I knew you could do it. I must tell your dad."

"I need to call Caro. This is so exciting."

Her mum returned indoors and Laura FaceTimed Caro, while staring at the landscape.

"Hi, Laura, what a nice surprise."

Caro's voice, with its soft contralto, sent a thrill tripping down Laura's spine. "I had to tell you. I've great news. Or I hope it's good news. Domingo Studios are going to fund my project—"

"Congratulations. You've worked hard, and you deserve it. I'm so pleased for you. Are you up in the hills?"

That seemed a shift change of direction, but Laura grinned and switched the camera to forward mode. "I was trying to paint the view, but it still looks like a cartoon with the hard lines around the mountains."

"That's just your style. Use it, explore it, it makes you *you*. The colours are a close match, and you've got some lovely depth and perspective. Wait, focus on that jam jar. Is that any way to treat your brushes?"

Laura switched the camera back to her and flashed a coy smile. "I was in a hurry to answer the phone."

Caro raised her eyebrow. That look, so arch, so sardonic, so Caro, made Laura's heart tango and her sex pulse. She loved her. What was she waiting for? Nothing was going to change. She didn't want Caro to slip between her fingers because she had pushed her away.

But no sound came out. She tried again. "I love you. Caro. I've been trying to tell you for days now. Weeks really, but I've been scared. I'm still scared, terrified you'll leave me or reject me. I know I mess around so I don't have to say anything serious, but I've known for a while now. I love you."

A single tear trickled down to Caro's cheek, making Laura want to reach through the phone and wrap her in her arms. "Hey, don't cry. I thought you'd be happy."

"I am. I can't believe it. But it's just your delight at your funding speaking, that's all. Tell me face to face when you get home."

Home. Laura flinched. England would never feel like home to her.

"I hoped you might come out here to paint and show me how it's done," Laura said.

"I'd love to."

There were such simplicity and certainty in the reply that Laura believed her. It would be all right. Caro would come here. She released the breath she'd been holding.

Her mum came bustling onto the terrace. "Your dad wants to speak to you to tell you how wonderful you are."

"Okay, Mum. I'm just on a call to Caro. I'll be with you in a minute."

"Don't worry. Go talk to your dad, and I'll speak to you tomorrow," Caro said and finished the call.

Her mum thrust the phone into her hand.

"Hi, Dad. Yeah, it's great." Laura basked in his delight whilst trying to ignore the discomfort in her stomach. Was Caro okay? Why had she cried when Laura said she loved her, and why didn't she believe her? Did she have cold feet? Laura took a calming breath. Everything was okay. Caro said she'd come and paint here. That was the perfect solution.

Chapter Thirty-Three

"ARTEMISIA, YOU KNOW LAURA'S coming back today?" Caro stroked the cat, and she purred with delight. It was as if she understood, and she nuzzled around her legs. She sat on the stool in the studio and appraised her painting. She liked her new style. It seemed to suit her shifting moods, less intense and grieving, more carefree and spontaneous. There was still the black fuzziness around the edges, but in the centre, bright and strong, was the love she had for Laura. She'd never thought she would love again, and yet she had fallen so hard and fast. That Laura hadn't been able to return it fully had been a surprise as her body language, her acts of kindness, and everything about their relationship sang love, but trust and rejection still had Laura in their grip. Caro would wait.

She stared at the canvas on the easel and nodded. Rebecca would be pleased. There would be enough to hang a new exhibition, especially if Rebecca lined up the commissions she'd promised. Caro glanced at her watch. Laura should have landed by now. She had offered to pick Laura up from the airport, but Laura had insisted she didn't want to disturb her if Caro was painting. A thrill of anticipation skittered down her spine. She was tempted to drive up to the airport and meet her anyway, but she'd probably pass her on the road as Laura came via taxi.

It had seemed a really long eighteen days, and she didn't realise how much she would miss Laura. She had even put Laura's coffee out some mornings before she realised Laura wasn't there. How weird Laura had sifted under her defences so easily with her ready smile and enthusiasm for life. It left Caro feeling naked and newborn. She had clung to her persona as a crusty widow for so long that she was having to reassess who she was in the world. What a surprise a different perspective made to her life and how it had completely changed her style of painting. Maybe she should paint up another of the sketches she had done of Laura dancing and make it completely abstract, just sinewy, sexy curves and vibrant colours, warm vermillion red and yellow. Did she dare risk that for a painting in the new exhibition? They had agreed the exhibition could be titled "Of Light and Love." It seemed fitting as a reflection of her journey out of grief and into love.

A car pulled up outside. She couldn't contain her delight as she heard a car door slam.

"Thank you."

Laura's voice. Caro practically skipped down the garden, creating frosty patterns on the path. She slipped off her shoes and padded through the house to the front door, her heart dancing double time. And then they were in each other's arms, kissing, and reconnecting, and whispering sweet nonsense. Laura was home. *Home?* "Come in, come in. Let me help with your bag." A surge of shyness slipped over her. "Do you want me to drop it in my room?"

Laura laughed. "No, it's only dirty laundry. I'll chuck it in my room." She grasped her bag. "I'll be down in a minute."

"I've made soup."

"Perfect."

But it didn't feel perfect. Something seemed odd, as if Laura was taking time to herself and wasn't certain about sleeping in Caro's bed. She tamped down the disappointment. Caro was eager to show Laura how she had made changes by putting away the painting of Yvonne, and all the knickknacks and Yvonne's television awards had been boxed away in the attic. It had taken Caro two whole days after Christmas, and now her room was neutral territory again. The entire house seemed to have lost the spirit of Yvonne, as though her ghost had melted into the brickwork.

Caro traipsed back to the stove and smiled when she realised Artemisia had followed Laura upstairs. It was so tempting to follow herself, but she had to respect whatever Laura needed. She stirred the soup to heat it through. She couldn't shake the disquiet that whispered in the periphery of her consciousness. Her heart was still doing double time, but less from excitement than from doubt and uncertainty. Did Laura have second thoughts about them? Caro could see a bright future together. She placed the best cloth serviettes on the table and sliced the bread, but still there was no sign of Laura.

Eventually she heard Laura's measured footsteps on the wooden floor and the echoing, lighter padding of Artemisia's paws. But there was none of the usual lightness in Laura's steps. Caro gulped and turned to greet her with an over-bright smile. "Soup's ready if you'd like to sit down. I've put Adele on Spotify but change it if you want."

"That's perfect, thanks."

Laura was being too stiff, too polite, too controlled. Adele was her favourite artist and normally, she would have raved with enthusiasm, or made some rude comment about opera, but this was uncomfortable. As they sat and ate, the air became thick with tension and the conversation was strained. Nausea bubbled up, and Caro couldn't stand it any longer. She took a breath in, but Laura dropped her spoon in the soup with a splatter.

"I need to say something, and I'm not sure what you'll think," Laura said. "As I told you, my project has been accepted by the Granada studios and they've offered me an excellent deal."

Caro's whole body sagged, thinking it would be something like this. Laura would have to go back to Spain in the summer. It extinguished hope like the last candle being snuffed out. And just as a candle smells stronger after the flame is extinguished, Caro's senses became hyperalert. "I thought you might consider living here. I've also got you an opportunity to pitch with Nutty Squirrel productions."

Laura squeezed Caro's hand. "Thanks, I really appreciate it. But I've already accepted Domingo's offer. It's too good to refuse. If the project goes well, they want me to take over the animation side of the studios. It's my dream job, and I can live at home and save a deposit for my own place, although Dad was talking about converting the barn at the bottom of their garden into a house for me."

Caro coughed as she tried to speak around the lump in her throat. Laura had decided and not discussed any of it with her as if she didn't matter at all. Did she even factor into her decision making? "Nutty Squirrel Studios have a great rep, and they're already linked into network distribution. I'm sure they would give you top dollar for your idea, especially if you have a counteroffer to dangle in front of them. They seemed really interested. And they're based in South Bristol too, so it would be an easy commute." Caro knew she was babbling and had to pull herself together. She inhaled and pulled out her courage from somewhere deep, as if she was fighting for her life, which in some ways she was. "Didn't you consider me at all in your plans? I thought we'd be together, discuss it together, and work something out that would suit both of us."

Laura smiled, but it seemed rueful and didn't reach her eyes. "I hoped you'd come to Spain with me. The light is wonderful, and we could easily set you up with a studio. I know we'd need to get you a visa which would be a pain, but we could do it. Dad says he knows a lawyer who specialises in all of that."

"But you didn't talk to me about it." Caro couldn't help her petulance. Relationships were so hard. Was Laura really saying she wasn't happy, just as Yvonne never had? A flare of anger intertwined with latent grief. "So, you're saying we're not enough? Are you really just going back for the role, or are you going back to your ex? Didn't she work with you?"

Laura fiddled with the spoon, and it made a grating sound against the soup bowl. "Yes, but it's not like that, and I've already told her I won't be with her. I can't trust her anymore."

"You spoke to her when you were in Spain?" Panic flickered in Caro's soul and mixed with the tight coil of jealousy. Why hadn't Laura mentioned that before in her texts and FaceTime calls? And was it just because she couldn't trust her?

Laura placed her spoon on the table and fixed her gaze on Caro. "She was in the meeting and came to see me afterwards to say she was sorry, but I told her we were over."

The jealousy uncoiled like a cobra. "I knew it. You're going back to her. She's much more your age. Besides, you've always loved her. You said she was your soulmate, so if you go back, you're bound to go back to her."

Laura frowned. "Didn't you hear what I said? I can't trust her as far as I can throw her. And I realised what I had with her is nothing to how I feel about you. I tried to tell you on the phone at Christmas, even if you didn't believe me, and I've been trying to say it every day since, but I'm still not sure you believe me. I don't know how else to say it. I don't love her, and I'm not going back to her. In fact, it's the one downside with taking the job that I have to work with her and Gonzalo."

"The one downside? So, leaving me isn't a downside?" Caro tried to be as cool as she could, but rage was buffeting the roof and she was struggling to hold it down.

"I don't want to leave you. I want you to come too. That's what I was banking on. It's the perfect solution." Laura rose. "You could paint anywhere. Wouldn't it be wonderful to paint in the hills?"

"But I paint people, not landscapes, in case you hadn't noticed." That was harsh, but the pain needed a voice, vicious and unrelenting. "Rebecca is setting me up with a series of commissions with the London glitterati. She's secured a politician and a couple of sports personalities. I need to be here. I was going to talk to you when you came back."

Laura looked deflated. "I didn't know that." Annoyance flashed across her face. "Hang on, you said I haven't told you about Spain, but you didn't tell me about the commissions. How is that different?"

"It's only recently been finalised. Besides, I could never leave this house, my studio. It's my home, my sanctuary—"

"Mausoleum, more like—"

"What do you mean?" Caro exhaled deeply. She needed to calm down before she said things she couldn't unsay. Laura looked so sad Caro wanted to sweep her in her arms and comfort her.

"Oh, come on, Caro. You have a shrine to Yvonne in your bedroom. You refer everything back to her. It's like having three people in the relationship. You've put her on a pedestal—"

"Like you've done with me, you mean? Do you know how trapping it is to live up to your expectations? I can't do it. I'm just a twisted woman who fails as often as she succeeds. Besides, I've cleared out Yvonne's things," Caro said.

Laura tossed down her serviette. "Bullshit. I don't fangirl on you. I love you for who you are, the real woman. But I can never compete with a dead woman. I'll never compare. Do you know how that makes me feel? Like I'm second best. Again."

Caro reeled back as if she was falling like one of Laura's animated characters tumbling into the abyss, and it felt as unbelievable. "What do you mean? You love me, or you're in love with me? I know you love my art, and you love posing for me, but that's not the same as being in love with me." Caro hated she sounded so needy, but the rage rippled off her in waves, crashing her hopes against the rocks.

Laura had turned bright red. "I should've known that you'd never leave the UK. You'll never love me enough. I was right not to trust you. Good night, I'm going to bed."

Laura slammed the door to the hall as she exited and left Caro staring at the uneaten soup. Her knees gave out, so she dropped onto the kitchen stool, hoping the food wouldn't make a reappearance. How had everything gone so wrong? Sorrow scoured her insides and hollowed her out like a tree bored out by a weevil. Realisation that Laura really did love her, or *had* loved her, washed over Caro when it was too late. Everything was too late.

Chapter Thirty-Four

LAURA STRODE UPSTAIRS TWO at a time and threw herself on her bed. MiniMe looked at her from the pillows, but Laura tossed her to the side. She needed to act the adult. So adult that she'd stormed out of a conversation like a moody teenager. Her rage subsided into shame and hurt. Caro would never love her enough. Just once in her life, she would like to be special, be the one. Even her mum loved her dad the best. She slammed her fist on the mattress. *Stop the pity party.*

She was stupid to trust again. Laura was always going to return to Spain, and Caro was always going to remain in the UK, so the split was inevitable. They could try a long-distance relationship, but that required trust, and Laura wasn't sure she could trust again. She'd been convinced that Caro would come to Spain. Caro had even said she would like to paint in Spain when they'd talked about it before Laura had gone home. How stupid was she?

Laura hugged the pillow. She had so looked forward to making plans for them both going back to Spain. She had even researched how they could get Artemisia safely into Spain. She couldn't stay here and see Caro every day, knowing it would end. Neither of them were interested in short-term flings. It was all or nothing.

It would be better if she took up Matt's now-empty room, then she could focus on her project and finish her master's. She was hurting enough now. How much worse would it get if they were together for six months and then split? There was no alternative. She would miss Caro, she would miss these lodgings and Artemisia, but she had to maintain her distance to protect her heart, and she couldn't do that if she was in Caro's orbit. There was something about her intelligence and enquiring mind, and her rarely seen laughter that entranced Laura. But it couldn't last.

Laura sighed and turned over to pick up her phone from the bedside table. She called Matt.

"Wassup?" he asked.

Laura could hear the TV blaring in the background. Did she really want to subject herself to that every night, rather than the calm of this house, the purring of Artemisia, and the companionship and passion of Caro? "Is that offer of the room still available?"

"Has your girlfriend tossed you out?" Matt asked.

A flash of irritation arose, and Laura squashed it down. "Nah. I've given her the heave-ho. We need to concentrate on our work, and I need to sit on your tail to get your help on the technical side and finish your own project. If you're still interested, Domingo may want to hire you for the project in Spain?"

"Cool. That sounds like a great opportunity, thanks. But I need to check with Kaylee."

That wasn't the reaction she expected. She thought she might get a whoop of excitement or a virtual high five. A splinter of guilt dug in hard. Matt was being mature by involving his girlfriend, whereas she'd just assumed Caro would come to Spain. She should have done the same, but she'd been so certain. Yet she was uncomfortable speaking to Caro, so she must have felt guilty about not discussing it with her. Caro had clearly meant a short-term visit to paint, but Laura had thought she meant for good. Talk about believing what you wish for rather than challenging assumptions. She should have asked what Caro wanted. Too late now. She'd blown it. "Okay. What about the room?"

"Yeah. I'll check with Rob, but I think it'll work. So the Studios liked the project then?"

Laura chatted about her visit then ended the call with Matt saying he would talk to Rob. She noticed shadow across the sliver of light under her door. Had Caro come up to talk? She couldn't. There was nothing more to say. She didn't want to trap Caro. She wanted her to be free, to be alive, to be the sparkling woman she had caught glimpses of. Caro couldn't be that person if she was with Laura. Better to slip out quietly and lick her wounds. Laura tried not to drop into the maudlin sense of low self-worth that she'd been so at pains to paper over with joking around.

The shadow moved, and Laura heard footsteps down the landing. Caro must have thought better of it. Laura had to set Caro free, even if it hurt like hell. But she had missed Caro so much over the last few weeks, she wasn't sure she could cope.

She rang her mum and burst into tears the moment she answered.

"Lolly Lumpkin, what's wrong?"

She shouldn't still need her mum at thirty, but she did. Kids always needed their mum, no matter how old they got. "Caro and I have split up."

"What? I don't understand. You said she'd live with you in Spain and paint. It seemed perfect."

"She won't leave her home."

"Didn't she agree before?" Her mum sounded puzzled.

Laura picked up MiniMe and cuddled her like a teddy bear. *How mature.* "I didn't ask her."

"What?"

Now she felt really foolish. "She said she'd like to paint in Spain, but she must have just meant on holiday. I thought she'd meant forever."

"But you didn't ask her?"

"No."

Her mum breathed in sharply. "How do you think that made her feel?"

Now her mum sounded like a therapist. "I know, I know, I don't need the lecture." Laura flapped MiniMe's arms. "I just thought she'd love to come to Spain. It seemed so perfect. Now she's pissed off with me because I just assumed, and she said she feels trapped by fangirl adoration and says she can't live up to my expectations."

"You could apologise."

"But that won't stop her from feeling trapped, and she won't change her mind. Her home is a sanctuary, and her room's a shrine to her dead wife. She'll never move on. I'll always be second best, and I can't compete with a dead woman. It's just like I couldn't compete with a man when Valentina had the affair."

Her mum sighed. "Even she realised she'd made a mistake."

"Maybe, but that's because Gonzalo's gone back to his wife, and I've been offered a big job. All I want is be seen for me, loved for me. Is that unreasonable?" She was one step away from self-pity, and nobody wanted to see that, including her mum. "I'm going back to live with Matt so I can concentrate on my project."

She said goodnight to her mum and switched off her light, but her argument with Caro churned around in her head and she castigated herself with everything she could have done differently.

Artemisia scratched at the door, and Laura rose to let her in. She peered out of the window, but there was no light spilling from the rest of the house, so Caro must have gone to bed. She had held her dream but had let it slip through her fingers like sand through a timer. Time had run out.

Laura looked online and booked the same cheap van hire she'd used before. She had no lectures the next day, so she sent a text to Matt and asked him to pick up the van in the morning and drive over.

All night, Laura fought with her sheets and cuddled Artemisia until she meowed for food.

"Shush, I'm not feeding you now. Go to sleep."

At six in the morning Laura crept down, because Artemisia was being such a pain. The kettle was still warm, and Caro had left her coffee mug prepared. Her breath caught at Caro's quiet kindness. She would miss that. God, she would miss her. When she looked outside, she saw the light on in her studio. Caro couldn't sleep either, then. She must have gone out very early, but whether she was working or trying to avoid Laura, Laura wasn't sure. She watered the orchid that was yellowing at the tips of the leaves, and the petals had become tissue thin. Caro wasn't lying about killing houseplants. It would probably wither and die now. Like their relationship.

She sighed and scribbled a note. "Thanks for the coffee. Sorry about everything. I've ordered a van, and I'll get out of your hair today. Sorry if you felt trapped. I never meant to. Please continue to play, and I look forward to seeing your career get back on track. Love Laura xox."

She remembered the first note exchanges they had had. Was it only four months ago? Her whole life had turned upside down since then. She still had Caro's first note to her, along with the sketchbook that she'd gradually filled. She even had a couple of mini-instructive scribbles of Caro's and the wonderful sketch on the hillside, which she would always treasure. Saying goodbye was hard. Laura hoped Caro would be around later so she could say it properly and apologise, but part of her hoped she could leave without seeing Caro again. There was no easy option, and cowardice was just another fault she could add to her list of shortcomings. She didn't deserve Caro. She didn't deserve love.

Chapter Thirty-Five

"So, DARLING, HOW WAS the big reunion? I'm surprised you're out of bed," Rebecca said when Caro called her.

"Oh, don't." Caro blinked hard to hold back tears. "Laura's gone, and she's not coming back."

"What do you mean? You were going to invite her to stay with you, and the Nutty Squirrel gig is all lined up?"

She stuffed her other hand in her jeans to stop it shaking and took a settling breath. Rebecca would understand. The weird thing about grief was that it had two components: the time you'd known someone and the intensity of the feelings you'd had. While the grief from Yvonne's death was a long, slow burn, Laura's departure was like a nuclear explosion, and Caro was in turmoil with its fallout. But she would survive, she would stand tall. She just hadn't imagined that Laura would be too scared to commit. Caro should not have made so many assumptions. They'd both been guilty of that.

"Caro, are you okay?"

She nodded, and a flash of anger ricocheted through her body. "Laura's going back to Spain when she's finished her master's. Originally, she planned to work here on the project for the Spanish company, but they want her to run the entire department, which means she needs to be based there. She assumed I would just drop everything and move out there. How can I? I don't see how I'd get a work visa, and what about Artemisia? I'd even cleared out all of Yvonne's stuff from my room, including her painting. It's all packed up in boxes." The dam that she'd been holding back broke, and she cried until she subsided into hiccoughing sobs. She felt like a wrung-out dishcloth.

"Oh, Caro, I'm so sorry," Rebecca said. "Come and stay with us for a few weeks. Bring your paints, because Hadley Wilks, that England cricketer who's just retired, is eager to have his portrait painted by you."

Caro didn't know much about Wilks, except there may have been some sleaze attached to him a few years ago. Something about taking bribes. Caro sniffed and blew her nose and considered the proposition. "He knows that I'd do the painting in two halves, with the face and props of his profession in the sunlight and his rump in the shadows would be whatever animal he's trying to hide?"

"Yes, I know, darling. I told him, and he seemed delighted."

Caro would never understand the psyche of celebrity culture. Some of Yvonne's colleagues had loved nothing more than to be the centre of even vicious gossip. "It won't be flattering."

"It all adds to his bad boy image."

"Seriously, if I paint him as a pig from behind, he wouldn't mind? I don't want to spend time and energy, and then he says no." How bizarre and intriguing. She could envisage how it would look. Caro loved symbolism in art. They were the emojis of their day, especially the old Dutch Masters, who painted bread and wine for religious symbols through to oysters and medlar fruits for lust and carnal knowledge. She could sprinkle in a few objects like that as an homage.

"I'll arrange a non-refundable deposit that will cover all of your materials and a sizeable chunk of time. If he doesn't love it, we can sell it in the exhibition."

Caro inhaled sharply. Laura had promised to attend that, but she doubted she would come now. "I see what you've done. You've distracted me from thinking about Laura."

"Maybe, darling, but it does sound like a rather good plan, don't you think?"

Caro contemplated it for a few moments. Would Laura come back? No, she'd been adamant, and there was just a scribbled note saying she was leaving. "What about Artemisia? I can't put her in the cattery for a few weeks. That's not fair to her, and she'd never forgive me."

"You can bring a litter box. The kids love her."

Caro sighed. "But Freddie's priceless furniture wouldn't."

Rebecca didn't disagree. "What about the children next door? Could they look after her? Aren't they friends with you now?"

Caro blinked back tears again. "They're Laura's friends because she plays—played—football with them. They don't feel the same about me and will probably revert to their previous pranks." *Oh, Laura, why did you go? You bring sunshine, but now my eyes are so dazzled, I can't see in the gloom behind.*

"You should arrange it. I insist. I don't want you moping around that mausoleum of yours."

Caro stared up from her bed at the bright patch on the wall where Yvonne's picture had hung. It seemed fitting that the space was now empty. "That's what Laura called it. She said that she couldn't compete against a dead woman in the relationship."

"She may have a point," Rebecca said.

"You're not much help."

"I'm offering you my wonderful home and a welcome distraction, which could be very lucrative. The more you paint, the quicker you can test your new style in an exhibition. Freddie says he has a slot in the gallery in May. What do you think?"

Friendly company, a change of scenery, and a chance to recalibrate after Laura was a good idea. As long as Artemisia was happy.

A few days later, Caro packed up her car to go up to London. Amelia and Riley's parents were happy with the arrangement, especially as Caro promised to pay a small amount for the kids to look after her. Given they already loved the cat, that was no hardship. Caro thought Artemisia would be upset, but she went straight to them without a backward glance. It might have helped that Amelia had Artemisia's favourite food in a saucer.

Caro squashed down her disappointment that her cat didn't seem to care, and she went back to playing Tetris with her art supplies. This was the next stage of her life, and she was grateful that Laura had been in her life, even if it was for a short while. How she missed her. Her heart hurt with every lonely beat like calling out in the wilderness to a mate who would never come.

Chapter Thirty-Six

MATT TOOK CONTROL OF the mouse and wiggled it to activate the screen. "Stop moping and go see her."

"I can't. I tried calling her, but her phone's switched off, and she's not replying to my texts," Laura said. Her stomach was in knots, wondering what Caro was doing, how she was doing. Really, she knew Caro would be hurt, upset, and angry. Laura should have tried earlier, but her stupid pride and embarrassment had held her back.

Matt gave her a hard stare. "Duh. That's why you need to see her. You're not getting your thesis written this way."

True, she was having difficulties writing. Having completed the practical side, she now had to evaluate everything. That felt weird given the project was already a commercial success. "Yeah, maybe I'll go, but not today. Will you come with me when I go to see Nutty Squirrel tomorrow?"

Matt wiped his hands on his Star Trek T-shirt he had picked up at Comic Con. "Are you still going even though you've split up with Caro?"

Laura looked back at the empty Word document to hide her sudden prickling of tears. She couldn't admit she wanted to go so she would have a connection to Caro, however tenuous. Besides, it was good to explore the possibilities with them as well. Since she'd left Caro, her stomach felt like she'd swallowed angry bees; she couldn't settle, couldn't sleep, and couldn't eat.

The following day, she and Matt arrived at the studios. Unlike the expensive headquarters at Domingo Studios, with its marble floors and receptionist, someone had tacked a hand-painted sign on the outside of a dockside warehouse with an ill-fitting windowless door that was propped open with a tin of paint. Not a good start, and an indication of how unprofessional they were. Laura cleared her throat and knocked on the open door. "Hello?"

As she entered, a tall lanky man, probably in his mid-fifties and sporting a huge grey beard, came to greet them. Matt stood on the threshold, fidgeting.

"Hi, you must be Laura and Matt. I'm Jeff Summers, the one responsible for this mess." He gesticulated wildly at the computers, partitioned-off stop-motion scenes, and puppets, including one of the eponymous Nutty Squirrel.

Laura tried to hide her dismay, even though she knew a number of animation studios ran on a shoestring and seemed to be chaotic. She had assumed because Nutty Squirrel was so successful, it would have been different.

"I know it doesn't look much, but Nutty Squirrel has great distribution over the networks. We're even doing a deal with Amazon Prime video, and that'll bring in lots of money."

It was curious he went on the defensive immediately, and he hadn't even asked about Matt yet. "This is Matt, my technical whizz. He's programmed my computer models to perform routine tasks. The models can be skinned and tweaked to allow for age, personality, and mood, so they're a lot quicker to set up and move, and therefore cheaper to produce."

Jeff shook Matt's hand. "Welcome. We always need technical skills. Let me show you around."

Everything was haphazard. The focus seemed to be one waist-high set that was flooded with three-point lighting. They photographed one key frame at a time, tweaking the model between each frame. There was an overriding smell of solvent and dust. Various people were introduced, but they seemed more interested in their work than talking to them. Jeff led them away, stepping over wires taped down with yellow and black hazard tape. Laura couldn't work here. She had heard that some animation studios liked an informal style to help the creative process, but this was madness. It was incredibly different from the internships she and Matt had had in Aardvark Studios, where everything had been sleek and sophisticated with high-end computers and the low hum of people engrossed in their work. That was what Laura aspired to if she took over animation at Domingo Studios, not this. Her back stiffened.

"Sorry if things seem a little chaotic. We're on a tight deadline for this new series for CBBC."

"If that's the case, do you have the resources to help produce my project?" Laura's boldness originated from the certainty of a job offer in Spain, but there was some room for overlap. Her mum always told her it was wise to keep her options open. Caro had said the same. At the thought of Caro, the bees in Laura's stomach stung. She pushed down the sadness and smiled at Jeff. She didn't want him to think she was dissing what they were doing; they had secured high-value contracts so they must be doing something right.

"Oh, I understood you would work on computers at home and just needed our contacts for access to the networks?"

Jeff led them into a partitioned-off office cluttered with papers strewn all over the desk. There were various models and puppets along the shelves and a huge cardboard cut-out of the Nutty Squirrel.

"That's true," Laura said and went to sit on one of the two faux leather office chairs strapped up with Gorilla tape.

"Just move the stuff on the chairs and pop it on the floor. I'd like to say it's not normally this bad, but that's not true. I'm not very organised, but I have the contacts you need."

Laura looked around the chaos. She couldn't work in this pandemonium, but she could use his contacts. If they had access to Amazon Prime, maybe they could have a reciprocal arrangement with Domingo Studios. "Is your distribution primarily in the UK?" She could see the Nutty Squirrel going down well in Spain. She could take that back to Domingo. They had great contacts in the gaming industry but not in broadcasting. This could be a way of short-circuiting access.

But she was conflicted. If she worked for Nutty Squirrel, she could be close to Caro. But her animation style wasn't hands-on stop-frame. She was a computer-based animator. The logical conclusion was that she would work with Domingo from Spain with all their facilities and funding but make links so she could distribute her project into the UK and maybe even Amazon Prime via Jeff. Equally, Nutty Squirrel could be distributed via Domingo Studios in Spain if the soundtrack was dubbed into Spanish.

Laura had to live in Spain. It would be impossible to live in the UK with Caro. She sagged at the realisation as the slim possibility slammed shut. Laura made an effort to smile as Jeff chattered on, and she had to affect interest in one of the models of a car cut in half to allow access at the rear. Matt nudged her twice to pay attention.

Fortunately, he covered for her and asked a couple of technical questions. They parted with a potential distribution deal and a string of possibilities to take back to Domingo. Bringing in more content and work for the dubbing actors should go down well with him.

"Are you going to draft an agreement?" Matt asked as they walked back to the bus stop.

"No. I need to talk to Caro, so I'll go there now."

"Want me to come with you?"

Her heart warmed at his generosity. He was taking Kaylee to the cinema later and would need time to change and work himself up to it, to approach it methodically and keep his stress levels down. He had come a long way from the shy, brilliant fellow intern she had met when she first fled from Spain. And now he was looking out for her. She squeezed his arm. "No, thanks. I need to do this alone. See you later. I shouldn't be late."

As she walked to the bus stop, a tight band of anxiety crushed her chest. Would Caro speak to her? She wouldn't blame her if she turned her away. Laura didn't know what to say, but she did know she had to see her. The closer the bus came to Caro's stop, the more agitated Laura felt. When she got there, she was tempted to cross the road and wait for the next bus back, but that was cowardly. And she wanted to be done with that kind of behaviour.

The house looked deserted. The curtains were drawn, and there was no sound from inside. Laura went through the side gate and towards the studio, but that was locked too. She scrabbled about in her bag to see if she had a pen and paper to leave her note. Was Caro away for the day? There was whispering and scraping as Amelia came up from the other side of the fence.

"Laura, you're back!" Amelia shouted. "Hey, Riley, Laura's back."

There was more scrabbling on the other side of the fence, and Laura grinned at them. It seemed ages since their football sessions. "Hey, you two, how are you doing? I came to see Caro. Have you seen her?"

"We're not supposed to say, but she's in London. We're looking after Arty Measles until she gets back, but we want to keep her. She sleeps on my bed at night even though she's not supposed to. Can you come back? It's no fun anymore."

"I miss you too, but I'm staying in Bristol now. Do you know what Caro's doing in London?"

"Painting lots of famous people, Mummy says."

"Oh." Disappointment dragged at Laura, and she had to lock her knees so they didn't buckle. Nausea bubbled up from her constricted stomach and she had to push it down. Caro was getting on with her life, and who could blame her given how Laura had stomped out. Even though she was painting again, it wasn't with Laura. She forced herself to flash a bright smile. "Do you know when she'll return?"

"Mummy says it could be weeks or months—"

"Years and years," Riley said. "It's so boring."

"Can you come and play football with us? I've been practising the Ronaldo chop," Amelia said.

"Really? Wow, I'd like to see that." Boxing away her upset to examine later, Laura walked around to the other garden. Watching the children play was certainly more entertaining than writing her master's thesis and was a welcome distraction from thinking about Caro and the hole in her own heart. Seeing the house so empty and reconnecting with Amelia and Riley had her yearning for Caro. A headache formed in her temples, dull and persistent. When Artemisia strolled up to her and rubbed herself against her legs, Laura fought back tears. How stupid to be upset at seeing a cat.

Laura picked her up, even though Arty Farty didn't like it, and buried her nose in the tabby fur. It was softer than she remembered. She even rewarded Laura with a raucous purr. "I've missed you too," Laura whispered so the kids couldn't hear.

Their mum came out to say hello.

"Hi, Gemma. How long is Caro away for?" Laura asked and received a scowl from Amelia, as if she didn't trust her. "Your mum may have more up-to-date information," Laura said.

Amelia shrugged, affecting nonchalance, and followed Riley inside to get a drink.

"She didn't say for certain. A couple of months maybe. It's going to be hard for Amelia and Riley to give back the cat after so long," Gemma said.

"I'm sure you can share her. She loves nothing more than having a bit of attention. Did Caro say where she was staying?"

"At a friend's house, I think."

"Rebecca?"

"That sounds about right. I'll tell Caro you called around when she gets back."

Laura had to leave now before she broke down or her headache swelled into a raging migraine. "Thanks. I ought to be going."

Sadness sharpened her sensitivity. Coming back had been a big mistake. It just showed how much she missed Caro. How stupid and arrogant to think she could do without her, but how could it work, unless they had a part-time arrangement? She'd come over here for a while and Caro could come out to Spain. She needed Caro in her life, even if it was only sporadic. How could she get through to her? The only way she could think was to contact the gallery Rebecca's husband owned.

On the way to the bus stop, she plucked up the courage to phone and introduced herself.

"Could you hold for a second, please?"

She heard a whispered conversation but couldn't make any of it out.

"Hello, I'm Caro's agent, Rebecca. How can I help you?"

"I was trying to get hold of Caro. I need to speak to her. It's Laura, her lodger. Ex-lodger."

Rebecca took a sharp intake of breath. "Well, Laura the ex-lodger, I have to say that Caro doesn't want to speak to you. You really upset her, and she's busy painting for an exhibition in a few months' time so doesn't need to be hassled—"

"Please, will you just tell her I called? I'd like to speak to her."

"Are you staying in the UK?"

God, did this woman know all their business? "No, but—"

"In that case, she definitely doesn't need to speak to you." The line went dead.

A few minutes later, Laura's phone rang. Had Rebecca passed on the message, anyway? She hardly dared hope and swiped to accept the call.

"Hello, I'm Freddie, the owner of the gallery, we met before." It was the man who'd been so charming when they met. "Caro will attend the opening of her exhibition, 'Of Light and Love' in May. I'll email you the details."

Her shoulders sagged, and she leaned against the bus stop. The exhibition was months away. "Is there any way you could pass on the message to Caro, please?"

"Not if I want to remain married, no. Sorry."

So Caro's friend was a ball-breaker, too. It was so frustrating. And she only had herself to blame. If she hadn't been so childish and stormed out, they could have had some time together and maybe even worked something out. The bus slowed down and stopped with a hiss of air brakes.

Laura stepped on, showed her ticket, and nodded at the driver, regretting the action since her head still throbbed. Now was not a good day for a conversation about the weather. She took her seat and all the last interactions with Caro turned around in her head, as if they would come to a different outcome.

Laura scrubbed her hands over her face. She'd blown it. What if she hadn't got the rejection in first so she wasn't the one being rejected? As if that hurt any less. She snorted, and a passenger on the seat across from her shifted slightly and gave her a sideways glance. All of her decisions had been wrong, and now she had to face the consequences. She stared out of the window into the gloomy grey afternoon that reflected her mood, the scene pixilating as she held back tears.

Her stop would be coming up soon, but she couldn't bear seeing Matt and Kaylee all loved up or deal with Rob's snarky comments, so Laura pressed the bell to get off earlier. She wandered through the Ashton Court Estate, paying only scant attention when she heard the roaring of a flame. A balloon gradually rose above the treetops and drifted slowly over the city.

Laura shrugged and reverted to studying the path as she walked. Normally, she would have been thrilled at the sight of a balloon, but everything had been reduced to one foot plodding in front of the other. A tremor rose in her chest, and she pushed it down. It was over. She needed to focus on her thesis, on her work, and life without Caro. The wait for the exhibition would be long and hard, but she would go, even if it was simply to say goodbye.

Chapter Thirty-Seven

THEY HAD UNLEASHED A media storm with the commissions. Controversy spilled from the arts page to the evening news. Caro hit the bitter Twittersphere by painting a national treasure as a vulture sitting beside a bowl of rotting peaches. How ironic that if Yvonne had been alive, she would've been discussing her own wife's work.

Rebecca bought Caro a new phone. "I'll handle the old one, darling. It's too hot and full of nasty messages you don't need to see. I'll set it up for you, don't worry."

The couple of weeks in London became a month, then three, and she had no time to return home before the exhibition. The media hysteria continued to boil and torch, and Caro's heart became icier.

Caro yearned for Laura with every cell in her body. She missed her as she mixed colours; she missed her when she sketched her *victims*; she missed her in the mornings when she had her first tea and again in the evening when food prep was efficient and serious, discussing the world news. With Laura, it had all been fun, and dancing, and joking.

Laura had to make the first move. She had made it very clear she couldn't be with Caro because she didn't want to be second best, and she was the one who stormed out. The hope that Laura would try and contact her slowly drifted away with each day. Had Laura gone back to Spain already? Hope liquefied and cooled into solid iron in Caro's gut. She picked up the sketchbook containing her pictures of Laura. She smiled at the attention Laura had given to Artemisia but tracing her finger over Laura's image turned the ache in Caro's heart to acid.

Caro scowled at her marked-out commission painting. She was like a battery hen, producing golden eggs to throw at people. Without thinking, she snatched the commission painting off the easel and replaced it with a new canvas. She needed to expunge her soul of grief. Caro painted fast and frantically, as if each stroke would serve to seal the wound in her heart. Why wasn't Laura in contact? Had they lost their friendship too? She wanted to tell Laura about the exhibition. However Caro viewed it, there was only one conclusion. It was over. Laura didn't love her enough. There was nothing more hopeless than unrequited love, to love and know that love is hopeless. But it wasn't unrequited as such. Laura just had different priorities. The judgement turned to ashes in her mouth. Caro couldn't give up her career either. It was like they were trying to harmonise a song in different keys.

Creativity comes at a cost to self, to soul, to love. Caro had lost it all. She needed to capture Laura's essence in this portrait to justify what she'd done by not following Laura to Spain. Laura's features emerged from the canvas like a goddess rising from the sea as Caro poured her emotion into every stroke. Passion, yearning, and regret coloured into the canvas. The radiance of Laura's smile made her shrivel and die inside.

Caro had just finished washing her brushes and stretching her back when there was a knock at the door. Caro glanced through the dormer windows. It had gone dark outside, and she'd only been vaguely aware of the change because the daylight lamps gave a false sense of time. The knock came again.

"Caro, darling, it's me. I wondered if I could have a word?"

Caro scowled. Rebecca had promised she wouldn't disturb her. She opened the door. "What is it?"

Rebecca burst in. "Darling, you'll never guess who, oh—" Rebecca stared at the painting on the easel, then at Caro.

Caro swiped at her face, only now aware that she was crying. Had she been shedding tears the whole time she'd been painting?

Rebecca squeezed Caro's arm. "Maybe you shouldn't paint your ex-lover if it upsets you so much? I thought you were painting the Morning TV woman portrait today?"

Caro stared at Rebecca. "I painted what I wanted to, what I needed to."

"I know, and it's beautiful, but the commissions are so lucrative we should capitalise on the trend before it fades. I was coming to tell you we have another commission, but I'll defer it if you've wasted a full day on this."

Rage rushed up Caro's chest and threatened to throttle her. She dried her brushes to give herself time to collect her thoughts into a coherent sentence. "Wasted? Have you lost your aesthetic eye, or are you so consumed with the ringing of the cash register you've forgotten what we stand for, what I stand for? What happened to not compromising on our art? Don't you remember we promised ourselves at college we would not sell out? Yet here we are." Caro pointed at them both then tossed the brushes into the jar and scrubbed her palettes.

"These commissions will keep you in your big house, or have you forgotten what it's like to be terrified you'll have to give up your sanctuary?"

Caro concentrated on removing a particularly stubborn globule of red vermillion that smeared and separated, dissolving into the water like blood. She didn't want to go there or think about giving up her home. She gesticulated at the portrait. "I remember you hassled me daily to get painting again. I am."

Rebecca's shoulders sagged, clearly upset at the accusation. Caro didn't want to hurt her best friend. "I'm grateful for your support. I know I'd be a nobody without you pushing for me," Caro said. Rebecca smiled. Sometimes it was easy to get that response. She should remember to thank her more often.

"And now look at you, on the evening news and everything," Rebecca said.

"I can do without the death threats. What's wrong with a vulture anyway? It's a vital part of the circle of life."

"Nothing, darling. Shall I make you a cup of tea? Sit down for a few minutes. Did you remember Freddie and I are going to the opera this evening?"

Caro nodded and vaguely remembered Freddie saying one of his friends had invited them to meet some potential new customers. Spending the evening schmoozing rather than talking about the performance was a waste of a good opera.

"Are you cross we didn't invite you? I promise you we'll go next week. I'll see what I can get tickets for and treat you. You need an evening off."

Caro watched the red-stained water flowing down the plughole. "I thought you said I'd just wasted the day?"

"I didn't mean it like that, darling. We just need to get as many commissions done as we can to put into the exhibition. People are more likely to attend the opening if they can see their own portrait. Freddie wants to make a big splash. He's arranging a string quartet to play as people arrive, and he'd like you to do a little speech. Not long, just a few minutes."

Is this what Caro had come to? She could have gone with her heart and followed Laura to Spain, but she'd chosen her art legacy instead. How ludicrous and sad that she would probably be remembered for her satirical portraits rather than anything else she'd done. Fate was perverse and uncontrollable. "I can't do any more commissions beyond the ones you've already set up. The money may be good, but it's crushing me."

Rebecca placed the mugs of tea on a side table, and they sat side by side on the chaise longue. "I heard what you said, so I've doubled the commission rate to reduce the demand. Somehow, it's just given your portraits an extra cachet. Why don't we just finish this batch and then you can go back home?"

We? Caro was torn. She wanted to see Artemisia, but everything at home reminded her of Laura. She had filled Caro's heart, broken down her defences one smile and food offering at a time. Laura may have already gone back to Spain. Caro swiped at another unbidden tear, hoping Rebecca hadn't noticed. "Is it all worth it?" Caro asked. She couldn't be like Rebecca. "Do you wish you still did sculpture?"

Rebecca took a sip of her tea before replacing her mug carefully onto the side table as if giving herself time to think and compose an answer.

"I don't know. Decision-making is never as simple as yes or no. I would never have been as good a sculptor as you are a painter, would not have made a successful career out of it, so the choice to quit was easier. I'd never have the same accolades. I've still got the Sunday Times piece that hailed you as a modern master. My delight now is in seeing others succeed. You, my other artists, my children, Freddie, and my work in my own business. It doesn't feel as though I've sacrificed. I've just enabled others to meet their goals. I promise you Carolyn Trent-Parker will never be forgotten."

Caro snorted. "All major art galleries have storerooms stuffed with paintings by unknown masters. And if they're forgotten, does it matter?"

Rebecca took Caro's hands. "What's this existential crisis about, Caro? You've never been so popular."

"Before this, I painted passion, and all that is beautiful in life and love in all its tempestuous glory. It's what I do and who I am. With these commissions I'm making snide commentary on people, feeding their vanity, and poking at the soft underbelly of society. It's satirical and mocking, yet this work is so popular and deemed more important. I can't do this forever; it's killing my soul one painting at a time."

Rebecca squeezed her hand. "You're just tired. Perhaps if you concentrated on the commissions, you'd be less exhausted. It's the typical pre-show flurry of activity. We could make the entire exhibition on the commissions and preliminary sketches."

Caro extracted her hand and locked eyes with Rebecca. "My portraits of Laura will be hung, or there won't be an exhibition at all."

Rebecca raised her hands. "Of course, darling. But the commissions are quicker with the photo sitting after the initial consultation." She gestured at the discarded canvas with the preliminary marks on. "I really want to include this next one in the exhibition, because she said she'll be there."

"I need a break." Caro stood and moved to the window. She peered through the small opening onto the grey roofs opposite. There was the constant rumble of noise that she couldn't drown out even with Wagner. Caro longed for the views of nature outside and the kids next door trampling on her begonias. Had she really become a hollowed-out painting machine with no heart and soul?

"After the exhibition, I'll take a break and go home." If Laura was still in the country, she would track her down, even if all they could salvage was a friendship. She clenched her jaw. No, hang that. She would follow Laura to Spain if she had to. What they had was not something to throw away without a fight.

Chapter Thirty-Eight

LAURA STEELED HERSELF BEFORE she opened the etched glass door to the gallery. A bejewelled crowd sparkled as they quaffed champagne. She looked down at her jeans and T-shirt looking drab and ordinary. Her leather jacket was semi smart, but she felt so out of place. Oh, well, she said she'd come, and here she was. The bell jangled as she opened the door, but it couldn't be heard above the din of braying, laughing glitterati.

To the left of the door, a mobile rack for clothes sprouted evening coats and bags. Although it was May, the evening was not warm, and presumably most of the attendees here would be off to the opera or dinner parties later. A man dressed in a dark suit and tie accosted her and blocked her entrance.

"Good evening, madam, may I see your invitation please?"

She'd never seen such a posh bouncer in her life, no tattoo or crew cut in sight. He was probably called Jeeves. From her inside jacket pocket, she handed him the crumpled email from Freddie that had followed his verbal invitation.

Jeeves raised his eyebrows and covered his disdain with a neutral expression. It didn't stop him from looking at her suspiciously.

"This is unusual. One moment, madam. Would you mind stepping aside a second."

It was a statement, not a question. A couple entered, the woman dripping with diamonds in a low-cut dress. They flashed their invitations, and Jeeves nodded them through.

He tapped his mouthpiece. "Mr or Mrs Zeltser to the front door, please."

God, this was embarrassing. She clearly didn't have the right clothes or look. Maybe she shouldn't have come, but she desperately wanted to talk to Caro face to face, and this seemed her only opportunity before she left for Spain. She had submitted her thesis and the final show was only three weeks away. She didn't have the right to ask Caro to give up this life with the arty set to follow her to Spain, so she needed to see her again to say goodbye.

A woman in a bright green cocktail dress, jade necklace, and earrings with matching four-inch heels came gliding across to the front door.

Jeeves put on a full-dazzle smile. "I'm so sorry to disturb you, but this young lady doesn't have an official invitation, just an email purporting to be from Mr Zeltser."

The woman looked from the email to Laura then back again. Then she nodded and smiled as though she were laughing at a private joke.

"So, you're the delicious Laura. I'm Rebecca, Caro's best friend and agent."

Great. Caro's gatekeeper. Laura nodded. Even if she had to push past the woman, she'd be coming in. *Start with diplomacy.* She gave her best smile. "May I come in?"

"Normally, people dress up for an invitation showing, but I'm sure we can make an exception."

Patronising git seems determined to humiliate me. MiniMe would certainly have said something, but Laura didn't want to make a scene. She just wanted to see Caro. Although how she would find her in this crowd, she had no idea. "Thanks," she said.

Jeeves became charm-incorporated now. "May I take your jacket?"

"No, I'm good, thanks." Seeing the forest of expensive coats, Laura imagined it would be a bun fight at the end. Besides, she had her wallet, train tickets, and phone in it. Laura stepped into the gallery area behind Rebecca, so tempted to pull a face behind her back. But that was too childish, and she didn't know who else would see her.

A waitress dressed in black trousers and white shirt approached Laura with a silver tray of champagne.

"Thanks." Laura took a flute.

Rebecca turned around and smiled as though she hadn't spent the last few months keeping Laura out of Caro's orbit. "Look around, and I'll let Caro know you're here. Although I'm not sure she'll want to talk to you."

"Please, I need to speak to her."

"And she needs to talk to people who'll give her a commission." Rebecca sighed and pointed at Laura's face. "I can tell by that look you think I'm being a bitch, but I'm really trying to protect her."

Laura contained a snort. "Can you let her choose if she sees me? Don't dress up the request, just tell her."

"Fine."

"Thanks."

Rebecca swivelled on her sharp heels and strode towards the back, nodding and making comments to people as she went until she disappeared into the crowd.

Curiosity about what Caro had been doing overtook Laura. To one side, Freddie was holding forth, talking to a gaggle of people, who were listening intently.

"As you can see, CTP has developed from the Florentine disegno oil painting style where everything was meticulously drawn beforehand, and has moved onto the Venetian colorito, more like a modern-day Titian. Note that she's done the commissions in acrylics, which is a much faster medium, and people have been lining up to have their portraits done. These are not ordinary portraits, as you will see. If you want to snap up the signed prints, there are only a few left."

Laura drifted away so she could examine the portraits for herself. Besides the commission portraits, there were various prints of the preliminary sketches. Most of the portraits already had a large red spot indicating they were not for sale, followed by a long tail of smaller dots showing the limited-edition prints had been sold, too. She laughed at the portrait of the cricketer, his face and torso in bright sunlight but with a pig's tail painted in the shadows. Laura read the title of the piece, "Howzat?" It wasn't difficult to interpret that Caro thought he was greedy and was mocking him. It was beautifully painted, though, so you could feel the human behind his eyes, observing, judging, and condemning. Caro had even captured that haughtiness in the accompanying sketches. She was so talented. Laura's heart picked up pace. It was such a joy that Caro was painting again, and if she had played some small part in that, it warmed her to her soul.

There was another room behind the main gallery with the satirical sunshine and shadow portraits. Laura avoided the main crowd and wandered in, then stopped short. She tried to catch her breath and forced herself to inhale deeply. She didn't expect to be confronted with an entire wall of her own image; dancing in the kitchen, looking out to the distant hills, cooking at the stove. In each one, there was such unfettered joy glowing from inside. Laura put her hand to her mouth when she saw a particular pair of portraits. The first was of her looking down, petting Artemisia with such affection, and the second portrait of her, identical to

229

the first, except Laura's head was raised, and she was staring directly at the artist, at the observer, with a shy smile and with love in her eyes.

It was obvious, with such raw naked emotion, that Laura felt so vulnerable, stripped bare, yet she still had all her clothes on. This was the sketch just before "Desire," when she was naked and crawling towards Caro, full of pent-up lust. Laura heated up and furtively glanced around to check it wasn't included in the exhibition. She exhaled with relief as she realised the rest of the paintings were not of her.

A woman next to her nudged her elbow. "Is that you?"

Laura didn't trust herself to speak, so she just nodded. She stared at the painting. It was as though all her layers had been stripped down like old varnish on an ancient painting, revealing the bright colours and the damaged canvas underneath, exposing the real Laura, bright, flawed, and irrefutably in love…and loved.

"Beautiful, my dear," the woman said, and touched Laura's forearm with a silky gloved finger.

As she moved away, Laura was unsure whether she was referring to the painting or herself. Perhaps she should slip out before seeing Caro. She had seen her truth and painted it to life in cadmium yellow and raw umber. Laura had never been so seen before, and it was terrifying. But this was what she wanted—to be seen, to be loved. And Caro had done that, before Laura had stropped off like some melodramatic teenager.

From next door, there was the sound of a knife tapping against a glass, seeking attention. She heard Freddie's voice, and the crowd headed towards him. Laura hung back at the threshold between the two rooms.

"Good evening, ladies and gentlemen. Thank you so much for making it here on this unseasonably cold evening. I can't tell you how delighted we are to let you have the first glimpse of CTP's latest creations, and I'm thrilled with the reactions I've heard while walking around. Most of the paintings have already been sold, but signed prints and sketches are available for those who missed out. I recommend you snap them up, as I have a further announcement. We have just heard from the Tate gallery that CTP's painting 'Howzat,' which you can see by the entrance, has been shortlisted for the Turner Art Prize."

There was a ripple of polite but enthusiastic applause.

Freddie cleared his throat. "If that doesn't persuade you to invest in one of these wonderful works of art, I don't know what will. I'd like the artist herself to say a few words."

From the crowd, Caro appeared in a smart business suit. Laura swallowed hard. Caro had never been so beautiful. The Vandyke brown of the suit picked up her dark hair, and her eyes shone bright, reflected in the royal blue of her silk blouse. She was stunning.

"Thank you all for coming out this evening. And thanks, Freddie and Rebecca, for all the support you have given me over the years. As some of you may know, my wife died nearly three years ago, and for a long time I couldn't paint at all. Rebecca and Freddie believed in me, by which I mean nagged me to keep going—"

Laughter echoed around the audience. Caro waited until it subsided. "But it wasn't until a young woman came into my life, a woman who was molten sunshine, who scrubbed away at my gloom and despondency one smile at a time. It was she who showed me how to enjoy life again by enjoying life herself. It is because of her that I was able to paint again. I was fortunate she put up with me and let me sketch her. They are the paintings and sketches you can see in the smaller gallery behind. Because of her, I found the inspiration to paint again and explore and develop my craft, which you can see all around you." A look of pain and sadness crossed Caro's face. "Unfortunately, I've never been able to tell her how much I owe to her—"

"She's here," said the middle-aged woman with the silk gloves.

Caro's eyes widened. Clearly, Rebecca hadn't told her that Laura was here. Why was Laura not surprised?

"I saw her in the other room. She's over there," the woman said.

The crowd parted, and Laura was aware of all the eyes on her, but the only set of eyes she cared about was Caro's. Her expression was unreadable, a mixed palette of emotions, from joy to doubt, to sorrow and hope.

Caro coughed. "Well, it seems I can say how much I owe her in person. Laura, thank you, I am privileged to have known you, been cared for and been inspired by you."

Laura nodded and blew Caro a kiss. The audience laughed and burst into applause.

"Please bear with me. I would like to speak to her in private but do stay for the champagne and nibbles. Thank you so much for coming."

Caro half-bowed and handed the microphone back to Freddie. She rushed over to Laura, as much as her high heels would allow. She slowed as she approached and seemed shy, as though unsure whether she could hug her. Laura decided for her and moved towards Caro, and they clung to each other.

"I've missed you," Caro whispered. "It's wonderful to see you. Freddie said he'd invited you. I hoped, I wished, but I didn't dare believe you'd come."

"Rebecca didn't tell you I arrived?" Laura couldn't help stirring it a little.

"No, but then she's been busy this evening."

"Hm." Laura wasn't buying that. Rebecca had her own agenda, and that seemed to entail keeping Laura as far away from Caro as she could, probably so Caro could continue painting without distraction.

"It's wonderful to see you. Please will you stay if I show you upstairs?"

Upstairs? What did she mean? Was she proposing they sleep together?

Caro laughed. "No, nothing like that. I've been using it as a studio for my commissions. It would just be great to talk. I need to say my goodbyes to people, but I'd love to spend some real time with you. I'm delighted you're here. Please don't rush away."

"Sure." What would she do anyway? She hadn't thought about what would happen after seeing Caro. How much she loved her came flooding back. She might not have expressed herself until it was too late, but it was so clear in the portraits. Caro led Laura to a set of stairs at the back of the building.

"Come."

Caro held her hand as if she was scared Laura would melt away. She led her up the concrete steps. It was nothing as glamorous as the gallery. The first floor contained offices. Caro led her up to the second floor and stepped into a studio, set up similar to the one she had at her home, complete with bench and chaise longue.

Whatever they planned to say next was lost as their lips devoured each other. Her yearning bubbled up, hot and excited, and spilled over into desire and need. Laura tugged at Caro's lower lip, and they moaned. The kiss was no longer chaste but raw, and needy, and getting hotter by the second. Caro trailed her hands up Laura's body underneath her T-shirt, leaving a trail of fire.

"I've missed you so much, and I would love to stay with you and make love to you now," Caro said when they pulled back for air. "But I need to do my duty downstairs. I promise I won't be long. Then we probably need to talk."

Laura stroked back the strand of hair that had fallen over Caro's eyes. She had forgotten the exact colour of blue they were, more grey blue than the cerulean blue of the sky, but the sparkle of joy was unmistakable.

Caro grinned. "Help yourself to coffee over in the corner, although it's not your extra strong sludge."

She brushed her lips against Laura's cheek in a whisper of a kiss that promised more, and then she was gone. Bathed in the warmth of Caro's gaze, seeing the evidence on the paintings downstairs, Laura knew with certainty that Caro loved her. She did a little twirl of delight. She would do what she could to make this work.

Chapter Thirty-Nine

DUTY DONE, CARO RACED UP THE STAIRS AND FLUNG OPEN THE DOOR. SHE melted into a pulsing mess, seeing Laura standing there in her makeshift studio. Out of habit, Caro turned the lock, then threw herself in Laura's arms. It felt so good to feel the warm snuggle of Laura's body pressed against her own. "Thank you for waiting. It's wonderful to see you. I thought I'd never see you again. Do you like your pictures?" She paused as she realised she hadn't let Laura answer. This was so unlike her. She was the quiet one, the one not to gush, but her emotions needed to take voice and to be spoken aloud, to resonate around the room and reach Laura's heart.

Laura laughed. "Well, that's a lovely welcome. It's great to see you too, and the pictures are so beautiful, and raw. Thanks for not hanging 'Desire.' I'm not sure I'm ready to see my naked, lustful self, or for the world to see it."

"I'd never betray your trust. I promised." Caro tried not to be offended, but what they had between them was broken now and no previous rules applied, so Laura was right to question it.

"Thanks."

Caro felt the warmth of Laura's breath. She was close, so close, it would be easy to kiss her again. Caro gazed into the depths of Laura's eyes, saw the longing there, mixed with regret and sadness, and maybe just a thread of hope. She mustn't kiss her. She couldn't assume the right, but she wanted the connection, the physical sense of warm skin on skin. Caro leaned her forehead against Laura's.

She tried to speak but nothing came, so she cleared her throat and tried again. "Much as I would love to take you to bed, I think we need to talk."

Laura blinked and her head bobbed against Caro's. "Vale."

"Let's sit." Caro pulled Laura onto the chaise longue. They faced each other, and Caro pulled Laura's hands into her own. "I can't tell you what it means to see you here. How did you find out the details and get an invite?"

"Freddie sent me an email. I phoned the gallery for details but wasn't sure he would send them. I was so happy when it came, although it was way too long to wait. I wanted to see you. I called at the house, and Amelia and Riley said you'd gone. You never replied to my texts, and I called, but I'm guessing Rebecca didn't say?"

Caro clenched her fist. *Damn Rebecca and her interfering ways.* "No, I'll speak to her about that. After the hate mail because of the vulture portrait, I got a new phone. I wanted to call to see how you were doing, but I didn't think I should —"

Caro could have tried harder to contact Laura but hadn't. Partly, she was scared that the momentum in her art would go, and she would be back to staring at empty walls, partly because Laura walked out on her. It seemed fitting Laura should make the first move. Why was she here? Was she coming to support, to apologise, or say she was leaving for Spain next week?

"I wanted to see your exhibition, but that's not why I'm here," Laura said, as though she had read Caro's mind. She looked down at their linked fingers. "I still love you, and I miss you so much." Laura waited until Caro met her eye before speaking. "Sorry, I made assumptions about you coming to Spain. I wondered if we could try a long-distance relationship. Although I'd really love to wake up to you every morning, I'd prefer you in my life part-time rather than not at all. What do you think?"

Caro exhaled the breath she'd been holding. "When you say long-distance, how often are you thinking we would get together?"

"I'd love you to spend the maximum time you can in Spain, but that's only ninety days in every six months. I'd come over here when I could too, and on the holidays, but I need to be in the studios most days." Laura looked so defeated, and her head drooped.

Caro released one hand and cupped Laura's cheek. She just wanted to run her fingers all over her and reacquaint herself with Laura's body. She knew how important it was for Laura to live together; there was a huge issue of trust when they were apart. It was as if she needed the tangible presence to believe it. Caro wanted to believe Laura could sustain that. "Are you sure you can do that?"

Laura held Caro's hand to her cheek but dropped her gaze. "I'd struggle with it," Laura said. "I need to wake up with you every day. If you're always leaving in three months, how can we settle, how can I settle? But I have to try. I can't live without you."

Caro stroked Laura's cheek. "Is it that, or would you find it difficult to trust me when I'm away?"

Laura shook her head and released Caro's hand. "I'm so fucked up. I have such an issue with rejection and intimacy. It's why I mess around so no one will look at the screw-up underneath the surface."

Caro frowned. "What do you mean, you have an issue with intimacy?"

Laura blushed. "You may not believe it, but I struggle being comfortable with sex."

Caro shook her head. This wasn't what she'd expected. "That's not how I've experienced you. Besides, real intimacy is about trust not sex. It's the trust when you know you can be vulnerable, and let someone see that vulnerability, knowing they won't use or abuse it, and that they see you for who you are."

Laura raised her eyes to meet Caro's. "That's why you're so special. You *do* see me. You stripped off all my layers. I need you. Can't you come and apply for residence in Spain?"

Caro wobbled. "But I can't leave my home forever," she whispered.

"We could get Artemisia brought over."

"She wouldn't be happy." Panic threatened to overwhelm Caro, her breathing was shallower and faster. She couldn't leave her home, not indefinitely. Or could she? She was part of the stones and hills, and they had always imagined growing old there. But Yvonne wasn't there anymore. Yvonne was her past, part of her retrospective. Laura was her future.

Laura shook her head. "No, I'm sorry. That's not fair of me to ask. Imagine if Michelangelo's wife had refused to go to Rome because she wanted to be close to her family. The world would never have had the Sistine Chapel frescoes. I can't do that to you, now you've rediscovered CTP. Your work's too important. That's not me fangirling. I don't want to restrict you or curtail what you do. I love you too much." Laura's eyes were shiny with tears. "Have we come to an impasse?" she asked.

The question stabbed at her, as if Caro's heart was about to be wrenched in two. She needed Laura, and it was through Laura's love that she came alive. She was no longer a numb zombie, staggering through life without purpose. There would always be a compromise, one would always have to give up something to be with the other. But it wasn't a compromise if Caro chose. Caro was in love and was loved in turn. They had the perfect mix of pigments that created the most astounding tone that was completely unique and beautiful. How could she choose anything else?

She interlocked her fingers with Laura's and held her gaze. "I want to be with you, and since that's in Spain, that's where I'd like to be."

"What about the house? Yvonne?"

"Yvonne is my past, and I'm putting that behind me. The house is just bricks and mortar. It was so empty after you left, yet everything there reminded me of you. We can work out what's best for Artemisia. I suspect she'll be happiest staying with Amelia and Riley. You are my present, my future. I love you and choose to be with you, if you'll have me."

Laura slipped her hands behind Caro's neck and gently pulled their foreheads together. "I love you. I want you."

Caro leaned in and pressed their lips together, softly at first, then open mouthed, their tongues clashing, hungry and desperate. The kiss unleashed Caro's arousal, which she had been holding onto tightly. This woman could bring her to her knees with want. Part of her felt guilty. Laura should be with someone her own age, not someone eleven years her senior. But the age gap had never bothered her when she was with Yvonne, maybe because she idolised her. This was much more even. Caro closed her eyes. She shouldn't be thinking about Yvonne now. Laura had been right in their argument. There had been three people in the relationship. Caro had moved on in so many ways, except for her stubborn need to be rooted at home. Not now. She was free, and that realisation lightened her soul.

Laura slipped her hand up Caro's blouse. Her warm fingers on Caro's cool skin scattered thrills through all her nerve endings. Caro tugged at Laura's T-shirt. "This needs to come off. And so do these." She unbuttoned Laura's jeans, and Laura wriggled out of them, letting them settle in a pile. Beneath, she wore a lacy thong, tantalising in what it concealed. "Nice, but also surplus to requirements."

They shared a smile, and it was like no time had passed at all. What a stupid waste of time. They should have been together.

"I'm sorry," Laura said. "I should have contacted you before. We could have met up, maybe done this."

Laura placed a hand on the sensitive skin below Caro's belly button that caused her core to thrum in anticipation.

"Shh. I could have too, but we didn't. We're here now. Let's enjoy it." Caro trailed her hands up Laura's arms and over her shoulders, noticing how goosebumps followed her path. "Are you cold?"

Laura shook her head, and Caro kissed the soft skin on her neck as they leaned back on the chaise with Caro on top. She slipped one finger over Laura's collarbone, which elicited a moan. Feeling more confident, Caro cupped Laura's breast and stroked her nipple through the cloth of her bra. Her nipple hardened immediately. Laura arched her back so Caro had more access.

"May I?" Caro gestured at removing her bra, and Laura stretched behind her back to unclasp it and let it drop. She pushed her breast into Caro's hand, as though demanding she be in control. Caro's own clit responded as she caressed Laura's naked flesh.

"You're beautiful," Caro said hoarsely.

"Fuck me. Make me come." Laura pushed down Caro's hand.

She spread her legs and rested one foot on the floor. Caro traced her fingers along the contours of Laura's body, over her belly button to the rough short hairs. She circled Laura's clit, teasing, not touching her where she wanted, but getting closer. And the thrill of Laura responding to her, being excited, straining to be touched, to be taken, made Caro feel alive and totally in tune with her.

"Please," Laura gasped and held Caro's hand to cup her clit.

"Is this what you want?" Caro obliged by dipping into the wetness, along her sex, then back to her clit.

"Inside."

Laura's lips found Caro's, and she pressed her tongue between her lips, as if instructing Caro how she wanted her fingers to be inside her. Caro obeyed and slid her fingers into Laura's folds and deeper, enclosed by Laura's hot wet body and eliciting another moan. Caro pulled back her head slightly to watch Laura, to check whether she was okay with the rhythm and the depth, and to take in the expression of desire and hunger on Laura's face. It was almost enough to send Caro shuddering into orgasm. She loved this woman and being here now, on this chaise longue above an exhibition celebrating Laura, it seemed so fitting, a culmination of desire, want, and fulfilment. Caro wanted to experience everything and remember it all, see the softness on Laura's face as she threw back her head when Caro's thumb brushed her clit, coaxing her pleasure from inside and out. Laura's body tensed as she teetered on the brink, and Caro raised the tempo until Laura bucked and cried aloud.

Caro gently removed her fingers and crawled up Laura's body, cradling her and pressing against her body as if to imprint the sensation into her memory forever.

"Mm, delicious, thank you," Laura said a few minutes later, all groggy and hoarse.

Caro was mesmerised by this beautiful woman stretched out, comfortable in her naked pleasure, and she didn't want it to end. She was warmed to her toes, and every nerve end tingled with anticipation.

"This is just the beginning," Caro said in a choked whisper.

Laura smiled, and Caro basked in the warmth of it. Their foreheads met and Laura's face blurred. She sank into Laura's perfume, her presence, her touch, and love lit the dark places in her soul.

Chapter Forty

As LAURA LAY SATIATED and deliciously sore in places she hadn't felt for a while, she was loathe to move, despite having to keep a foot on the floor to remain balanced in place. Caro must have been reluctant to move too, as she pulled a throw to cover them and snuggled closer on the rather narrow chaise longue.

Up in the attic room studio in Mayfair, above where Caro's exhibition was coming to a close, it felt like a little space just for them. Laura hoped all the attendees had dispersed into the cool May night to attend their opera performances or dinner parties, so she and Caro could indulge themselves, exploring each other and reacquainting themselves with each other's bodies. She had forgotten how lean Caro was, or maybe Caro had been working hard over the last few months and lost some of the weight she'd gained with Laura's cooking. Caro tended not to eat when she was absorbed in her painting and judging by the array of pictures in the exhibition, she had been very busy. A flutter of guilt crossed her consciousness; she should have been here to look after her.

Caro laid her head on Laura's breasts. "I can't believe you're here. I missed you."

The sound vibrated in Laura's body, like Caro was purring rather than speaking, and Laura sighed. "Mm, me too."

"Do you want to stay here all night? Or we could find a hotel close by?" Caro raised herself up to loosen her tight bun and shook out her hair.

It tickled Laura's belly as she lay back down again. "I can't move. You've worn me out."

"I thought you youngsters could go all night," Caro said and stroked Laura's nipple till it hardened to a peak.

Arousal stirred again. "Maybe, if you give me a minute—"

The door knob rattled.

"Caro, hun, are you okay? Why is the door locked?"

Rebecca. Laura should have known she would come and chase Caro down. The door creaked with the knocking. "She's not going to go away, is she?" Laura whispered and snuggled under the throw.

Caro shook her head. "Go away, Rebecca. I'm busy."

"Don't be silly, darling, you can't be painting now. We want to celebrate a very successful exhibition. I'm coming in."

"Stop. No."

Too late. The key rattled in the lock and Rebecca pushed her way into the room, brandishing a bottle of champagne and glasses. "What are you hiding up here for? You're a triumph!"

When she caught sight of Laura, Rebecca's smile slipped like melting ice cream. Laura waved but gripped the throw to cover her dignity.

Caro sat up and turned rigid against Laura's flesh. Laura hadn't seen her so angry since the first day they met. She was so glad she wasn't the target of Caro's wrath.

"How dare you come barging in here? You've no idea of boundaries—"

Rebecca flushed the colour of beetroot, a complete contrast with her jade green outfit. "How was I supposed to know you'd be up here," she glanced at Laura with a raised eyebrow, "entertaining? I'll wait for you in the offices."

She turned on her four-inch heels and clattered downstairs, leaving the door swinging open.

Laura's giggle started with just a small vibration in her chest, until it expanded and she couldn't contain it any longer. Gradually Caro's body relaxed and she also laughed, but not in the same unrestrained way Laura was snorting, desperately trying to control herself.

"Come on, giggler, we'd better go downstairs and battle it out with Rebecca. Unless you'd prefer to wait here?"

"And miss the showdown at the O.K. Corral? You've got to be kidding." Laura threw off the covers and began to pull on her clothes. Caro snatched up a robe from the back of the door and stomped downstairs, while Laura hurriedly zipped up her jeans as she followed barefoot and tried to keep up.

They accosted Rebecca in her office with the green leather chairs and oak desk that took up a huge amount of space. Rebecca poured three glasses of champagne and placed them on the coffee table between the chairs. "I thought we'd be more comfortable in here. Dom Perignon?"

Of course Rebecca would have one of the most expensive champagnes.

No cava for her, although Laura couldn't really taste the difference. She nodded as she sat, but Caro was rigid beside her and perched on the edge of the chair.

Caro punctuated the air with her pointed finger as she spoke. "Why didn't you tell me that Laura had arrived tonight or inform me that she tried to contact me before?"

Rebecca looked down and smoothed her slinky sheath dress. She took a few seconds to compose herself before looking Caro in the eye. "I was trying to protect you. I didn't want you to get hurt—"

"You wanted to protect your income stream, you mean. I needed you as my friend first and foremost, not my agent."

"Don't you remember how distraught you were after Yvonne died? You were broken and hardly existing, and it almost finished you. It was heartbreaking to watch and painful to help pick up the pieces. You can't go through that again. You've been through enough." Rebecca glared at Laura. "You said you were going back to Spain, so you'll just hurt Caro again. She can't cope with another loss—"

Caro's hands balled into fists. "That's not for you to decide or judge. You've deliberately tried to keep us apart."

Rebecca swung around to face Caro, "I was only trying to look after your best interests…"

"I can look after myself. I trusted you to give me any relevant information, and you failed me. You're too controlling."

Laura squeezed Caro's hand. Caro's mouth was a taut line and was probably reflected in Laura's. For the first time, it felt like they were a team, facing the world together, and it warmed Laura to her toes.

Silence stretched for a few seconds as Rebecca stared from Caro to Laura and back again, cleared her throat and mumbled, "Sorry."

Finally, Rebecca realised she'd gone too far and that if it came to it, Caro would clearly choose Laura over her. Despite how badly she had behaved, Laura couldn't help feeling sorry for her.

Perhaps Caro did too as she relaxed in the chair and said, "I needed you to be a friend, my chosen family. I wanted you to look out for my happiness." Caro caught Laura's eye for a second and smiled, then swung back to face Rebecca. "I want you to be happy for me that I've found love when I never thought it would come again. You also owe Laura an apology."

Rebecca physically crumpled, before pulling herself together. "I do want you to be happy, Caro, and not just because of the painting. I am sorry, to both of you, for keeping you apart and for barging in. I'll go now and leave you with this rather nice champagne."

She stood up and smiled at Laura. "Would you like to come back to stay at our home this evening, Laura?"

"How can she feel welcome there after the way you've treated her?" Caro asked before Laura could answer.

She was amused and comforted, despite being able to stand up for herself. It was the first time she had someone fighting her corner and it gave her a thrill that Caro cared.

Rebecca nodded then slipped her phone out of her clutch bag. "Perhaps I can help make amends by seeing if The Athenaeum has a suite available for tonight? It's where most of our VIPs stay when they come to town."

Without waiting for a reply, she turned her back and spoke rapidly into her phone.

"Are you okay?" Caro asked.

"Apart from annoyed about the interruption? Yes. A night in a hotel is a start, but I won't forget. We could have been together for longer, although I could have made more of an effort to contact you."

That Caro had stood up for her and taken Rebecca to task made her feel loved and protected in a visceral way. She knew it in her bones. They would make it work. For the first time ever, she felt like number one. Her parents were always so wrapped up with each other, she always felt slightly on the outside, always wanting what they had but never believing it was possible, and she didn't even want to think about Valentina. She had tried so hard to cover her previous hurt with a veneer so bright and shiny no-one would look beneath, but Caro wasn't fooled.

Caro had pulled back that veneer and peered into her soul when she painted her, when she didn't take Laura's shit of using MiniMe as a literal prop, when they shared their passion of art and discussed their differing opinions, and when Caro saw her for who she truly was, flawed and floundering. These last few months had been so hard. Laura had only survived by throwing herself into her thesis and the project and hammering down the loss in her heart. It would be hard to cope with the enforced absence until they could work out the visa situation, but now she trusted that Caro would wait and would be there for her.

Rebecca returned her phone to her bag and inclined her head. "Okay, it's all sorted. You have one of the suites overlooking Green Park. They're expecting you anytime you want. I'm sorry again, and hope that over time, Laura, you'll get to know me and forgive me."

"Your offer's generous, but you can't buy our forgiveness. I feel hurt and angry that you put money before our friendship, and honestly, it will take time for me to wholly trust you again."

Caro seemed completely calm as she spoke, as if she was discussing what they would have for supper, but Laura could feel a slight tremble in her arm.

The hope in Rebecca's eyes dimmed, and she twisted her wedding band around her finger. "Oh. I see. Will you take the suite anyway as they'll charge it to Freddie's account?" She bit her lower lip. "What can I do to earn your trust and friendship again?"

"I don't know. Right now, all I want to concentrate on is making up for lost time with Laura."

Rebecca blushed again as if she was suddenly aware she had disturbed them. "Sorry. Please don't be too mad, Caro. Call me when you can."

She almost bowed as she retreated, carefully closing the door behind her, with a finality that could have portended the end of a friendship. Laura hugged Caro, trying to expel the hurt expression but Caro trembled.

"Are you cold? Maybe we should take this to the suite? I've always wanted to stay in a really posh hotel. It seems a shame to let it go to waste." Laura smiled, but Caro was just staring vacantly at the recently shut door.

"Rebecca betrayed me. I don't know if there's a way back from that."

Laura stroked Caro's jaw, which was clenched so tight it must hurt. "I understand. You once said that real intimacy was trust. I think I know what you mean now. Trust is so important. It's what I struggled with for so long after Valentina. I thought I'd never trust again, but I trust you."

"Do you?" Caro seemed surprised.

"Of course. How Rebecca treated you was hurtful. But give it time. You've been through a lot. She knows she messed up, and she's trying to make amends."

Caro exhaled noisily. "True. Come on. Let's get dressed properly just to get undressed again when we get in the suite. Did I tell you I love you?"

"You can never say it too many times. I love you too. Do you think they'll put chocolates on the pillow?" Laura asked.

Caro kissed Laura's nose. "Chocolates, flowers, petals on the bed, champagne cooling on ice. You deserve it all."

"Thank you." And she knew Caro meant it. They would face the long absences and the re-joining, the joys, and disappointments together. Now she had a special someone. The knowledge made her shiver with delight.

Chapter Forty-One

Three months later

CARO PLACED THE PICTURES back-to-back and front-to-front with foam at each corner, creating a suspension between them for minimising damage in transit. In a charitable mood, she would say it was good of Rebecca to take all her pictures into storage, not in Mayfair, of course—that real estate was way too expensive—but in a more sceptical mood, she would say it was so Rebecca had a ready supply of finished works of art to sell. It said something about the sorry state of their relationship that she no longer trusted Rebecca's motives. Before, she would have just thought she was being a great friend, but she'd been naïve. Now, she didn't know. Rebecca had tried so hard to burrow her way back into Caro's life. Yet, staying with Rebecca when Caro had commissions to complete in London had been tense. Even the kids asked what was going on between them before scurrying off into another room.

She sighed and wrapped the stack of pictures in cardboard before unwinding the parcel tape with a satisfying whiz and carefully sealing the package. She thumbed out the bubbles of air, smoothing down the tape and sealing her future. A few artists only used bubble wrap, but this method protected the art just as well and was reusable, unless the cardboard got soaked.

She looked up at the clouds. It should be fine, as it was a cool early autumn day, where the light was softer and the first tinges of red ochre and cadmium orange tinged the leaves. It was not unlike the first day Laura came into her life. A thrill of excitement rippled through her and she inhaled softly. She needed to keep calm and not get distracted that it was only seven hours and thirty-three minutes until Laura's plane landed. She was definitely going to the airport to meet her, even though Laura had said she would catch a cab, but she wanted to see her as soon as possible. It had been a long three weeks since Caro had been in Spain. The constant toing and froing was beginning to take its toll. But no more. Yesterday she had picked up various documents and identity numbers from the Spanish Embassy for her to enter Spain on a visa that would give her temporary residence.

Caro attempted to hold down the rising tide of guilt. She should have told Rebecca that she was leaving in the next two weeks, but she hadn't wanted Rebecca to try and dissuade her. Would Rebecca react as her agent or her friend? Their relationship had been too blurred in the past. Yet she missed their friendship and its easy banter, and Rebecca had been there for her after Yvonne died.

Rebecca, Freddie, and the kids had been Caro's chosen family for so many years that she didn't want to leave on a sour note. Forgiveness wasn't easy even when life was simple. There was always a giving up, whether that was ego or hurt or righteousness, and is that what she wanted to hold onto? The answer was no, but she didn't know if Laura would forgive Rebecca. Would that be an issue of friction between them? She hoped not. Laura. It was still seven hours and thirty-one minutes until her plane landed. How did time pass so slowly when she was waiting? She needed a distraction.

Caro sighed and knelt to place her sketch books into clicklock containers. She came across the last one she had made when Yvonne was alive. This sketch book had been well thumbed when she was grieving and had been one of the tangible items she had clung to so hard she had practically had to prise open her fingers to let go. A bit like her heart. Yet Laura had done that, and now they were about to start a new phase in their life together. Excitement and anxiety warred within her. She wished her Spanish was better. She was very grateful that the solicitor had smoothed through the visa process as the forms were incomprehensible, but wondered what else she would struggle with. Laura would be beside her though, and that made her heart expand, quashing the fear. Carefully, she smoothed out the cover of the sketch pad and placed it into the box, like putting Yvonne aside as an earlier part of her life. She would also wrap up the nude painting of Yvonne that was in the attic and give it to Rebecca, with the instruction that it could never be hung or sold.

There was a knock at the studio door.

"Hi, Rebecca. Come on in."

The door squeaked open, and Rebecca popped her head in. "Hey, Caro, do you need a hand?"

Rebecca was still so formal and respectful, it was like being addressed by a stranger, not her best friend. She just wanted that friend back. Caro rose and Rebecca kissed her on both cheeks, but it lacked her usual warmth. "I'm just packing up the last of the sketch books now. Would you like a tea?"

Rebecca placed her hand on Caro's arm. "I'll make it. Are you going to tell me why you're putting all your paintings in storage? We're happy to have them, of course. Please don't tell me you're going to stop painting again?"

Caro shook her head.

Rebecca's smile faded. "Unless you're emigrating to Spain?" They locked gazes. "You are, aren't you?" At Caro's nod, Rebecca clutched her chest as if she was stopping her heart from exploding. "Oh. What about a visa?"

"As of yesterday, it's all sorted. For the next year, anyway. It'll take me much longer to gain citizenship."

Rebecca stiffened against the bench. "Is that what you want?"

A flash of irritation flickered, but Caro quelled it. Rebecca was bound to be surprised, shocked, and unhappy about it. "Yes. It is."

"And you've planned and organised all this without letting me know?"

The hurt in Rebecca's tone was clear, and Caro placed her hand on Rebecca's to still it. "Yes. I knew you'd be upset and try to stop me, so I kept it from you. And to be honest, I wasn't sure how much I could trust you, or rather how much I could trust your motives. Would you respond as my friend or my agent?"

"I, I…" Rebecca looked upwards as if she was attempting to quell tears, then lowered her eyes to meet Caro's. "I only ever wanted you to be happy and to do the best for you, as my friend. It also happens that when you're happy you get absorbed in your painting, which is what I want as your agent."

Although she looked contrite, Caro wasn't ready to let her off just yet. "So why did you stop Laura from contacting me?"

Rebecca huffed out a breath and seemed fascinated by the bench. "I thought you'd be upset if she left for Spain, that it wouldn't last, and I'd be picking up the pieces, again. And if I'm really honest, I was a bit jealous." She stared at Caro. "I'm not proud of myself. It's just that I'd been so important in your life for so long, and I could see my role being supplanted. I'm ashamed, and it's resulted in you pushing me away completely, which is the last thing I wanted. And now you're leaving. I'm sorry. I can't undo what I did, but I regret it every day."

She missed those regular phone calls too. "Think how much you've saved on phone bills," Caro said, trying to lighten the mood. It was hard to see Rebecca being penitent and trying to atone.

Rebecca shrugged. "All inclusive contract."

"And now I've had no nagging, I could get on with painting." Caro smiled so Rebecca realised she was joking and trying to steer the conversation towards safer waters. "I miss my friend, and I miss Freddie and the kids too. I forgive you, but I don't know if Laura will."

Rebecca gave a wry smile. "I can understand that. But if you forgive me, that's a start. Can we hug it out?"

Caro stepped into Rebecca's arms and was enclosed by the scent of expensive perfume. She relaxed a little, glad they were on proper terms again.

Rebecca pulled away. "Now I'll go and make you that weak and watery tea while you finish up."

"That's what Laura calls it." Caro warmed at the thought of Laura but didn't dare glance at her watch to have it confirmed that only a few more minutes had passed. Rebecca exited, and Caro turned to the packing.

It didn't take long to fill and label the large boxes. She hoped they would keep them safe. They would load up the specialist removal van later, so she headed over to the kitchen where she could see Rebecca opening every cupboard door, presumably trying to find something. "What are you looking for?" she asked.

"Sweeteners. I used to keep them by the coffee."

"Oh. Laura reorganised when she was over here one weekend, and I think she put them by the sugar." Caro stretched over and rattled the small container. "I'll finish off here, if you want to sit down."

"Okay." Rebecca settled herself by the kitchen island.

The kettle had just boiled when the doorbell rang. Rebecca looked at her. "Are you expecting anyone?"

Caro poured the boiling water into the mugs. "No. It's probably a delivery for next door."

"I'll get it." Rebecca walked down the hall to the front door.

She heard a woman's voice after the door opened. It sounded like Laura, but it couldn't be since she wasn't due for another six hours and fifty-seven minutes. Not that she was counting. She stirred the tea and heard Rebecca's footsteps approaching.

"Who was it? A delivery? One or two sweeteners?" Caro asked without looking around.

Arms slid around her waist, causing her to jump. "Coffee, of course. As strong as you can make it."

That voice, that touch, that scent of Laura. Caro swung around, hardly daring to believe it. "Laura! What are you doing here?"

Laura's embrace almost crushed the breath out of her. Or maybe Laura just took her breath away. Then they merged into tongues, and hands, and lips as they desperately reconnected, trying to make up for all the missing days apart.

Laura cupped Caro's face in her hands when they paused for breath.

"I caught an earlier flight. I couldn't wait any longer."

Caro's heart beat fast. "I'm so excited to see you. I asked Rebecca to come so I could distract myself from waiting. I've been packing up my pictures and counting the minutes until you arrive. Somehow, the final day is too hard, and I can't settle on anything." Caro could hardly speak through her broad smile.

"I know, I know. I was so impatient to see you."

They kissed again and the world righted itself like some gigantic gyroscope. Laura was here. Caro pulled back. "I'd better get Rebecca and rescue her tea before it goes cold, and I'll make you some sludge." Unwilling to loosen Laura from her grasp, she held on to Laura's waist and reached up to extract another mug. Laura shimmied out of her hold to grab the lockable tin that held her precious coffee and dug in her spoon into the rich smelling grounds, precisely measuring way too much. "It's safe to come through now, Rebecca," she called out.

Within a few seconds, Rebecca appeared at the door.

"Come in, sit down. We won't bite," Caro said, handing over Rebecca's mug.

Rebecca flicked her gaze at Laura then back to Caro.

Laura laughed. "I promise I won't bite either, although I am pretty famished. I don't suppose you have anything to eat, do you, sweetheart?"

"Only the cinnamon polvorones your dad gave me when I left."

"You haven't eaten them yet?" Laura looked genuinely surprised and affronted.

"I wanted to save them for a special occasion."

Laura snorted. "You mean you've forgotten to eat for the past few weeks."

Caro felt the blush burn her cheeks.

"Yes, she does that, then wonders why she loses weight," Rebecca said and took a sip of her tea.

Laura beamed at Rebecca. "Right. My first mission is to fatten her up a bit."

"I'm not a pig getting ready for market, you know." Caro pretended to be offended but was delighted that the two of them seemed to be getting on, even if it was at her expense.

"I'd say more a turkey, wouldn't you, Rebecca?" Laura asked.

Rebecca laughed. "Well, she certainly hates Christmas."

"Hey, that's not fair. I always join in the games."

Rebecca paused with her mug halfway to her lips. "Although she never knows the answers in charades."

That was true, but it never seemed to matter. They always did boys versus girls so she was just a spare woman in the family games, contributing very little, but no one minded. She would miss spending time with them all at Christmas and wondered if they would come out to Spain.

"I remember she'd never heard of Bridget Jones' Diary," Laura said, like the mischievous traitor she was.

Caro made to hand over Laura's coffee, but then held onto the mug as Laura reached out. "Just to set the record straight, I didn't recognise the quote. I had heard about the movie."

Laura stuck out her tongue and grabbed the mug, lifting it like a trophy when she wrested control from Caro. Rebecca laughed at their antics.

As she turned to pick up the biscuit tin, Caro smiled to herself. It was good to see the tension soften between them; it made it easier. Although she would need to change that now. Opening the old biscuit tin holding the polvorones, she presented it to Laura then Rebecca. "I've told Rebecca that I've got my visa and will be leaving for Spain within two weeks," Caro said, and Rebecca's smile faded.

"I'll miss you," Rebecca said, her eyes shining with unshed tears. "But I can see you're very happy together." She twisted on her kitchen stool to face Laura and looked her straight in the eye. "I'm sorry I kept you two apart. I...I..."

Laura nodded. "You thought you were protecting Caro. I get that." Her face broke into the most beautiful dazzling smile, that warmed Caro to every cell in her body. "Love finds a way, gives a motivation to overcome all obstacles—"

"Even interfering friends?" Rebecca asked.

"Especially that." Laura raised her mug as though it was a glass, and they clinked mugs as though proposing a toast.

Caro's shoulders relaxed, grateful that Laura also had decided to forgive Rebecca, or at least put their differences behind her. She was so good at putting people at ease. That charm had certainly worked on her.

"Apart from a distraction for Caro, are you here en route to surfing?" Laura asked.

Rebecca glanced at Caro as though checking it was okay to tell the truth. "No. I came to collect Caro's pictures and sketches to store or sell off."

Caro leaned over and intertwined her fingers through Laura's. "Including 'Sated' and the sketches of Yvonne."

Laura's head snapped up, and she searched Caro's expression with wide eyes.

"Those aren't for sale, but it's time to stop them holding me back," Caro said.

Laura squeezed Caro's fingers with her soft, warm hands. "Thank you."

Arousal sparked deep in Caro's gut. She wanted to be alone and reconnect on a deeper level. That would have to wait, and she needed to focus.

Laura must have felt the same, because she abruptly looked away and scanned the kitchen. Her gaze settled on the rather sorry looking orchid, its leaves bleached ochre and all but one of the flowers shrivelled from purple petals to gossamer, a breath away from disintegrating.

Laura sighed and turned to Rebecca. "Are you any good with plants? Because this one is an herbaceous serial killer."

Caro couldn't deny it. It's not as if she hadn't warned Laura, but she had kept it going much longer than she anticipated.

Rebecca nodded. "I'll see if I can rescue it."

A rattling from the kitchen door had them all turning in their seats and a tabby cat strutted in, delicately placing one paw in front of the other like a high-class model.

Laura shrieked and dropped to the floor to pet her. "Arty Farty, you came to say hello." She showered her head with kisses.

Rebecca raised an eyebrow at Caro. "You seriously let her call her that?"

Caro shrugged. "I didn't get much choice, and Artemisia loves it. Laura's the only person she seems to gravitate towards. Laura and the kids next door." As if to emphasise Caro's point, the cat jumped into Laura's lap and started purring like a saw mill. Caro smiled at the sight. "I think it's the childish energy Artemisia resonates with."

Laura stuck out her tongue. "Hey, I can adult."

Caro stretched down to kiss Laura's head and pat Artemisia. "Says the woman who makes a living devising children's cartoons." They shared a loving glance.

"What are you going to do with her?" Rebecca indicated the cat, not Laura.

Both Caro and Laura sighed simultaneously. "We've decided she'll be better off staying here with Amelia and Riley next door. She's too old to adjust to a new environment."

Caro hoped she wasn't too old to change her environment too, then she looked at Laura and the overwhelming rush of love swept over her like a tide. Laura was home. Even if home was shifting location. She was swapping the soft autumn light for the brightness of the southern sun, and she basked in it.

"I'm sure you want time for yourselves," Rebecca said, breaking the gaze Caro and Laura shared. She picked up her bag. "I'll ask our painting removers to come down first thing tomorrow, so everything will be clear. What about everything else? Do you need help with that?"

Caro was touched by Rebecca's contrition and sensitivity; she was clearly trying to make amends. "Thanks, that's perfect for the specialist removers. We have international removers arriving late tomorrow afternoon to pack up the rest of my stuff, but thank you for the offer."

Rebecca looked so forlorn, Caro reached her hand out to touch her forearm. "When we're settled, maybe you can come over—"

"And bring the teenagers too," Laura said and smiled.

That she was so forgiving and welcoming warmed Caro's heart.

Rebecca coloured. "Are you sure you know what you would be letting yourself into? They're not the easiest to wrangle."

Laura grinned. "I can't believe they're any harder to wrangle than a group of nerdy animators who seem intent on going off on various techie tangents."

Rebecca's face softened. "Thank you, Laura. Now I'd best be off. I'll text you when Dan and his team will arrive."

Caro drew Rebecca into a genuine hug. "Before you go, do you know if any artists would like to rent my house and studio? I was going to put it on the market but wondered if you'd like to have first refusal for any of your contacts."

Still holding on to her, Rebecca said, "Leave it with me. And thank you. I'm glad we're friends again."

Caro pulled back. "So am I. Drive safely. Send my love to Freddie and the kids."

"I will." Rebecca hugged Laura, put her mug in the sink, and picked up her bag and the pot plant. "I'll see if I can save this," she said then exited down the hall.

"Thank you," Laura shouted after her.

The outer door clicked behind Rebecca, and they were together, alone, hours before she expected Laura to be here. Laura was in her arms before Caro could catch her breath, and they merged into kisses and caresses. Caro vaguely realised she hadn't made her bed this morning. Changing the sheets was another of those tasks she had listed on her distraction check list to do before Laura arrived. But it didn't matter, Laura was here, and she wouldn't care.

"I couldn't wait. I had to be here and sod the expense. Now I'm busting for a pee, so I'll go and freshen up, then shall we go for a walk up the hill?"

"But we've got so much to do before the movers come—"

"Which we'll do this evening and tomorrow. Please indulge me."

How could Caro deny those puppy eyes? "Sure."

Laura fluttered her eyelashes. "Do you want to bring a sketch pad and can I borrow one?"

Then it clicked what Laura was up to, and warmth spread over Caro at the thoughtfulness. It would be wonderful to see her favourite view one more time. "You're going to recreate the first walk we took when I sketched you."

Laura grinned. "Maybe. See you in a few minutes."

She was gone with a whirlwind, tossing life and laughter into every corner, scattering light into all the dark places. Seeing Laura leave the room, Artemisia gave up in disgust and clattered through the cat flap to see her new servants. A pang of sadness at leaving her cat behind gripped her heart. But there was so much to gain being with Laura. She inhaled and rummaged amongst the boxes for her sketching satchel and spare pad.

Within half an hour after the bracing walk up the hill, they stared out over the countryside. It was too misty to see over the Bristol Channel to Wales today, but the fresh air was exhilarating. Laura settled herself just to the side of Caro as she had previously, the perfect model, in three quarter pose, looking out across the valley. Caro smiled.

After twenty minutes sketching, Laura stretched her hands above her head. "How are you getting on? Can I see?"

Caro glanced at her drawing. She'd really caught Laura's expression, which could only be described as anxious, possibly because she was chewing her bottom lip. She felt the warmth of Laura's body behind her before she enveloped her in her arms. Laura's hot breath on her neck caused goosebumps down her body.

"I love you," Laura breathed into Caro's ear. "It seemed fitting to come up here, because that's when I realised I was falling in love with you, that I wanted to cherish and protect you, that it was more than a fangirl crush."

Caro settled into Laura's embrace and closed her eyes to absorb the comfort and familiarity of her scent. "I love you too," she whispered, her words almost lost in the slight breeze. "You fell in love with me then? But I was devastated, at my worst point and a complete mess. Everything I thought was true was a lie."

Laura squeezed her shoulders. "You showed such courage to face that. It was also the day you broke through and started sketching again."

Caro nodded. "That's true, you inspired me. Thanks for dragging me up here one last time." Her eyes flicked open as a thought occurred to her. "Is everything okay? You seem nervous." She pointed her finger to Laura's expression on the sketch.

Laura cleared her throat. "I wish I could use MiniMe—"

"No. I'm so glad that horrible puppet is in your office where I can't see it."

"I promise she'll stay there. Okay, right…"

Of Light and Love

There was fumbling behind Caro, and she strained to see what Laura was doing. She slipped a small box from her pocket and held it out.

Caro spun around as she realised what it might be. Laura took a step back, pulling back the box. Anxiety washed across her face, and her eyebrows raised as if in hope.

She cleared her throat. "I know you said you'd never marry again after Yvonne, but I was hoping, maybe, you'd consider marrying me?"

An explosion of conflicting emotions scattered around Caro's mind. It was too soon. She said she'd never go through that again, but Laura shone her joy in her darkest places. She had already committed to Laura, to move countries, to start again with a different language and culture. Surely this was just the final step, the finishing stroke, the highlight in the eyes to bring a painting alive?

Laura's brow furrowed deeper, and she was biting her lip so hard the skin was stretched.

"Yes," Caro said. "I'd love to be your wife." She opened her arms, and Laura collapsed into them.

"I thought you were going to say no," she said into Caro's chest.

Caro pulled her closer, then pulled Laura's chin up to kiss her.

"Of course I'd say yes. I'm honoured. Now are you going to show me what's inside the box?" She couldn't resist the teasing. She'd never seen Laura so flustered, or relieved. Her shoulders finally relaxing, and the tension shifted from her body as she opened the box, where a sapphire solitaire ring glistened in the light.

"I hope it's okay. I tried to match the colour of your eyes, but it's too dark, too blue. I think it should fit, but the jeweller promised me we can take it back if it needs tweaking. Maybe I should have waited and we could have chosen together—"

Caro placed the ring on her finger and admired it. "It's beautiful, thank you." She took Laura's hands in hers and fixed her with a loving gaze. "This place has always been a favourite. Now it will have an extra special meaning, inextricably linked with this perfect moment, with you."

Laura blew out a heavy breath and smiled at last. "I'm so glad you like it."

"I love it. Thank you. I can't wait to start my new life with you. You're my light, my love."

Epilogue

Eighteen months later

CARO LOOKED AROUND THE restaurant at the faces, some familiar, others she had met for the first time; they had come here just for her and Laura. She glanced at Laura, her wife of one hour and a giddy thrill shimmered through her. Laura glided around the sea of people, spreading smiles and laughter like fairy dust, making everyone feel seen and welcome, and it made Caro glow from the inside. When Yvonne died, Caro thought she'd never be happy again, and certainly never love again, yet Caro's heart had never been fuller with love than it was now.

Laura looked over, and her focused gaze elicited such a mix of delight and desire that Caro wanted to tell everyone to stay and enjoy the party while she and Laura disappeared to enjoy their honeymoon night. She raised her eyebrow and blew a kiss. Laura jumped as though to catch it and placed her hand over her heart.

"I love you," Laura mouthed.

Before Caro could respond, Amelia tugged at Laura's skirts. She smiled and answered Amelia's question like it was exactly what she wanted to do at that moment. And knowing Laura, maybe it was. Caro was touched the whole family had come to Spain for the wedding. Amelia said Artemisia was being looked after by a friend while they were away, and he sent daily photos to reassure Amelia, and she had passed them on to Caro. The latest picture of her old cat sprawled out on various toy cars and dolls made her laugh. It looked really uncomfortable, but Artemisia was the very picture of repose. "I don't suppose you miss me one bit," Caro murmured, but she was glad that Artemisia was content with her new servants.

Laura's boss came over and shook Caro's hand. "Congratulations. It is good to meet you at last. We all like to see Laura so happy."

Caro met his smile. "She makes me happy too."

He nodded. "Did she tell you that her series, Charlie's Questions, has been nominated for the European Children's TV awards?"

He was actually the fourth person to inform her of that today, and it was typical of Laura to be modest. "So I've been told."

Domingo patted her arm. "Laura tells me the model for Charlie's cat is your cat, Arty. She is the favourite toy from the show." He grinned.

No doubt she had made the studio a lot of money. At least Laura hadn't called her Arty Farty.

"I will leave you to your next guests. Congratulations again."

"Thank you," Caro said, as he reached for another glass of Cava and moved away. Everyone had been so friendly since she'd moved to Spain and they all adored Laura, so by association, welcomed her too. It was a stunning place to live and work.

A hand on Caro's shoulder made her jump. "You seem at home here, and happy, I might add," Rebecca said.

"I am. I've never been happier."

Rebecca looked surprised. "What, even with Yvonne?"

Caro frowned. Why was Rebecca bringing up Yvonne on Caro's wedding day? No, she wouldn't react. Rebecca had taken it quite hard when Caro said she was going to marry Laura and live in Spain. She eyed her friend to see if she was being sarcastic, but her expression was open, as if she was curious and slightly baffled. Rebecca had never really got Laura, or perhaps she had hero-worshipped Yvonne. "It was different with Yvonne. She was all drama, thunder, and lightning, and everyone had to take notice of her. I was pulled to the excitement and flattered she chose me. But I wasn't the right person for her, in the end. Laura is the noon sun that shortens my shadows, and warms me with her joy, and brings out the brilliant colours of everything around me. You should know that. You've seen my latest paintings. And I really don't care that they aren't selling as well as my old style, and before you ask, no, I'm not going back there. I've found light and love, and yes, I'm happy."

Rebecca flung her arm around Caro's shoulder in a rather drunken side hug. "I'm so glad for you, Caro, and I wouldn't dream of suggesting you go back to your old style. I just miss your friendship."

"We'll be coming over often, and I hope we can both stay with you." Caro wrapped her fingers over Rebecca's hand and knew they were okay again.

"Always. Now I'd better wrestle that alcohol off Jack. His one glass has increased to two, and I don't want to explain to the hotel why a teenager has thrown up all over their expensive suite."

Caro grinned and sipped the cava. It was typical of Rebecca and Freddie to stay at the Alhambra Palace, the most luxurious hotel in Granada, where the likes of Eva Peron and the Dalai Lama had stayed. And it probably had the best view over Granada, other than from the Alhambra itself.

Caro looked around for Laura but couldn't spot her as Laura's mother sidled up to her. "Hi, Mandy, have you seen Laura?"

Mandy threaded her arm through Caro's. "She's been asking for you, and I said I'd get you."

Concern washed over her, and her heart picked up tempo. "Is everything okay?"

Mandy smiled, and the same dark eyes as Laura's took Caro's breath away.

"She just wants to see you. Come with me."

Caro let herself be led away by her new mother-in-law. They left the high terrace of the restaurant overlooking the city and made their way through cool, dim corridors to a small courtyard, where the glare made a sharp contrast. Mandy pulled Caro past the fountain, fed by gravity from higher in the mountains and designed to keep the place cool in high summer. She didn't have time to admire the Moorish architecture with its curls and arches before Mandy took her into another building with dark corridors.

"Are you kidnapping me?" Caro asked and grinned. She hadn't been in this part of the restaurant before.

Mandy tapped her arm. "Behave, and you'll be glad you came with me. Spanish weddings are a marathon, not a sprint, and this will last for hours. A little lie down will do you good, while everyone is getting pissed on the dancefloor."

She winked at Caro, making it very clear that she expected she and Laura would *not* be having a nap. "I also wanted to say thank you."

Caro kept her head down to hide the blush. "For what?"

"Making my Laura happy. I've never seen her like this. I thought she would never recover after…well, you know. It's wonderful to welcome you to our family, and we're delighted you'll be living here. And we're honoured to have a famous artist in the fold."

Caro waved away the compliment. "Laura makes me so happy, I can't tell you."

"I know, dear, it's written all over your face." Mandy paused in front of an ornate dark wood door and knocked. "Laura, I've brought the parcel you wanted."

Parcel? She'd been described in more flattering ways.

"Thank you. Let her come in," Laura said.

Mandy indicated for Caro to enter and squeezed her hand. "I'll see you later, dear."

With a tremble of excitement and nervousness, Caro opened the door. "Hello?" Instead of being in her white bride's dress, Laura was naked on the bed, surrounded by delicate white orange blossoms. The heady, exotic scent and the sight of Laura, welcoming and available, overwhelmed her.

"Lock the door behind you. I'm changing from my English dress to my traditional Spanish black dress for the rest of the afternoon and evening, but I thought you could help me dress. Eventually."

The look Laura shot Caro was sultry and did strange and wonderful things to her. She pressed her legs together as if that could stop her arousal.

Caro blew out a long breath. "You're gorgeous. I've been lusting after you all day."

"Good. That's the idea. You've too many clothes on. Hang them on the floordrobe or the chair."

Caro frowned. "The what?"

Laura laughed. "On the floor, just hurry up. Come and join me."

Caro didn't need a second invitation. She divested herself of her specially tailored formal suit and hung it over the back of the chair, then stepped out of her underwear and tossed it on the floor, eager to be free of its constraints. Her hands shook slightly as she crawled up the bed and into Laura's welcome arms. "You've got goosebumps. Are you cold?" Caro asked, wondering if she should pull up the blanket.

"No. Hello, wifey," Laura whispered and pulled Caro close.

"Hello, yourself."

Laura traced Caro's face gently as if she was exploring her for the first time. She trailed kisses down her neck, sucking on Caro's collar bone in a way that made her shiver with delight. She surrendered to Laura's touch willingly and tried to hold on as long as she could; she was fit to explode already. If Laura continued sucking at her nipple, she wouldn't last much longer without needing Laura inside her. But she wanted to pleasure Laura first. "Let me make love to you, wife," Caro whispered.

"My pleasure."

Laura's words vibrated against Caro's breast and Laura's giggle played through Caro's body, making all her nerves tingle. She kissed her way down Laura's body and hovered just above her clit.

"Please," Laura whispered.

Caro needed to touch Laura and have her tongue on her, in her, confirming to Laura she was loved. Laura was so beautiful with her eyes closed and her head thrown back. Entranced, Caro melded into a mess of arms and legs, the taste of salt, the waft of orange blossom, sweet perfume, and the heady scent of sex. Laura came with a throaty scream and lay back for a few moments.

"Come up here," Laura said huskily. "We're not done."

Caro crawled up Laura's gleaming body and kissed her hard. Laura moved her hands all over Caro, eager and devouring. The pulse of fingers and folds, swollen throbbing clits, flesh on tingling flesh, hot and lathered, urged them on, fast and frantic to the edge of desperate wanting, at the crest of too much to bear. Then Caro caught the wave and rolled with an ear-rushing, gushing release of ecstasy and a shuddering toe-curling wash of delight.

Joy bubbled over with Caro's orgasm, and she sank back, laughing like she hadn't for a long time. Laura giggled too, then belly laughed. They lay entwined for a few minutes.

"I suppose we ought to go back," Laura said. "Do you think they'll miss us?"

"On our own wedding day? No."

They looked at each other and burst out laughing like naughty children. But Caro didn't care. She embraced her inner child now; Laura had taught her that. Life was bright, exhilarating, and intoxicating with Laura by her side. This was her new beginning. She had stepped out of the shadows, and now she revelled in a world of light and love.

Author's Note

I really hope you enjoyed reading *Of Light And Love*. If you did, I'd be very grateful for an honest review. Reviews and recommendations are crucial for any author, particularly one just starting out. Just a line or two can make a huge difference.
Thank you.

What's Your Story?

Global Wordsmiths, CIC, provides an all-encompassing service for all writers, ranging from basic proofreading and cover design to development editing, typesetting, and eBook services. A major part of our work is charity and community focused, delivering writing projects to under-served and under-represented groups across Nottinghamshire, giving voice to the voiceless and visibility to the unseen.

To learn more about what we offer, visit: www.globalwords.co.uk

A selection of books by Global Words Press:
Desire, Love, Identity: with the National Justice Museum
Times Past: with The Workhouse, National Trust
World At War: Farmilo Primary School
Times Past: Young at Heart with AGE UK
In Different Shoes: Stories of Trans Lives

Self-published authors working with Global Wordsmiths:
E.V. Bancroft
Valden Bush
Addison M Conley
Emma Nichols
Dee Griffiths and Ali Holah
Helena Harte
Dani Lovelady Ryan
Karen Klyne
AJ Mason
James Merrick
Ray Martin
Robyn Nyx
Sam Rawlings
Simon Smalley
Brey Willows

Other Great Butterworth Books

Warm Pearls and Paper Cranes by E.V. Bancroft
A family torn apart. Love is the only way forward.
Available from Amazon (B09DTBCQ92)

Let Love Be Enough by Robyn Nyx
When a killer sets her sights on her target, is there any stopping her?
Available on Amazon (ASIN B09YMMZ8XC)

Lyrics of Life by Brey Willows
Sometimes the only way to heal someone's heart is a song from you own.
Coming June 2023 (ISBN 9781915009265)

An Art to Love by Helena Harte
Second chances are an art form.
Available from Amazon (ASIN B0B1CD8Y42)

Caribbean Dreams by Karen Klyne
When love sails into your life, do you climb aboard?
Available from Amazon (ASIN B09M41PYM9)

Nero by Valden Bush
Will her destiny reunite her with the love of her life?
Available from Amazon (B09BXN8VTZ)

The Helion Band *by AJ Mason*
Rose's only crime was to show kindness to her royal mistress...
Available from Amazon (ASIN B09YM6TYFQ)

That Boy of Yours Wants Looking At by Simon Smalley
A gloriously colourful and heart-rending memoir.
Available from Amazon (ASIN B09HSN9NM8)

Judge Me, Judge Me Not by James Merrick
A memoir of one gay man's battle against the world and himself.
Available from Amazon (ASIN B09CLK91N5)

LesFic Eclectic Volume Three edited by Robyn Nyx
Special edition raising funds for the DEC Ukrainian appeal: available
from Amazon (ASIN B09V39LW2W)

Made in the USA
Monee, IL
18 September 2023